THE HORNS OF RUIN

Tim Akers

THE HORNS OF RUIN

an imprint of **Prometheus Books**
Amherst, NY

Published 2010 by Pyr®, an imprint of Prometheus Books

Cover illustration © Benjamin Carré.

Inquiries should be addressed to
Pyr
59 John Glenn Drive
Amherst, New York 14228–2119
VOICE: 716–691–0133
FAX: 716–691–0137
WWW.PYRSF.COM

14 13 12 11 10   5 4 3 2 1

Library of Congress Cataloging-in-Publication Data

Akers, Tim, 1972–.
    The horns of ruin / by Tim Akers.
        p. cm.
    ISBN 978–1–61614–246–9 (pbk.)
    I. Title.

PS3601.K48H67 2010
813'.6—dc22

                                                                2010029659

Printed in the United States of America

To my own Bloody Jennifer, who fights like a girl

CHAPTER ONE

They came for us one at a time, came to kill the last servants of the dead god Morgan. I had lost brothers and sisters before, to battle or old age. Scions of Morgan die all the time. We're warriors. Now we were going to die in alleyways, in our homes, in crowded theaters and empty hallways. They came to kill us, and we didn't know who they were.

They came for me and Barnabas while we were walking through the city, on our way back to the Strength of Morgan from an errand at the Scholar's prison, the Library Desolate. Well. Mostly they came for Barnabas. I just happened to be there, escorting him. It was me. I'm the girl who let the old man down.

He looked good that morning. Healthy. He always looked better out of the monastery. Those old, empty stone halls did little more than weigh him down. Open air, even the dirty air of a crowded street in the city of Ash, always put a smile on his face. He was smiling that morning. This was before the hidden deaths, before the murders and betrayals. Before we knew what was happening. He was the first one they came for, and we didn't know they were coming. Not yet.

We walked down the road, and the crowd parted for us. Barnabas was in his formal robe, a deep maroon hemmed with gold thread, and carrying the staff of his office. Symbolic armor clattered on his shoulders, and the cuffs of his robe were stamped with golden scale mail that shimmered in the morning light. His knuckles bore the calluses of a life spent fighting and working, the twin paths of the scions of Morgan. White hair and wrinkled face sat on a frame thick with muscle and iron hard. Even in the waning days of our Cult, there was glory in the office of the Fratriarch, and Barnabas Silent looked every inch the part.

As proud as I was, I wished he'd left the formal robe at home. I was dressed in my battle-day simples. Pride was fine, and glory was better, but both of those things were bought with attention. As the Fratriarch's only guard, I could have done with less attention. Of course, whatever attention I avoided by dressing simply, I gave up with my holster and sheath. But a girl shouldn't go out half dressed.

"It's a matter of state, Eva," Barnabas said, his voice as gentle as mist at the foot of a waterfall.

"I said nothing, my Elder."

"You did," he said, nodding. "In the way you stand, in the movement of your eyes. In the weight of your hand upon your bullistic. You do not wish to be here."

"It's not my fault you like to get dressed up, old man. No, no, I'm happy to be here. Thrilled to be walking through the city with the holiest man I know, just me as a guard. Not like we have any enemies, Barnabas. Not like the Rethari are massing at our borders, or their chameleon spies have been dredged up in the collar countries. No, not at all. This is ideal." I sped up a little to intercept a group of children who had blundered into our path. The Fratriarch smiled and patted their heads as we passed. They stared at us, whispering. "I just wish you'd brought more guards. Maybe an army or two?"

Barnabas watched the children, his face equal parts gentle happiness and melancholy. He turned back to me.

"The Rethari are always massing. It's what they do. And as for their spies? We used to make stew of their spies. Besides, we have no other guards, Eva. It's a matter of state. We go to seek the aid of our godbrother. Only Elders of the Fist and Paladins may attend. Among the Elders, Simeon was busy, Tomas and Elias are napping, and Isabel cannot be more than ten steps from her library, for fear that one of her books go unread."

"I saw Tomas, just before we left."

Barnabas nodded absently. "Yes, yes. Not napping. Tomas does not . . ." He smirked and shrugged. "Tomas will not be involved in this. And of the Paladins, Eva?"

I grimaced and looked around at the passing crowd. A pedigear weaved past us, its clacking engine momentarily drowning out the perfectly good awkward silence.

"You are the last Paladin of the dead god Morgan, Eva. There are no more, and likely never will be," he said, patting my hand. "I am the Fratriarch, and you are the Paladin. Let us attend to our business."

He walked off. I sighed and followed.

"Yeah, let's just make a parade of it. You and me," I said quietly, adjusting the hang of my revolver at my hip. "Maybe I should have rented an elephant."

"Elephants don't belong in cities, Eva," the Frat said, gesturing broadly to the crowded streets and towering glass buildings all around. "It's not humane."

"To the elephant? Or the city?"

He laughed deeply, and I smiled and caught up. In younger years he would have pinched my cheek or patted me on the head, as he had those children. But now he was the Fratriarch and I was the Paladin. We walked side by side through the city of Ash.

"If it's a matter of state, then we're going the wrong way. Alexander will be at his throne today, in the Spear of the Brothers." I pointed across the road. "That way, in case you've gotten senile."

"It is," Barnabas nodded, "and we are not going there."

"You said—"

"Morgan had two brothers, Eva. We are going to visit the scions of Amon."

I stopped walking, frustrating the crowd. Barnabas continued on, nearly disappearing into the throng before I snapped out of my shock.

A whole column of elephants wouldn't be enough, nor stone walls. Nothing would make me feel safe in the halls of Amon the Betrayer.

Ash is a funny city. Not funny, like rag clowns and puppet shows. Funny like it shouldn't exist. Funny like it should collapse in on itself in a cloud of shattered glass and burning streets. My kind of funny.

It goes back an Age, back to when the Feyr were the race-ascendant rather than mankind, when the Titans ruled the skies and the earth and the water all around. Before there were people, maybe. I don't know. But it goes back to the Feyr.

What is today the city of Ash was once the capital city of the Titans. Their throne, their birthplace, a city of temples and totems and grand technology. The name of that city is lost to us, but it nestled in a crater, like a giant bowl of stone sprinkled with buildings and roads and carved riverways. We really don't know why the Titans and the Feyr fought their little war, but they did, and that war came to the city in the crater.

The Feyr were masters of the elements. They made water out of nothing, fire out of air. They could sink mountains and freeze the sun in the sky. That's the story my momma told me, at least. Scratch that. That's the story my nanny told me. So the Feyr came to the crater, to the city of the Titans.

They burned it, then they drowned it. Two deaths for one city. It was enough to win the war, and more than enough to scar the Feyr forever. They filled the crater with a lake of cold, black water, and that lake was choked with the slick ash of the dead city below. It was a wound on the soul of their kingdom, the greatest sin they ever committed. In time they tried to atone. They built temples of wood that floated on the lake of ash, trying to suck the sickness out with their prayers.

And when war came to them, when mankind rose up and named their gods and came marching with swords and totems of their own, this was the last place the Feyr stood. Afterward, mankind made a city on that lake, built up from what was left of the charred temple-rafts of the Feyr. Amon the Scholar crafted engines that supported more and more structures, more buildings and roads and people. It became the capital of the Fraterdom, the impossible engines always churning against the lake to keep us dry.

It's a crazy way to build a city. Three hundred years, and that lake is still black as night.

I escorted the Fratriarch into the shadow of the Scholar's ominous prison. The Library Desolate was a dark wound on the city, its stone and steel walls still blackened from the arcane battle that washed across it generations ago. Whenever rain or time cleaned off some portion of its edifice, the citizens of the city of Ash would gather to ritually scorch the stone black again, as it had been burned when the outraged legions of Morgan descended upon it to slaughter the priesthood of Amon the Betrayer, for the murder of their god. That was a tradition we kept. The roof sprouted a cancerous rash of glass domes, their panes smeared with ash and chipped black paint. The last House of Amon the Betrayer lived in permanent night. The Cults of his brothers Morgan and Alexander saw to it.

We were met at the gate by a servitor of Alexander. Morgan had held this guard a century ago, until our numbers dwindled and the godking Alexander stepped in. He had ordered all records of our time in the prison destroyed. Security, he insisted. As though a scion of Morgan would sell those secrets. As though he couldn't trust the servants of his own brother. Though trust is what got Morgan killed, so I suppose it wasn't without reason.

The servant was a pale man, whiter than his robe, his bald head shinier than the dull silver of the icon around his neck. Not the cream of the crop, here at the prison. He looked us over with lazy interest, then spun up the clockgeist beside him and pulled the speakerphone to his mouth.

"Names?" he asked over the clockgeist's quiet howling clatter. I stepped in front of Barnabas.

"Eva Forge, Paladin of Morgan and sister of the Fraterdom. I demand entry to the house of my brother by my right as scion of Morgan."

He looked up from my breasts, then down to my holster, then up again to the two-handed sword slung over my shoulder.

"You'll have to leave your weapons at the gate."

I sneered and snapped out the revolver, flipped it once in my hand, and spun the cylinder open. I presented the clacking wheel of bullets to him and began to invoke.

"This is Felburn, heart of the hunter, spitting fire of the sky. Morgan blessed the revolver as a weapon of his Cult at the towers of El-Ohah, when the storm cracked the stones of that place and the cannons of his army cracked the sky. This weapon was beaten from the iron of the mountain of the Brothers, the land of their birth. The bullets are engraved with my soul's name, and blessed by the Fratriarch of Morgan on an altar of war." I snapped the cylinder shut, passed the barrel across the pale man's heart, and slammed it into my holster. "I carry it, whether I live or die, through fire and fear and foes. I leave it nowhere."

"Well, I . . . uh." The Alexian grimaced and shuffled his feet. Barnabas leaned out from behind me.

"Don't ask her for the sword," he said, then banged his staff against the narrow stone walls all around. "It's a much longer show, and there's not really enough room for the full production. If we step outside for a moment, though, I'm sure she'll be happy to demonstrate. Eva?"

I reddened and chewed my jaw, then glanced over my shoulder at the old man. He was beaming. He stepped around me and tapped his ceremonial staff to his forehead, like a fisherman hailing a passing boat.

"I'm Barnabas, Fratriarch of Morgan and First Blade of Alexander's dead brother. If you don't know who I am, then you can be damned. I have an appointment."

The color, what little of it there was, left the servitor's face. The clockgeist chewed out an answer that he didn't really hear. He nodded and the gate opened.

The pale-headed man locked the gate behind us, shuttered the cowl on the clockgeist, and escorted us into the library-prison of Amon the Scholar. We followed a long brick tunnel deep into the complex, the way lit by the Alexian's gently humming frictionlamp. There were no other guards, no other gates, but suddenly the tunnel opened up into the mitochondrial complexity of the Library's stacks. We were among the Amonites. I bristled, and the articulated sheath on my back twitched with insectile anticipation, like a spider testing its web. Barnabas sensed the change and put a broad hand on my shoulder.

"Silence," he whispered. "These are the tame ones."

"It's the tame ones I don't trust," I answered, but left my blade where it was and tried to relax.

They moved among the stacks in absolute silence. Their black robes looked like wrinkled shadows, and they kept their heads down. A few paused in their grubbing among the books to turn our way, but the sight of a Paladin of Morgan sent them scurrying.

"They wander around like this?" I asked. The servitor nodded his bald head, though he did not turn to look at me.

"They are bound to this place, my lady. Their books, their equipment. The shrine of their god, fallen though he may be. They would not leave."

I looked around at the close walls, the wooden ceiling, and the stinking, pulpy stacks of books on their sagging shelves.

"I would. First chance I got."

"Well. Perhaps they don't have that, either." The servitor fingered a loose coil of chain that hung from his belt and chuckled. It looked like a woman's necklace that had lost its stone. There was carving on the links, but I couldn't make out the pattern.

"I would prefer *they* wore the chains, servitor," I said, resting my hand on my revolver. The stacks were narrow and close, like a maze of wood and leather. It felt like an ambush. "Better to have them in cages. If we still ran things, it'd be cages."

The servitor stopped walking and faced me. The Fratriarch walked another half-dozen steps then idled to a halt. He flicked a hand through a book that was resting on a nearby podium, his eyes distracted. So old, in that moment. He looked like a forgetful grandfather. I pushed the thought aside and faced the servitor. He stared at me with barely veiled contempt. No, not veiled at all. Just contempt.

"In chains, madam? In cages? Tell me, are all the scions of Morgan so nuanced in their approach?" He whipped the coil of thin chain from his belt and held it at shoulder height. "What was the escape rate when Morgan held these halls? Do you know, even?"

I held the smaller man's gaze, leaving my face as dead as possible. He fingered the chains with idle malice. The Fratriarch ignored us. When it became clear that I wasn't going to answer, the servitor continued.

"We have had none, my lady. Not one. Chains rust. Cages can be shattered. The bonds of this world fail us. Faith in metal and stone is inevitably faith squandered." He sneered, his tiny eyes wrinkling over his ugly nose. "You should know that, Morganite."

I would have struck him, if the Fratriarch hadn't been there. The flat of my blade or the barrel of my bullistic, he deserved nothing less.

Patience. It was a speech I heard a lot from the Fratriarch. From all the Elders. Patience. I put my hand flat against his chest and prepared to invoke. He grimaced and clenched the chains in his fist, then spat out something arcane. The stacks erupted in screams, all around, echoing between the rows of books like thunder in a canyon.

My sword was in my hands without a thought, the pistons and hinged arms of the articulated sheath pivoting it over my shoulder and into my ready grip. I dropped into a guard position and began invoking Everice, Mountain among Streams. The servitor laughed. The Fratriarch looked on with grim disappointment.

Black-robed Amonites stumbled from the stacks, spilling to the floor in shrieking agony. They writhed at the servitor's feet, their eyes wide with terror and pain. I stared at them in horror, then fascination. The Amonites had chains of their own, thin and flat, made of some dull gray metal and arcanely etched. Our guide loosened his grip on his chains, and the screaming stopped.

The servitor stood over them, the coil of chains dangling loosely from his open palm. The Amonites lay in a heap, panting and mewling. The room smelled of offal and disgrace.

"Cages rust. Metal fails." He returned the coil to his belt. "We bind the soul, my lady."

He turned and walked away. The Fratriarch looked sadly down at the pile of Scholars. There were old men among them, and children. He gave me a look, then followed the Alexian. I surrendered my sword to its sheath, then left the Amonites to struggle to their feet and disperse. There would be words from Barnabas for that provocation.

"Not my fault he's a jerk," I muttered. He ignored me.

The small corridors and tight stairways continued for a while. I lost track of our turnings, though it felt like we were going higher. Groups of Amonites watched us from the shadows, eyeing the heavily armed woman and the old man with his fancy staff. The servitor they ignored. He hurried ahead of us, opening doors and securing locks. Well, at least they used locks sometimes.

"How did that work?" I asked the Fratriarch as we crossed a broad chamber. I kept my eyes on my feet, only daring to glance quickly over at the still furious Fratriarch. "How did he do that to them?"

Barnabas did not answer immediately. When he did, it was with a deep sigh and a quiet voice. "How does your armor work, student?"

I stumbled to a stop. Student. He had not addressed me in that way since . . . since I was a child. I hurried to catch up.

"Master, I meant no—"

"I asked a question, and I await an answer."

"I . . . Master. The symbol of the armor is the armor."

"The idea of the armor, you mean. The soul of the armor," he corrected. He let out a long sigh and looked around at the dingy walls. His eyes held distaste, even pity. "We draw on the noetic power of Morgan's armor, and it protects us. We draw on the noetic power of his strength, the greatness of his deeds, the collective memory of his courage." He waved a dismissive hand. "This is the same. The Healer has built a prison into each of them. Chains would bind the flesh. The noetic power of chains, the memory and symbol of chains, though— that binds their souls."

I thought about that. It troubled me. The strength of Morgan, his courage and his bravery, his victories in battle—these were the things that gave us our power, our invocations. Each of our powers had its basis in some part of Morgan's story. Everice, Mountain among Streams, for example, is a defensive stance. When invoked, the scion of Morgan can face multiple threats at once, her attention divided equally in all directions. It draws its power from Morgan's actions at the Battle of Everice, when his line had been overwhelmed by the Rethari hordes. Morgan had stood alone against waves of scaled Rethari warriors for a full day, striking each of them down with a single blow. To the rest of the army, heavily pressed and unable to relieve their god, Morgan had looked like a mountain in a flood, battered from all sides but unyielding.

I wondered what bit of Alexander's history the power of the chains came from. Nothing widely known, it would seem. All the gods had their secrets, of course, revealed only to the highest scions. Still, it was a strange power for Alexander the Healer.

"Master Barnabas, I beg forgiveness for my actions. The presence of so many of the Betrayer's scions—"

"Forget it," he said wearily, and then smiled. "There is a duty here, and a purpose. These people do not serve Amon the Betrayer." He stopped and fixed me with his pale eyes. "He did many things. It is by his hand that this city was raised, and by his servants' hands that it still stands. His tools drove back the Feyr and forged the Fraterdom. The Betrayal was one act, as horrible as it was. One act. They worship the god that he was. Not the murderer he became."

"Is that supposed to be enough?" I asked.

"It must be. Amon is dead. Morgan is dead at his hand. Of the three brothers, only Alexander remains. There is nothing more we can do."

We stared at each other, master and student, elder and orphan. The Fratriarch sighed and turned to the servitor, who was waiting at the foot of a staircase. I followed, as I always follow. The Cult of Morgan was not mine to lead.

We continued in tense silence up a tightly coiling spiral staircase, dusty shelves of books on all sides, until we emerged into a much larger room. The Fratriarch and I stumbled to a halt, wide-eyed.

We were on a broad terrace that was, itself, part of a cavernous space of books and dappled light. This single room was a gash that ran the height of the building, steep walls that stepped outward in terraces and narrow walkways, polished wooden railings and trestles arching across the gap, their paths illuminated by warm frictionlight and, amazingly, the natural sun in delicate patterns. I followed the thin light up to the ceiling. Several of the domes that we had seen outside yawned over this grand chasm, their chipped black paint letting in a bright constellation of sunlight. And everywhere I looked, the walls, the rooms that opened onto the cavern, the walkways that wound treacherously across, all of them were lined with bookcases. They seemed to burst organically from the wood and stone, like strata of musty intellect crushed into gilded pages by the weight of the building.

The servitor hurried to a cabinet by the edge of the terrace. It was a dark wooden contraption with many tiny doors, each one cryptically marked with letters of the Alexians' secret language. The bald man ran a finger along the cabinet, then snapped open one of the doors and drew out a long wooden dowel, jangling with loops of chain. He looked up and saw us in rapt distraction.

"The Grand Library. Surely there are records of this place in your monastery?"

"The godking had our records burned when his Cult took over the prison a century ago," Barnabas whispered, then looked at the servitor. "He didn't trust his brother's church to hold the secrets."

"Trusting his brother Amon led to Morgan's downfall, eh?" the servitor said tersely. "Perhaps Alexander did not wish to make the same mistake."

I stepped to the bald man and placed a hand on his shoulder. "You should watch your words in the presence of people like me."

"You should watch your hands on the body of your godking's servant, woman."

The Fratriarch placed his staff between us, and we parted. I went to stand by the railing. This guy was getting on my nerves more than he should. Something in the air of this place made me uncomfortable, like a battle shifting under your feet before you can do anything about it. I put my elbows on the railing and stared down into the shelved chasm.

The floor of the library was dark and far away. A bristling forest of frictionlamps cast a ring of dim light around the perimeter, but the center of the floor was a slippery shadow of darkness. That void seemed to writhe with shivering currents. I struggled to focus on that strange expanse. Suddenly there was a disturbance and something smooth and gray rose from the floor. It slid quietly to the edge of the darkness, casting out ripples. I saw a pier, then, and tiny figures casting lines. A depthship, surfacing from the water.

"They have access to the lakeway?" I asked.

"No, no. There are wards. The lake is there for our use." The servitor shook his head. "They could no more travel it than they could fly out that window. Settle down."

The city of Ash was unique in the world, in that it floated on a great lake. Ironically, the many fabulous machines, each as large as a country town, that churned and lifted and stabilized the city were the design of Amon the Scholar. In this he had not betrayed his brothers, for those engines still kept the city afloat all these centuries later. But as much of the city lay below water as above it. This submarine section was linked by long passages of steel and stone, known collectively as the lakeway, navigable only by depthships. In places it emerged in underwater chambers, or let out into the black deeps of the lake itself.

To have an open passage to this network in the middle of a prison . . . well. I found it strange.

"I don't care if you've nailed their tongues to the floor, Baldie. I don't care about your chain tricks or the fact that these bloody bookworms probably can't even swim. The second we're out of here I'm filing a motion with the Council to have that 'way sealed and your access suspended until such time—"

"Are you here to add anything of value to these proceedings, or is your sole purpose in this matter to run your mouth and lose your temper and make pointless threats that you have no ability to carry out?" he snapped. He left the open cabinet and stuck one pale, thin finger in my face. "Because I'm beginning to suspect that you're nothing but a good sword and a great rack!"

"Yeah," I said, thoughtful. "Yeah. That's all of your wisdom I'm going to take."

I flared invokations: the Sundering Stone, the Wall of the World, Hunter's Heart. My sword was in my hands, bleeding light and smoke and fire. The Alexian took a step back, and his form was fraying at the edges as he chanted the defensive invokations of the Healer. Barnabas stepped between us, then cracked me across the head with his staff. My invokations dropped.

"Child," he said, and nothing more. Over his shoulder, the servitor of Alexander looked on with amusement. I returned the sword to the tiny, clasping hands of the sheath and took a stance of meditation.

"You should teach your children better, Fratriarch. A servant of Alexander knows his place in the presence of Elders." The servitor whipped his hands and the invokation fell, his body snapping back to wholeness like a spring. Barnabas rounded on him.

"A servant of Alexander should know his place," he snarled. He poked the pale man in the sternum with the staff. "Wet nurse, or bed maid, or hearth servant." Poke. "Not provoking the scions of Morgan." The Fratriarch crowded the servitor, stepping in too close and then following him as he retreated. "God of War. Champion of the Field. Heart of the Hunter. Do you understand?"

"That woman is . . . she is—"

"She is a warrior, an anointed Paladin, a scion of Morgan. She is a dangerous person." He put an old hand against the servitor's chest and gave him a slow, powerful push. The pale man stumbled back. "As are we all, dangerous people."

The servitor trembled against the cabinet, staring at the Fratriarch. He looked between us, then picked up the chained dowel that had tumbled from his hand.

"We have business, Fratriarch. There's no need for this to get complicated."

"It always is, servitor," Barnabas said. His voice was tired. "It always is."

The bald man scowled but returned to the cabinet. He fingered the dowel, then unclasped a length of chain and handed it to Barnabas.

"Some of the chains express an aura of restraint, drawing on the souls of any who have been bound. We use those for crowd control. Other sets are attuned to specific individuals. Since your request was for a single subject, this is probably the best."

Barnabas took the chain. It was a narrow loop, not more than six inches in loose diameter. He twined it around his fingers and squinted. "How does it . . . Ah." The old man looked disoriented for a moment. Startled, I stepped forward and put a protective hand on his elbow. Slowly he regained his bearings. He looked at the servitor. "You didn't have to hurt them at all, did you?"

The bald man shrugged.

"Well, where is he?" Barnabas looked around, then stopped. "She. Yes, I see. Like this."

He raised the chain, his fist clenching around the flat, dull links. A figure rose from a table on a nearby terrace and crossed over to join us. She was a young woman, a girl really. The dark robes of the Cult of Amon hung loosely on her frame, but she had her hood down. Her hair stuck out in thick, black curls, startling against her pale skin. She kept her eyes lowered. The chains that hung around her shoulders looked very new.

"A child? Did our request not stress the importance of our need?" Barnabas asked.

"This one is . . . gifted. Unique. Have faith in Alexander, my friends."

"My knee will bend to him, sir," I said, "but my faith belongs to Morgan."

The servitor shrugged again, laughter dancing in his eyes. "As you say. If this girl will not serve, I'm sure we could reprocess your request. It would take some weeks, of course."

"Don't toy with us, Healer." I looked the Amonite up and down. A pretty thing, if frail. Battle would break her. "What's your name?"

"Cassandra," the girl said. Her voice was quiet.

"You can incant the histories of Amon? The rites of the Scholar?" Barnabas asked.

The girl looked between us, then raised her arms and locked her fists together in front of her small breasts. Her voice, when it rolled into the quiet of the Grand Library, was a different creature from the timid ghost that had given her name as Cassandra. It was rich, resonant, touching in the deep places of my mind. The words spoke of stress lines and inertia, gear periods and energy reserves. It was the language of clockwork, the language of machines and engines arcane. It had a rhythm to it, smooth, churning, driving forward from beneath my skin and through my bones to a peak of momentum and mass and energy.

"Hold," Barnabas barked, and the girl stopped. I came out of a stupor I hadn't realized I was in. The room was changed. A table by the cabinet was disassembled, the old form cut away into gears and chains of wood. It was some sort of machine now, clockworks and cranks and long pistons of polished maple that gleamed in the half-light of the glass domes above. A gentle cloud of sawdust hung in the air around us.

"Do you see, now, the futility of locks, Lady Paladin?" the servitor asked. I stared at the wreckage of the newly made engine.

"What's it for?"

The girl shrugged. "It goes around," she said. "It is an engine merely for the sake of engineering."

"We've seen enough," the Fratriarch said. "She will do."

Our departure had none of the idle tension that marked our arrival. The servitor chatted happily with the Fratriarch as we made our way through the book-hemmed labyrinth. I walked beside the girl Cassandra, my hand on my revolver.

"So, what is the purpose of your request, Frat Barnabas?" the servitor asked. "One hundred years, the Cult of Morgan doesn't step foot in the Library Desolate, and suddenly you make a request for one of our guests. Some project, I assume?"

"What business is it of yours? She will be returned to your charge, brother."

"As you say. Though, to be honest, with your companion I wouldn't be so sure. Small matter to me. I love the Amonites no more than you do. A matter of curiosity, is all."

"Then curiosity it must remain." Barnabas folded his hands at his waist, indicating resolve. The subtlety of his action was lost on the servitor.

"Plumbing trouble, perhaps? The Chamber of the Fist is hip deep in used toilet water, eh?" The servitor beamed and chuckled. He looked back at me. "We have plumbers in the city of Ash, you know. No need to deal with the folk of Amon for that."

"As much as I appreciate the assistance of the godking in this matter, I'm afraid our reasons must remain our own," the Fratriarch said.

"Have the scions of Morgan so lost faith in his brother Alexander, then?"

"As you said," Barnabas stopped and turned to the bald man, "it was faith in our brother Amon that cost Morgan his life. And gained Alexander a throne."

The servitor smiled stiffly, then nodded and led us out.

CHAPTER TWO

he streets outside were busy. We began the long walk back to
the Strength of Morgan, leading our black-robed charge. The
girl kept her head down as we walked. I stayed in the front, my eyes
on the crowd.

"Eva, we should speak about your outburst in there," Barnabas said
after we had walked several blocks. Took him longer than I expected.
Old man must have been tired, from all the talking and the making
nice to that bitch servitor.

"Which one?" I asked without looking back. Didn't like having
the Fratriarch out in a crowd like this. I liked it even less as his only
guard, but he hadn't wanted the sort of scene that an armed convoy
would have caused. I didn't care about the scene. Hell, I just wanted
more swords, more guns, and more eyes on the crowd. The Frat was
probably right, though. Too much attention. Besides, the Cult of
Morgan was spread awfully thin. The days of armored columns were
behind us. I stopped daydreaming about a glorious caravan of fellow
Paladins and snapped back to the conversation. "That man was trying
to piss me off. I obliged."

"Not much of a task, Eva. Listen." He plucked my sleeve and I
stopped, but I wouldn't look at him. These talks were bad enough
without having to see the expression in his watery old eyes. "The Cult
is waning. We need to preserve our relationship with Alexander and
his scions. He's the last of the brothers still alive. Without his support,
we'd be adrift. We'd be dead."

"Is it too much to ask that he honor the memory of his dead
brother?" I turned, glaring at the Amonite before settling my gaze on
Barnabas. His eyes were old and tired. "That his scions treat the Cult
of Morgan as something more than a curious relic from antiquity?"

"He honors us. Without him——"

"Honor? He drags us out for parades and holidays. He has his court jester write poems in Morgan's memory, then he steals our recruits and dedicates them to his own Cult. He's strangling us with bloody honor, Fratriarch."

Barnabas winced. The crowd around us had slowed, gradually becoming aware of who was standing in their midst, and what these rare individuals were arguing about. The Fratriarch bent his head to me and spoke in a furious hiss.

"He does not steal recruits, Eva. Morgan is dead. Amon is dead. Of the three Brothers Immortal, only Alexander remains. Parents do not dedicate their children to the service of a dead god."

I looked around at the silent crowd.

"Mine did," I said, then marched off. The pedestrians melted away from me, anxious and afraid.

"Aye, girl. We know," Barnabas said quietly, then glanced at the Amonite and motioned her forward. "Come on. She'll leave us if we let her."

I made them struggle for a minute before slowing so they could catch up. I was a little embarrassed to have walked away from the man I was supposed to be guarding, but I was a little more pissed that he'd lectured me in public. We walked in tense silence for a while, then I drew up next to the Fratriarch.

"So why are we doing this?" I asked, nodding at the quiet girl in her black robe and dull chains. "We've had no need for an Amonite for one hundred years. Why now?"

"It is a matter for the Elders, Eva."

"Well. Let me know if this one is lacking. I can be persuasive."

The girl looked up. Her face was impassive. "I will serve you, scion of Morgan. But not out of fear."

I snorted. "As you say. Just keep in mind that—"

"We're being followed," Barnabas said under his breath.

And we were. Of course we were. Damn Barnabas's fault for calling me out, and that damn Alexian's fault for being a windbag and giving me a good reason to get in trouble. That was my first mistake of the day, I think. Probably not the worst. I pulled our little group to the side of the road, grabbing the girl by her thin shoulders and pretending to shake her. Like we were arguing.

"Where are they?" I asked. The girl kept staring at me, indifferently. Barnabas pulled my hands away from the girl.

"They've passed us now. Probably more around and they're just handing off the tail." I looked up at his face, then followed his eyes down the street. Two men in bulky overcloaks, the hoods up, were strolling casually along. They turned a corner and one of them spared us a glance. His face was cowled, a ventilated metal mask covering his nose and mouth. His eyes were much older than his body suggested, and there were strange markings around them like tattoos. The pair disappeared behind a building. I looked back at Barnabas and the girl. She was still staring at me.

"Distinctive couple," I said. "Not terribly sneaky."

"They snuck up on you," Cassandra said.

I grimaced, but ignored her. Barnabas was looking up and down the street.

"They were pretty obvious. Maybe just trying to spook us?" I asked.

The old man shook his head. "There was something different about them, right up until they passed us." He twisted his staff in his hands like he was wringing a towel. "I didn't see them either. Not at all. For all that they stuck out, I didn't see them."

"Invokation of some kind?"

"Something."

I looked at the girl again. "Maybe the sworn rites of Amon the Betrayer?" I asked. She flinched, but her eyes did not leave mine. "One of your assassin friends, come to collect his girl?"

"The Betrayer's invokations are proscribed," she answered. "They are not recorded, they are not practiced. They are not known, to me or any of my brethren."

"Sure, honey. Everyone believes that. You're all innocence and knowledge. We get it." I turned to Barnabas. "What do we do?"

"There won't be any more. The Amonites' shadowkin work alone, or in small teams. If those are truly Amonites of the Betrayer . . ." He trailed off. "We should find a Justicar's post. Get an escort."

"What happened to not causing a scene?"

"That was to avoid attention." He gathered himself up, holding the staff in front of him like a plow. "We seem to have attracted attention."

"Nearest post is five blocks. North, north, west, follow the iron stairs," Cassandra said, as though reciting scripture. "We can be there in two minutes."

"You just happen to know that?" I asked.

"We maintain the city. We know the streets."

"Very well," Barnabas said. I put a hand on his shoulder, then made my second mistake.

"North is out of our way," I said. "The Strength is east and south."

"The nearest post—" Cassandra began.

I interrupted her. "We're going south and east. There are posts along the way."

Barnabas shrugged. I unholstered my bully and quickly invoked the Long Reach, the Iron Teeth, and Balance of the Songbird. The cylinder hummed as the etched rounds in the revolver glowed with power. Weaker invocations, but they were the only bullistic rites I had. I was a girl of the blade, but this wasn't the place for that much steel.

"We'll move fast. Elder Frat, you and the girl move side by side. Stay ahead of me. If I yell, you drop. Unless I yell something about running. Then you run."

"Shouldn't you be in front?" Cassandra asked. "Leading us, or something?"

"Bitch Betrayers come from behind. If I can see them, I can shoot them. It's a pretty simple system, really," I said, then crossed the bullistic over my chest and nodded. "Let's get going."

We moved out into the crowd, which was rapidly dispersing. Crowds smell trouble. In this case, maybe the crowd saw a heavily armed Paladin of Morgan with her bully out, escorting an old man and an angry girl, all of them looking nervous and a little trigger-happy. Barnabas invoked as we went, something I didn't know. An almost invisible force washed out in front of us, lapping around our legs and trailing in our wake. I had no idea what he was doing, but it made me feel better to hear the old man chant and see the blessing of Morgan around us. It made the crowd nervous, but that was okay.

Four blocks, six, then ten. The old man's voice was faltering. There really should have been a Justicar's post by now. Barnabas finally stopped invoking and just moved, taking long, deep breaths that shuddered as we walked. I hadn't seen any more of the Betrayers, but I didn't expect to. The crowds were pretty much gone. I kept looking up at the buildings we passed. Betrayers were blade-men, but what if they hired help? What if they hired a sniper? I was jumping at shadows now, and the empty streets were not calming me down.

We stumbled into an empty square and the Fratriarch stopped by the dry fountain at its center. He leaned against the concrete and hunched over. His breathing sounded bad. The girl stood next to him with her hand on his shoulder, looking for all the world as if she cared. He couldn't go on, though he would try if I asked him.

"We aren't going to make it like this," I said. Barnabas didn't answer, his thick shoulders heaving as he tried to get his breath. I looked at the girl. "Where's the nearest post now?"

"Same post. It's just twice as far away now."

"There's got to be one closer. Why the hell am I asking an Amonite where I should go to hide from another Amonite?" I started to pace around the fountain. The buildings surrounding us were part of the old district, tired and stone and settling into themselves. Faces in the windows quickly disappeared. "This is ridiculous."

"There have been a series of post closings in the last six months, mostly for maintenance issues," Cassandra said, again as if she were reciting holy writ. "The southern horn of Ash has been particularly hard hit, as the base level of that part of the city has been settling into the lake at an unusual—"

"Stop it. You don't say two words together all the way here, and now you're giving a lecture. I don't need a lecture on city infrastructure. What I need—"

There was a roar that filled the square, and the ground shook. I dropped to one knee and aimed my bully before I realized it was just the monotrain line. Tracks ran across the northern edge of the square, the elevated rails held up by rusty iron trestles that seemed to grow out of the brick of the surrounding buildings. The train rumbled past, filling the square with clattering noise and a wind that smelled of hot metal and burning grease. When it was gone I looked at the girl.

"The nearest mono station?" I asked. She nodded, and we helped the old man to his feet.

The mono lines of Ash travel the city in wide, sweeping arcs, like the cogs of a giant clock. Riding one is never the most direct way to your destination, but it is certainly the fastest. I ran up the stairs at the nearest station while Cassandra and Barnabas struggled to keep up. I caught the car just before it was leaving, kicking everyone out of the forward compartment and holding the door while the Fratriarch got on. Some of the passengers grumbled and then got on one of the other cars. A lot of them took one look at my bully and just waited for the next line. I watched everyone who got on the other car after us, then pulled the compartment shut. We rolled out of the station with a groan.

"I used to ride the train, when I was a boy," Barnabas said. He sat with his eyes closed, his head leaning gently against the car window as we bumped up to our full speed. "My mother and I would take it to the northern horn, to visit the docks. She made a brilliant fish chowder, every Sunday."

"They had trains back then, old man?" I asked. "I always pictured you growing up in a cave, maybe with a mule or something to carry you down to the rock store."

"We had trains, Eva. And revolvers and elevators and hot water." He smiled, and his face filled with wrinkles. "We were very civilized people back then."

"These lines were laid by Amon the Scholar, in the hundredth year of the Fraterdom," the girl said. She was standing, leaning against the wooden frame of the window, one hand on a leather loop that hung from the ceiling. "He laid the lines and built the centrifugal impellors that power them with his own hands."

"Was this before or after he murdered his brother Morgan on the Fields of Erathis?" I asked. "Oh, right, it must have been before. Because afterward we hunted him down, chained him into a boat, and burned him alive. So it must have been before that, right?"

She didn't answer at first, swaying with the movement of the train, her eyes on the city as it ripped past.

"Yes," she said eventually. "It was before all of that. But not much before."

We rode in silence for a while, the Fratriarch breathing quietly in his seat, the girl watching the window. I paced the length of the car, my boots wearing down the already heavily worn carpet. It had probably been nice carpet, once. I cancelled the invokations of the bullistic revolver and just paced. I kept looking back at the other passengers in their cars, but they made a point of not raising their eyes from their newspapers. I was glancing back when the light hit, so at least I still had my eyes when it happened.

It was a fast shot, traveling from my left and going toward the front of the car. It came in through the windows like a lightning flash, first behind us, then keeping pace, then ahead of us and nearly gone. I was just glancing over my shoulder to see what it was when the sound came. Tearing, like ripped cloth. The tracks shook and then everything was washed in red and gold and a terrible, terrible sound.

We fell. I hit the carpet hard and slid all the way to the front of the car, slamming to a stop with my shoulder against the wall. The girl slid into me, screaming. Barnabas ended up against the benches. He was the first to his feet. I pushed the girl away and stood. Cassandra lay on the floor, burbling and wailing. When she rolled over I saw that her right hand was a mangle of skin. There was no blood, but the bones were broken, and there were long, angry friction burns across the palm and back. Her thumb was pointing in several wrong directions.

Outside the car, there was smoke and metal. Something had hit the track. The creosote-smeared wooden spars of the tracks were burning with chemical brilliance, thick black plumes of smoke rolling off in heavy waves to the street below. The rails themselves were as tangled as the girl's hand. We were off the tracks and leaning in dangerous ways. The other passengers were screaming. I was screaming, too.

"Get up and away from the windows. Get off the car!" I yelled. In the cars behind us, people were slapping open the emergency hatches and riding the telescoping chutes to the ground. I started toward our own chute just as the car torqued under some unseen force. All the windows popped, then the ceiling peeled open like a scroll. Fat coils of rope, three of them, landed on the floor around us.

They landed in a rough semicircle. I turned my back to the Fratriarch, pushing the whimpering Cassandra behind me. The girl stumbled to the ground, cradling her limp hand against her chest. I hurriedly invoked armor and strength, sketchy bindings that I could snap out without thinking. I didn't have time to think. Gold lines traced the edges of my greaves and pauldrons, and the air around me tightened. The runes of my noetic armor settled down to a warm glow. As invocations went, they were weak, but there wasn't time for anything fancy.

Our assailants wore armor, actual armor, though it was roughly formed. Their faceplates were flat and plain, two bulbous gogglelike eyes over a voxorator grate. The metal of their breastplates and pauldrons was dull gray, sheened like oil on water. Wickedly barbed blades snapped out from their armguards. They attacked without saying a word.

I laid into them. My opening strike was to the left, scything past the first brute's guard with the weight of my attack. The blade struck his shoulder, denting metal and drawing a staticky shriek from his vox. He collapsed to the floor, and I followed the force of the blow, letting my sword swing low. My momentum rolled me over the fallen warrior. I came to my feet. This separated me from the Fratriarch, but their attention was fully on me. *That's right, watch the dangerous bitch. Don't worry about the old man.* The two remaining guys were nicely lined up. I turned the flat of my blade toward them and invoked.

"Morgan stood at the gates of Orgentha, broken city, broken wall. He stood in the stones and bones of the defenders; he stood before the spears of the invader." My voice was flat and quiet, grinding like stone in the grist. This was a new invocation for me, and I had to focus to draw into the past and pull out the power of Morgan's story. Hard lines of energy danced around my legs, light cutting in spirals through the train's dusty interior. The attackers stared at me impassively with their glassy eyes. I hurried, binding the invocation as quickly as I could. "Three days he stood against them, alone, shield as a wall, sword as an army. The city stood. He stood. The Wall of Orgentha."

The long, complicated length of my sword flashed, the power springing from the floor and coalescing against the blade. I swept it down and a brickwork of light traveled across the train, cutting the Fratriarch and Cassandra off from the attackers. The bug-eyed men looked the wall up and down, its light winking brightly off their lenses. When they looked back in my direction I had moved. I stood at the rough opening that had been torn in the car, swinging my sword in the slow circles of a balanced guard.

"Wall behind you, sword before you," I snarled and smiled. "Nowhere to go, boys."

The fallen attacker stood slowly. He moved his arm sparingly, and the dents around his shoulder leaked blood. He watched me warily. Odd curls of cold fog wisped out from under his mask.

"Three to one?" I asked. Their absolute silence was getting to me. "I am comfortable with those odds, now that I don't have to worry about the Fratriarch." I slid from balanced guard into a more aggressive stance. "Let us settle our differences, as warriors do."

The air filled with the roaring drone of engines. Behind the shimmering wall, Cassandra's eyes went wide, even around the shock. The Fratriarch grimaced, then put a hand on the girl's shoulder and began invoking. Reluctantly, I glanced behind me.

A dozen more, their bulbous green eyes bright as they arced toward the train from the ground on columns of black smoke. These men wore two barrel-wide burners on their backs, flame flickering around the turbine blades as they whined forward. Couldn't hold off this many. I looked back at the Fratriarch.

"Go!" he yelled. His voice was muffled behind the wall of light.

"If I leave you, the invokation will unravel."

"Girl, I have my own tricks." He planted his staff and leaves of metal began to tear through the ruined carpet from the car and swirl around him like a tornado on an autumn day. The leaves slapped together into a rough, hollow column around the Fratriarch. He drew the girl close to him. "Morgan on the Fields of Erathis, Eva Forge. Remember."

The last metal flake fell in place, and I dropped the wall. Light continued to flash from the column. Other invokations, other wards. The Fratriarch was Morgan's First Sword, his greatest scion in the world, I reminded myself. One of the framework towers that held the monotracks up over the city was nearby, and I jumped to it from the car, leaving the old man to take care of himself. Third mistake. That was probably the big one.

I clambered down as the flying goggle-men adjusted their trajectories to intercept me, jumping the last twenty feet. The arcane strength of my legs cratered the cobblestone street when I landed.

Morgan on the Fields of Erathis. A fateful thing for the Fratriarch to say, I thought as I jogged away from the elevated tracks. There were small crowds of injured civilians still clambering down from the train and dispersing into the city. Trying to get away from the fighting. Lots of screaming, lots of blood, but there were no threats among them. No hidden assassins. It made me think briefly about the Betrayers. This was nothing like their usual attacks, their small teams, their knives in the backs of their enemies. No time for that now. The distant moan of emergency sirens echoed beneath the urgent roar of the burnpacks of the attackers that were even now descending to the ground. They landed in the streets, fire and smoke haloing around them, scattering the already panicked civilians like leaves before a forest fire. I ducked into an alley.

In some ways, Erathis was Morgan's greatest battle. The Rethari horde that had been rolling through the northern provinces spread out when it came to the unpopulated Erathisian grasslands. Morgan led a cadre of Paladins on a monthlong campaign against the horde. They traveled on angelwings, hitting the Rethari in unpredictable places with crippling force and speed. Morgan led his company against the Rethari weaknesses, and also against their strengths. Wagon trains and armored columns fell to Morgan's blade. They even tore down a couple of the Retharis' divine clockwork totem-men. The Rethari gods cracked under Morgan's assault.

I watched the bug-eyed men spread out, searching for me, ignoring the civilians. The three up top called down in strange, static-laced voices from the train above. Outnumbered but mobile, I moved, searching for a weakness to strike. The comparison that the Fratriarch made was apt. As always, there was wisdom in his words.

I circled away from the elevated track, lacing new invocations into the air around me as I went. My armor tightened in memory of Morgan's Hundred Wounds, and my blade gleamed as I bound it with the Sundering. My step lightened as I invoked Morgan's march against the city of Ter-Trudan. When I felt appropriately buffed, I returned to the site of the crash from a different direction. Three of the strange men were standing in the wreckage of the ruined building, glass grinding under their feet. One of them was carrying some sort of heavy bullistic, awkward loops of ammunition twisted around his waist and shoulders. The street was thick with smoke and the sharp smell of idling burners. I came at them low to the ground, running forward in a squat, silent, hiding in the smoke of their burners until I was upon them.

"The Warrior stands!" I shrieked as I rose from the smoke behind them. I had one in half before he could raise his blades. The second offered feeble resistance, batting away my attack with his bladed gauntlets before he succumbed to a trio of armor-crumpling strikes across his chest.

Thunder rolled between the buildings as the backpedaling gunner slewed his bully around and let tear. Smoke vortexed out in whipping tendrils as the slugs ripped toward me. The hardened air of the armor invokation shuddered, knocking the breath from my lungs. Each shot hammered a little closer, the shell of my protections shimmering in protest. The metal of the noetic armor gleamed with heat as the friction of the attack sluiced off of them, the runes entangled within them failing one by one.

I went to one knee and rolled, buying seconds as the gunner corrected the stream of fire, his shots skimming off the edge of my protective shell. He dug up cobbles, shards of stone cutting my legs as I focused my defense on the impossible torrent of lead and fire. I braced my heels and sprang forward. Slugs hammered across my blade, nearly knocking it from my hands. Only the blessing of Morgan made me strong enough to hold on. The tip of the blade nicked the barrel of the gun and his aim faltered, stitching a line into the building behind me. I brought the sword around, and the backswing struck the firing chamber. The gun exploded, washing away the last of my protective invokation in a wall of fire. The gunner staggered back, windmilling the shredded rags of his arms. I stepped forward and struck him cleanly through the chest.

"Damn unnatural weapons," I spat. My hands and legs were

shaking, and curls of smoke wisped up from the tired runes of my pauldrons. I went to one knee. There was blood and ash in my mouth. The air around was a ruin of smoke. The static voices of the fallen man's comrades began to drift from the surrounding alleyways. I struggled up. My chest felt like a trampled wicker basket.

Morgan, on the Fields of Erathis. His greatest victory. The hordes of Rethari undone, the grasslands fed with their dark blood, their gods shattered into wreckage, their armor broken. The Fraterdom saved, all by the hand of Morgan.

But also by the body of Morgan. The Fields of Erathis, where treacherous Amon crept through the night, among the smoke and the confusion and the bloodletting. As Morgan slept, he came. Jealous Amon, the Betrayer, the assassin. Morgan on the Fields of Erathis, murdered by his brother.

I blinked sweat and fear from my eyes and slipped away. More of the strange men came into the square. More bullistic weapons, more bladed gauntlets. More than I could handle on my own. I looked up at the mono car, where the Fratriarch still waited, bound by his wards, shielded. For now.

Morgan on the Fields of Erathis. An apt description.

CHAPTER THREE

They were beginning to panic. You could see it in the way they clustered under the tracks of the elevated train, hear it in the strange squealing language of their voxorators. The sirens were getting closer, the emergency response teams rushing to rescue the injured from the monotrain accident. Several of the strange men had set off to intercept the sirens. That would bring an armed response, and they knew it. Time was running out.

Nothing they had was going to cut through the Fratriarch's wards. And it was clear that he was their target, from the way they kept close to the train, the way so many of them kept climbing up and arguing and then climbing down. The way they looked up nervously to the car dangling from the ruined tracks, flaring light and dull explosions marking their failed attempts to get inside Barnabas's shields. No way they were going to do it. No way I could let them do it.

When I stumbled out of the square, there was no immediate pursuit. They clustered under the train and regrouped. I did the same in a quiet alleyway, weaving invocations into armor and strength, flaring power along the length of my blade, cursing myself for letting the Fratriarch out of the monastery without a full guard. For letting him outside at all. I would get one chance to make it right, I knew. One chance to go in and cut them down before the old man's wards failed. Balancing act between recouping my arcane reserve and guessing how long Barnabas could last. Lots of unknowns in that equation, so I played it dangerous and went back in before I was fully invoked. No use being at full strength if they got away with the Fratriarch while I was buffing up in some corner.

I crawled to the edge of the roadway behind some wreckage from the mono derailment to see how my strange little friends were progressing. The goggle-faced crew was under the tracks, talking and pointing. As I watched, a couple of them shrugged their burnpacks more firmly on their backs and walked to the center of the square. The wide, loud turbines began to cycle up. Hot, stinging air washed off them in oily waves.

Going to get help. Going to get bigger explosives, or cutting torches, or . . . Brothers knew what else. Going to get one of their renegade Amonites, probably, to Unmake the whole damn car until they could pry the old man out by his teeth. I couldn't let them go. If I was going to stop them, it had to happen now, or not at all. Now.

I had already incanted the Rite of the Stag Hunt for speed, Morgan's Journey and the Long Stand to keep the fatigue far enough away, and, finally, the Walls of Alteraic. I didn't have the words that the Fratriarch could manage, or the more complicated invocations of the bullistic revolver that came with devotion to other paths, but I sparked up what I knew, and came in burning like a flare. The sword is my path, the sword my fire and my strength.

I came out of cover at a blind sprint, the wide, flat steel of my sword held up over my head. They were facing away from me, the barrel-like engines of their burnpacks blocking my approach from their view. Halfway across the courtyard, my legs hammering the cobbles like iron pistons, I began to yell the invocation of the Mortal Blade. It doesn't last long, and you have to wait until the last second to flare it or it runs out before you run out of enemies. Plus it's nice for the intimidation.

"I bind myself to the Champion, the Warrior, the battlefield, the blade!" I intoned, my flat, arcane voice grinding out like an avalanche of steel. As I spoke, fat red sparks rolled off my weapon like crimson leaves in an autumn breeze. The air around me coiled with power. Red and black flecks coalesced in front of me, plowing forward as I ran. "I bind to blood, to fire, to steel, to grave! I bind myself to battle and the war eternal! For Morgan, dead and unending!"

They saw me, too late.

The near one turned, raising the intricate double blades of his gauntlets into a guard that would never withstand such arcane fury. I cut him down, the blade sliding in an easy cross against his chest, his blades and his arms falling away as he crumpled to the ground. His companion took one look at the invokations roiling over my noetically armored body and fired the turbines on his burnpack. Flames and heat filled the square and a plume of smoke boiled down to the cobbles.

I rushed toward him, my blade catching the fleeing warrior on the shoulder. He twisted, his control of the 'pack wavering as he sluiced sideways. I punched forward with the blade, strength and force coming from my hips, my legs. The tip of the wide sword parted his chest and drove back into the whining furnace of the turbines. A tongue of flame lashed out from the man's chest, charring the scream that died on his lips. I whipped the sword out in a backhand slash. The turbines ruptured, tearing the man apart.

The explosion battered my shields, framing me in angry fire, flames of blue and red that tore up into the sky. The shock wave rippled up into the towers that surrounded the square. Glass shattered into a diamond snow that crashed down to the cobbles. Glittering shards flaked across the remnants of my shield, building up a shell of starry light shot through with skeins of furious red.

The glass settled into a field of sharp light, reflected from the sun above. The cataclysm of the explosion echoed through the canyons of the city. The bodies of the two men lay twisted under the tiny glass flecks.

I turned to the men standing beneath the elevated tracks and raised my sword in salute.

"I bind myself," I said quietly, gasping with the effort of the invokations and the fight, "to battle. The blade. The grave."

The last misty shards of glass shuffled to the ground. They crunched under the knobby treads of my boots like broken bones. In the shining light that reflected off the broken-tooth windows far above, the courtyard was silent. The goggle-eyed men and I stared at one another. *Before they gather themselves*, I thought. *Before they recover from watching me blow one of their comrades into rags of meat and ash. Before I collapse from the strain of the attack, from the sheer arcane weight crushing my lungs and straining against my bones.* Before I became something I couldn't control.

I moved, and the air shimmered around me as I ran. Waves of force tore away from my sword as I swung it into a variable guard-to-strike position. The stones under my boots boomed as I rushed them, rushed them like an avalanche broken free from the mountain of god. My scream was meaningless and terrifying, full of incoherent rage, full of pain and anger.

I moved and they fell back. Dropped their weapons, their guards, their formation, and fell back. But not fast enough. Never fast enough. The first one I caught on his heels, his sword held forgotten by his knee. Two more fell before any of them held a guard worth avoiding. I burned bright, flaring my invokations for quick results. Had to break them fast. I couldn't win a long fight, not against this many.

Another down, arm and shoulder split from his chest, the heat of my blade curling up in wisps of smoke from the edges of the wound. My head was a dull roar, little in it but the form of the sword and the rage of murdered Morgan arcing through my bones. Something lurked at the edge of my attention, though, something begging to be heard through the fire of the battle. The next one managed a guard block and counterstrike as my mind raced.

Blood. The blood. I raised my sword warily, sparring with the warrior. The others were circling. Another one came at me and I fell into a dual guard position without thinking about it, cycling my sword in broad, sweeping arcs, finally finishing the first attacker with a cut to the inner thigh that slid through bone and whirled up into the stinking mess of his guts. He folded, and I spun around to give my full attention to the second man. I held my sword in front of me.

The blood hung on the wide blade like lumpy mud, smearing across the sun-bright metal in uneven streaks. Old blood, cold blood, blood that had clotted and cooled and stiffened like tar.

Dead man's blood.

I looked at the man at my feet. He sat on the ground, a clumpy pool of thick gore spilling out of his burst gut. His voxorator squealed in mindless complaint, then he raised the gauntlet of his right hand and drove the blade into my knee.

Pain burst through my leg like a wildfire, and I shrieked. The tip of his weapon skidded off the hazy shell of my invoked shield, but was thrust hard enough and came close enough that it drew blood and scraped bone. Still screaming, I brought the sword down. Put the blade into his head near the base of the sword, then drew back, slicing, running the dull metal of his helmet along the full length of the sword in a long, rasping strike that slid through metal, bone, and meat. Tar-thick blood spilled out. A swirling tendril of fog followed the blade through the wound like smoke snatched by the wind. Frost glittered along the blade, and then the man fell back. Dead. Finally.

The others were on me in a breath. Seven or eight of them, and it was all I could do to stay in one piece. Blades slipped through the waning shield, the power of the invokation stressed by the explosion and the sheer number and ferocity of their attacks. I was able to sneak in a handful of guard strikes to legs and hands that would have crippled living men. These things, these warriors, these cold-meat, dead-blood monsters . . . they fought on. Glittering frost and gummy blood slopped from their wounds with each strike. I retreated, foot by foot, shifting my stance closer to the edge of the square. When I got to the mouth of an alleyway I dropped the rest of my arcane bindings and flared the invoka-tion of the Rite of the Stag Hunt, pushed it into my legs, and leapt away from contact with the dead men in a series of long, ground-shuddering steps. I slid around a corner and started to run in a staggering gait.

I was spent. By the time I disengaged, I counted five attackers left. Just as many more were limping off, arms or legs mangled beyond use. Still too many in my present condition. As I ran the final invokations wisped away, leaving me drained. When the Hunt faltered, I stumbled to a halt against the side of a building to catch my breath. Hell, it was all I could do not to lie down and tremble into sleep. I slid to the ground, sword tumbling to the stone of the street.

"What the hell is going on back there?" I gasped to the empty street. My hands shook as I wiped the clods of blood away from my sword with a rag. Tired, bone-tired. Scared, too. I tried to go through the meditation of assessment, struggling to focus against the ham-mering of my heart. Blood leaked from my knee, both arms, a dozen smaller cuts, and a deeper wound that had scraped my ribs. The invokations that had wrapped me away from these things were gone, and now the flesh was back and full of holes. My hands hummed from the constant striking of metal against metal and yielding bone. I fum-bled open the first-aid kit from my thigh pocket and bandaged up as best I could. I didn't have it in me to invoke the Binding of Flesh just now. Didn't have anything left. I wiped the blood from my hands and threw the rag to the ground.

I struggled to my feet. Tired, scared. Unsure of the tactical situation. Had they gone for help? Had they gotten at the Fratriarch? More important, why in the name of the living Brother was I fighting dead men, and what did they want with the Fratriarch? I was used to fighting alone. I expected to fight alone. Just not dead men, and not with the life of the Fratriarch on the line. And he was back there, alone with the girl. With the Amonite. Those wards of his wouldn't last forever.

I jogged toward the wreck of the monotrain, taking a longer, circuitous route back. The streets were quiet. I held the double-handed sword in a loose grip, hugging it close to my body. So tired, afraid I was going to drop it, but more afraid that if I sheathed it I wouldn't be able to draw fast enough if one of those dead men jumped me.

Creeping the last few yards to the square, I invoked a weak shield and snuck up to the corner. The courtyard was empty.

I moved carefully around the wreckage of the fight. The civilians were long gone, obviously, but where were my attackers? I reached the elevated track and reluctantly put the blade away, then started to climb. The iron trestles offered good handholds, but I was drained to the bone. Twice I nearly fell before I was able to scramble onto the track.

The car leaned dangerously away from the courtyard, probably unsettled by the burnpack's explosion or some other tampering by the undying assailants as they tried to pry Barnabas from his shell. I stepped inside carefully, this time holding the revolver in shaky hands. There was a body in the entrance, the scarred metal of the dead man's armor rimed with frost. I put a boot into his shoulder and turned him over.

His chest had burst open, the grim smile of ribs clenched behind the metal. That same tarry blood lined the wound, but where there should have been heart and lungs, there was a glass cylinder. A piston cycled slowly inside the glass, a plunger of leather and brass that rose slowly before settling to the bottom of the tube with a metallic sigh. Up and down, slowly. Breathing.

I drew back the hammer of the ordained revolver and sighted along the barrel, then fired a slug into the dead man's chest. The glass popped and a cloud of fog erupted out, twisting up to the revolver before dancing across my chest and filling my face. Startled, I gasped for air and swallowed a century's cold lungful of ancient, stale breath. It tasted like metal caskets and the frozen memories of tombs, buried in stone and ice. I staggered back, coughing until my lungs were clear. Shivering just as much from the memory of that breath as from the cold, I stepped into the car.

The floor was charred. Not an easy task with metal. The seats were nothing but twisted wreckage, the windows all blown out, and the Fratriarch's column of metal was gone. Where it had been, the floor was clear, spotless. There was something at the edge, a tiny dot of color against the dark metal. I bent down for a closer look. Just a drop, really. I put a finger to it and it burst, splattering across my nail. Holding it up to my face, I twisted to get a better look in the light from outside the car.

Blood. Real blood, red and warm and slippery between my fingers. The Fratriarch was gone.

My earliest memory of the Fratriarch is one of my earliest memories, period. I was in a car, the interior warm red leather, the woman sitting next to me dressed in a tight gray dress, her face covered by a white lace veil. My mother, I think, or a woman who was mourning my mother. I had the feeling of coming from some complicated ritual. Something that I hadn't understood, but that everyone around me took very seriously. Very sadly. Later in life I told myself it was a funeral. It could have been anything. I remember not understanding, but also not being afraid.

It was raining outside. The car drove through parts of the city I didn't know. More than that. Drove through a city I didn't know, like I didn't know what cities were. I knelt on the seat and looked out the window at all the close-together houses, the tall buildings, the crowded sidewalks. So many people. Something in my memory compared this to long gardens, carefully manicured, perfectly empty. Even the trees of my memory were empty. No birds, no squirrels.

The woman sitting next to me pulled me to the seat beside her, wrapping my tiny hands in her long, cold fingers, pressing them into my lap. I looked up at her, but she was facing forward. Watching where we were going.

The driver was a man, just another man, gray coat and hat and gloves. He drove stiffly. I pulled on my mother-mourner's hand, straining to look out the window, but all I could see were the rain-streaked clouds and the stony tops of buildings.

The car stopped and the man got out and came around to our door. The woman looked at me for the first and last time, then released my hands. The man opened my door. A wave of rain washed into the car, spattering across the deep-red leather. I shied away from the sudden cold and wet. Afraid to ruin my dress and my little hat. The woman put a hand on my hip and slid me out. I stumbled on the runner and nearly fell, catching the man's pants leg in a twist of my fingers. He closed the door and went around to the front again. I looked back at the car, water beading across its beetle-smooth black shell, its engine huffing quietly in the rain. I was getting soaked.

A square, like a courtyard, but shabbier. I don't know what I compared this place to, to consider it shabby. There was a statue, a high wall that surrounded the circular drive, an iron gate that was open. I was standing in the lee of a grand high building, made of old stone and curving smoothly away from the ground like a big old egg. It looked like the coldest, hardest place I'd ever seen. There was a door that looked tiny, but only because it led out from this enormous place. A dozen half-circle stairs led up to the door, and there were two men in simple gray robes standing close to the building, out of the rain.

The car roared to life behind me, and I turned just in time to see it roll through the iron gate and out of view. How did I feel about that? Surprised? Relieved? Cold. Mostly I felt cold.

The closest man tossed a cigarette into a puddle and shrugged his hood over his head, then ran out into the rain to me. He was a large man, his shoulders wide as blocks, his face wrinkled and smiling. Like he enjoyed running in the rain. He leaned over me, cutting the rain off with his bulk, then held out a wide, flat hand to me.

"Miss Eva Forge? Welcome home. My name is Barnabas."

"Barnabas what?"

He shook his great head slowly, happily. "Silent. But never mind that. We don't have use for more name than that, here. Would you like to come inside?"

I looked back to the gate, where the car had driven off, then up at the friendly man and his enormous face.

"My name is Eva Forge," I said.

"Of course, dear. Now come inside."

His hand smelled like nicotine and oil. I held it and walked back to the door. He took tiny steps at my side, hunching down and keeping the rain off my nice, new hat.

I burst through the door and swept into the foyer. The Alexians had given me a white linen cloth to clean up with on the way over, and I tossed it at the stony feet of the idol of Saint Marcus and made for the holy nave. The whiteshirts who had given me a ride clustered anxiously at the door, afraid to enter but anxious to see the scene.

"Tomas!" I yelled. "Isabel! Any of you bloody old . . . lordships, if you please. Tomas!"

"You rode in on every siren in the city, Eva. You don't have to yell," Tomas said from the engraved stone archway that led to the Chamber of the Fist. "We're gathered, all the Elders. Let Barnabas come inside and we can talk about whatever it is—"

"Talk later. He's been taken."

"Taken? Who?" He dropped his cigarette and ground it out with an old, oil-stained boot. "The Fratriarch?"

I brushed past him, not sparing a glance toward the open door of the Chamber. Out of the corner of my eye, I saw the upturned faces of the rest of the Elders. There was a relic of armament next to the Chamber. I threw back the cowl and began rummaging through the offerings.

"They came at us after we left . . ." How much did he know about our business? What had the Fratriarch told him? Barnabas had said nothing to me of our business, and I was his guard. But these were the

Elders. "After we left the Library Desolate. There were two guys, following us, and then—"

My hand strayed to the dark wood tray of bullets. I hadn't seen those two again, I realized. The two bulky men with their metal cowls and tattooed cheeks. They had been following us, for sure, but they hadn't been in on the attack.

"Then?" Isabel asked. I looked up. The whole Fist of Elders was standing around me, eyes wide. Only Simeon, his dark face impassive, seemed to have gotten past the shock. He shouldered Tomas aside and began gathering bullets from the tray. I snapped out of it and joined him, pinching them into the empty cylinder of my bully.

"Then we were attacked. Strange guys . . . metal faces, goggle eyes. Never seen them before. They fought me off and took the Fratriarch."

"The Rethari have struck us here, in the city?" Tomas said, his voice trembling with rage.

"Not Rethari. Forget the field reports, Elder. I know those war drums have been beating for months, but these guys weren't the scaled bastards. They were men." I sighted the weapon, and made sure there hadn't been any damage in the fight. "They were machines."

"And the scholar?" Isabel asked.

I stopped what I was doing and looked at her. "The girl?" I asked.

"Yes, the Amonite. What became of the Amonite?"

I stood there, silently, watching Simeon load shot into his antique revolver. The rest of the Elders were clustered tight, nearly trembling.

"The hell with the Amonite," I hissed. "Barnabas is gone, Isabel. Your Fratriarch has been taken."

That broke the spell. They stepped back, Isabel nearly fluttering with anger.

"I am an Elder of this Cult, Eva, and your sworn master. You will not—"

"Next time, Izzy." I slapped the cylinder of my revolver shut and holstered it, then walked briskly to an anointing tub and dipped my sword into the water. It came out shimmering, the remaining dead, cold blood of the Fratriarch's kidnappers rolling off in clumps. "We can have this spat next time, when I have a day or so to listen to your holy nonsense. Today, right now, while we're talking, Barnabas is in enemy hands."

"Of course," Tomas said. "There is no time. We will convene the Fist and contact Alexander's representatives. The city must be mobilized."

"Sure thing," I said, then all but ran out into the street. The giant wooden door, carved with the histories of the scions of Morgan, greasy and worn with time and neglect, slammed closed behind me.

Felt good to be on the move again. To be mobilized.

The representatives of Alexander. The Healers, the whiteshirts, the nurses. Alexians. They had to be contacted, right, because they wouldn't otherwise notice the gunfight that just broke out in the middle of their city? Sure. It was a whiteshirt patrol that had given me a ride from the crash site back to the Strength of Morgan, and another patrol that was tearing hell to the godking's palace. Probably to amp up their own security.

I love my Elders, honest to Brothers, but they've gotten old. Even Elias, hard as stone, isn't going to do much more than carry that revolver tucked into his belt while he putters around his highgarden. Doing things was up to the Paladins, and these days, that was me. Just me.

I swung into the whiteshirts' wagon, crouching on the bench so my sword wouldn't bang against the wall. The Justicar sat across from me. His head was wreathed in a communications rig. I tapped the shiny iron band across his eyes and leaned in.

"Any word?" I yelled.

He opened the rig and gave me an angry glare. "It wasn't on, lady. You don't have to yell."

I slapped the rig, knocking it fully off his head, then grabbed his collar and put my lungs into it.

"Any! Word!"

"Gods, okay, okay. It's not like . . . Okay, it's exactly like that. Hold on." He picked up the rig and spun it up. "There's been some kind of interference today. Something wrong with the channels. But no. Your Fratriarch hasn't been seen. Not him, not the convoy of flying corpses that you say took him. Just one wrecked train and a lot of scared citizens."

"This is why you were late? Why I had to fight off the whole stinking pile of them myself? Your . . . channels were interfered with?"

"Yeah, that's part of it. These things go out, sometimes. Bad timing."

"Terrible timing. The worst timing." I leaned back in my seat and cursed as my articulated sheath rattled against some gear, knocking it to the ground. "Can we go somewhere, already? Can we just . . . just turn that siren on and let's go?"

"Where are we supposed to—"

"Go," I howled, then leaned forward and slapped the siren on. The rest of the patrol piled into the wagon and hauled the doors shut. We sat there in the wailing of the siren, the Justicar and I looking daggers at each other. Finally, he sighed and turned to the driver.

"Get us to the Harrington Square station. We'll check in with the land line there, see where we should deploy."

The wagon lurched forward.

I smiled at the Justicar. "It's a good start, sir. A good start."

"Glad you're happy with it."

"Happy enough. Your name's Arron, right?"

"Owen," he said.

"Owen. You're doing fine, Owen. Alexander would be very proud."

"To hell with that," he said, then twisted back to the driver. "And turn that damn siren off."

CHAPTER FOUR

The station was a squat brick building, sprouting a crown of heavy communication wires that crisscrossed the city like a spider's web. Inside it was hot and crowded, everything painted a dull, chipped white, the paint applied sloppily and thick. The air smelled like kitchen cleaner.

We checked in with Owen's patrol coordinator and were told there was no news. We checked in with headquarters. No news. A runner came from the Strength, specifically to tell us that there was no news.

The Fratriarch of the Cult of Morgan was missing, and no one knew anything more than that. I gave my interview to one of the representatives from the palace of Alexander, a real efficient-looking guy in a suit who asked brief questions and got brief answers. When we were done he folded up his notes and walked out of the station. Everyone seemed relieved when he was gone.

The city was busy enough, that's for sure. The printsheets were stuttering out of the vendors splashed with big, black letters: FRATRIARCH OF MORGAN KIDNAPPED. Every time I got up to pace to the door, one of the whiteshirts would put a hand on my shoulder to say that their boys were on the case, they had people working leads, that it was best if I stayed put and let them do their work. I felt caged. I felt like those Amonites in the Library Desolate must feel, only I hadn't signed up for it. It was well past noon when I gave up being patient and kind, and decided to go ahead and be a Paladin of Morgan. It was my nature.

"I'm going," I told Owen as I marched to the door for the fifth time that hour. They had tried to take my sword and bully when I got there. They settled for the bullets on my belt, and a promise not to draw steel. More for their own good, I think. Owen followed me to the guard station and tapped his foot while I checked out the ammo. I examined the bullets. All in order.

"You can't do any good," he said. "We've got people. Let them do their thing."

"What thing are they doing?" I asked.

"Interviewing people. Searching the scene of the crime."

"Scene of the crime. Like someone's precious bike was stolen." I slapped the cylinder shut, opened it again, spun it, slapped it shut. Nervous. "This isn't stolen property. This isn't even a murder. It's an act of war, Justicar."

"We don't know that. Honestly, we don't know much of anything. This stuff takes time, Eva."

"Time. Right. We're just awash with time. Probably a whole twenty-four hours before they kill him, right? Isn't that what the statistics say?"

"For a normal kidnapping, yes. But this isn't a normal kidnapping—"

"That's what I've been saying! Brother-damn hell, Justicar, we should be turning this city inside out."

"There's . . . we don't want to upset the populace." He looked back to the den, to the bunch of officers milling about desks and talking into clockgeists. "We don't want to scare anyone."

I sighed, like a steam engine bleeding off pressure.

"I'm going out."

"You can't," he said, trying not to sound timid. Well. Trying to sound forceful, I guess.

"I can't."

"There are orders. I was trying to tell you, but . . . it's complicated. We're supposed to keep you here."

"Whose orders?" I asked, twisting the grip of my bullistic in cold, sweaty hands.

"From the top office. From the god himself."

"Alexander?"

He nodded. "There have been threats. Warnings. Someone's saying they're going to kill off the Cult of Morgan."

"Someone," I said. "Someone said that. And you're keeping me here, keeping me safe."

Again, the nod. "Got word just after we reported in. The Strength of Morgan is on lockdown. Most of our men are focused on that, and finding out who made the threat."

"And keeping Alexander safe, no doubt. People start bumping off his brother's Cult, can't be long before they come for him."

Owen looked down and shrugged. "Security measures have been taken. Tightened. Sure, we're stepping up protection."

"Between guarding Alexander's precious white ass and keeping the Strength on lockdown . . . Owen, do you have anyone looking for the Fratriarch?"

"We're prioritizing resources, Eva. We have to. There are people looking, sure, but—"

I laughed, an angry laugh that cut the room to silence. He stood there looking at me, gaping, face white as his sloppy white desk. "I like the part where you were going to keep me here, Justicar," I said, shaking my head. "That's good."

I turned and kicked the door open, splintering the lock some idiot had installed. The street beyond was mostly empty. People were home by now, getting ready for dinner. The first shades of dusk were starting to dust the city in gray.

"That's real good," I said, and walked out into the city to find the old man.

Owen took some liberties with his orders, modifying "keep her in the station" to "try to keep up with her," and came along. Members of his patrol, too, though not the whole group. I had the feeling that frantic calls were being made back at the station. Not my problem.

"Where are we going?" he asked after we had walked the first five blocks at a brisk pace. These guys were used to rolling around in that stubby battle wagon of theirs. "I mean, are you following some kind of plan, or are we just going to kick in doors until we find your guy?"

"You guys could do with some door-kicking practice," I said. Honestly, I didn't have a plan. I just didn't like the idea of sitting on my hands. Didn't want to admit that to these whiteshirts, though. I ambled to a halt and pretended to fuss with the hang of my holster while I thought about where we were and where we might be going. The patrol stood around me, looking nervously at the dark windows and shadowy alleys.

"You don't have a plan, do you?" Owen asked.

"I have a sense of direction," I answered, folding my arms across my chest. "A sense of purpose. And, as you've noted, I have some experience kicking in doors."

"But no plan," he said.

I grimaced. "Not yet. I prefer to develop these things organically. That way I don't have to fight my own presumptions when the situation changes."

"Yeah," he said. "Don't think, just jump."

"Look, if you'd rather be back at your desk, I'm not keeping you here."

"Yeah."

We smoldered at each other, then he shook his head and sighed.

"We have to start somewhere. What was the first strange thing you noticed about that fight?"

"That we were going to the Library Desolate. That we were talking to Amonites. That it was the Fratriarch doing all this, rather than some attendant or man-at-arms."

"Or woman-at-arms," Owen said. His patrol was getting antsy. I was getting antsy.

"Don't be smart. It was a weird bit of business."

"I agree," he said, "but I don't think that'll help us find your man. Unless what he was doing might have something to do with why he was taken."

And of course I hadn't considered that. To me, the business was bad but it was just business. In my mind, the enemies of the Fratriarch (and of the Cult of Morgan in general) didn't need a reason to do the things they did. They were crazy. They hated us. They looked for opportunities, not reasons. Consequently, I looked for ways to prevent those opportunities rather than debating the reasons behind them. I shrugged.

"Maybe. You want me to list the dozens of factions and principalities who might have a grudge against the Cult of Morgan? We've killed a lot of people in our generations."

"Might be easier to list your allies," he said.

"I don't keep that list."

"You're a real bright spot in my day, Eva Forge. So." He looked around at the dingy square where we were having our little head-to-head. "You want to pick a door to kick in, or shall I?"

"We're not kicking in doors," I said. The idiot patrollers actually looked relieved. "Maybe you're right. Maybe it was related to what we were doing."

"With the Amonite? Probably. I mean, you have to admit, it's kind of strange."

"Yeah. And there was that tail, the two guys with the tattoos around their eyes."

"The who?"

"The two guys. I told your bureaucrat all about it, during the interview."

"That wasn't in the report," he said, then started digging in one of his pouches, eventually producing a wrinkled square of paper. "'Subject picked up a tail shortly after leaving L-D,'" he read. "That's the Library Desolate."

"Yeah. I remember being there."

"Right. Anyway, picked up a tail, took flight, opted for the train out of consideration for the Fratriarch's health."

I grabbed the paper and scanned it. It was a summary of our interview, leaving out a lot of the details. I gave it back to Owen.

"Close enough. The tail was two guys, bulky, wearing cloaks. They had some kind of . . . armored cowl over the lower half of their faces, and they had tattoos around their eyes."

"You didn't think to mention that kind of detail in the interview?"

"I did. It's just not in your report. I mean, how much detail does a patrol Justicar need, really?"

"I guess. And those were the guys who attacked you later?"

I shook my head. The report hadn't described my attackers, either. I didn't feel up to it, right now.

"Different guys. I guess I never really thought about the disconnect. You think that's important?"

He shrugged. "I think it's interesting."

"You want to base your investigation of the disappearance of the Fratriarch on 'interesting'?" I asked.

"Well, interesting is all we've got. Where was this?"

I told him, as best as I could remember. It wasn't close. At first the whiteshirts looked nervous, as they considered that kind of hike, but Owen spun up his rig and called in for a wagon. They were all very happy about that, and sat around talking about how happy they were until the wagon clattered into the square and we all piled in and made our way south, toward the Library Desolate and the place the Fratriarch and I had first run into those weird guys with their eye tattoos.

The square where Barnabas and I had stopped with the girl looked less sinister when I wasn't being pursued. The fountain was still dry, and the dark windows of the surrounding buildings looked empty rather than menacing. The monotrain rails that ran along the perimeter were quiet. All service had been stopped on this circle while the attack was being investigated and the tracks repaired. I sat on the edge of the fountain and looked around.

"Only a few hours," I said. "You wouldn't think the place would look so different."

"Perception colors reality," Owen said. "Looks the same to me."

"You're familiar with this place?"

"It's on our patrol route. It kind of always looks like this."

"Hm. Could have used you this morning," I said.

"It's a long route. We only get through here once a day, I guess. But yeah, sorry we weren't around."

I shrugged and stood up. "Let's not pretend it would have made that much of a difference."

I walked around the perimeter of the fountain, looking for anything out of place. Just cobbles and street trash. This was the last place we had rested before making the final push to the train. Last chance anyone following us would have had for an ambush. Either no one had been here, or we had moved before they pulled the trigger. I didn't think that likely. We probably lost our pursuers in our rush. Resting here had probably given them a chance to catch up, to figure out where we were going. The Library Desolate loomed darkly to our west. I turned that way and started walking. The whiteshirts followed.

We had run this part of the route, and I didn't remember much of it. Twice I had to stop and backtrack, after taking lefts when I should have taken rights. I didn't remember making a lot of turns, but walking the path now, it was clear that we had been dodging around like a rabbit in the shadow of a hawk.

"You plan your escape routes as thoroughly as you plan your rescues?" Owen asked at one point as we clumped back to the road we had just left. "Because this is either a very cleverly devised route, or you guys were just running scared."

"The Fratriarch does not run scared," I said. "But no, we didn't plan this. We got spooked."

"You should have gotten an escort," he said. "We would have walked you home."

"That came up. Frat didn't want it."

"That might have been a mistake."

"One of many, Mr. Justicar. Just one of many."

We ended up at the row of shops where Cassandra and I had pretended to argue while the two peculiar men passed us by. We got there just as night was taking the city of Ash in its grip. The moon was barely over the horizon, painting the high buildings all around with silver light. The sky was clear, and our breath puffed out as fog. Reminded me of the coldmen. Lots of stuff reminded me of those freaks today.

"This is it. Our planned route continued around this corner, up to the Terrace Boulevard, and then home. Long walk, but straight, and lots of people." By now the Terrace would be empty, but the high lamps that lined it would still be burning white. "Those two spoiled that." I indicated their path with my hand. "Came right through here and around that corner. We took off, back the way we just came."

"And you said they were big guys?"

"Bulky. Never got a look at what they were wearing underneath those cloaks. Could have been armor."

"Hm." Owen paced the street, his patrol sticking close to the wagon. All the perimeter lamps on the stubby wagon were burning, bathing the vehicle in a circle of light. Good thing this wasn't a residential district, I thought. "It seems weird that guys like that would be tailing you. They sound kind of obvious to me, like they'd stick out in a crowd."

"There was something about them. Something . . ." I waved my hand, looking for the thought. "Something arcane. Like they were shielded. We just didn't see them."

"Amon's Betrayers are supposed to be able to do something like that," one of the whiteshirts said, from the safety of the wagon's wide double doors. "Walk through the night like shadows, and you don't see them until they've put the knife in your back."

"Your momma tell you that, Travers?" Owen said. "That's what they do, just before they steal the candy off bad little boys. That's what I heard."

"I'm serious," I said. "Fratriarch said it, too. Something about them we couldn't see."

"Well, okay. If the Fratriarch said it. But I'm still pretty sure Travers there is just passing on fables." Owen walked down the street, his hand on his sidearm. "This way, you said?"

"Yeah, around the corner. They even looked back at us as they went."

"Stealthy couple of guys, making eye contact and sporting facial tattoos. I don't know how y'all ever picked up on it."

"Stop being an idiot," I said. "If this is how you're going to be, you and Travers and your damn truck can just pack it up and go back to your station. File a report about your mothers, or something."

Owen chuckled. "Prickly, prickly girl. Come on, folks. The strange men went this way."

"Not like they're still going to be there," I said.

"Hope not," Owen answered, then went around the corner. I followed. None of the other whiteshirts moved.

This road began to ascend gradually as it led up to the elevated boulevard that cut across this part of the city. Another late addition to the city's architecture, the boulevards served as direct routes for the foot and pedigear traffic that most citizens used, especially those who couldn't afford the monotrain service. We followed it up for a while. Eventually the wagon clattered around the corner behind us, the patrol walking carefully behind it in a loose semicircle.

"Brave bunch of boys you've got there, Justicar," I said.

"They do okay. They're good guys. This is just a . . . kind of strange situation."

"Walking around at night with a woman?" I asked, looking back at the patrol. They were young, holding their weapons tightly in their skinny hands. "Yeah, it looks like it'd be a new thing for most of them."

Owen chuckled. "You're probably not what they think of, when they think like that."

"Likewise," I said. "And this is where we stop."

"Oh, be cool. I'm just—"

"You're still walking when I said stop. So stop." I knelt down and peered at the ground, then looked around. We were at the mouth of a narrow alley that had a thin trickle of water running down a gutter in its middle. The cement at my feet was splattered with something dark. I put a finger to it. It was cold, and gummy.

"Get those lights up here."

The boys obliged, after a few miscues and misunderstandings. I moved out of the way so the wagon could get good light on the street. It was spotted with dark, muddy blood. I looked up at Owen, then nodded down the alleyway.

"Put the wagon here, focus the beams down there," he said, directing the patrol. The wagon turned tightly on the avenue, its tall tires showing a remarkable agility. The whiteshirts mostly stayed behind its bulk. "Get out here, guys. Come on. Stand over here, like we practiced for building entry."

They did, eventually. They really were just kids, and not that well armed. There was a single bullistic and his ammo guy. The rest had thick staves with blades that snapped out of the top, should a riot turn political. I waited until they looked ready, then decided I'd be waiting all night. I pulled Owen close.

"I don't want these guys getting in my way," I said.

"They won't. Unless you decide to run away, of course, and then you might trip over them."

"Be nice. But be out of the way more."

He nodded. I drew my bully and crept into the alley.

You can't sneak up on the dead. I smelled it pretty quick, going down that alleyway. The air was rimed with ice, and stank of dead meat and old blood. Oil, too. I found them in a little alcove off the alley, the entrance boarded up. Someone had kicked the door in. I went back and got Owen and his boys.

The room was filled with about a dozen of the coldmen, all deader than they had started out. Lots of injuries, from severed limbs to ruptured skulls. The wounds were savage. Something an animal might have done, or a madman. Someone had put a blade into their chests and smashed that glass and leather piston. It was that old air I could smell, air that tasted like the breath of tombs.

"Lot of 'em," Owen said. "And well done for. Your tattooed friends might be on our side."

"Or against these guys. Which might be the same thing. Or it might not." I kicked through the corpses and their shattered weapons. "What's this look like to you?" I asked, toeing a complicated metal box.

"Some kind of communications rig," Owen answered. He knelt down next to it and fiddled with a few dials. The top folded out into some kind of array, orbits of metal and wire telescoping open like a mobile. "Not too different from ours. Don't see any input or output jacks, though. Like it's a receiver with no speakers."

He folded the box away and got two of his boys to take it back to the wagon. One of the whiteshirts was in the alley, spinning up the Justicar's rig to call in a team to cart off the bodies, when the ground began to rumble. We all knelt down and looked up.

The makeshift room was open to the sky, hidden only by a collection of pipes and other business from the surrounding buildings. I hadn't given it much of a look when we got there, distracted as I was by the carnage and the stink. Now that rumbling grew into a roar and the sky was blocked out completely as something rushed over our heads.

The monotrain. We were tucked away just under some of the elevated tracks, our teeth rattling as the train went past. When it was gone I looked at Owen and jerked my chin up.

"Which circle was that?"

"Must have been the Hamilton Stone," he answered. "You were on the Pershing when you were attacked."

"They meet up," I said. "Those circles intersect, north of here."

"Yeah."

There was some junk in the alleyway, crates and an old discarded manifold. I dragged those into the room and piled them up, then clambered to the level of the tracks.

"You really shouldn't do that," Owen said.

"You'll make a great mom someday." I pulled myself onto the tracks and squinted around.

As with all buildings in the city, the surrounding structures had an open framework at the level of the train. It wasn't necessary, as the impellor could go right through them, but people didn't like living in the constant surge of those engines, and why build walls if you don't have to? I felt that surge now, my bones vibrating as it pulsed through me. There, between the iron grid of the open buildings, far away at the center of this particular monotrack orbit, I could see the impellor tower, shimmering sickly in the moonlight.

"They were waiting," I said. "Waiting for us to come by."

"How could they know you were coming this way?"

I looked over at Owen. He had clambered up beside me, his hands white on the railing at the edge of the tracks.

I smiled. "You really shouldn't be up here," I said.

"Gods help me if I implied you would make a good mother someday. Gods in heaven help me."

"They couldn't know. Whether they were waiting for us to come by the boulevard, or ride by on these tracks." I shook my head. "They just couldn't know."

"Unless someone told them. Someone who knew where you were going and how best you might get there."

"Someone from the Library? Maybe. But we didn't come this way, even though we planned to. And they still found us."

"Not this batch, though." Owen looked down at the mess of bodies, and his nervous patrolmen trying to organize them. "But another. Which means they could have been watching multiple routes."

"Which means we'll find other groups like this, watching other tracks?"

Owen looked thoughtful, twisting to peer along the track and around at the city. "Maybe. Maybe if we make a map of other paths you could have taken. I've had enough fun up here, for now."

He climbed down, leaving me alone with the periodic pulsing of the distant impellor. The rails began to rumble again, and I sighed and followed him down. The train came by a minute later, but I barely heard the roar.

This is how I usually spend my nights when I spend them with men. We crawled through alleyways, we rumbled down boulevards, we stopped monotrains so we could walk on the tracks and poke through alcoves and cringe when the impellor's invisible surge washed through our bones. It was filthy.

We found two more places where we'd been watched, where someone had sat and waited for the Fratriarch to come by. Mostly they were improvised rooms, cobbled together from driftwood or old crates, hidden in alleys and under tracks. We found another of those communication rigs, this one still active. We shut it down and took it. I felt something when I was close to it, like a voice in my blood, but then it faded. There were signs these guys had been there for days. At one place we found a body, some old guy who must have stumbled on their hideout and paid with his life. He'd been dead almost a week, wrapped in some kind of sheeting that masked the smell. We even found a lookout on the closest waterway, accessible only by depthship or a really good set of lungs. The last place we looked was along the Pershing circle, trying to find where the guys who had actually attacked us were hiding. It was almost dawn.

It was an easy place to find. Just had to figure out where we were when they had attacked the rails, and then backtrack a little bit. It was a nest, built into the open gridwork at the level of the train, shielded from view by barrels taken from a local distillery. There was no communications rig here, just some kind of tube that was charred at both ends and smelled of gunpowder. From here I had a clear view of the crash site, and the surrounding square. Patrols milled about, whiteshirts circling nervously and black-robed Amonites working on the track. I sat down on the little platform and swung my legs over the edge.

"So," Owen said, sitting beside me, "what do we know?"

"We know where they waited. That there were a lot of them, spread out all over the city. They knew we were coming, and how."

"Not necessarily. We've only looked in places we knew you could have gone. There might be other sites like this, all over the city."

"That's a cheery thought."

"Yeah," he said. "Means there could be a lot of those guys."

"We also know that someone killed some of them. Either because they were following us, or knew we were being followed." I rubbed my face and looked down at the street, far below. "That's something."

"Really, we still don't know much of anything," Owen said.

"We know the Fratriarch is missing."

There was a shout, far away, and we both looked up. In the distance, there was a commotion around the crash site. Amonites were rushing away, all of them running toward a white-robed man who held one hand high in the air. They threw themselves at his feet. The other Alexians at the site were milling about. The tracks and other buildings blocked much of our view.

"They've found something," I said.

Owen stood and spun up his rig, the swirling orbits of the helmet closing around his head and eyes as it tapped into the communications grid.

I didn't wait. I jumped to my feet and, invoking a little trick from the book of Morgan, leapt the distance to the track. I ran along the rails, toward the crash site, bully out, heart pounding.

CHAPTER FIVE

They were gathered around a crater in the ground. The Amonites were fully leashed, lurking unhappily behind their Alexian master on the far side of the square. There was a yellow tape barrier around the crash site, lined with a handful of curious passersby, though more were gathering as the search team became increasingly agitated. It didn't help when I boomed down the tracks, glory wicking off my boots as I leapt to the ground in full combat gear. I'm a crowd pleaser.

The investigator in charge, a bald-headed, frail, middle-aged man in an impeccable Alexian robe, waved me to a stop. Then he put a hand on my shoulder as I passed him and, eventually, hurried after me as I closed on the crater. He was sputtering.

"We don't know the full extent of its power, my lady, and think caution is best."

"Full extent of what's power?' I asked. There were a number of craters in the ground, all of them from my fight yesterday. Already yesterday, I mused. How long did the Fratriarch have? "What did you find?"

"It's . . . unclear. An icon, perhaps. It might be nothing."

"Nothing, huh? That would be in line with the rest of your findings." I reached the crowd of whiteshirts who had gathered around the crater and muscled my way through.

It was far from nothing.

The crater was shallow. I didn't remember it from the fight—at least, I didn't remember doing anything dramatic in this particular spot. Close to the tracks, but not where I had engaged the two burn-pack soldiers. My line of retreat had been . . . over there. This hole could have come from something the coldmen had done while they tried to get to Barnabas and the girl. The sides of the crater were charred, and most of the indentation was filled with rubble. The cobblestones here had been pulverized but left in place, like a giant cube of ice crushed in a bowl. The Amonites had been clearing it out, from the looks of things. And among the shards of stone was an icon, torn from someone's ceremonial robe.

We all wear icons, the scions of the three Cults of the Brothers Immortal. My armor is an icon, as are my sword and revolver. Very practical icons. But I wear others, noetic symbols of the power of Morgan. An iron fist pendant at my neck, the bound copper wire around my wrist, tattoos on my chest and legs. There is a holy symmetry to my symbols, brought to arcane life by the power of Morgan. The Fratriarch jangled with the icons of the holy Brother.

This was not his symbol, not a symbol of Morgan or of Alexander or any of the other minor sects dedicated to inchoate powers of significant events or famous battles. This was a symbol of the Betrayer. Amon, in his aspect as murderer and assassin. It was a pendant, silver clasping the gnarled blade of that darkest aspect of our darkest god. No wonder they had the Amonites so tightly reined.

"Is there any doubt now that the Betrayer was involved?" the inspector whispered at my side.

I holstered my revolver and looked back nervously toward the pack of Scholars at the far corner of the square.

"Did any of them touch it?" I asked.

"One of them found it, but swears it did not reach his skin."

"Contain him. You'll need to keep the rest out of the general population until you can confirm they were not infected."

"We know the rites of infection, my lady." The inspector sniffed and waved a hand at some of his fellow whiteshirts. "We will do our duty."

"Whatever." I bent to the icon and dusted the debris away from it. It had been embedded in a cobble, like a stone pressed into hot wax. I removed the penetrated cobble and slid it onto the ground. "Some force that was."

"Your battle was mighty, my lady."

"I had nothing to do with this," I said. "Those weren't servants of the Betrayer I was fighting. Not scions, at least. Evil creatures, perhaps, but there was nothing . . . blessed about them."

"Who, then? The Fratriarch?" the inspector asked. Doubtless remembering the old man who walked in the parades. Not exactly a figure embodying power.

"What is it?" Owen asked, running up. He skidded to a halt and looked over my shoulder at the stone and its infernal decoration. "Ah. Oh . . . huh."

"You are a man of culture and insight, Justicar. What do you make of it?"

"You did not speak of scions of the Betrayer, though we all suspected they were the power behind the attack."

"Suspected," I said, nodding. "But unknown."

"We can lay that to rest, it seems. How did it get here?"

I craned my neck to look up at the elevated track. The damaged car had been removed, and the twisted support towers were being rebuilt. The tracks themselves looked solid enough.

"A fight," I said. "The icon gets ripped off in the heat of battle."

"When, though? You stated that the Fratriarch was locked away in a column of steel, and the coldmen could not break him out. Then you returned and he was gone. They were all gone."

"They didn't break him out." I stood, looking around at the damage of the square, seeing lines of force and advance in the arrangement of wreckage. "He fought his way free. There was a body in the door of the car. I never really thought about how it got there."

"So he might be out there, free?" Owen turned in a slow circle, gazing around at the buildings on the square as if the Fratriarch might be looking down at us from some terrace. "We should organize search parties."

I snorted. "You should? Maybe a day ago, when I first came to you with this. No, he didn't get away. The living Fratriarch would have returned to the Strength of Morgan, no matter his condition. He battled, and was defeated."

"Who could do such a thing?" Owen asked, quietly.

I kicked at the stone-wrapped icon of the Betrayer, then looked up at the Justicar. "They have a history of it," I said, and walked off.

Behind me the whiteshirts started making plans to contain the Amonites, seal away the icon, and continue with the repair of the site. I walked over to the nervous pack of Amonites. There was an Alexian with them, his fist white around a jumble of those soul-chains. He was a thin man with a weak chin, but large, strong hands.

"Which one was it?" I asked.

He volunteered himself, before the whiteshirt could compel him forward. Another small man, though wide and strong. There was grease under his nails, and calluses on his hands. His skin was the color of worn leather. For all his strength, he quivered under his hood.

"You found the icon?"

"Yes, my lady."

"How?"

"I was . . . I was repairing the cobbles, my lady. As ordered. I was clearing out that ditch there, and turned a stone. The icon was there."

"Did it call to you?"

"No, ma'am. I heard nothing from it. I'm not . . . attuned to such things."

"You are a scion of the Scholar," I said. "You are attuned to his symbols."

"That aspect of the lord Brother . . . of Amon . . . such symbols are forbidden, as they have always been." He shuffled his feet. "And even if they weren't, I'm not . . . gifted, my lady."

"You can't invoke?" I asked, surprised. Rare for someone to swear to one of the gods without showing some noetic talent. Rarer still for that someone to swear to Amon.

"No, my lady. I worship with my hands, and my back, and my mind."

I stood quietly in front of him, looking for some lie in his broad, sun-scrubbed face. There was fear, but who was to blame for that? I turned to his keeper and nodded. When I turned around, Owen was two steps behind me.

"Scaring the witnesses?" he asked.

"Questioning them. I believe that's your job, of course, but someone has to actually do it."

"It is my job, Eva. Leave it to me."

"If I had, Justicar, where would we be? Kicking our heels in that lovely station? Drinking coffee, perhaps? Maybe we would have been able to question this man there, after someone else had found him and brought him to us."

"Better that than rushing around the city all night," his voice was steadily rising, "chasing ghosts and digging through bodies. There are people for these jobs—"

"We are those people, Owen. I am that person. I let the old man down. I will not sit and wait."

"You're overexcited. It's time we were back at that station. There is much to report on," he said, and put his hand on my wrist. Oh, mistakes, mistakes. Such glorious mistakes.

I pulled his hand toward me, until his knuckles brushed my belly, then flipped my hand over and grasped his elbow. Rotate, hip-check, and then toss. He hit the ground like a sack of flour, and then I was past him, turning from his rapidly reddening face and walking briskly to the taped barricade. The crowd that had been gathering at the yellow tape line was staring at the furious Justicar and the Paladin who had put him on his ass. Not every day that you got to see the scions of god fight, not since Amon had been bound and burned and drowned. So they stood and gaped. I gave them a smile and a short salute, and let them have their look.

All but one of them. A girl, twisting her face quickly away from the barricade, slipping shoulder-ways into the press of bodies, squirming through. She was dirty-faced, skinny-armed, the thick matte mane of her dark hair pulled back in a messy tail that spilled in curls across her shoulders. Black robe, black hood pulled back, the sleeves torn away to disguise the garment's origin. She wore an Amonite's robe. The girl. Cassandra.

She was gone, and now the crowd was staring in horror at me, at the bully I had pulled and was now pointing at them, at the space where the girl had stood, my finger tight on the trigger. They began screaming. Understandable, considering the mad fury in my face. The murder in my eyes.

The Justicar ran up next to me and put a hand on my gun arm. Without thinking I shrugged my shoulder into his chest, cracking the hilt of the still-sheathed blade across his teeth, then hooked his flailing arm and hip-checked him into the crowd, all without thinking. Reaction, and my hunter-mind was finally smoothing through the shock and anger. I put a heel into Owen's chest as I jumped over him and into the seething crowd. In pursuit.

I locked down the dozen questions that pushed for space in my brain. How the girl had escaped her chains. If she knew where the Fratriarch was, what had happened, if he was still alive. Why she came back to this place. Locked it down and ran.

The crowd thinned out after the immediate press around the barricade, but it was still a busy street in a busy city. Vendors and pedigears and carriages filled the streets, along with a loose river of pedestrians. Most of them were oblivious to the chase, only a few looking behind them in confusion as the girl ran past, wondering why she was in such a hurry. I pushed past them, following the invisible line of the Amonite's path through upset carts and startled citizens. I was as gentle as a tiger is to grass, as quiet as lightning before thunder's wake. I still had the bully out, barrel up, ready to snap forward should a shot present itself. Too many people, though. Too much interference. The girl stayed ahead, a glimpse of black robe or the bobbing cascade of ringlet hair the only sign that I had not lost my quarry.

One clear look, the girl rushing into an alleyway between two ill-maintained buildings. I slid to a stop at the entrance. It was clogged with junk, and absolutely dark. A rapid hissing sound, then a thump. There were no other sounds of flight, no footsteps, no panicked breathing, no debris being shoved out of the way by a hurrying girl in the dark. Iron groaned in the blackness, and something fell from high up, dancing against metal as it dropped. Silence again.

I slid the bullistic into its holster and drew the blade, then stepped into the shadows and invoked the Torches of the Fellwater. My eyes began to glow with a pale, bluish white light that wisped in twisting tendrils across my cheekbones and into my hair. The bright street behind me washed out into brilliant light, but the alley resolved into blocky grays and blacks. I slid forward, sword at guard, looking for any sign of Cassandra.

The alley was cluttered with a carefully constrictive jungle of trash. The stone walls to either side were lost behind cardboard boxes and stacked iron pilings, tumbling down on the ground like a child's game of sticks. I stepped between them carefully, maneuvering between piles of junk, doing everything I could to keep the sword in a guard position. No sign of the girl. I looked up and saw that there were platforms above, suspended from a rough framework of metal tubing that was anchored into the hidden wall, behind piles of junk. A rope dangled loosely beside the rough structure, still slithering with recent movement. Quick climber, maybe.

"What is this place?" I asked myself quietly. This was not just a haphazard collection of trash in the crevices of the city. This had been built and hidden. Peering up into the alley's heights, I was momentarily blinded by the strip of early morning sky. I blinked the image away, startled into dropping the invokation of night sight. Darkness shrouded me, but in the few seconds before I lost my vision, I thought I saw a form flitting between platforms, high above.

Squinting, I felt my way to the rope and gave it a tug. It pulled down loosely in my hand. A pulley, or something. The end of the rope on the ground was heavily weighted. So it was some kind of escape route. One end of the rope was tied to the ground, the rest hooked over a pulley high above with the weight dangling from it. Run up to it, cut the rope, and hold on as the weight dragged you up. Simple, and completely one-way. I tugged the rope once more, hard, and the other end of it cleared the pulley high above and fell heavily to the ground. It was a lot of rope. She could be anywhere up there. Sighing, I felt my way to the nearest platform, then reluctantly put away the blade and started to climb.

The way was tough. It might have been easier with more light, but even then the handholds were irregular and ramshackle. The Fellwater was very difficult to power up once it had been snuffed. There was something in the story about spies dousing the spare torches in swamp water, so that the army had been blinded when they tried to switch the blazes out. Details of history could be inconvenient sometimes. I cut my hands on raw iron, and scraped my cheek and shins on loose stone that slid free when I put my weight on it. The framework tower creaked and shifted around me.

Thirty feet up, I paused. I sat cross-legged on a platform, my tired hands resting on an iron pipe that served as the bottom rung of a rickety ladder. Still trying to convince myself that this ladder was worth climbing, that this was the way Cassandra had come. She could have cut the rope and then hidden, and how would I know? A false path, maybe? Or did the Amonites have some sort of technology that deadened the sound of a stack of lead smashing into the ground? Who knew? Who knew what those bastards were actually capable of doing?

At the very least, I was curious where all this structure had come from, and where it led to. Curiosity was losing out to grim practicality, though. The girl could be anywhere by now. She could have kept running straight through the alley, past the false path of the elevator. She could have just hidden, waiting for me to get high enough before dashing back out into the street and away. Even if she was up here, if she had taken the makeshift elevator she could have gotten awfully high awfully fast. It just didn't seem likely I would catch up with her. I sighed and started preparing myself for the descent. Owen would be along soon, with his patrol and his wagon with its spotlights. We could surround the building and conduct a tedious, pointless search. Maybe even find some evidence that Cassandra had been here, hours ago. It was the best I could hope for, once the quarry had been lost.

I was considering if it would just be easier to shield up and jump when the girl's face resolved out of the shadows across the way like a half-moon sliding from behind the clouds. She was sitting on an intersection of iron braces, her legs tangled in the crossbars, her arms looping casually over her head. I jumped up into a low squat and went for the bully.

It was the fastest I had ever heard the Cant of Unmaking invoked. The girl whispered a heavy chant that rolled across the chasm in waves of power. The pistol began to come apart in my fingers even as it cleared the holster. Bolts shivered free of the weapon, jangling like loose change as they were joined by the cycling rod, the hammer, finally the cylinder itself. The barrel followed the quick trajectory of my draw, spinning like a knife across the alley and smacking into the girl's shoulder. Cassandra winced and stopped her cant, but all that I held was a loose collection of familiar pieces that wouldn't jigsaw back into a bullistic, no matter how tightly I gripped them. Let them go and drew the blade, yelling.

My first step found the weakness in the tower, my boot kicking free a bar of metal, quickly followed by an avalanche of metal pilings that shuffled into the yawning darkness below. I gasped, trying to steady myself, but everything I touched loosened and slid away. Across from me the girl looked terrified, her wide eyes watching each piece fall. Cassandra's own perch began to falter, and she scrambled higher. I was too busy with my own gravity issues to watch her go.

The Cant of Unmaking must have clipped the tower, because the structure that had supported me all the way up here now folded away like a magician's trick knot. My platform tipped and I was falling, dropping a few feet before I slapped against another platform which in turn clattered free. Soon I would be swallowed by an avalanche of loose boards and spinning pipes. I looked across the alley and saw that the other structure was still standing, its platforms and struts loose but in much better shape than my own tower. A long way, but no other choice. I screamed and jumped and fell and closed my eyes as the air whipped past my head and I was falling, falling, *crunch*.

My teeth sang with the impact of the tower. I crashed through a thin wooden railing and onto a platform several levels below where Cassandra had been sitting. Blood filled my mouth and the air left my lungs, but I pushed myself up to a kneeling position. Across the alley my former tower collapsed like a castle of dust, the roar of metal and wood deafening in the tight canyon between the two buildings. A cloud of debris swirled up from the ground, choking me and stinging my eyes. I covered my face and spat. The platform under my feet swayed but did not give way. I looked up for the girl.

The structure was starting to lose hold of itself. Bits of it clattered down into my face. Wooden planks folded and spun as the bolts that held them shriveled away. Through the rapidly growing openings above me, I could see a door into the building that had been left open. There was light. A pale hand slipped out and pulled the door closed, rusty hinges flaking as it squealed shut. The structure around me groaned and leaned into the open alleyway.

I scrambled higher, reaching the door in half the time I thought possible. There was a narrow iron balcony around the door. I stepped onto it, my fingers grasping the door's round handle. My boot wasn't off the ramshackle ladder for more than two panicked breaths when the structure shuddered and shuffled off into the darkness, collapsing in on itself in a horrible cacophony that roared in my head long after it had joined its fellow tower in the alley below.

I turned to the rusty door, laying my hand against the rust-spotted paint, listening. There were voices, many of them, yelling and arguing and making demands. Asking questions. I heard fear in those voices. I heard terror.

My hunter's heart roared to life, and I began to invoke the Rites of the Blade.

I am outside of myself in moments like this. The deeper I dig into the heart of Morgan, the more of his life and his story I let flow through my blood, the less Eva I feel. The less . . . civilized. There is a raw fire in it, the invocations wrapping around my bones and burning through my flesh as the heart of my god flares into me. It's like dying of joy.

I wreathed myself in Everice, the Hundred Wounds, the Rites of the Winter War. Smoke and sparks of red and hate roiled off me. I chanted the warrior's dedication, and the steel framework of the balcony sang as the air collapsed around me, hardening in coils of power. Hunter's Heart grabbed me, and I howled in perfect happiness. The sword was in my hands, the enemy was before me. But first, the door.

Steel splintered and brick tore under my boot. The passageway beyond was narrow and dark. The force of my passage dug runnels in the walls, and waves of angry light whipped in my wake. The voices had become . . . urgent. I pushed through the hall and into the cheap wood-frame door at the end. It burst like a dry leaf. They were beyond it. Screaming.

Amonites, all of them. They had ditched the robes and chains, but I could tell. I could smell them. Could smell the grease under their fingernails, the oily smoke of burnsaws in their hair and clothes. The fear. Mostly, I could smell the fear.

The room was a tight labyrinth of head-high walls that ended long before they reached the ceiling. They looked cobbled together, made from bits of junk that only coupled under an Amonite's careful hand. The air smelled of sweat and burned food. It smelled like a crowded home, like diapers and stale sheets. I stood in the foyer of their hovel and flared my shields. A wave of force puffed out from my core, scattering paper and pottery. The Scholars were running. As they should.

"I am here for the girl!" I boomed, my voice distorted and fey through so many invocations. "What runs will be run down! What hides will be dug out!"

A scattering of shots sparked off my armor, children with hand-guns firing from the corners of the trash-built home. I pushed at them, weaving my sword through an invokation of force that crumpled the walls and splintered their bones. I was burning it way too hot, but Morgan was on me and vengeance had taken my heart. All I could think of was the old man, and not letting him down again. I was a little blood-sick from yesterday's fight, but I just rode it out.

I stepped over the bodies, scooping up and holstering a discarded revolver as I went, and shoved through a flimsy wall. It fell into a kitchen and toppled a pot of boiling liquid, then caught fire against the heating element. Soup hissed as it steamed away, filling the air with the smell of fried meat. A pocket of Scholars scampered from cover, crossing the rapidly burning kitchen and diving through a door across the way. The last one turned to spit a cant into the room. The stove tumbled open, its tank spilling thick, heavy flames onto the floor. I laughed and followed, the fire whimpering to a halt at the edge of my shielding. More shots banged off me from behind, but they were light caliber. Nothing to worry about. I was on the path, and they were just trying to distract me.

"The girl, Cassandra! She is all I ask of you, Betrayers!"

The first real resistance came from a trio of older men, still wearing the tired remnants of their robes, their belts of service tight across their chests and jangling with tools. They fell in around me and began to unmake the room, throwing together half-realized constructs and hurling them to die at my blade. They dropped a cage of pipes around my shoulders, tightening it until it clenched the articulated sheath like a lover. My blade thudded dully into the steel, suddenly harder than any building's conduit had the right to be. Runes writhed across the surface of the metal as one of the Amonites chanted a rite of strength.

I rolled against the cage, slipping one shoulder between the bars, regretting it as the metal pinched closed against my pauldron. A whirlwind flurry of tiny automatons buzzed across the floor, scampering up my legs in tiny, razor-barbed steps, cutting their way to my face. I screamed, flaring a shield that crisped the toys but left my larger defenses weakened. The cage tightened again, and now I was staring at the tip of my own blade as it was crushed against my chest. The trio of Betrayers was chanting, tighter and tighter, my breath coming in grunts and starts. Forcing my hand.

I burst, spiking hard into Morgan's power, the wreath of his incarnation manifesting in blue and black fire. The cage held for half a breath and then it was gone, and along with it most of my invokations. My sword fell to the smoldering floor and I dropped to my knees, drawing the bully as I crumpled. The trio closed in.

My first shot took one in the knee, the second stopped his heart. They started in on the Unmaking, but they weren't Cassandra and I was fast. I emptied the cylinder, killing the second Amonite. The last one abandoned the cant and just ran. Good thing. I dropped the revolver and fell to my hands and knees, heaving bile and spit. Too much invokation. I probably should have eaten some breakfast, too. Gotten some sleep. It's hard to be a god on no rest and a little wine.

The room was wrecked. The half-walls were mostly burned and crumpled, shattered framework turning to char from my final invokation. There were clothes burning, and bodies, and the remnants of furniture. I spat the last of the vomit from my mouth, wiped off and holstered the revolver, then dragged myself to my still-warm sword. My hands burned against the metal.

"I gotta learn to dial that glory down," I gasped. "God or no god, I need to keep that tight."

The girl was gone, I was sure. Doors slammed open, feet hammered on concrete. Fading. The only voices I could hear were organized. Calm. Directing an evacuation. I looked at the two dead Amonites, the ones who had almost taken me. Scholar had his own Paladins, I guess. And the last of this little convent of Amon was getting away. I stood and started toward the next room.

Evacuating, all right. In a hurry. Clothes and various personal items were strewn across the floor, possessions hastily packed, weapons loaded, and food gathered. How long had they been here? It had the feel of a place that had been lived in.

The escape hatch was about halfway around the room, a tiny steel door that looked like it belonged on a depthship. Rusty iron wheel in the center, pressurized glass window. I tried to undog it, but the wheel wouldn't budge. Too much of Morgan had left me to force the issue. I looked around for something large and metal for leverage.

The wreckage of the room was little help. The inner walls were flimsy, little more than plywood braced up with scrap. There were no beds, just piles of clothes, a couple mattresses that were intricately stained, and a crib, but it was smashed. The only metal was in the kitchen, in the form of old and worn-out utensils. The spoons were almost flat.

Amonites always had tools. I went to the bodies of the two Scholars who had slowed me down. Wrenches, hammers, ankle-pliers, all clean and stored carefully on their belts. I took the biggest wrench I could find and tried the hatch, but there was no budging it. It was invoked, for sure. I went and put the wrench carefully back in the guy's belt, then walked around the room one more time. Looking for weapons, I guess. Looking for signs of an underground conspiracy bent on kidnapping the most powerful man in the Cult of Morgan.

Stuffed toys. Pots. A stilograph of a girl, standing on the stairs of an old house in a field somewhere. The girl was just turning toward the camera, not yet aware that her picture was being taken. She had a hand against her face, half in the act of brushing a curl of long, blonde hair out of her eyes. I put the stilo down and looked around.

Children, and old men, and mothers. This was a home hidden between empty spaces, carved out of junk and refuse and the forgotten things of the city. Occupied by the desperate remnants of an outlaw church. They could be escapees, or simply Amonites in the wild, some splinter Cult left over from before the Betrayal. Who knew? This was more an orphanage than a bandits' den.

But the girl had been here. And where the girl was, there might be clues to where the Fratriarch was. That was all I had.

I sat cross-legged on the floor and laid the sword across my knees, then fumbled a vial of oil from my vest and prepared to anoint the blade. Outside I heard Owen's amplified voice booming down the alleyway. Looking for me. It would be a while before they got up here.

"Long hunt," I whispered, to myself, to the Fratriarch, to the girl. "Gonna be a long hunt."

CHAPTER SIX

"Are you going to hit me again?" Owen asked. He was standing in the middle of the wreckage of the Amonites' hideout, holding the remnants of a child's teddy bear.

"Are you going to touch me again?" I asked.

"Probably not."

"Okay then."

He looked around the room, at the torn walls and scorched floor, at the two body bags and the trail of blood that led to the escape hatch. Men were working on the hatch with burn knives, fat sparks cascading down like a fountain. The Justicar shook his head and threw the ragged doll into a pile of other toys and assorted personal items that his men were sifting from the wreckage.

"You make quite a crime scene."

"Takes practice. How else am I supposed to get your attention?"

He looked at me funny, then shrugged. "Well, I mean, there has to be a better way. I would send flowers, but I wouldn't want to receive flowers, so—"

"Stop it."

"Uh . . ." he sputtered.

"Stop talking like we're friends, or compatriots, or whatever the hell is going through your head. I waited for you because there's a lot of trash to pick up in this place, and I didn't want to do it myself."

He went red, looked to see which of his men were listening, and then took two quick steps closer to me. He nearly punched me with his finger, but held back. That wouldn't have been good for either of us.

"Listen. I don't know what the hell's wrong with you Morgies, but this is serious. Bad things are happening. And every time we try to help, we get this attitude like you don't need us. But you do. You need

Alexander more than you need Morgan right now. You're never going to find your Fratriarch without our help. Best you remember that."

"Remember?" I did a casual thing where I pushed his finger out of my face, pulled him a little off balance, and then brushed my fingers against his chest just hard enough that he had to take a step back. "Alexander isn't ever going to let us forget. How he hunted down Amon, tried him. Put him to the torch. We won't forget."

"Then why—"

"Another thing we won't forget, Owen, is how he declared amnesty for the Betrayer's scions. Locked them in the Library Desolate, kept them alive. Used them. They built the weapons that made us obsolete, Justicar. Those damn chain guns, the valkyn. Whole armies of peasants with rifles that make the Warrior's Path irrelevant, all courtesy of the Librarians Desolate. Long as they didn't study the Path of the Betrayer, they could keep worshipping their dark old god. We remember."

He grimaced. "These are old arguments. I won't have them with you. And if you're too stubborn to help me find your Fratriarch, then it's on you. His blood is on you, Eva Forge."

He walked away to supervise or something, but I stayed where I was. His blood was already on me. It didn't matter what anyone else did.

Men were going through the junk that had been crammed into the various nooks and crannies of this place. I went over to watch. It looked like a dozen households all jammed together. So much mismatched stuff. New clothes for young children, patched clothes for older children, women's hair combs, men's razors, cheap pottery, broken tools. Nothing too nice. Some pictures, laid out in a neat grid by the investigators. None of them looked to be of the same people. Children and wives and gatherings of friends, some birthdays, some formal portraits. All of them worn at the edges, wrinkled from being carried in pockets. Well loved. None of them were of the girl.

There was a yelp behind me, then a heavy thud. The hatch had broken free, still hanging from one hinge but mostly open. Two Alexians rushed forward with a third man between them. An Amonite. I found Owen nearby.

"You'd let one of them in here?" I asked. He shrugged. "What's he going to tell his prison mates? He must know what this place is."

"Probably. It's not like they don't know they have brothers in the wild."

"Not what I was told. The priest who met us at the Desolate claimed there had been no escapes since Alexander took charge of the prison."

Owen laughed. "Sure, no escapes. Whatever he says."

I wanted to ask more, but the Amonite was going into action. He invoked slowly, his long chant rolling through the room. Eventually he raised heavy arms to the hatch and lifted it, ever so slowly, off the floor. With the hinge realigned, he was able to pull the thing open and rest the heavy metal door against the wall. His attendants secured the metal, then took the man by the arms and pulled him away. The Amonite didn't look around at the wreckage as he walked, but for all the world he had the posture of a father at his daughter's funeral.

With the hatch open, the room suddenly stank of lakewater. Owen's men were already through the door, pointing around with lamps and talking excitedly. Owen followed them through, then came back.

"This is extensive," he said, his voice eager. "They've been here for a while, and they planned well. Look at this." Then he disappeared back through the hatch. Reluctantly, I followed.

The room beyond was small and metal, like the inside of a ship. There were racks against the near wall, but they were empty. Plenty of disturbed dust made it clear that something had been stacked here. Supplies, probably.

There was a spiral staircase leading down. Some of Owen's people were rushing down it, their voices echoing up from metal depths along with the smell of the lake. I took out my revolver and followed. Owen laughed when he saw the bully in my hand. Let him get shot, then. His call.

The staircase went for a while. It became disorienting, spinning down in darkness and metal, the only light coming from our lamps. I would rather have invoked my eyes, but they would be no good around those lamps, and Alexians had no similar trick to help them see in the dark. Hell, half these men weren't even sworn scions of the Healer, anyway. It felt like we were spinning forever down into the city.

The end came in another small room, almost identical to the one up top. The air was cold and the walls leaked rust. There was another hatch here. When we threw the wheel the bolts undogged easily and the door creaked open. It hadn't been used much.

"I'll go first," I said. "There might be traps."

"There could have been traps anywhere on our way down," Owen said. "Why now?"

"You don't trap the start of the path your people are going to take. You wait until the way opens up a little, then put something a bit to the side." I took the nearest man's lamp and snapped it off, then indicated that the others should do the same. They looked nervous about that. "If you're in a dark place, it's good to set a trap that's triggered by light. That way you're sure it'll go off, eventually."

They looked at each other, then at me, then at Justicar Owen. He shrugged. The lights went out, one by one. When we were wrapped in cold, dark air, I invoked the Torches of the Fellwater. Everything settled into shades of gray.

I crept to the hatch and peered through the opening, my bully held loosely against my thigh. Nothing blew up, so I stepped through, leaving the hatch open just a crack. The ground under my feet was springy, like wooden planking. The air smelled of tar and water. Slowly I was able to make out the space. It was big and round, like a massive pipe that had been capped. We had come down against one wall. There was a dock, maybe ten feet on each side, held up by tar-sticky pylons. Everything else was water. There were coils of rope and an antique seaman's lamp lying on the dock.

Either some kind of depthship had been waiting for them, or they had breathing machines that let them swim out. I thought about all the toys upstairs, and the abandoned canes. Children and old men. Probably a ship.

I sighed and started to turn back, but something caught my eye. It sparkled among the ropes, and it takes a very special thing to sparkle when there's no light around. Ignoring the bedtime story I had told Owen and his boys about traps, I went over and picked the thing up. Let's be honest, any trap made by an Amonite was going to be miles too clever for me to figure out.

Happily, there was no trap. Just a necklace, draped carefully across the coil of rope. Dangling from my hand, it turned slowly, an inner light snaking out from its heart. A simple triangle, wood braced with iron, etched in bronze, suspended from an iron chain. I knew it well. It belonged to the Fratriarch.

They left it behind. She did. She left it for me to find. I held it up, letting it shimmer in the unlight of my invoked eyes. How had she gotten it? Ripped from his throat as he struggled? Dropped from his dead fingers? Left behind as he fled? Where had it come from, and where did it lead?

"He gave it to me, if you're wondering," she said. Behind me.

I spun, bully whipping around the small dock, seeing nothing but black wood and blacker water, not a glimmer of movement. Nothing.

"Where the hell are you?" I spat. Voice down. Didn't want Owen and his boys to hear me and come storming in. No telling what she'd do.

"I am here," she said, from everywhere. "What are you going to do when you catch me?"

"It's what *you're* going to do, bitch. You're going to tell me what you did with the Fratriarch. You're going to tell me where he is, who has him, why. You're going to talk. You're going to wish you had never gotten away."

"You make it sound so . . . appealing." Her voice was breathy, near and then far, always quiet. "Maybe I won't let you find me."

"Let? Let! I'll find you, girl. I'll hunt you from here to Everice, to the halls of the Rethari swine. I'll kill every Brother-damn one of your ragged friends that get in my way, and every one of them that doesn't. I'll find you wherever you hide."

"Yes, I suppose you will," she said. There was a crackle, and her voice changed. Became more real, more local. "And I can't have that."

A sound came from above, a winch unwinding rapidly. I cleared the floor with my bully and drew my sword, switching guard directions as quickly as I could breathe. She dropped into the middle of the dock, some kind of mechanical pulley in one hand, the trailing edge of a rope in the other. The rope disappeared a dozen feet above the ground, as though it was magicked into thin air. A mask hung around her throat, dangling across her white clavicle like a necklace. A very complicated thing, with speakers and breathing tubes and wide buckles that had been unclasped. She snapped the rope and it fell, like a magician's trick.

"I just can't have you chasing them. You're a monster, Eva Forge. If I can keep you out of their lives, I will. It's all I can do."

I lowered the bully at her chest and snarled. She held her hands up in surrender, dropping the rope and the pulley. I motioned to the mask, and she worked it free from her neck and sent it clattering to the ground. No other weapons that I could see.

"You should gag me, if you're worried."

"I'll leave the worrying to you. Owen, you can come out now," I said, pocketing the pendant. The hatch swung open and Owen and his boys exited, sparking up their lamps as they came. The room looked pretty much as it had under the influence of the Fellwater. Gray and cold and wet. Cassandra squinted at them, and I realized she had been seeing without light. Not something I knew about the Scholars. Now I could see that her right hand was in some sort of glove, metal laced into flesh. I remembered seeing that hand after the wreck, bending all sorts of wrong.

Owen started when he saw the girl, then gave a crisp nod and motioned to his boys. Always the leader. They surrounded her, guns held at her tiny chest. She made no move.

"Where did the rest of them go?" he asked me. "Was there a ship?"

"Beats me. Probably. You think all those kids swam out?"

"Seems unlikely." He turned to Cassandra, who was staring blankly up to the ceiling. "What do you say, kid. Boat?"

She didn't answer.

I shrugged. "Yeah. So. They have a boat."

"Maybe someone . . ." He paused, cocking his head at a curious angle. "Huh."

"What?" I asked, then a gunshot echoed sharply down from the spiral staircase. Yelling, more shooting, then feet on metal. Owen grabbed me as he ran by. I shot the girl a look and then followed up the stairs.

The staircase was chaos. Lots of people rushing down, a couple of us rushing up. The ones coming down were hurt. Blood on their faces, or their shirts. One guy was dragging a body. The limp's head was bouncing on each metal step, thumping meatily and leaving bits behind. I made a note not to get shot on a staircase, or at least not get shot in such a way that some fool felt compelled to drag me out.

The firefight was on us quick. Heavy bullistic fire came in short bursts, answered by weak revolver shot that was again quickly drowned out by the heavy stuff. The first shots came ricocheting past us shortly after we left the lower room. Not long after that, I heard those static-laced voices, methodically working their way closer to us. I stopped.

"What are you doing?" Owen asked. "We've got to get up there."

"Up there is coming down here," I said. I cursed myself for never learning many rites of the bullet. The sword had always been a nobler path, but I kept finding myself in places where it just wasn't appropriate. "The rest of your team is dead."

"You don't know that," he said, nervously. Something in his voice . . . He hadn't lost men before. That's tough. I looked him in the eye and waited for him to actually see me.

"Justicar. Your team is dead. All that's left are those boys behind us. And all we can do is take care of them."

He looked up the stairs, grimacing and twisting his hands around the short shotgun he had slung out. More shooting, much closer. Hot bullets traced a row of dimples into the wall just above us. He nodded.

Once we were on our way down, it went fast. Those things, with their static voices and cold-piston hearts, must have sensed us. Must have known there were few of us left. The fever of the hunt was on them. I knew the feeling.

"Get your men in the water. Maybe the Amonites swam out, and there's a quick path that we just can't see."

"There are injured. They'll drown."

"Drown or get shot," I said. "Now get 'em in the water."

On the dock, the few remaining Healers were milling around. *Alexians aren't cut out for this*, I thought. *How did we ever let them take charge? Who left them in the big-boy chair?* This crowd had done a bang-up job of getting the injured all lined up and field triage accomplished, but most of them had dropped their weapons. Those who were still walking around were pretty badly hurt themselves.

Cassandra knelt by the edge of the water, staring nervously at the door. She had a guard or two, but those boys looked more scared than her, and she looked pretty scared. I pointed at her.

"Don't you try getting away in all the excitement. This bit'll be over soon, and then we have business."

She nodded at me, or at least in my direction. I turned my attention to the defenses, such as they were.

Owen got into an argument with one of the older guys. It was pretty clear that no one was going into the water any time soon. I closed the hatch, but the lock was on the other side. A couple of the Alexians saw what I was doing and tried to help. That's when I saw the other Amonite.

He was sitting cross-legged against the wall, staring at Cassandra. It was the guy who had opened the hatch for us, Owen's pet Scholar.

"Hey, aren't you on the wrong side of this door?" I yelled. He shrugged, then stood and came over.

"Would you like me to go out there, or would you like me to close that door?"

"Can you close the door, and then maybe drown yourself?"

He sighed, then placed one palm on either side of the pressurized window and began to invoke. All of our frictionlamps guttered, which is unusual for normal, mechanical lights. The air around us seemed to swell and grow heavy, like we were moving through molasses. His words stretched out in time, long syllables rolling out of his mouth and sticking in the air, their weight and density drawing us in. The room seemed ready to collapse.

Everything snapped, the whole world rushing at the space between the Amonite's two palms. I lurched forward like a drunk on a ship, and the room lurched with me. We were in sudden vacuum, without sound or breath, the instinctive panic burning through my lungs before I even realized I couldn't breathe. The door crumpled like a child's toy and I felt an instant of betrayal, before I realized that the egglike hatch had flattened out and molded itself with the frame. The whole door was solid metal now, wrinkled and hot. Only the window remained intact, untouched among the violence.

"That will do," the Amonite said, then shot me a dull look and returned to his seat. He went back to staring at the girl. She couldn't bring herself to look at him, at his chains.

"How the hell will we get out of here?" one of the badly injured men asked. I shushed him. One problem at a time.

And our first problem came up pretty quick. Through the window I saw pale blue light, and then the wide goggle eyes of the coldmen. I couldn't hear their static voices, but I could feel them, itching through my bones. It felt like I could taste that breath again, centuries dead. I put away the revolver. At least here, on the deck, I had room to swing some blade.

"Everyone stay behind me. If it gets bad, jump in the drink and go under. If they come for you . . . swim."

"Swim," Owen said, "and pray to Alexander for deliverance."

"As you like," I said. "But mostly I would swim."

Hammering at the door, now. A slow, patient, heavy stroke that rang the metal like a bell. The whole room echoed from the impact. The water behind us lapped against the dock. I drew my sword and began to invoke, drawing a semicircle on the ground in front of me and feeding it what power I could. What power Morgan could give me.

The door burst like a shell, spitting hot metal across the dock, hissing as it struck the water. The debris arced off the flimsy wall of my shield. I kept my sword crossed over my chest, chanting the ritual of protection as hard as I could. When the explosion settled into nothing more than smoke and cinder I dropped the shield and rushed forward. Owen fired a shot into the roiling smoke from behind me, then cursed as I got in his way. I trusted my steel more than his lead.

They came out of the gaping hole in the wall, the jagged wound of the hatch. The coldmen. Their eyes were luminescent in the smoke and steam. White fog vented out of their faces, frost riming the blades of their greaves. They lurked, like animals stalking into the light of a campfire. Their eyes flashed, and then I was on them, screaming.

They fell stubbornly. I put the blade into chests, shoulders, thighs, drawing harshly back to pull the sharp edge of the sword through their flesh as I retreated. I heard and felt the remaining Alexians firing their weapons into the flanks of the horde of coldmen who spilled out of the door. Hot white lances punched into dead skin, rupturing bone and metal. They kept coming. They always kept coming.

I dove in and out, slashing and giving ground. There wasn't a lot of ground to give. Their wrist blades were sharp, and I had no shield to protect me. The wide blade of my sword got mired in a rib cage; another of them punched metal through my coat, slicing skin. The holy-forged form of my noetic armor crumpled under the assault like a child's toy. I let go of my sword with my right hand and punched the one in front of me twice, fast, reeling him back, then drew my bully. I started firing as soon as it cleared the holster, putting the first shot into the long bone of his shin, splintering it as the bullet went from knee to heel. My second shot cracked open his hip. I whipped the revolver up, slamming the thick barrel into his chin, cracking it like a wishbone. He fell back, taking his blades with him, out of my skin and my coat.

The sword came free when I put the tip of the revolver I had stolen against the offending rib cage and blasted it away with three quick shots, then holstered the bully and cleared the space around me, swinging metal into bone. There were so many of them, and we'd been pushed back nearly to the edge of the dock. I was losing sight of the ruined hatch. I lost sight of the girl, too.

"Justicar!" I yelled, looking around for the scion of Alexander. He was off to my side, trying to reload the fat cylinder of his shotgun. "We're going to have to make a move here awfully quick."

"We'll keep fighting, Paladin. Until we're out."

"That's not going to—"

The air cracked around me and I stumbled. The planks of the dock went crazy. The world was moving, sliding farther into the water. Away from the hatch.

The dock must have been damaged in the explosion, or the girl had cut us loose. I spun around, looking for her. Nothing. The dock twisted on its supports and pulled free of the wall, slapping against the water. We started to sink in cold water and earnest.

The wounded screamed, those awake enough to register the danger. Several rolled off and disappeared into the water, soundlessly. The coldmen didn't seem to notice, just kept fighting, pressing, coming. I fought on, because it was what I knew how to do. The water made it to my ankles, my knees, the shocking spike of cold into my crotch taking the breath from my lungs. The platform was tilting and I slipped, ashy water splashing into my mouth and eyes. I hauled myself to my feet.

I lost sight of Owen, of the other Alexians, of the walls all around. A couple of the frictionlamps bobbed on the surface of the water, a couple more glowed dimly as they sank beneath the waters. I saw the girl, once, refastening the mask that she had surrendered, her eyes panicking as the water rushed up around her throat and into her still-open mouth as she slid beneath the surface. Hands clutched at me, and I cut them, unsure if they belonged to the coldmen or my dying companions. My attackers gabbled at me in staticky panic, falling beneath my blade or stumbling off the platform to disappear. The planks under my feet began to shift as the whole structure lost integrity, forgot that it was supposed to be stable and flat. I was standing on a loose bundle of boards, and the bundle was coming apart. I tried to pick out the ruin of the hatch, but could see nothing but blackness and the swallowing darkness of the water. I picked a direction, lurched toward it, thrashing against the water to try to stay up, then stepped off into an abyss, into oblivion.

The water swallowed me, and the darkness, and the cold.

CHAPTER SEVEN

The corridor was a tube of slimy brick with gutters on both sides of a narrow iron walkway. There was no light, other than the soft glow coming off the Healers' runed cuffs as they invoked over the bodies of the nearly dead. I was on my back, shoulders arched uncomfortably over the mass of the articulated sheath. The corridor ended in a waterfall that fell silently, held back by some hidden force. I sat up. Owen saw me and came over.

"Careful now," he said. He passed a palm over my head, whispering some invokation of anatomy. He had put on his Healer's rings, a dull silver cuff for each finger, and they glowed a dim blue as he watched me with nervous eyes. "That was an unusual method of drowning."

"What happened?" I asked. My head felt like it had been stuffed with kindling and then used to start a particularly stubborn fire. The Justicar put his palm against my forehead, shook his head, then began to invoke. His skin was cool and wet, surprisingly soft. I closed my eyes and lay back against the damp tunnel wall. "Where are we?"

"Under the water," he said, then broke contact. The pain in my head dampened to a soft roar. "There's some mechanism in the water that dragged us in here. You should be fine until we get to the surface."

"A force?" I sat up again and looked at the waterfall. The water flickered light. I could detect a pulse in my bones now, not unlike the feeling I got standing on the monotracks, staring at the distant tower of the impellor. "This is how the Amonites got away?"

"Probably. Clever kids, those Scholars." He stood up, hunching under the curved brick ceiling. "We can talk about it later. I've got people to attend."

"Did our wounded get through?" I asked.

"Some of them. There must be a point in the water where the field is most effective. We just brushed it. Lucky, really." He started to turn away, then paused. "Some of those . . . things came through, too. We cut them and threw them back."

"What about the girl?"

He nodded down the hallway. "Yeah. We've got her guarded, best we can. Took her toys away and made her drowsy." He rubbed his knuckles around the cuffs, like an old man worrying the arthritis from his bones. "She's scared, Eva."

"Yeah. I scare people."

"Not sure it's you. Not sure it's any of us." He pulled one of his cuffs off, buffed it against his shirt, and put it back on. "Anyway."

I nodded, and he returned to the row of bodies lined up along the center of the corridor, checking pulses and invoking his rings. I eased myself into a more comfortable position and did a quick inventory of the meat. One of the Healers had already patched me up, Owen or one of his boys. I felt pretty good, for a girl who had just fought off a horde of dead men, followed promptly by a short period of drowning and unconsciousness. My sword was in its sheath, either returned by one of my fellow survivors or plucked out of the water by the articulators as it fell out of my hand. Watching the sheath do its thing could be creepy sometimes, like watching a spider pounce across the tense strands of its web. But it was good at what it did.

"How much of the city is like this?" I asked myself, quietly. The waterfall at the end of the hallway looked like a living painting, an artifact from the time of the Feyr. Might even be that old, though most of their ancient city had been torn apart after the siege. "How many burrows are there, for our little Amonite friends to hide in?"

"He did build the city," Owen said. He was sitting against the curve of the wall behind me, still rubbing his hands. "Who knows what Amon laced between the walls?"

"These guys do, obviously." I looked up at him. "If I can't get the girl to talk, maybe we should have a chat with your friends in the Library Desolate."

He shook his head. "We've found places like this before. Hidden rooms, empty tunnels. Sometimes evidence that someone had just left, or maybe provisioned the place like they intended to come back. We've interrogated the captive Scholars about it. Nothing."

"There are no plans for the city, somewhere?"

"Sure. They were in Amon's personal library. The one you guys burned to the ground."

"Ah. Well." It had happened in the angry days between Morgan's murder and Amon's capture. "Sorry about that."

He shrugged, then pulled off his Healer's rings and dropped them into a satchel on his belt. "We should get going. A lot of these guys can't be moved, and they're beyond my abilities. We'll have to bring a real Healer down here."

"Sure." I stood, then looked around the corridor. "Can your guys watch the girl?"

"Cassandra. She said her name is Cassandra."

I looked at him in the dim light of the waterfall. He wouldn't meet my eyes.

"Can your guys handle her?"

"Sure. She's out. Come on."

I nodded and checked my pockets. "I think I lost my gun. You see it?"

"Nope. Then again, I lost ten guys and whatever evidence those monsters destroyed on the way. So maybe I wasn't looking too hard for your gun."

He spoke quietly to one of the Healers he was leaving behind to watch the injured, then pulled a frictionlamp from his pack and started down the corridor. I followed, balancing my way past the line of dead and injured that took up the center of the path. We walked that way longer than I expected. Cassandra was at the end of the row, three Healers crouched around her, taking turns touching light fingers to her temples, her wrists, her ankles. She was out. She looked a lot paler in the frictionlight than I remembered. Once we were past all the quiet bodies, Owen and I walked in silence and shadows.

The brick tunnel led to a series of ladders that ended in a monostation on the city's inner horn. It was pretty clear that these were maintenance tunnels. There were doors that led to rooms that were nothing but machine and conduit, loud, hammering rooms that looked as if they'd been running for generations and could run for generations more. Several times the tunnel filled with vented smoke or steam, only to ventilate just as suddenly through hidden ports.

Also plenty of signs of recent traffic. Someone had bled all over one of the ladders, someone else had thrown up in a cubby-room off the main drag. There were abandoned clothes, a bag of dinnerware thrown to one side, even a muzzleloader that probably hadn't been fired in years, propped up between two pipes. There was plenty of dust, too, but it had been disturbed. This passage was ancient and hardly used. It was an easy trail to follow.

"How many people know about these places?" I asked. It was the first thing either of us had said since we'd left Owen's people behind. "Amonites come down here for maintenance, remember it when they get away from your zero-escape-rate Library?"

He shook his head thoughtfully. "Probably not. Maintenance is a problem. We know these passages exist, we just don't know where they are. Long as something doesn't break, we don't worry about it."

"And if something does break?"

He shrugged. "We dig to it."

Once we were on the surface, Owen disappeared to coordinate the rescue party. They closed off the monotrain station and filled the new-found tunnel with men carrying lamps and shotguns. I waited until the girl was brought up, arranged an escort for her back to Alexander's royal court where she could be questioned about the Fratriarch's disappearance, then lost interest. I had been gearing up emotionally for a hell of a chase, and it had just ended in a flash. There was still the Fratriarch to find, and these coldmen to figure out, but for now I was between tasks. I caught the last mono the Healers let stop at that station and began the long series of circular orbits and exchanges that would get me back to the Strength of Morgan.

I sat alone in the plush cabin of the mono, staring at the pendant Cassandra had left for me on the dock. It was the Fratriarch's, though not something associated with his office. More accurate to say that it belonged to Barnabas, the man I knew, rather than the Fratriarch I served. He had been wearing it as long as I'd known him, which had been forever. As long as I can remember, at least.

Did this mean that she knew where he was? If her compatriots were holding him captive, he would be bound and nearly naked. The icons of the faith are powerful tools for channeling the invokations of Morgan. My sword was an obsessively precise mimic of Morgan's own blade, the Grimwield. Same with the revolver. My armor, the pauldrons and gauntlets and greaves, all mirrored Morgan's battle dress, at least in style and spirit. At the higher levels of the faith, the icons became more obscure and more genuine. The staff Barnabas carried had at its core the driftwood staff that Morgan had carried with him into the mountains during the Thousand Lost Days. Many of the pendants and charms that the Elders wore or had stamped onto their robes reflected some aspect of Morgan's personal life. Some were genuine, some were decoy, to protect the secrets of Morgan's life. It was only knowledge of these things that powered them, and that knowledge was carefully guarded by the ranks of the initiated.

So they would have stripped the old man. Of his robe, his jewelry, even that ancient staff. This pendant would have been taken from him, too. The girl could have lifted it from the stash of his belongings, feeling some regret perhaps over her involvement in his kidnapping. It didn't make any sense.

Soon enough, the Chanters of the Cult of Alexander would find their way into the girl's brain, and then we'd know. It was a slow process, but she didn't seem the type to give it up to fear or intimidation. I sighed and rested my head against the glass of the window. I'd know, soon enough.

The invisible fingers of the impellor swept through the train, setting my bones to vibrate like fine crystal for the briefest of moments. I remembered the feeling in the tunnel, of something lurking in the water producing the same wave under my skin. Pushing me out of the water and into that tunnel. Out the window I could see the impellor tower, set in the middle of our perfect-circle track. I imagined the impellor itself, like a battle hammer, rotating swiftly through its cycle, giving the train a little push and then passing on, each little push building up momentum until the whole mono moved. I had no idea how it worked, how the impellors from the other towers didn't interfere with this one, how the transfer from one circle track to the next was handled. None of it. No one in the city understood it. Except the Amonites. The wave passed through my bones again, and I sighed and closed my eyes.

I didn't like the idea that was forming in my head. It wasn't the Amonites, or at least not the local breed that I knew. The people I had seen lived in squalor. They lived to survive, and they lived with their families. They didn't have the kind of technology needed to take down the Fratriarch. And I'd seen no sign of the coldmen, until the end. Certainly I'd seen no sign of the Cult of the Betrayer, no one who would have carried the icon we had recovered melted into the cobbles at the crash site. And the coldmen showing up . . . what did that mean? Why had they shown up? Were they reacting to my attack, coming to defend their masters, or did our paths just run parallel? Were they looking for the girl?

I pulled the pendant on over my head and tucked it into my shirt. It was warm against my breasts. I held my hand over it for a while, and stared out the window at the towers that moved us around the city of Ash.

The disassembled bullistic revolver shone golden in the heat of the forge. It was spread out on an anvil of trueiron, each piece set with ritual precision. A row of bullets lay below it, balanced on their casings, like tiny soldiers at attention. I had looked down at this spread a thousand times. At my side, my hands itched to go through the motions of assembly. Not yet.

Tomas stood behind the anvil, dressed in the leather robe of the Blacksmith. He held the ornate hammer of the role in both hands. We were both sweating hard. Tomas looked uncomfortable behind the anvil. This was usually Barnabas's job, but he wasn't around. Tomas lifted the hammer and weakly struck the anvil near the barrel of the weapon. Still, the metal pieces of the weapon jumped.

"Eva Forge, Paladin of Morgan, why have you come to the Blacksmith?" the old man intoned.

"To arm myself," I answered.

He struck the anvil again, a little harder.

"For battle?"

"Forever."

Again, hammer to anvil, again a little harder. The anvil sang and the pieces of the revolver jumped. They would have shifted if they had not been locked in place by ritual and rite.

"Do you swear yourself to the struggle of Morgan?"

"I swear myself to the battle, the blade, the bullet."

Hammer. Anvil. Light runes glowed faintly across the shell casings of the bullets. Lines of arcane light began to itch their way across the pieces of the revolver. My fingers ached to answer them.

"Do you swear yourself to your brothers of Morgan and to your sisters of the Champion?"

"I swear myself to the monastery, to the legions of the Warrior, until the grave."

Tomas lifted the hammer over his head and struck again. The room was filled with the music of the anvil, and the arcane lines of the revolver nearly outshone the molten gold of the forge behind him. When he struck I could feel the echo of it in my feet.

"Bind yourself now to this weapon, the Terrorfel of Morgan. With it, you must carry the battle, follow the hunt. You must serve the scions of Morgan—"

And I realized he was off script. I looked up. His eyes were full of furious rage. He stared through me, glaring with such hatred that I nearly staggered back.

"You must serve your Fratriarch, whatever the cost."

I was lost for a response. Words left me. I put a hand against the anvil to steady myself and was shocked at its chill in this place of fire.

"Forever," I finally managed.

He raised the hammer high above his head and struck as if he meant to shatter this anvil that had stood here for a thousand years. The head bounced off the smooth black surface, the shaft leaving Tomas's hands and rebounding to fly up and drag the hammer back up into the air. It scattered the pieces of my new revolver. The runes of binding screamed through the air as they were bound to my soul.

"Forever," he said, quietly, then walked out of the ritual chamber.

I did my best to avoid Tomas after that. Not sure what his problem was, whether he was angry with me for failing the Fratriarch, or if he was trying to impress upon me the gravity of the situation. As if anyone understood it better than me. Then again, the more I looked into this whole thing, the less I understood. Bull on, I thought, and the clarity will come. Bull on.

I didn't like what I was finding with the Amonites. Everything about the Amonites' little hiding place was incompatible with a secret conspiracy committed to overthrowing the city's religious hierarchy. So while it was my first inclination to blame the Betrayer's feral children, I just didn't see it in that group. The only thing I wasn't sure about was that escape route. Awfully sophisticated. Even Scholars would be hard-pressed to throw together an impellor on the fly, especially one that could move people. Near as I knew, the technology didn't work like that. The monotrains had some kind of receiver in each car that was specially tuned to the impellor. You could feel the waves go by, but it wouldn't push you around. Not like that thing had.

I had nothing else to do. Alexander's Chanters would do their weird little trick to Cassandra, and we'd know what she knew about the Fratriarch and the free scions of Amon. It wasn't the fastest process, and took a great deal of energy from the godking, so it was not a rite that was lightly used. Until I heard from them, though, I had no other leads to pursue. And the Fist of Elders was locked away in the Chamber. Well, three of them at least—I could hear voices behind the door, Simeon and Tomas and Isabel arguing and reasoning and just . . . yelling. Elias was missing when I gave my initial report and the others had been in no mood to answer my questions. Wherever the hell he was, he doubtless had his reasons, and it didn't seem likely that the rest of them would grant me even a brief audience for a while.

Getting back to the cistern was easy. The whiteshirts were all over that hideout now, taking lithos and cataloging the debris. Not as much debris this time, though. The coldmen had come through here on their way to killing a bunch of Owen's men, and they had done their share of damage. The whiteshirts were heavily guarded, two guys with bullies for every one scratching in a notepad, and even then they looked nervous. I waved my way through and went downstairs.

The spiral staircase was dented and bloody. Everything smelled like blackpowder and burned metal. Where the hatch used to be there was a crosshatch of yellow opening out onto the water. Two guys in a collapsible raft were beginning to dredge for bodies. They came over at my signal. Probably glad to have a break from dragging the bodies of people they knew out of the water.

"What have you found so far?"

"Six of us, two of them," the guy with the hook said. "It's not as deep as we thought."

"What about the machine?"

"Keeps fouling the hook. Pushing it around in the water."

"You know where it is?" I asked.

"Sure," he said. "At least, I know where we're avoiding."

"Good enough. I want it up."

"The machine? That's, uh . . ." He looked around at the raft, his length of rope, the crude, bloody hook. "That's a little more than we can manage with this equipment."

"Then get some better toys. I want that thing on the surface."

"Okay, okay. Soon as we get the rest of our boys up—"

"They'll still be dead, whether you fish them up now or let them marinate overnight. Get on the rig to your boss and get whatever equipment you need down here. That machine's going to be dry and tight in the next hour, or I'll know who to yell at."

"Lady, listen—" he started.

I stopped him. "No, no, not worth it. Trust me, it's not worth getting on my bad side. You're a tough guy, I get it. They don't give this kind of duty to a softie. But I'm the last Paladin of Morgan, and for now that's the highest authority you've got." I pointed at the water and then jerked my thumb in the air. "Up. Now."

He sighed, gave his partner a bitch look, then pulled the raft ashore and clomped up the stairs. The other guy looked at me for a while, then shrugged and lit a cigarette.

"I was tired of dragging up bodies," he said. "This is fine with me."

"Glad to be of service."

He laughed and nodded, then leaned back in the boat and closed his eyes.

"Anything's better than fishing for your friends, lady. Don't mind us."

It wasn't what I expected. They sent a couple divers down, hooked the machine, and then dragged it up onto a temporary platform of rafts, lashed together and anchored next to the ruined hatch. Owen must have heard my name going through the static of the communication rigs because he came down just as they were dragging it out of the water. The impellor waves kept fouling the lines, pushing the whole load into the wall. I stood on the slowly bobbing platform with my arms crossed, waiting.

"You cause a lot of trouble," Owen said.

I nodded. "I get things done, though. Covers for a lot of bad manners."

"If you say so. But listen, maybe next time give me a call when you're going to change people's orders and requisition Alexian equipment," he said, standing next to me on the platform and watching the work. "I can get this stuff done without so many ruffled feathers."

"Is that your job, now? Make sure Eva doesn't piss off too many of your fellow Healers?"

He shrugged, and then we were quiet for a while as the machine was finally pulled free of the water. It spun crazily on the lines, like a bottle rocket on a string. With a little effort and a little luck, they got it down on the platform. The rafts immediately began tugging at their anchor. I stepped away from the stream of force echoing out from its side and moved closer for a better look. The impellor wave was rippling the air like a heat mirage.

Several things. I had never seen an impellor this small. The enormous devices that ran the monotrains were as big as houses, where this one was maybe fifteen feet long and half that in width. They were also immensely complicated machines, sprouting conduit and gears and various . . . flashing things. Machinery wasn't my strong point. But they looked like big machines.

This did not. This didn't look anything like what I expected. It was almost organic, like a smooth seashell, rippled and furled, with whorled apertures of some glossy, fluted material that was colored with the deepest blues and reds I had ever seen. It was a beautiful engine, if it was an engine at all.

I put my hand against its side. The surface was cool and soft to the touch, denting slightly from the pressure. My skin began to vibrate in time with the waves of impellor force.

"Is there a control panel somewhere?" Owen asked.

I blinked and turned to him, then looked around the smooth shell of the impellor.

"No, nothing I can see. It looks alive, doesn't it?"

"It started talking to you, Eva?" He smirked, circling carefully around the artifact. He paused and then put his hand against it, standing opposite me. "Here we go."

I felt a momentary surge of panic along my spine, and then the impellor waves fell out of rhythm and subsided. The artifact lay there on the platform, inert, like an instrument just put aside by a master. I stepped back and crossed my arms, fighting a chill.

"Any idea what it is?" I asked.

"An impellor, isn't it? Sure felt like one." Owen rubbed the hand he'd touched to the device. I walked around and saw what he'd activated. It was some kind of indentation in the side of the artifact, almost like a handprint but somehow wrong. Too small, and the fingers were . . . strange.

"Maybe some kind of new design," I said. "Might be these runaway Scholars have more resources than I thought, if they're cooking up stuff like this."

"It is the oldest design," a voice said behind me. I turned and saw that a couple of Owen's boys were bringing an Amonite onto the platform. It was the same guy who had sealed the hatch for us.

"You survived," I said. "Hope you didn't have to fight or anything inconvenient like that. Or did your dogs know not to bite one of their master's boys?"

He ignored me and went to the artifact. His hands trailed along the flutes of the apertures like an artist tracing a line in a painting. When he was done communing with the thing, he turned to Owen, sparing me the briefest look.

"It is not a made thing. Or at least, not made by the Scholar's Cant."

"So it's something they found?" I asked. "Or something they stole?"

"Something they stole," he answered, still not looking at me. "Or perhaps something they bought. This is a Feyr device."

"The Feyr make impellors?" Owen asked.

"The Feyr can make anything, if they decide to. Or they could. The time of the great Feyr fabricators ended when the Brothers Immortal destroyed this city and cast down their gods. But yes, at one time, this was made by the Feyr."

"So it's old. Maybe something they dug up out of the city. Any ideas where they would have found a thing like this?" I asked, walking to stand in front of the Amonite. I plucked the hem of his hood, so he couldn't avoid looking at me.

"That is not what you are asking. You are asking if I have any ideas about where they might have gone, or where you might find others of their kind. In this, you know as much as I do," he said. His eyes were lined with dark concern, and he nodded up toward the abandoned hideout, far above. "You have seen that place, as have I. Where do you think they might be, now that you have turned them out of their home?"

I grimaced, and put my hand on the artifact. It was cold now, the skin stiff. I paced around it, examining it, running my hand across it.

"The Feyr, huh? It's an interesting lead. Can't imagine it has anything to do with the Fratriarch, though." I looked up to see the Amonite's eyes still following me. Creepy bastard. I shrugged at him, then motioned Owen's people over. "He's not being helpful. Get him out of here."

They led him away, leaving me alone with Owen and the artifact.

"This mean anything to you?" I asked him. "That they had a Feyr device like this?"

"Like you said—probably something they just found. What do you want me to do with it?"

"You guys probably have some kind of warehouse for stuff like this, huh? Why don't you put it there?"

I paused as I heard footsteps hammering down the stairs behind me. Some problem with the Amonite? Turning, I saw one of the whiteshirts push aside the barrier tape and jump down onto the platform. When he saw me, the guy's face went white and he averted his eyes, then made a beeline to the Justicar.

"Something to report?" Owen asked. The man nodded, then looked back at me. "Something private?"

"No, sir. Not private. Just . . . she's not going to like it."

"You think you can possibly tell me something that's going to make my day any worse than it already is, son?" I asked.

Owen held up a hand. From the stairs there was a quiet peal of sound, a clamoring that echoed down the steel and stone from the street above.

Sirens. To hear it down here, the world must be screaming with sirens.

CHAPTER EIGHT

*E*lias was a gardener. A strange enough thing in the Cult of Morgan the Warrior, and stranger because he had practiced this art since childhood. On campaign as a sergeant in the god's army, the mud in front of his tent was groomed and raked, accented by potted plants and lines of tumbled stone. His barrack post crawled with vines. Even on watch, he took time to prune the hedges on his route. And now, as an Elder of the god, he kept a terrace on the tall, wind-wracked heights of the monastery, the stone floor crowded with loamy planters and ivy-covered trellises. He slept between rows of dirt, his bed under a canvas roof, the mud under his nails fresh.

When he woke up that morning, it was to stiffness and pain. It had been a late night. Arguing with Tomas, arguing with Isabel. Trying to get Simeon to take a side or at least express an opinion. Missing Barnabas. Missing his voice in the argument, his leadership, his strength. Mostly, though, just missing his old friend.

Outside his simple room, the wind whipped coldly over the terrace. The sun was a white disk of hammered silver behind the clouds. It wouldn't rain today, but it felt like it should. Like the air needed cleaning. Elias shivered as he slipped from his morning robe, stretching strong, wrinkled arms in the chill air as he assumed the poses of the warrior. When he was done with the morning ritual, the old man put on loose pants and a leather jerkin, and began the daily rite of weeding and tilling that would settle his mind and gird his spirit.

He was there, kneeling beside a planter of herringheart, trowel in one hand and a fist of dirt in the other, when they came for him. That they would find him here was inevitable. It was where Elias was, at this hour, on these days.

That they would strike him here, high up in the Strength of

Morgan, steps from the Chamber of the Fist, on the holy stones of the Warrior god. That was unthinkable.

He fought. Even caught unawares, even unarmed, unarmored, uninvoked. With nothing but the hammer-strength of his old, wrinkled hands, hands that had planted and nurtured and struck stone and metal and bone. He fought, and he killed. There was more blood here than belonged to an aging Elder of the Cult. There was enough blood here for three men, soaking into the mud of the crawling vines, slicking the water of the artificial pond. More than enough blood. But only one body.

He lay where he had fallen, the trowel still in his hand. Its edge was dull and nicked. Bloody. His fists were pulverized. The bones of his face lay haphazardly under the skin. Deep cuts traced across his chest, his arms, his legs. He had fought, and he had lost.

I knelt beside him. It had been hours before they found him, and hours more until they had gotten word to me. Alexander's men stood nervously around the monastery. They had failed. The other Elders gathered to take the body into the quiet halls of the Warrior's Rest. I helped them carry, along with a couple whiteshirts. Afterward, we met in the Chamber of the Fist. Tomas was furious. Divinely furious.

"We agreed to stay because you said the Cult of Alexander would protect us," he said, his voice a hammering monotone, the fury just under the surface. "We agreed to stay because you said we would be safe."

"Since when do Morganites do the safe thing?" I asked, quietly. It wasn't my place, but there weren't many people left whose place it was. "Why are we hiding under a blanket of white?"

Tomas didn't answer me directly, but Simeon and Isabel drew back uncomfortably nonetheless. There were whiteshirts present: the two who had helped carry Elias's body to the Rest, a couple patrol-level authority figures, and the Elector of our district. Guy named Nathaniel. His armor was pearl white and trimmed with gold and silver. He looked glorious, for a nursemaid. All of them sat behind a table, the third side of the Council's usual triune arrangement. There were enough empty seats, now, that we could afford the space.

"We had the exits covered, my lords, and regular patrols. The Elder wouldn't have a guard. He refused us," Nathaniel said, his gauntleted hands folded casually on the table. "There is only so much we can do for you."

"Aye, and you've done it," Simeon said. "We've had enough of your help, highness. You may take your leave."

"Your pardon?" the Elector asked, cocking his head to one side like a schoolchild. "We are here to guard you, Elders. If this can happen with us here, what will happen if we were to leave?"

"I can't imagine it being much worse than this," Tomas said. "An Elder of the Cult was murdered today, sir. Your presence did not prevent it. Therefore, it is no longer necessary."

"There's no need to be stubborn," Elector Nathaniel said. "There's enough trouble without you getting stubborn."

"There's enough trouble without you strutting down our hallways and mucking up our relics," Isabel answered. Her voice was calm, but she sounded like a mother correcting a child. "We've had well enough of that. Eva had the right of it, I think. You will not take the necessary actions. We must see to ourselves."

"I will not—" the Elector began, standing.

"You will not tell us our business, nor make any claims to our safety," Tomas said, standing, yelling, hunched forward with both strong, wrinkled hands flat on the table, and the Council stood with him. Even old men and women can stand strong when the need is great. Especially then. "The Sword of Morgan cut a path for this city. It was on his steel that the Fraterdom was built. I'd thank you to remember where you are, and to whom you are speaking."

"I'm speaking to a dead man, if you kick us out!"

Tomas raised his eyebrows and leaned back.

"I have decided to take that as a threat, sir. You will vacate these premises immediately, or you will face me in challenge. Do you accept?"

"This is . . . it's a circus," the Elector huffed. He gathered the paperwork he had brought with him, the sheets rattling in his hand as he clenched them angrily. "A circus. A farce. A mummer's play. You have left your senses."

"And you have still not left the building," Tomas answered, then drew a short, flat blade. Its surface was black, and did not reflect light at all. He balanced the tip on the table and worked his thin, bony fingers over the hilt. "There is little time left, child."

"Gods! Gods in heaven and water, and whatever's in between." The Elector snapped a salute to his men, then motioned them out. The evacuation was precise.

"Boys," Tomas called, as the two who had helped carry Elias followed their lord out. "A moment."

The two paused, nervously. Tomas nodded to them, though he was still fingering that awful blade.

"You bore the weight of my brother, Elias. For this I thank you. The Sword of Morgan go with you, and carry you through the battle that is to come."

They stared at him in silence, then looked at each other with wide eyes.

"The Sword of Morgan," they intoned, then hurried out.

"Still recruiting?" Isabel asked.

"Hm. Well. Brother knows we could use the help," Tomas said. He hid the knife away and turned to his fellow Elders. "We must see to our defenses, and then pray our brother down. Eva, if you would take first stance?"

"I have things to do, Elder. I'd like to catch the bastards who are doing this."

"And catch them you will," he said, looking at me with narrowed eyes. "But first you will honor your brother Elias. Or are the rites of Morgan lost to you?"

"They are not," I answered. I wasn't looking forward to hours of meditation in the Rest, but I had no choice.

"I thought not. Elders," he said, looking back to the two remaining members of the Council of the Fist. "We have much to discuss. I will have food brought."

I left them to it, returning to my room to don the ceremonial garb of the Cult. The rest of my day was spent in quiet contemplation of the rites of Morgan, and the passing of his brother, Elias. The world went on without me. I hoped Barnabas would forgive me, and swore to honor him, when his time came.

They had argued for hours. It was the kind of argument where everyone knows that none of them is going to win. The room was quiet. No one was looking at anyone else.

"I have served the watch," I intoned, holding out the gold-etched ceremonial sword. "I pass you my brother's sword, that the watch may continue."

Tomas and Isabel didn't move. Simeon moved further away, turning his back to me and futzing with some fruit on the Council's triune table. I sighed and took a step into the room.

"Come on, folks, someone has to stand the next watch. Elias can't hold this sword."

Tomas sighed and stuffed his fists into his robe, then turned to Isabel. She nodded.

"Elder Simeon," Tomas said, trying his best for Barnabas's commanding voice. It wasn't a bad try. "I believe that this is your watch to stand."

"She has to know, Elder," Simeon said without turning around. "You can't expect her to continue like this."

"She will know."

Simeon turned and faced the smaller man. "When?"

"Stand your watch, Elder. For Elias."

"And Barnabas, if we keep this up," Simeon said under his breath. He marched to me and took the sword, not once meeting my eyes. When he was gone I tried to get Tomas to look me in the eye, then Isabel.

"This is the part where you tell me," I said.

Nervous looks, and then Tomas waved a hand.

"Follow me, child."

Tomas went before me, Isabel behind. I couldn't help but feel that I should be carrying my bully, or at least a knife.

They took me to the solarium. In our glory days, this space had doubled as a ballroom for formal events. Now it was just dusty, and a nice place to watch the stars. Night now, so the wide, domed ceiling of glass glittered with the diamond sky and the wash of alchemical light from the surrounding glass towers of the city. We were high in the Strength, above the fortified chambers, above even the terrace where Elias had fought his last. The solarium was a luxury of the Strength, not found in the other fortress monasteries of Morgan. Not that there were any left in the countryside still dedicated to their original purpose.

Tomas paused by the door and spun up the broad frictionlamps that ringed the glass dome. The room filled with amber light. The marble floor was unevenly dusty, and the air was cold and stale. I waited for Tomas to finish his business with the lights, watching Isabel walk further into the room. She reached the center and then orbited the inlaid compass rose, very slowly.

"No waiting around, girl," Tomas muttered as he passed me. "We've a lot of business tonight."

We joined Isabel at the center. He held up a hand for me to stop, just on the edge of the compass. Isabel came to stand beside me. Tomas kept his eyes on the floor, focusing on the dusty marble. Then, strangely, he raised his arms in benediction. And he danced.

It was a slow step, heel and toe and careful forms that moved him around the compass rose to an unheard tune. The dust puffed around his feet and stained the hem of his robe. Isabel put a hand on my elbow and tugged me slowly back. One revolution he danced, and then the floor opened and a platform rose into the room, panels sliding and clicking like a magician's disappearing box.

The platform was small and pyramidal, rising to waist height at the center. On the highest part there was a cylinder of banded iron, like a thousand pistons bundled together.

"How many years of dances and balls held in this room, and no one just happened to step that path?" I asked, my voice a whisper.

"It is an invokation," Tomas answered. He was out of breath, and a sheen of sweat beaded on his pale forehead. "Something you will learn, in time."

"So. What is this thing that we have hidden behind our god's secret life as a dancer?" I asked. Steps led up the gentle slope to the platform. I ascended and put my hand on the cylinder. It was about the length of my arm, and four times as thick. Heavier than I anticipated when I picked it up.

"You will need to invoke," Isabel said. There was a hint of amusement in her voice. I ignored her and hefted it to my shoulder, then tottered down the stairs. Isabel shook her head, then invoked under her breath and plucked the cylinder from my grasp. She set it on the ground, and we all stood around and stared at it.

"We don't know," Tomas said eventually. "It arrived, unseen, in the Chamber of the Fist. Two weeks ago."

I knelt beside it. The complicated bindings of my ceremonial doublet creaked as I looked the device over.

"These are Amonite markings," I said, running my finger over a band of runes along one edge. "This is the language of the Scholar."

Tomas took a deep breath and then exhaled a deeper sigh.

"It is," he said.

"Why is this in the Strength, then? It is the engine of a heretic. It should be taken to the Cult of the Healer and destroyed."

"Yes," Isabel said darkly. "It should."

"It should, but was not," Tomas answered, testily. "On the word of the Fratriarch."

"And what came of that?" Isabel asked. They were starting their argument again, as if forgetting I was in the room. "You fought him, Tomas. It was your vote that we destroy it. Immediately."

"Yes, it was. But the vote still stands."

"What vote?" I asked. "What the hell are you people talking about?"

Tomas and Isabel stared at each other, lost in old conversations. When they broke their stare, the tension in the room snapped.

"There was a great deal of discussion on this subject. The Council voted." Tomas circled the cylinder, then placed a hand on its cap, running a finger around the Betrayer's runes. "And that vote still stands."

"For now," Isabel answered. "But Elias is dead, and Barnabas, most likely. The Council needs to be re-formed, a new Fratriarch ascended, a new vote—"

"Whoa, whoa, hang on. Barnabas isn't dead, not yet. Unless you've got his body in some chandelier or stuffed behind your wardrobe, he's still the Fratriarch. And I'm still his Paladin. Whatever the old man decided still stands." I looked angrily down at the cylinder. "Even if we don't like it."

"We will see. This is a time of emergency, Eva." Isabel placed a hand on my shoulder. "We must take extraordinary measures in times such as these."

"Or we could stand by our vows, and serve the Fratriarch." I fixed Tomas with my gaze. "As we swore."

"Yes, yes. As we swore. Either way, you won't get a vote, Paladin. This is a matter for the Elders. And this," he said, motioning to the device, "is the heart of it."

"This is what got Elias killed? Do we even know what it is?"

"Not really. As you surmised, it is an Amonite artifact. Some kind of storage device, perhaps, or a map." Tomas took a step away from the thing and clasped his hands behind his back. "Amon was always fond of keeping knowledge in machines. But really, we don't know what it is, or where it came from."

"And you didn't turn it over to the Alexians because . . . ?"

"Because we did not know where it came from. It was given to us, to the Cult of Morgan. Not Alexander."

"So this is some kind of pissing match, Elder?"

"Alexander abuses the knowledge of the Scholars, Eva," Isabel said, stepping into our conversation from where she had been observing from the side. "He keeps them as pets, milking them for whatever benefit he can manage. Whatever will further his power."

"Are you feeling empathy for the Librarians Desolate, Lady Elder?" I asked, smirking. "Doesn't sound like you."

"Not empathy. I don't think they should be kept at all. Alexander allows the worship of Amon, Morgan's murderer, to further his own needs. He speaks to us of justice, but only as far as is convenient for him. He promises us revenge, and then allows the scions of Amon to live in captivity, so that they might build him weapons, and grow him armies of peasants."

"Weapons that have contributed to the downfall of our Cult, Elder? Is that your concern?"

She stepped close to me, her breath a mix of spice and sweat. Her finger hammered into my chest, inches from Barnabas's pendant.

"My concern is that the servants of the Betrayer are allowed to live, when our god Morgan lies dead."

"Regardless of fault," Tomas said, "we do not wish to further Alexander's knowledge of the ways of Amon. Whatever knowledge this archive contains, it is for us, not him."

"And that's why we were fetching the girl," I said. "In the hope that she would be able to decipher the device, and further the cause of Morgan."

"That was the Fratriarch's hope," Tomas answered. "We were opposed to it, but . . . he's the Fratriarch."

"Was," Isabel said. I rounded on her, but she held up her hands in peace. "And shall always be. Settle, girl."

"So why are you showing me this?"

"You should know what caused all of this. Barnabas's kidnapping, the murder of our brother Elias. Whatever is to come. We all felt that you should be aware of the cause."

I nodded to myself. That was the reason they were willing to tell me, at least. I suspected there was more going on, more that I wasn't being told. I would speak to Simeon, later, and get his side of their disagreement.

"And why was Elias killed?" I asked. "Did he have some secret knowledge of this device, or something?"

"We don't know," Tomas answered, shaking his head slowly. "Someone is warring against us. We assume they are aligned with the Betrayer. Perhaps trying to recover this device, or destroy it."

"They're welcome to destroy it," Isabel spat. "I don't want this Scholar filth in my monastery."

"If the Betrayer wants it destroyed, then isn't that reason enough to preserve it?" Tomas asked. Isabel took a step back, looking at him with confusion. He nodded at the question in her eyes. "This is not as simple a question as I would like to believe, Isabel. The more troubles develop, the more questions I have. The less sure I am of my earlier vote."

Isabel grimaced, then hefted the device with her still-invoked strength and placed it back on the platform. Without a signal that I saw, the platform folded intricately back into the floor. When it was smoothed away, Isabel turned to Tomas, fire in her eyes.

"Do not speak to me of complicated answers, Tomas. This course will see us all killed. Alexander fails us. Amon will lie to us. It is only in Morgan we can trust."

"Morgan is dead, love," Tomas answered, quietly. Isabel spat, then whirled and marched out of the room.

Tomas watched her go with sad eyes, then put a hand on my shoulder.

"How will we stand, if not together?" His voice was very quiet. "We must speak of your duties, Paladin."

"What would you have of me, Elder?"

He turned to me, his clear blue eyes wet and bright.

"The girl is in the hands of the Chanters," he said, very carefully. "What does she know?"

"She can chant a hell of an Unmaking, Elder. Beyond that," I shrugged, "that's what the Chanters are for, aren't they?"

"It matters to us, Eva. It is important. We cannot go back to the Library Desolate and simply withdraw another. Besides," he drew close to me, "this girl, she was with the Fratriarch when he was taken. Might have been involved in it."

"Yes. I hope she can lead us to him."

"Lead us? Perhaps. But we must know how it happened. Who is responsible. And worse, Eva . . . what did he say, there at the end? What if she escaped, ignored by whoever it was that took Barnabas. What does she know of why we summoned her? She surrendered to you, did she not? Why would she do that?"

"To preserve her fellow scions, I think. It isn't unreasonable."

"That is not the action of a Scholar. Of a Betrayer. She must know something of the archive, something of Barnabas's reason for visiting the Library."

"And if she does?" I asked.

"The Chanters will know. And then Alexander will know."

I crossed my arms.

"Is it that important, Elder? That we endanger the search for the

Fratriarch, perhaps cost him his life, to keep this thing hidden from Alexander? He is our god's brother, after all."

"As was Amon." He pulled away from me, shuffling slowly to the center of the floor, his head down. He traced a pattern in the dust with the toe of his old boot. "It is important, Eva. It was the Fratriarch's will. He knew the danger, when he went to the Library alone, with only you as his guard. He knew, and accepted it."

"What are you asking of me, Elder?"

"To do the Fratriarch's will. To obey him, as you swore to obey him." He stopped his scuffling and looked up at me. His eyes were sad. "Alexander has the girl. Bring her to us."

It didn't really matter what I thought. The Elders were going to do what they were going to do. I had never understood Cult politics, the secrets we kept, the secrets the Healers kept from us. Never understood why either of the Cults put up with the bloody Amonites, either. There must be other ways to keep the city running, besides the Betrayer's slick invocations. Again, not my decision. Not my business. The Elders were going to do what they were going to do. And I was going to do what I was going to do.

I stopped in my rooms only long enough to shed the stiff ceremonial gear for a pair of jeans and a cotton T-shirt, boots for a loose pair of meditation slippers, then set out to roam the higher halls of the monastery. I was bone-tired, having been up all night searching the city for signs of the coldmen, then much of today standing watching over the dead body of Elias. But I couldn't sleep. Too much on my mind, and more on my heart.

My feet shushed along the cold slate floors of the monastery. The corridors were spottily lit, and the rooms were quiet. The monastery had been built to house two strong Arms of Paladins of the Champion, five hundred men, plus four times that number of support staff and lesser initiate warriors. Add in the Father Elders, the Fraternal leadership, the holy seers and anointed champions . . . nearly three thousand souls had called the monastery home, in comfort. Not a barracks, nor a mendicant's hovel, the monastery was the height of the holy order of Morgan's warrior church. Had been, and still was, though the Cult was dwindling.

There were fifty of us left. And most of that corps were aging Elders and middle-aged initiates who had never achieved the status of the blade. There were warriors among them, brothers- and sisters-at-arms who were fit to guard the doors and march in the hallways, maybe even carry a charge in the field. But of the Paladins there was one. Me.

The corridors of the monastery twisted up, narrower and higher, the living chambers occasionally interrupted by empty defensive towers and unlit muster stations. The weapon racks were left empty. I wandered until my feet took me to the highest part of the egglike monastery. I went outside to stand on the Dominant, the narrow platform atop the egg that, in time of war, would serve as the Fratriarch's station.

The Dominant was a smooth plane of stone, about fifteen feet in diameter. The edge was sheer, without even a low wall to protect its occupants from tumbling off. The platform was a fixture on all Morganite strongholds across the peninsula, most of which now stood empty or in ruin. From this place, the master of the stronghold would direct the defenses when the enemies of Morgan and the Fraterdom laid siege. Open to the field of battle, and with a perfect view of the armies below, the master would stand in clear sight of the enemy. The only things protecting him were the hard invokations of Morgan, incanted by his personal guard of Paladins. Such was their power that their words could turn away bullistic shot, clouds of arrows, even the early cannonades that were just seeing use near the end of Morgan's life.

I sat on the edge of the platform and dangled my legs over, resting my heels against the smooth curve of the stone wall as it arched away. So easy to slide off. Slide off and down, to fly into the city without a sound. I leaned back on my palms and let the cold of the stone leech into my blood. The Strength of Morgan, safe in the city of Ash, had never seen siege. Probably never would. But the view from the Dominant was still spectacular.

The monastery sloped out and away like a black moon. Few of the windows were lit, fewer of the chimneys curled smoke. The monastery sat like an eclipse in the middle of a city of light. All around, bright towers of glass reached starward, their surfaces shot through with the witchlight of the Amonites. Even at this hour the streets were alive with traffic. The golden rails of the mono shimmered as the trains sped by. Crowds moved below in silence, too far away to hear. Life went on. The city of Ash went on.

I stood and stretched, pacing silently through the five stances of the Brother Betrayed. Circling the Dominant, the forms flowing through my arms like shadows flickering on a stage. I kept my eyes closed, my fists open, my breath coming in long, deep cycles. Muscles relaxed into the comfortable ritual of the forms.

"You should be sleeping," a voice said from the center of the Dominant.

My empty hands stopped inches from his throat, the strike rising up from my heels and through twisting hips, automatically snapping out what would have been a killing blow had my mind not recognized the voice.

"Elder Simeon," I said, finally opening my eyes and looking at the old man over the stiff splay of my palm. I relaxed and stepped back. The Elder remained standing and still, as though he had never been in danger. As perhaps he hadn't. The Elders spoke the deepest secrets of the Cult of the Warrior. Even infirm, they had their powers. "Forgive me."

"It is your forgiveness that must be given, Paladin. I checked your room, but you were gone. I came here to . . . collect my thoughts." He stepped away from the stairs, trailing out toward the edge of the platform. "And perhaps my memories. I did not seek to disturb you."

I closed my stance and faced away from the Elder, putting some distance between us. Old men didn't climb that many stairs without a purpose. Especially this old man.

"You treat me well, Simeon. Always have." I squatted down onto my heels, resting my arms on splayed knees. "So be honest with me. What was Elias's vote?"

"His vote?" he asked. "On the archive?"

"Yeah."

"So they've told you about that, at least. What else?"

"What else should I know, Elder?"

He folded his arms into the wide sleeves of his robe and nodded toward the cityscape.

"He was with Barnabas."

"He wanted to reach out to the Amonites," I said, mostly to myself, mostly fitting the pieces together in my head. "To learn more about the device, without telling Alexander."

"Yes." He nodded. "That was his hope."

"Might not that be why he was killed?"

He became very still. "These are dangerous suggestions, Eva." He turned toward me. "The Cult has enough enemies without digging them out of the monastery."

"This is what I know, Elder. Someone delivered that artifact to the Strength. Someone kidnapped Barnabas and killed Elias. In every case, these unknown someones had pretty excellent knowledge of the business of the Strength. Who knew where the Fratriarch was going, and why? Who knew we had the artifact, or that a vote was taken to determine its fate? Who knew where those votes lay?"

Simeon did not answer me. Did not need to answer.

"And let me extend that thought. I know Tomas voted against it. Isabel made her will known. She has no tolerance for the artifacts of the Scholar. So, two against. Barnabas voted for investigating the artifact. As did Elias. Two votes to two. Leaving only you, Elder."

"Aye. I was with Barnabas."

"And now you fear for your life, as Elias should have feared for his. And now we must ask who held the knife. Who could be trusted, and now cannot?"

"Surely you do not suspect the Elders?"

"I am not threatening the Council of the Fist. I'm not accusing you, or Tomas, or Isabel, of anything. There are others in this monastery, other powers at work in the city. What I am saying, Elder, is that I will pursue this hunt wherever it takes me."

"You must be very careful, girl. We do not wish to show weakness—"

"Enough, Elder," I snapped, flushing at my own rashness. He took a step away from me. "I do not know what you are doing, but I do know that you are doing something. Tomas sent me to watch over Elias so he could talk to the other Elders. He sent you away so he could talk to me in Isabel's presence, and show me the artifact. And now you are here, to speak with me alone. Perhaps to speak against the Elders, perhaps to sway me in my decision regarding the artifact. It is a careful game, but I will not play it with you."

"Paladin . . ." he hissed, then paused. Two long breaths we stood there before he gave a sharp nod, then retreated to the spiraling staircase.

When he was well and truly gone, I relaxed from the fighting stance I had unwittingly assumed, then continued with my stances of meditation. I should not have spoken out to the Elder like that. But then again, he should not be trying to play games with the hunter on her trail.

CHAPTER NINE

My first glimpse of battle came on my tenth birthday. Tomas brought me to the train, and rode with me as far as it would go. We took the smaller elevated mono, in its unerring orbit, out of Ash and to the lakeside terminal. There we boarded a landlocked train, huffing and snuffling and groaning as it gained slow momentum out of the station. Tomas bought me jerrycakes and soda that the vendor mixed right at the cart, and let me sit by the window. When we were close, he helped me get into the custom-fit steam suit, the pistons and boiler huffing like the train. I didn't have the noetics yet, and I was too young to wear a man's armor.

There were ladies on the train with us, accompanied by their gentlemen. They wore silk dresses and carried picnic baskets. The Rethari Incursion was still a curiosity, like a page of history that had torn free and was rampaging among the peasants. Only we didn't really have peasants anymore. But the ladies boarded the train with their picnics, and their men carried folding chairs, and they sat in their leather-upholstered compartments and talked. Mostly they talked about me, in ways they thought I couldn't hear.

I clambered out of the train and followed Tomas down to the field, and to Barnabas. People were already saying that he'd be the next Fratriarch. He would make a good one, I thought, though he was getting a little old. Something I didn't understand—why we waited until a man was old to make him Fratriarch. Best grab them while they're young and full of fire. Old men settled into patterns. They smelled. Fratriarch Hannas smelled, at least, and his bony hands were like the gnarled roots of trees. I hoped that making Barnabas Fratriarch wouldn't do that to him. I couldn't imagine him that way.

The Rethari were gathered together, their scaly legions lined up in cohorts, their cohorts rallying to standards and champions. Just like any other army. I looked out across them and found the totem-men. Their gods. I laughed at such foolery, but Tomas hushed me. I picked out Barnabas. At the lead, of course. Without his helmet, of course. His great white mane of hair snapped in the wind, like a totem of winter snow trapped in a field of summer. His hair had always been white, long as I'd known him.

The men followed him. I understood that. I would follow him, if Tomas let me. If I could get out of this ridiculous suit and wield the blade, if I knew the rites of armor and bullet. Someday.

The Cult of Morgan carried the charge. As was our right. But we did not carry the day. It was glorious, down among the flashing swords and dancing warriors. It wasn't until later, when I stepped that dance myself, that I would learn of the grim filth of war. The death, the stink of men and women voiding themselves as blades burst guts, as bullets shattered teeth and opened skulls like ripe fruit. From here it was beautiful. Down there it was glorious too, but not in a way the ladies in their silk would understand.

We carried the charge, but did not win the battle. The Rethari were driven back, then folded around the tight knot of the Cult of Morgan like a fist. Our legions fought, but the enemy were many. Their totem-men scythed into us. Living gods, or unliving. They cut into us. I watched the scions of Morgan fall back, drawing tighter and tighter to Barnabas's standard, to his wild crown of white hair and the swirling arc of his hammers. I stepped forward, but Tomas put a hand on my shoulder.

"Sometimes there is loss, Eva," he whispered. "Perhaps that is today's lesson."

But it was not. There was thunder, and the common levy advanced. Set shoulders lofted bullistic rifles like a bristling forest of metal and wood, which then erupted in fire and smoke. It was the greatest sound I had ever heard. The valkynkein swept forward on iron treads, tearing into the soft flank of the Rethari force. Thunder and lightning and the sharp stink of cordite as the conscripted warriors of the city of Ash advanced. Warriors. Farmers, fish sellers, tailors, beggars. But armed with the Scholar-crafted weapons of the Royal Armory. They were unstoppable. They put fire into the Rethari, and the scaly legions fled.

Their totem-men tromped away, their heavy feet digging into the bloody mud of the field. The battle was carried by common men, and the weapons of Alexander and his pet Scholars.

That was the lesson of the day.

I woke up, startled by the sound of the maid pushing dust down the hallway outside my door. I stood naked and shivering in my room, bullistic in hand, listening to her brush, brush, brush her way until she turned a corner and the sound faded. I had been sleeping, but I had not been sleeping well. Dreams of the Fratriarch, of Elias, both lying cold and dead in the Rest. Of them rising up and calling after me with static voices that scratched against my bones like the song of the impellors.

My fingers shook as I got dressed. They shook as I cut my breakfast in the quiet mess hall, shook until I stuffed them into the pockets of my pants and hurried away from the Strength. This was before dawn. The sky was just barely light, and the streets were empty.

It was a hell of a thing the Elders were asking me to do. The Cults of the Brothers Immortal had their differences, as the Brothers themselves had their differences. Petty things that brothers do, whether or not they are gods. More so for Morgan, Alexander, and Amon, since they were born human and became gods through their actions during the war against the Feyr. Petty things, and serious things, and in one case at least, murderous things. But ever since Amon had betrayed Morgan, since the Cults of Morgan and Alexander had hunted down their wayward Brother and put him to the torch, enslaved his Cult, and harnessed their wisdom . . . ever since then, Morgan and Alexander had stood close. Whatever grievances we had against each other were insignificant beside the Betrayal.

So what were we doing now? Hiding an artifact of the Betrayer in our monastery, acting behind the Alexians' backs, risking the life of our Fratriarch to preserve that secrecy. These were the orders of the Elders. And now they were asking me to break into Alexander's palace and free an escaped Amonite. An Amonite who might know where

Barnabas had been taken, who certainly knew something of what had happened to him. All to keep the scions of Alexander in the dark. It made me . . . uncomfortable. But that was my vow, reiterated to Tomas just yesterday, burned into my heart since I had been left at the door of the Strength.

I wandered the city of Ash in quiet contemplation, wandered as the city unfolded around me, as the night fell to morning, and morning became day. I was wasting time. But my hands had stopped shaking, at least.

I felt better, the closer I got to the Strength of Morgan. That old building always gave me peace, nestled darkly among the bright glass-and-steel towers of the city. It was a place of dense power and ancient strength, like a foundation stone from which an entire world could be built. I had built my life on it. Easy to forget its majesty in my trouble.

I paused along the wide boulevard that circled the Strength, resting beside a vendor cart at the edge of a stream of pedigears clattering over the cobblestones. The Strength rose above me, its egglike shape exaggerated by its height and width. The stone of its walls was intricately carved with friezes from the history of the Cult, its sides interrupted by terraces and gun platforms and wide glass windows on the higher levels that glittered in the sun. On the far side I could just make out the walled driveway where I had been turned over to the Cult as a child. And, facing me, the wide mouth of the recessed portal that led to the main door of the cathedral. Against the height of the Strength that door looked small, though it was ten feet tall and made of thick wood. The arched portal was easily thirty feet high, and bounded by statues of the warrior-saints. At our current strength, we couldn't afford the processional guard that traditionally stood at attention. That door remained closed but unlocked, even in this time of trouble.

What was not unlocked, and never open, were the sally ports that ringed the monastery. Solid stone doors, hidden in the seams of the holy carvings, openable only with invocations and secret knowledge. Which is why it caught my attention when the farthest sally port I could see cracked open and a single figure slipped out. Whoever it was scurried across the mostly deserted boulevard and disappeared into the press of buildings on the other side.

I was invoking before I fully understood I was moving, and moving before half a breath had left my mouth. The boulevard was never crowded these days, not since the Strength had lost its prominence as the spiritual center of the Fraterdom. Nothing got in the way as I sped along the edge of the buildings, each step faster with every invokation of speed and the hunt. By the time I reached the place where the figure had disappeared I was flaring power in a coruscating aura of glory. I turned the corner and turned my Morgan-blessed senses on the trail.

Whoever it was, he was running invokations, too. My senses were baffled by a muffled aura of misdirection. The street twisted under my feet, the buildings that should be so familiar fading from sight to be replaced by a nondescript facade of unknown houses and featureless walls. The sky closed in. Even my sense of balance took a tumble. I braced myself against a building that I'd never seen before and looked around. Behind me, the Strength was lost to sight. The average citizens who had the misfortune of traveling this street at this time stood dumbfounded in the road, unsure of where they were or where they were going. I passed them by, pushing through the subterfuge of the invokation with the burning eyes of the hunter. Faint hints of the figure's path called to me, disturbances of air and power that could only be detected by the sharpest of eyes. Morgan's eyes, blessed to me.

After that initial surge of misdirection the trail settled down. Traces of invokations hung in the air where my target had jumped a fence or passed, ghostlike, through an intervening wall. A couple times I found myself following ghost tracks and had to walk back and pick the trail up again. Twice I spotted the figure. Nondescript robe, shuffling through the crowd that had gathered in front of a fish vendor. Once he was in the clear, there was some sort of commotion in front of the shop that drew everyone's attention but mine. With no one looking, the shuffling figure jumped gracefully up a fire escape and disappeared into the alleyway beyond.

He was better than me. In a pure chase, speed against speed, invokation to invokation, he would have outdistanced me in a breath. It was only his apparent need for subterfuge and the occasional crowd that was slowing him down enough for me to keep in range.

My pursuit took me deeper into the city, away from the harbor horns and to the opposite shore of Ash. These were the oldest buildings, the first structures the Fraterdom had raised after the defeat of the Feyr. I kept catching glimpses of the Spear of the Brothers, the marble tower that had served as the seat of power before the three Cults had split and settled into their own domains. After the betrayal of Amon, Alexander had returned to the Spear to build his throne, leaving his Cult's Healing Halls to the administration of his scions and declaring himself the godking of all mankind. When it was built, the Spear was the tallest structure in all Ash. Now, like the Strength of Morgan, the Spear was dwarfed by the glass-and-steel towers of the modern metropolis. Ironic that Alexander sat humbled by the technology created by his policies toward the Scholars.

We did not go to the Spear, however. The figure skirted the edge of the administrative district, keeping to the old town and transportation hubs, more than once ducking into shops and then out the back door without speaking to merchant or customer. People seemed unphased by his passing. There were a couple more instances of the disorientation, when it felt like the world was being squeezed through a tube and everything became unfamiliar. If my quarry was a scion of Morgan, he was reeling off invocations I had never heard of, much less learned. I felt the Betrayer's hand in this. My pace quickened, driven forward by curiosity as much as my warrior's training. I wanted this target, wanted to hunt him down and drive him to the ground.

Our path began to orbit a cluster of buildings. I slowed down. The figure was looking for tails, checking and double checking his path. I had him well in sight now, but there was no getting any closer. We circled that cluster of buildings once, twice, and then he stopped in front of one particular place. White walls, plaster chipped and old, windows shuttered, but the iconography still maintained. One of the original missions of Alexander, its glory faded, its doors long closed. But not to this man. He crept silently to the door and laid a hand against it. Something happened, an invocation or a signal, and the door opened. Before he went inside, the figure looked up and down the street, then disappeared into the darkness. I saw his face.

Elder Simeon, son of Hatheus, holy scion of Morgan.

Simeon walked slowly through the darkened hallway, discarding the invokations of stealth and speed that he had been wearing since he left the Strength. He was unarmed and unadorned, as the relics of the Cult would have too readily marked him as a scion of Morgan. His clothes were plain, and he wore no emblems around his neck or at his wrists. One of the most powerful men in the city of Ash looked like little more than a shopkeep, caught in the bad part of town.

The hallway opened into a tall central room, a domed space off which various arched doorways led. Light came from a scattering of frictionlamps around the room, flickering under minimal power. A second-level terrace overlooked the main room. The floor here was a mosaic of tiny earthen tiles, but so many of the pieces were shattered that the picture was lost. Simeon scuffed his foot across the fragments, frowning. He looked around the room, then drew something from his pocket. A pendant. He held it aloft and incanted something under his breath. A pulse rippled through the air, and the shadows shifted.

"We are here, Simeon of Morgan. There is no need to shout."

The voice came from the terrace. Simeon turned to face the speaker, though he couldn't see him. He kept the pendant held high.

"I didn't want to meet like this, Malachi. There are too many eyes."

"Our eyes, Elder? Or your own?"

"Both. Come out, Healer."

A shadow detached itself from an archway and passed between two lamps. The man was trim and proper, white armor laced with gold and linen. He wore the armor well, a man accustomed to fighting as well as parade. A brace of daggers twinkled at his belt, and his gauntlets glowed with the subtle power of the Healer's icons. His face was smooth and young, though his eyes looked like the eyes of a doll. His lips were too big. Golden hair cascaded across his shoulders. His icons marked him as a High Elector of the Cult of Alexander. It was Nathaniel, who had early on been put in charge of the defense of the monastery, and whom the Elders had kicked out.

"Is this better, Warrior? Both of us in the light."

Simeon took a step back, breathing a curse. "I have had business with you, Elector, and put you aside. I am used to dealing with Malachi, of the House of Sutures. Where is he?"

"This matter has been elevated, as have I. I am in charge of this investigation now. The Council of Blood is deeply concerned about the possibility of their brothers of Morgan acting behind their backs, and have asked me to take a hand to it. So, tell me." He leaned against the railing. "What news, Elder?"

"They are not acting behind your back so much as acting in their own interest. You must understand their—"

"They are hiding an abomination of Amon. That was your report, no? That is why you came to us originally?"

"I came to Malachi because we are old friends, and things are getting out of hand. Your involvement is unwelcome."

"My involvement is at the behest of the godking, Elder. Now, tell me, what is happening in the House of Morgan that you would call such an urgent meeting with your friend?"

Simeon looked nervously around the room, then settled into himself.

"They have tasked the Paladin to retrieve the girl in your care. The Amonite. They believe she will be able to help them interpret the artifact."

"And why don't they get another Amonite? There are plenty."

"They do not wish to alert Alexander to their purpose. They wish the artifact be kept a secret."

"Mm." Nathaniel paced the terrace slowly, hands behind his back. "And the Paladin? How does she intend to retrieve this Amonite?"

"I don't know. We give her a loose leash."

"You should tighten it. There are enough troubles in the city without a Morganite kicking in doors and starting fights on the monotrain."

"She was attacked. The Fratriarch was kidnapped!"

"Regardless." He stopped and looked down at Simeon. "Control her."

"Two things, Elector. One, it doesn't work like that. She doesn't work like that. Two, you must remember that I am an Elder of Morgan. I will not be taking orders from your Cult, godking or no. I am here as a courtesy, because I think things have gone off the tracks."

The Elector stared at him with a dead face, then entertained the briefest of smiles. "Of course. Forgive me. I so rarely meet another of my standing. So this . . . Paladin. She will attack the Spear and save the young girl?"

"Perhaps. Your best hope is to hide her. A Paladin of Morgan is not something to be fought."

"We have our defenses. I am shocked that one of your Cult would seriously consider attacking the throne of the godking." The Elector flipped his hand in the air, as though dismissing a cloudy day. "Strange times."

"She would, if that is the only way for her to protect her Fratriarch. And your defenses? They are the defenses of a Healer. The Warrior will find her way through."

The slightest of smiles again, and then the Elector continued pacing.

"Of course. Additional precautions shall be taken. Any insight on what happened to Elias? I assume you are running your own investigations."

"I . . . I think Eva may believe that it was an inside job. That he was betrayed by one of our own."

"Really? You should be careful, then, Elder, sneaking out of the Strength for shady meetings with the scions of Alexander. Does she suspect us, then? You lot are always blaming someone for your troubles."

"Excuse me?"

"Oh, for the decline of your order, the loss of your Fratriarch. Like when you threw my detachment of guards out of the Strength. A wise and deeply considered move, I am sure."

Simeon flushed and clenched his fists. The Elector was a much younger man, but he wasn't familiar with the fury of Morgan. Either that, or he was suicidal.

"I came here for your own good, Elector. For the good of the Fraterdom. If you'd rather take your chances with the Paladin, or the Amonite, then you are free to do so. But there is no cause to insult me."

"Insult you? No, no. That was not my intention." He paused again and leaned lightly against the rail. "We will take care of the girl. She will tell no secrets, either to Alexander or any of his children. And as far as chances go, I think you will find that we are not prone to taking them at all. Leash this one."

A shadow darted out from one of the passageways around the central room, skipping over the shattered mosaic and striking the Elder before he could raise his old hands. The shadow resolved into a man, bound in gray with an iron mask across his face, crudely molded to give the impression of a nose, eyes, a mouth. These features twitched as he attacked, as though laughing. He held a knife in each hand; wide, flat blades that flashed across the Elder's chest with such speed. Simeon gasped and stumbled back, then invoked a weak shield that could not hold long against such an assault. As the Elector looked on, another half-dozen figures entered the room from various doors and hidden chambers, closing on the old man. They were all similarly dressed, and all bore the icon of the Betrayer.

I intervened.

I had used a lot of energy keeping up with Elder Simeon. I was tired. My reserves were ragged from three days on the hunt. It had been like a long, running battle, a battle fought more in retreat than advance. So when I saw that first knife go into Simeon's chest and draw back with the Elder's blood all over its blade, I felt a moment of fatigued vertigo. Hadn't been preparing for a battle. I was like a scout who found herself too far behind enemy lines, suddenly thrust into the fight, without hope of relief. Desperately in need of relief.

But the Cult of Morgan was out of reserves. There were no more armored columns of Paladins waiting in the barracks, no more legions of Initiates of the Blade and Bullet filling the training grounds with the noise of their practice. The battle was joined, and there was me. There was only me.

I drew my sword, incanted a scant few invocations of armor and strength, then drove my blade through the skylight I had perched beside and leapt to the Elder's aid. I hadn't been there for the Fratriarch. This was a doomed battle, but I would be there for Simeon. And then there would be none to take my place, but this is what warriors do. It is what we know.

I fell past the terrace, and was pleased to see a look of distress on

Nathaniel's face. The Elector, or whatever he was, whichever God he was sworn to. Time for that later, if there was such a moment in my life. I landed in the middle of the mosaic, shattering brittle tiles in a ripple of sharded dust. The assassins stopped for a fraction of a breath, their murderous attention drawn from the Elder to this new threat. Simeon made a sign with his hands, a benediction of forgiveness, then collapsed against a pillar and used the last of his strength to invoke something hard and impenetrable. I was alone.

"One fewer that we have to hunt down, my brothers," Nathaniel sneered. "End this one, and then finish Simeon." He had drawn one of his daggers, a small, sharp thing of silver. He pointed it at me and laughed. "It will be good to be rid of this one."

They came at me in fluid attack. As soon as I engaged one he would melt away and I would find a knife at my back, probing the defenses of my sword forms. I had to be careful, never expending too much on offense so that my defense could remain solid. It was a mobile battle. I was glad it was my last. There was no need to hold anything back, no need for a reserve in anticipation of the next fight. There would be no other fight. I would die with the blood of a Betrayer on my sword, and that was enough for me.

"Morgan stood against the thousands," I incanted, leveling my sword against my foes. *This is how the invokations of Morgan should be sworn,* I thought. *In battle, with blood on your steel and adrenaline in your lungs. We should burn down the monasteries and build a world of battlefields.* "Their spears struck at him, and he stood. Their shields defied him, and he stood." One of them came at me, blades low and then high. His mask was a twisted visage of glee and malice. I blocked the attack and swept my sword back at the inevitable blindside attack. Metal found flesh, and I turned to see one of the assassins crumple, his lifeblood pumping out over the holy forged blade of my faith. "Their legions attacked him. He stood. Forever, on the hill of Dre'Dai-mon, on the eve of Cuspus, against the forces of chaos. Morgan stands. The Warrior stands."

The noetic power of Morgan wrapped around me, somehow drawing from the frenetic energy of my final stand. Or so it felt, to me. For years I had practiced a religion of forms and maps, studying the great battles of my god and my brothers. That time was past. The time of battles was upon me, and my faith was purified for it. Deep veils of power engulfed me, and the strength of Morgan filled me. I laughed with heartfelt joy, with gleeful abandon. My last battle, forever.

One down, but there were more. They were incanting their own rites of power and strength. I knew nothing of the forms of the Betrayer. The last time the Cult of Morgan had drawn steel against the scions of the Assassin, Amon was still alive, and Morgan was only freshly murdered. There had been pockets of resistance after the pogrom, but mostly we fought the enemies of the Fraterdom. The Feyr, the Rethari, the Yongin. People whose gods were waning, or had not yet fully ascended.

Best not to wait for them to find their forms. The closest one was incanting some story about the secret places of the Assassin, ritually invoking the hidden knife, the false partnership, the dark alley. It seemed to me that their powers were limited to the unexpected strike. They were here. I knew them, could see them. This was a battle now, not an assassination. While he spoke with the power of his lungs, incanting ancient rites of betrayal, I shuffled forward and brought the full weight of my double-handed sword against his skull. The tip split his forehead, parted his eyes, and ended the business of his mouth. He fell like a rag discarded by a servant. I exulted in the directness of Morgan.

His fellows howled like scalded cats and rushed me. *Excellent*, I thought. *They abandon the shadows. This is the place of Morgan. In the light, in the field, in the battle fully joined.* I danced between them, parting tendons from bone, opening flesh and revealing marrow. They hesitated, and I brought them the glory of battle. Morgan surged through me, as though he reached out from the grave to give his servant strength against the Betrayer. Of course. This is what I worshipped, the fallen warrior, the betrayed god. This is the battle I was consecrated to fight.

It was not enough. I ended two of them and maimed another. Perhaps he would find a beggar god, that one. But there were too many. I overextended. Too much offense, and one of their blades parted my armor and put barbed steel against my bone. I staggered back, and another found its way into my shield. They came at me like waves of hail, battering me and then falling back. One of them circled the room, cracking open the frictionlamps and snuffing each element. Soon, I was battling in the dark. The only light came from the invokation of my armor, noetic runes flaring in the shadows. It was not enough. They appeared before I could react, struck, disappeared. My defense forms were not enough. I fell back to the Elder, where he huddled behind his shield, comatose, blood seeping from his wounds. It would make a nice statue, I thought. The Paladin, last of her kind, standing between the darkness and the light. I would be content with that. They circled, and I invoked the last of my strength, then began to write the ballad of my death.

They intervened. I did not know them, though they were familiar to me. The two I had seen, just before the attack on the Fratriarch. Bulky men in cloaks, armored cowls over half their faces, hoods down, tattoos banding their eyes. They fell from the roof, just as I had. They carried weapons, in each hand a punching dagger that folded out from hidden places, expanding and growing even as I watched. Their eyes flared brilliant light as they landed. Their incantations were of absolute power, spoken in the words of ancient languages. Again, the Betrayers paused.

The first that stepped to the new attackers was cut down. The second as well. There was no third attack. The rest jumped away, the shadows swallowing them even as the newcomers lifted their arms and filled the dome with light. The Elector was gone, the gold trim of his cloak flitting around a corner even as his servants disappeared.

I stood in a guard position. They raised their hands to me, then nodded in the direction Nathaniel had taken. I shook my head and went to the Elder. His shield flickered and disappeared like a wisp of smoke under my hand. His breath was ragged.

"Eva. I didn't know who they were. I didn't realize."

"Enough, Elder. What has happened here?"

"The girl. They will end the girl. She must be saved."

"From Alexander," I said, grimacing. "He seems to have it in for us."

"I don't know," Simeon gasped. "I don't know who these people are, or who they stand with. But the girl must be saved. We have made so many mistakes, Eva. She must be saved."

"We've made nothing but mistakes, Elder." I stood, wavering as the power of Morgan left me. "But I will do what I can."

"What you must, Paladin. They have taken her to the Chanter's Island."

I nodded and looked around. The men were gone. I turned to the archway the Elector had taken, touched my sword to my forehead, and remembered Morgan as he lay dying on the Fields of Erathis. I had found the scions of the Betrayer. They would not escape me.

CHAPTER TEN

Owen really had been sent to look after me by his boss. I wasn't sitting in the local station more than five minutes before he came rushing in. Like he was just in the area. Sure.

"Gods, Forge. You look like hell."

"Hell is filled with trite expressions," I said, wincing as I stood. "You my ride?"

"I don't think you're going anywhere. Honestly, you're barely able to stand."

"Yeah. That's why I called for a ride." Truth was, I had stumbled into this station to give them the word on my Elder. They had rushed out with medical bags and trauma machines, out to where I had told them Simeon was lying. They hadn't come back yet. In the meantime I had sat down, and just hadn't gotten around to standing up again. Long as Owen was here, though, I figured he could make himself useful. "Let's get going."

He tugged at the leather shoulder strap of my holster as I tried to get by. I turned to him.

"Seriously, what went on out there? I've got reports on the rig of a roughed-up Elder of Morgan and a lot of dead bodies."

"That's what happens, usually. One of us, lots of them." I rested against the counter for two long breaths. "Is he going to be okay?"

"The Elder? I don't know, honestly. Who is it?"

"Simeon. He was out there . . . talking. Trying to do what he thought was the right thing." I looked Owen briefly in the eye, then tugged free of his grasp and started toward the door. "Anyway. We've got some ground to cover."

"There more bodies you need to lead me to, Paladin?"

"Not yet. But there will be." That got him to follow me.

The ride over was quiet, quiet as it can be in a patrol wagon with blaring sirens. The Chanter's Island home wasn't too far, but it was a lot farther than I was going to walk. On the way I gathered what strength I could. Meditated. Thought about Simeon and Elias, put down by Betrayers' blades. Barnabas. Wherever he was. I thought about those strange tattooed men, and the cold, dead eyes of the coldmen as they came at us in the Amonites' cistern.

"What happened?" Owen asked, sternly. "What are you driving us into, Eva? What am I going to lose my boys to this time?"

I opened my eyes and looked down the length of the wagon. Owen's patrol was strapped in, trying hard to keep their eyes forward, the fear off their faces. Trying, and failing. Some new faces, to replace the boys we lost in the cistern. Owen sat next to me, his hands crossed over the biggest, widest shotgun I had ever seen. Boy had upgraded. Not so much of the Healer in him now, perhaps. That was good.

"Who attacked the Elder, Eva? Must have been a hell of a thing, to take down one of your old men."

"I don't know. Seems to be more and more common all the time. As to who they were . . . I'm not sure. I don't know, and I'm praying like hell that you don't know them either."

"What's that supposed to mean?"

"One of them was dressed as a High Elector of your Cult. Guy's name was Nathaniel. He was in charge of security at the Strength, around the time that Elias got killed." I gave Owen a sharp look.

"You're saying a scion of Alexander attacked you? That's . . . it's not true. It can't be."

"No, not saying that. I'm saying it looked like that. But him and his dogs, they were Betrayer kin. They bore the icons, and they had the invokations. Amon's folk, and no doubt about that."

The wagon got tense. Owen leaned close to me, his voice a harsh whisper.

"Eva, if what you're saying is true—"

"Forget it. Forget I said anything. If it's true we're going to have to root the whole damn Cult out again, I know it. We thought we had them nice and safe in their black robes with their chain-bound souls. Lazy. That's our mistake, Healer. We got lazy."

Everyone settled back into their seats and listened to the sirens for a while. I didn't have to tell them what we might be going into. We all knew the stories of the Betrayer. We knew this was the kind of fight that ended with one side all dead and the other with plenty to mourn.

The Chanters sect of the Cult of Alexander has its own island. It's the kind of thing you really hope for, when you're setting up a mysterious religious order. Your own island. This particular island was really just a floating tower, much more of it below the water than above, bobbing peacefully in the wide bay that was formed by the two horns of the city of Ash. It looked like an iceberg of stone, held in place by a flat ring of landing platforms and docks that met the face of the water.

We took a ferry over, cranking up the wagon and bursting along the dock with our sirens blaring as soon as we touched the artificial shore. The Wardens of the Chanter's Isle didn't know what to make of that, other than to give us funny looks and stay out of our way. Good enough for me.

The main gate of the Chanters' detention facility was a facade of unbroken marble, smooth as the first snow. The wagon chattered to a stop where the gate was supposed to be and the patrol piled out, Owen in the lead. Beside the gate there was a marble figure, the barest features of a face on a square column. I walked up to it and tapped it on the forehead. Disrespectful, but I never was much of a fan of the Chanters and their pretty little tower.

"Hello, inside. We'd like to come in now. Okay?"

The column shivered and the face moved. You could taste the understated irritation.

"Entrance to this facility is limited to the highest initiates of the Cult of Alexander, godking of all Ash. All others must request special privileges. These requests may be filed—"

"Eva Forge here. Last Paladin of the dead god Morgan." I bounced my sword lightly against the figure's face. "Open up."

"Entrance to this facility—"

"For the love of the Brothers," I swore, then bent at the knee and incanted something from my childhood. A trick we only used when the brothers weren't looking. Mostly strength, but a lot of brute violence, too. I put my shoulder against the pillar, grunted, and pushed. The whole thing creaked and then splintered at the base. I was still smiling to myself when the pillar tore free and went spinning against the smooth marble wall.

"What the hell was that?" Owen asked.

"Morgan used to knock trees over with his shoulder, when he was a kid," I answered. "He wasn't always a god. But he was one hell of a strong kid."

"And you have an invokation for that?"

"Not something they teach you in the sanctuary, but we figure it out." I stretched my back and smiled. "You can only use it for frivolous things. For giggles. You probably don't have anything like that in the Healers."

"Nothing about knocking trees over, no." He squinted up at the quiet wall of the Chanters' tower. "And I'm not sure your trick got us anywhere with our potential hosts."

"Well, yeah. Probably not. But it needed doing. It's not like that conversation was getting us anywhere either."

"New plan. You're not the one doing the talking from here on out."

And, of course, that's when the marble gate cracked open and the Chanters came out to see who had knocked over their pet statue. I turned to Owen and smiled.

"Newer plan. We skip the talking part next time."

"Gods and Brothers above," he said, sighing. "Why do you encourage her?"

"Who did this thing?" the lead Chanter asked. She was wearing a dress of iron plates, sewn onto cloth of steel and rattling like loose shingles as she moved. There was a mask over the lower half of her face, a series of baffles that stole the power from her voice and diffused it into the air like wind chimes. The soft glory of her words did not match the fury in her eyes.

"If you'd been listening," I said, raising my sword to repeat the ritual of forehead knocking, "I am Eva Forge, last Paladin of—"

"Right, right." Owen stepped in. "I am Justicar Owen LaFey,

sworn scion of our lord Alexander. I am escorting this Morganite to an appointment with the Amonite, Cassandra. You are holding her here at our will."

"Cassandra," the woman answered. "Yes. She is in ritual right now. You may speak to her when it is complete."

"We'll speak to her now," I said. "I have reason to believe that there are Betrayers among you, working to kill the girl."

"Betrayers? In the House of the Chanter? No, such a thing is impossible."

"Look, I'm pretty much going to insist on seeing the girl, and standing guard over her." I rested the tip of my sword on their nice lawn, threw my arm over the hilt, and smiled. "So you can get over that and just let me in now. Please."

The Chanter glared at me, then at Owen, then at the rest of the world.

"You will see the girl," she said, sharply. "But that is all. The ritual is not to be interrupted."

"It's a good start, but I need to do more than see her. I need to know that she's safe."

The Chanter held a hand up to me, as much a warning as a benediction. "Silence, woman. Walk with me."

We walked. The marble gate closed behind us. Owen's patrol kept close to him, right up until one of the Chanters made a sign and escorted the boys away. Owen gave me a look, then went with them. I was alone with the creepy Chanter girl and her mask of chimes.

"You have been to the Chanter's garden before," the woman said in her breathy, muffled voice.

I shook my head. "No. Never had reason to come around." We entered the inner court of the castle, and even I'll admit it was a beautiful place. Topiaries and pebble-lane mazes that wound around marble fountains and statues that looked like dancing chandeliers . . . it was eerie. Nightmare in a tactical fight, too. I'd hate to try to hold a line among all the hedgerows and tiled canals. "Nice place, though."

She gave me a strange look, muffled surprise wiped away with a blink.

"Never had reason. I suppose not." She kept her hands in the sleeves of her robe, but I could see her fists bunching under the fabric. "No need for Morgan in a place like this."

Our path led us away from the gardens, then opened onto a shallow lake with a bed of copper. There were rafts on the water. I squinted at them, and could barely make out short, thin men with large heads working the lines.

"Are those Feyr?" I asked.

"They are visitors. Let us call them guests."

I looked beyond the lake and saw marble walls and guards, if Chanters with ornate poles could be called guards.

The woman noticed my attention. "They can leave when they want, whenever they are able. We guard against them, that is all."

"They're that dangerous? Those guys are all around the city."

"What they are is not dangerous. What they are doing . . . Never mind. It is no matter to the House of Morgan. You are here to see the Amonite, yes?"

"Yeah. You cracked her yet?"

"Cracked, no. But we have begun a conversation that may lead to the story we need." She led me away from the lake and into a building, finally. All these open spaces inside walls felt so unnatural to me. "Is that why you are here? For a progress report?"

I hadn't really thought about that. I was there to pry Cassandra out of the Chanters' creepy little hands and get her back to the Strength. I don't know when my thinking on this had changed. When I had started feeling more in union with the Amonite than the Healer. It wasn't like I didn't trust Owen. Completely.

"I'm here to see her, to make sure she hasn't been mistreated." I adjusted the holster on my belt. We were in a long, arched stone tunnel. The air was cool and wet, and I thought maybe I could smell the lake. "There have been threats."

"We don't threaten, Paladin. That is not our way."

We walked in silence, our boots crunching on the gravel path. She and I meant different things by threat, I think. There was more to the process than physical violence. It was the kind of thing that could be ugliest when it was pretty.

"Eva. My name's Eva Forge."

She glanced over at me, a little surprised, then nodded. "As you say."

"And I suppose you don't have a name?"

"Names are part of the Song, and should not be given away."

I grimaced and stuffed my fists into my robe. "Now you tell me," I muttered.

She shrugged and gave a light, lilting laugh. "We will each have our advantages in this, Eva. That is the way of these things."

There was no more talking. This tunnel led to another, which led to another. We crossed brackish ponds and moist fern gardens, passed under open skies and stone ceilings until we came to a final dark moat, and a castle at the center. I looked down and saw that this was lakewater, deep and black.

"All these walls and paths and buildings, and your final barrier is open to the lake?" I asked.

"There are other barriers. There is more to this place than walls and gardens, Eva."

"And I still don't know your name, and you're throwing mine around like a shuttle. Harsh."

"Lesea," she said. "This way."

The bridge was narrow and slick, as though it was carved from a single rib of the world's biggest fish. Lesea went first, her hands held slightly out as if for balance. The building that I had mistaken for a castle was really just a dome, spiked with towers like the head of a mace. The door was a disk of iron that rolled aside on geared teeth at the Chanter's signal. Soon as it was open I could feel their damn Song, itching into my blood. The water of the moat rippled away from us. We hurried inside and the door settled shut with a gasp of air pressure. The Song was louder in here, but not in a way that you could hear. The air vibrated with the Chanters' words, pure as honey and sharp, like a broken chime, beaten into a knife. This is why they got their own island, kids. The city folk wouldn't put up with this on their streets.

The domed building was really just a series of airlocks and pressure chambers, and each opened door layered on the discomfort in the air. I could actually hear it, now, could feel it in my bones and in my teeth. The articulated sheath seemed to cringe on my back, like a crushed spider. It was the hardest thing not to just draw steel and start shooting. Anything to drown out that mad Song.

The Chanters come from a narrow arc of Alexander's life story. An unhinged time. Becoming divine had been tough on the three brothers, and they each dealt with it in their own way. Alexander's place in the divinity meant he was particularly sensitive to the pain and sickness of men, and his initial reaction was to try to heal all of it. Noble, but foolish. Morgan did not try to win all the battles, only the one before him. But Alexander locked himself up and tried to sing a song of healing that would spread around the whole world. To say that he failed would be . . . well, polite. He went mad. The song he tried to form ended up forming him, as he tapped into deeper and older powers than he could ever understand. When he broke free from it, the song continued, and became the subject of worship for certain of his followers. They etched it, and it cut them, and together they became the Chanters.

I always felt like the Song was getting the better part of that conversation, between scion and invokation. It seemed as if the Chanters had to form their whole lives around this thing that they barely understood, much less controlled. They got farther and farther away from their service to Alexander, and became more and more their own thing. A separate thing. But the power that this service gave them, my Brother. I didn't think Amon's captive Cult was going to invent something to replace them anytime soon.

We stayed far enough away from the central chorus, where the Elders of the Sect kept the Song, trading off watches to rest their voices and their minds. The visitors' chambers were in the perimeter of the dome, though still too deep for my comfort. They weren't really built for comfort though, I guess. Lesea led me down a long hallway of circular doors, each vibrating like the stops in a pipe organ. I just kept my eyes forward, my hands at my sides. The woman next to me seemed completely at her ease, of course, and I saw that an unnoticed tension had left her face. She looked a bit drunk, actually.

Cassandra's door had its own little hallway, and the drone grinding out from it was something I could feel in my lungs. Lesea paused before she opened it and looked at me over her shoulder.

"Your shields will not help you in here, Paladin. But I would brace yourself, nonetheless."

I gritted my teeth and clenched my fists into knots. She nodded, then opened the door.

Cassandra was in chains, draped from heavy iron manacles and a collar. She was on her knees, her head bowed, her eyes closed. I would have thought her asleep if she hadn't turned her head at our entrance. There were four Chanters with her, one at each of the cardinal points, three men and a woman. They were singing through her, the drone of their voices whipping her robe and hammering her bones. And yet she looked calm. In the whining harmony I could hear a voice, nearly subsonic. Asking questions, about the Fratriarch, the Betrayer, the kidnapping. The murders. Not direct questions, just bringing up images and then abandoning them, like a dream that you forget with your first breath in the morning. Yet these dreams were carried on hammer blows. They spoke at the level of thoughts and spirit. I caught myself mouthing what I knew of the Fratriarch, intoning the story of our first meeting, our first fight, our first lesson together. The last time I had seen him. That I was worried he was dead, that it was my fault.

Cassandra was silent, cocking her head to listen.

"She is unique in this," Lesea whispered to me, though I wasn't sure she was even talking anymore. "We have never sung a song like her."

"Do you question many Amonites?" I asked, each word a gasp.

"We rarely have the opportunity, not since the Betrayal. They are always difficult. Such clear thinkers. Not like . . ." She paused.

"Morgan. I know. All fire and emotion. Will she talk?"

"She talks all the time. Just not about things that we want to hear."

As if to demonstrate, Cassandra raised her head and spoke to us, her eyes still closed.

"It is a series of mathematical thirds, iterated and then reiterated across a platform of subsonic patterns. I would call it beautiful, I think, in other circumstances." Finally, she opened her eyes and looked at me. A little surprise. "Eva?"

I didn't answer her, and in time she shut her eyes again. The singers did not stop. Lesea plucked at my sleeve, and I happily turned away and followed her into the hall.

"So you see she is well," the Chanter said. Her voice was strangely the same breathy whisper here, amidst the din of the Song, as it had been in the quiet garden above.

"I need to speak to her, still. Alone."

"No," she said, and her voice raised a little, gaining an echo and a vibration that unsettled me. "You do not. You are here for other purposes, Eva Forge. I feel the dissonance in your blood."

"Oh, that's just distaste, lady. Now get her out of those chains and give us a little privacy."

We stood, staring at each other in the cacophonous hallway, unmoving. Finally, she nodded and motioned me away from the door.

"She is in ritual now. I will not interrupt that. But we may sit, and talk this through." She turned and walked down the hall. When I followed her, she glanced over her shoulder. "Can I get you something to drink?"

"Whatever you've got," I said. "And plenty of it."

What they had was black wine, served in crystal that hummed between my fingers. We drank it in the quietest room I had been in since I had entered this damned building. The walls were three feet thick and the door was like a tombstone, rolled aside by pistons as thick as my waist and then sealed from the inside. Still I could hear that music, running through my bones.

"How do you people stand it?" I asked, my face buried in the wide mouth of the wineglass. "It's like living on the monotrain."

"Hm. Yes, I suppose it would be. But this is something you grow to love." She paused to drink. When she raised the glass to her mouth, the fluted chimes of her mask shuffled aside. Her lips were painted black, and she had the most delicate bones. She was careful not even to breathe when the mask was retracted. "You would have loved it, I think. Had you been born to the right path."

"We don't choose our paths, Lady Chanter. Not any more than they choose us."

"How very fatalistic. Appropriate for a warrior, I suppose."

I drank my wine and listened to the music in my bones. She tried to start a couple conversations, but I wasn't liking it. This place wasn't for me. It wasn't for Cassandra, either. Lesea was halfway through describing something about octaves and the high calling of the Chanters when a noise played its way through the horrible chorus, a noise that gave even the good Lady Lesea pause.

To me it just sounded like more of the Song, at least at first. The background noise of earthquakes. But then I noticed the Chanter had stopped talking, and was sitting perfectly still with her head cocked to one side, wineglass halfway to her mouth. Then I noticed that the chorus had kicked it up a notch, rising in waves and tides of pure noise.

Something tore through the chorus, like a jagged line of fire in a forest of dry grass. The Chanter dropped her glass and stood. The mask of chimes snapped open, revealing a perfect mouth and teeth white as tile and sharp as knives.

"Stay here," she said, and her voice ripped from her throat like barbed honey. "I'll be right back."

I stumbled at the sound of her voice, my glass tumbling to the floor, warm black wine splashing across the plush rug. I slid boneless from my chair, my skull vibrating, my fingers numb. By the time my eyes cleared the room was empty, and the door was sliding shut.

I struggled to my feet, using my sword as a crutch, leaning against it as I swayed in the wake of Lesea's impossible voice. Even I could hear the chaos in the Song outside. A great deal of divine violence was being done, at octaves that barely registered to my mortal ears. I dragged myself to the door, checked to see that it was locked, and slid back to the floor with my back to the wall. Time for the trick.

The bullets clattered as I dropped them to the floor, emptying the cylinder with a flick of my wrist. I loaded two blanks, special rounds we kept to scare the hell out of crowds. Two rounds.

"Morgan, god of war, lord of the hunt," I intoned. "Your breath is smoke, your mouth is the grave. Your skin is fire."

My skin stiffened and then sprouted the tiniest scales, blackening as the invocation spread across me. It wouldn't last long, but I didn't need it to. I held the bullistic next to my ear, said a little prayer for Barnabas and Cassandra, closed my eyes, and pulled the trigger.

Sharp pain, and then the sound of the world was sucked away into a humming maelstrom of silence. Quickly I switched hands before I lost my nerve, held the gun next to my other ear, and pulled the trigger. A lesser noise, but still great pain. I stood. My eyes were burning with powder. The scales had flashed away in the heat, but my face was blackened with powder. Warm, thick blood poured out of my ears. The world around me was silence. I could still feel the Song in my bones, but not in my head. I flicked the two rounds onto the ground, reloaded my bullistic, then exchanged weapons and invoked a silent rite of guidance.

In absolute, deafening silence, I opened the door and stepped out into chaos and fire.

CHAPTER ELEVEN

A man lay outside the door. His mask lay shattered by his face, and there was blood coming from his mouth. I stepped over him and walked down the hallway, in the direction I had come from. I found the source of all the violence just around a corner.

Even deaf to the Song, I could still feel it, feel the tension in its octaves and the crashing rhythm of its power. Before there had been a serene majesty to it, but now it was swollen with fear and violence. Whatever the Chanters were weaving, it was born of desperation.

I came around the corner and found that the Chanters' dome was being unmade. Some great power had split the dome in half, and the two sections were grinding together. My half of the building was sinking. Above me, I could see the floors that had once been parallel to my own, crumbling as they rose up into the air. Looking down, I could see the cracked heart of the building, the ornate wooden chamber of the Song, where the Elders of the Cult held watch over the ancient hymn. Smoke rose up from that chamber. On all sides, black water from the lake was spilling into the structure.

And with the water, hordes of the coldmen. They remained limp as corpses as the water carried them sloppily over the moat's edge, pouring into the building, spilling out over the floors and hallways that were suddenly revealed to the sky. They became animate only as they reached stone, dragging themselves to unsteady feet, then drawing out their blades and rushing into the structure. None had reached my floor yet, but they seemed intent on gaining the heart of the building, where the Song warbled and raged.

This was unexpected. I had come to try to convince the Chanters to turn Cassandra over to my custody. Failing that, I was going to steal the girl, and consequences be damned. At the worst, I was concerned that the Betrayer might try to assassinate her while she was in the hands of Alexander's people. Since Simeon had arranged his meeting with an Alexian friend, it seemed likely that the Cult of the Betrayer had infiltrated Alexander's power structure. If they could lead an Elder of Morgan into a trap, surely they could arrange to have a prisoner of the Chanters killed without causing too much of a fuss.

But this? There was more force here than had been used to kidnap the Fratriarch. Surely the girl wasn't more important than Barnabas? Was she?

The details would matter later. For now I was on a sinking island, swamped with undead warriors, and stone deaf. There was so much destruction that I could feel it in my bones, in my meat, but my mind was wrapped in a thick cloud of roaring silence. I tried to invoke and stumbled on the words. Power would not come to me if I couldn't form the words of the invokation. I was alone, and I had to get to Cassandra.

Cassandra was somewhere above me, in the half of the dome that was thrusting up into the sky like a new mountain range. Assuming they hadn't moved her while I was drinking black wine with Lesea. Assuming she wasn't already dead, wiped out in the first strike that had torn the dome asunder. Assuming.

The water continued to rise around me, and some of the coldmen spotted me and lumbered over. There was something different about these guys. Less armor, more flesh. Their skin was bloated, crisscrossed with deep cuts that had been hurriedly sewn together with thick leather cord. They still had the goggle eyes and the staticky voice boxes, but these were bolted crudely into their faces. Their weapons were just as wicked, though, just as sharp. They rushed me.

It was a poor-quality fight. I swept the length of my blade under-hand, pushing the tip about four inches into the first guy's belly and drawing it up his chest until I got to his chin. His ribs popped like a cheap zipper. He stumbled back and I maintained the sword's momentum, passing it overhead and then laterally. I put steel on his neck, near the base of the blade, driving straight through the meat and bone and coming out the other side with most of the weapon's speed still intact. I went to one knee, rotated, and drove the blade right through his companion's thighs. They fell away from me, falling bone-lessly into the dark water that was beginning to pool around my ankles. Quick fight. These guys didn't have the constitution of the coldmen I had encountered before.

But there were a lot of them. More than I had the time or patience to deal with, frankly. Let the Chanters guard their home. Before any more of the hastily stitched dead men could waylay me, I slid down the ruined chasm of the dome. Tiny waterfalls followed me, and avalanches of shale. When I got low enough, I was able to jump across the chasm, landing in a heap among broken instruments. I was low enough that I could see the fight that was boiling around the breach in the central chamber. Chanters, badly outnumbered and dwindling by the second, swarmed by the clumsy coldmen. I think there were Feyr among the defenders. Strange, but a puzzle for another day.

I climbed the rumbling incline of the shattered dome. The ghosts of sounds were starting to penetrate my head, even though my eardrums must surely be blown. The Song was such a violent thing, but even it was drowning in the groan of the building, the tectonic explosions and shifting architecture of the island. I looked down and saw water bubbling in the chamber below, working its way through organ pipes and articulated voice machines. I shivered and climbed on, as the Song began to fade from my bones.

When I got to the level where I thought Cassandra might be, I slid into the corridor. This whole half of the structure was leaning away from vertical, and once-level passages had become more like amusement park rides. Below me, the singing had stopped, or at least fallen to a level at which it no longer penetrated my deafness. The air was thick with dust. There were bodies on the ground, caked in dirt and their own blood. I couldn't tell if these were Chanters or their attackers. It didn't matter. I slid past them and down into the crumbling structure.

The lights were failing. I tried to invoke the Ghosteyes, but the words were thick on my deafened tongue and the invokation failed. Wisps of bluish light splintered out from me, scattering around the room before disappearing. I crept along, mostly blind, completely deaf, nothing but my hands and the weight of my sword to guide me. Something shifted far below and the floor tilted a little more. I wondered if it was an Amonite engine that kept this place up. I wondered if the scions of the Betrayer, Amon the Murderer, would know how best to disable the work of their god.

Someone stumbled out of the shadows and took a swipe at me. I punched him with the pommel of my sword, swept his legs from under him, then held my elbow across his throat until he stopped struggling. I raised his face up close to mine to get a better look. One of Cassandra's guards. Glad I hadn't just sliced him open. I wasn't quite at the point of taking up arms against all the scions of the Brothers Immortal. Not yet. And it looked like I was getting close to where I needed to be.

Sure enough, the next corner was familiar. A frictionlamp glowed dimly on its bracket, just outside a very memorable, very heavy door. I tried to invoke again with a little better success, coming away with enough strength to wedge the door aside. The guards were gone, but Cassandra remained, limp on the floor in her chains.

I said her name, then again, louder. She looked up, nodding when she saw me. Her lips moved, but I couldn't hear her. I pulled one of the chains taut, laid it out against the stone, and took an invoked swing at it. My swing struck as much stone as steel, and there were sparks. It was enough. One of the chains snapped open. With the loop broken, Cassandra was able to gather up the rest of the links and stand. She was as free as I could make her in my present state. I sheathed the blade and put my arm around her. Leaning on each other, we struggled out of the room and back into the hallway.

She leaned her head against me and spoke some more. I couldn't hear her, so I shook my head. She put her forehead directly against my head, the vibrations of her voice getting through my throbbing silence.

Thank you.

"Sure thing," I said, or I think I said. And that's when they hit.

It was a whole cadre of the coldmen, the true breed, the ones who had kidnapped the Fratriarch. They came out of the deeper parts of the building, boiling up from the darkness, their eyes glowing blue and green as they rushed us. The girl fell off my arm, or I pushed her, and the bully was in my hand. I stitched lead into the first couple of them, and then they were too close. In one motion I holstered the bully and went for my sword. The blade cut them as I drew it, the articulated sheath spinning the sword under my arm and into my hands. The corridor was too narrow and too precarious for truly fancy forms. I kept one hand high on the blade, on the weighted, dull length of steel that was there for just this purpose, striking mostly with the middle of the blade and thrusting with the tip. Trap with the hilt, push back with the middle, spear into black blood and cold flesh with the tip. Repeat. They fell around me.

Deaf, so I never heard the explosion that almost ended us. The floor jumped, and we all slid in a tangle of living and dead, deeper into the drowning building. Water, dark and cold, swallowed me. I pushed to my knees, then my feet, scything all around me at the grasping hands. I saw Cassandra burst from the water and swim to a tangle of metal at the center of this new pool, then wondered how I could see, then realized that the roof was gone and above us was yawning sky and sun.

The coldmen kept coming. They clawed out of the water and came at me. I was without invokation, without strength or shield. All I had was a childhood spent with a sword in my hands, a girlhood under the heavy eye of the Elders, lived in service to my god. It would have to be enough.

The trick is to keep the blade moving. A sword like this is only heavy if you try to stop it, or change direction, or carry it on a thirty-mile march in the woods. I have done all of these things, and I have learned to keep the blade moving in a fight. If you do it right, the only thing that will stop your blade is bone and meat and metal. And the only way to keep that from happening is to keep your blade very, very sharp. I have done that since I was a little girl. Sharp and heavy and always moving, and the strength that comes from thirty-mile marches.

I led with the pommel, bullying the blade into the air with my off hand on the blade rest, then launched the sword into a wide, scything swing that spun me around. This was before I had even gotten to the coldmen. Something to get the momentum going. I planted my feet, holding the hilt loosely in my palms to maintain the arc of the blade without getting twisted around, and just kept the sword moving. It was a training form, honestly, to build strength and familiarity with the weapon. As a child I had done it with a length of wood capped with lead. Today I did it to stay alive.

When the speed was good I shuffled forward and pushed the orbit of the blade into the nearest coldman. It cut into him at the knees, the shoulder, crossing back to open up his belly and finally splitting him from neck to nuts. He fell in many pieces, the way a plate does when struck by a stone.

I kept the motion up and two of them jumped me. There was water here, always rising, and as I shifted my weapon from front to back it kicked up tails in the muck. I could barely keep track of the blade's path, but my heart knew it instinctively, adjusting to skim off of armor without losing momentum, hardening my arms when the metal was about to find flesh or bone, always compensating for the motion of the enemy and the crazy tilt of the collapsing dome. All in complete silence.

The more of them that came at me, the less I felt the form of the blade and the more of it happened without thought, without direction. Two fell, then three. A fourth joined them and the blade moved on. I was sure that I was cut, but could not feel it. There was blood in the air, black blood and red, cold blood and warm, but all I felt was the joy of the blade's dance and the opening of meat. They came and they fell away, they rushed and they fell away. The world around me was nothing but the path of the blade.

It was over before I realized it, over and I was still dancing. No one else came to fall against my steel. I did another pass of the room, arcing and scything and dancing, the water kicking up all around me, the air whistling against my face, rustling my hair. No one left but the separated fallen at my feet. I gave the sword one last whirl and then grounded it tip first in the earth, and all the wounds rushed at me as the momentum of the dance left me, shuddering through my arms and the blade and into the ground. I collapsed against the hilt, struggled to stand, heaving breath and life all over my blade.

There were many wounds. I had not come through cleanly, but I had come through. Leaning on the sword, I looked around the room. At the half-submerged bodies of my enemies, at the tangle of metal and stone in the deeper parts of the pool. At Cassandra, just standing up from behind a column of brick. She looked frightened. I understood that. She was talking. I didn't understand that.

A shadow passed over me and I looked up. Above us, a great section of the dome peeled away and, slowly, gracefully, bent toward us. To flatten us, to bury us under a world of brick and stone and metal. All that, and the building was going to kill us.

Suddenly, Cassandra was beside me. She put one arm around me and threw the other one up, as though shading me from the sun. Power surged through her. I watched as the wall leaned down to us and then, suddenly, the avalanche of tumbling brick stiffened. Around us the stones formed a dome as they fell, stacking tight. The Cant of Making.

I looked down at Cassandra, and her eyes were fire blue as she intoned the Cant. Her hair whipped around, as though blown in a wind that came from inside the girl. Even her clothes, the cuffs of iron, her metal collar, all hung as though without gravity. Even I felt light.

Before the new dome had finished forming, she threw an arm out in the direction we had come, back up to the top of the building. A physical shock wave, very concentrated, shot out from her hand. As it traveled, the avalanche of collapsing architecture formed around it. It burrowed a tunnel into the sky, bricks lining up and clattering together like metal suddenly magnetized. The avalanche roared around us, the ground shook, but that tunnel formed and held in the span of a breath. Far away, at the end of the new tunnel, I could see a ring of blue sky. The earth settled, and it was still.

She collapsed in my arms, sobbing. My own strength was gone, but I lifted her, and she lifted me, and together we struggled up the tunnel and out into the light.

Owen grasped my head in his hands, palms against my ears, and began to invoke. My skull burned like a coal. When he released me, long, gummy strands of blood trailed from his palms to my ears. I could hear again. It was loud.

"That was a very bad idea," he yelled, though I could barely hear him over the rest of it. "I mean, a good idea, but a bad one too. We probably could have made some earmuffs for you, or something."

Owen had found us huddled in a ruined gazebo, on the shore of the copper lake where I'd seen the Feyr on my way in. The little men and their boat were gone, and the copper lakebed was punctuated with blast marks. The water had drained away. There was a lot of burning topiary, too. It looked surreal, burning green horses and spirals crisping away to nothing while I watched. This was as far as we were able to get in our condition. Owen and his patrol of Healers were fixing us up, one at a time.

"Where'd they take you?" I asked.

"Visitors' center. More like a holding cell for the curious. When that thing hit, though, everyone started rushing toward the center. We just followed."

"What was it?"

"You tell me. You came out of where it struck."

I looked over at Cassandra. Her face and arms were bloodless, and the two Healers who were attending her kept their voices low. I saw that her ruined hand was still sleeved in that contraption of steel I had first seen in the alleyway. How long ago had that been? Weeks? Days?

"I don't know either. We were inside, deep inside. Whatever it was cleaved the hell out of that sanctuary of theirs." I sat up and rubbed my head. "Doesn't make a lot of sense."

A flight of valkyn screamed by overhead. The city's defenses had finally responded to the attack, and the island was swarming with Alexander's peasant army. Back in the dome the Song had been replaced by a chorus of gunfire and muffled explosions. The whole island was shaking.

"You don't want to go back in there, do you?" Owen asked, nervously.

"I'm a Paladin of Morgan, idiot. Of course I want to go back in. But my sworn duty is to her, and her safety." Cassandra was sitting up now, looking around like a child woken from a nap. That Making had taken it right out of her. "How long until they hit Alexander directly, you think?"

"What?"

"Whoever these guys are, they're doing this for a reason. They started with Morgan. Maybe because we're the weakest, maybe because we have some trick that could stop them." I thought of the archive, but didn't mention it. I didn't know how that played into this game yet.

"Now they've moved against the Chanters. Arguably the Alexians' greatest weapons, thrown into disarray."

"This is not the time for this conversation," Cassandra said. She was struggling to stand. I rose and pulled her up by her injured hand, to test its strength. She grimaced, but the hand felt strong.

"Did you do this?" I asked, holding on to her sleeve. Her hand rested in a glove of wires and pistons, each joint articulated by minuscule gears that twitched and shimmered with motion, even when her hand was still. It reminded me of my sheath.

"The family didn't have any healers, and little medicine." She pulled her hand away and hid it in her cloak. "I did what I could."

"Does it hurt?" Owen asked. "I could do something for it."

"No, thank you. I'll be fine."

A series of thumps resounded out of the new chasm at the center of the island. Something deep inside the artificial ground collapsed, and the home of the Chanters clenched in on itself. Sirens began to wail in the distance, like the horns of the final battle sounding the ruin of the world. I grabbed Cassandra by the shoulder.

"This is the part where we run away," I said. "Come on."

We were not alone in our intention. The civilian population had been fleeing the island since the disturbance had started. They were now joined by the broken legions of the city of Ash, the valkyn arcing high overhead, the foot soldiers trying to find the boats they had come in on being turned aside by unit commanders who insisted the battle wasn't yet lost. The only ones not running were the coldmen. They pursued, their stitched bodies clamoring forward even as the ground gave way and they fell into the waters of the lake.

We stopped at the crumbling edge of the island. The wall had peeled away, and raw machinery bristled out of the ground, trailing into the lake. Owen was on the communications rig, trying to find us a ride.

"It's a rout," he spat, "and the boats are already gone. They evacced the civilians when they dropped off their units." He pulled off the rig and peered at the city. I could see a flotilla of transport boats steaming toward the docks. "Ten minutes at least, before they get empty and turn around."

"Where's our boat?"

"Commandeered to assist in the evacuation." He nodded to the distant fleet. "It's in there, somewhere."

"You got any holy tricks that involve walking on water?" I asked him. He shook his head. "Well. How about swimming? How does everyone feel about swimming?"

"A city on a lake, populated by gods, and people are trying to swim to shore." Cassandra slipped between those of us who had gathered at the rough edge of the water, and raised her hands to the sky. She invoked.

"Amon and his Brothers Immortal were at that time traveling across the land, meeting with the leaders of the people to warn them of the coming fall. In time they came to a great river, deep and swift. Morgan and Alexander argued how best to cross it, and while they argued Amon gathered wood, and rope, and pitch." She clapped her hands together and then pointed them down at the water. The surface of the lake boiled and churned. "He built for them a great ship, which carried them across the river, and later to the far islands, and the people of heaven were with them."

The girl raised her hands and something loomed in the dark water. It broke the surface with much trouble, listing and pouring water out its sides. It was a boat, covered in black sludge. Those few surfaces that were clean looked to be charred wood. Eventually it settled on the water, and Cassandra hopped lightly into it.

"Nice trick. You sure that thing's going to hold us all?" Owen asked.

"Weren't you listening? It's been to the far islands. It should be able to get us across this pond here."

"This is Amon's ship?" I asked. "What happened to it?"

"Not his actual ship, no, but a noetic representation of it. And the ship hasn't been the same since . . ." She shrugged. "You know."

We boarded and the boat started across the water. Owen took me aside.

"Since what?"

"Amon's death," I answered. "They bound him to that ship and burned him alive. It sank eventually, with him still screaming."

"Ah." He looked around the charred hull and winced. "Cheery."

"It's not so bad," Cassandra said. "At least we aren't swimming."

The boat lurched in the wake of another explosion from the Dome of the Song, and I grasped its side. The wood came away in damp splinters in my fist. Hard to forget that the story arc of this particular vessel ended with its owner burning alive and sinking to the bottom of this very lake.

"Not swimming *yet*," I corrected.

The boat made the short journey across the bay, docking along the inner horn. From there it was just a short mono ride back to the Strength. Owen left us at the station to report in. The civilian guard and their Alexian supervisors were in an uproar over the attack. Understandable. No one knew what had breached the dome, or where all those newly stitched coldmen had come from. It was unnerving, to maybe have an army floating under the city.

The Strength of Morgan was dark when we got back to it. Day was mostly over, and the old folks didn't keep the lamps burning deep into the night these days. Not even on days like this. The noetic bonds on the front door were intact, so I invoked my way inside and led Cassandra to the main mess. I found the remains of a meal in the kitchen, gathered up what looked serviceable, and took it out to the girl. While we broke our fast, I left my revolver on the table, next to my plate, the barrel turned ever so slightly toward Cassandra. We ate in silence.

"When are you going to tell me what happened with the Fratriarch?" I asked.

"When are you going to ask?"

I put down my fork and leaned back in my chair. "I'm asking."

She nodded, pushed aside the remains of her stew, and then took a long drink from her bowl of warm beer.

"Can I get a cigarette?"

"You smoke?"

"No." She shook her head. "But my lungs do."

I went out to Barnabas's study and fished up a cylinder of cigarettes and a lighter. She cut free a short length of cigarette, tapped it tight, and lit up. The lighter was an antique, a disk of torsion-driven element that heated up a ring of brass at its center. It took a couple pumps to get it hot, and it smelled of summer tar, but it reminded me of the old man. She tossed the lighter on the table and watched the smoke billow away.

"So. What happened?" I asked.

"After you left it was bad. We could tell when you were getting close because they would leave us alone for a while, but most of the time they were just hammering on us. It cost that old man, to keep his shield up."

"That old man was the Fratriarch of Morgan. He could have held it up forever."

"No. He could have lasted a long time, I'm sure, but there came a point when . . . when he had to make a choice. It had been a while since you'd been by to draw them off."

"Hadn't been that long. I was hitting them as hard as I could."

She looked at me for a long time, breathing in coals and breathing out smoke.

"It had been long enough. He decided to run for it, before he was too weak to run at all."

"That was a bad decision," I said.

"Maybe. But it was his decision. He invoked a shield onto that pendant and gave it to me, then he peeled back his metal column and broke out into the car. There had been an explosion a minute earlier, and they had slowed down quite a bit. We thought maybe you were nearby. That we could hook up with you and run together."

"I had just left. Thirty seconds earlier—"

She cut me off. "Doesn't matter. They were distracted enough. He killed the couple who were in the car and made it to the tracks. There were a bunch in the courtyard. They saw us and started shooting, and we jumped the other way." She tapped off the cigarette and swallowed. "They had someone waiting."

"Who?"

"Betrayer. One of the true scions of the Assassin. He might have been there the whole time, for all I know. Just . . . stepped out of the shadows and struck the old man down."

"So he's dead. Barnabas is dead."

"Not that easy. He fell and then he rose. There was a hell of a fight."

I remembered the icon of the Betrayer we found melted into the stonework, by the wreckage of the train. It made me proud, the old man going out like that.

"And that's how you got away. Your Betrayer buddy recognized one of his fellow Amonites and gave you a pass."

She stubbed out the cigarette. Folded her hands on the table in front of her. Stared at me.

"I don't really care what you believe. I escaped because he ignored me. Didn't care one lick about me. All he wanted was the Fratriarch. Honestly, that's all he could handle."

"So you ran? The old man fighting his last and you just ran."

"That's what he told me to do. He gave me the pendant and told me not to stop, no matter what happened. He told me to find you and get back to the Strength of Morgan. That the Warrior Cult needed me more than I could know."

"That's all? That's all he told you?"

"We were busy."

"Well, you got the running part down. Why didn't you come find me, like he said?"

"You didn't seem the understanding type. I didn't think you'd believe me, especially once that Betrayer showed up."

"I'm not sure I believe you now." I stood and gathered the dishes, then threw them in a wash bin and stretched. "Not sure I have much choice, though. So that's the last you saw of him. Fighting the Betrayer."

"That's the last I saw."

"Well. Here we are, I guess. Doesn't answer most of my questions."

"So you're not going to kill me?" she asked.

"Honey, if I were going to kill you, it would have happened a long time ago. You can relax."

She let out a long sigh, then drew and cut another cigarette. Her hand was shaking as she touched paper to the lighter.

"I'll work my way to relaxed, someday. You're not an easy lady to relax around. So what now?"

"Now we talk about why the Cult of Morgan needs you."

"What about Barnabas?" she asked.

"Barnabas is the Fratriarch of the Cult of Morgan, and the Warrior's True Sword on earth. He will have to take care of himself." I fiddled with the revolver I had left on the table while we ate, then picked it up and slid it back into the holster. "For now at least."

Footsteps hammered up the stairs behind us. Lots of them, and there was shouting. I motioned the girl back into the kitchen, then tossed the table on its side. Owen's lucky he was the first one in, and that the light was good enough for me to recognize him.

"What the hell, Healer? You want me to shoot you?"

"Not yet. You need to get out of here."

"This is the Strength of Morgan, consecrated from ancient days to be the home of the Warrior's Cult." I spat, then stood. "Maybe you should be the one getting out."

"Alexander has declared the Cult of Morgan apostate. He claims that Simeon was conspiring with the Betrayer, that Morgan is working hand in hand with the outcast scions of Amon. That you're responsible for the attack on the Chanters today, and want to overthrow the Fraterdom."

"That's crazy. I was there, Owen. You were there. You know we didn't have anything to do with that attack."

"You don't understand. He's saying that you personally are responsible for the attack. There are Chanters saying they saw you in the wreckage, that the breach was some kind of Warrior's invokation."

"You're kidding."

"Why do you think I'm here, Eva? The building is surrounded. Patrols are working their way through the lower halls now, searching for you. I'm supposed to arrest you."

CHAPTER TWELVE

We rushed up the corridors, higher and higher, Cassandra and Owen serving as the tail to my little comet. The halls were awful damn quiet, and dark. Empty.

"Where the hell is everyone?" I barked as we rushed along the hallway. "We've got enough food here for about a week. More if we get out of the city and can trap." I buckled up the pack I'd gotten from rummaging in the mess and tossed it to Cassandra. "You're the kitchen girl now. And you'll want to carry a weapon. You got any rifle training in you?"

"You think they spend a lot of time gun-training the scions of Amon the Betrayer?" she asked.

"Guess not. But it's a good thing to have. Here." We stopped at one of the few muster points that were still provisioned. I rattled through the cupboards and brought out a stubby Mots-Misley shotgun. Crowd-control stuff, but it could be plenty loud. "Even a Scholar couldn't miss with this thing."

The girl slung it over her shoulder, stuffed cartridges into the pockets of her robe, then looped the food packet onto her back. I saw that she was still carrying the cylinder of cigarettes.

"You've got the old man's lighter?"

"Uh, yeah. Sorry. I can put it back."

"We'll need it. Never did learn to conjure fire. That's more a Healer trick."

"I'm standing right here," Owen said. "Don't pretend I'm not coming with you."

"You're not. You're already in trouble for warning us. I won't have you going apostate."

"Is this something we pretend to argue about and then I do whatever I want, or do we pretend to argue and then do whatever you want?"

"We pretend to argue and then I threaten to beat the tar out of you."

"Fair enough." He nodded. "What am I supposed to tell my unit commander? That I chased you down, found you, then lost track of you?"

"Something like that," I said, then stepped smartly in and put my fist under his chin. He dropped like a sack.

"You two are close," Cassandra said. "I hope we're never that close."

"Not a chance. Look through his pockets for anything useful," I said as I turned and ran down the hall.

"Where are you going?" she yelled after me.

"Gonna try to find the rest of my Cult." I turned a corner and then, under my breath, "Some son of a bitch has to be left. Can't all be gone, can they?"

Trick was, they were. Trick was, a lot of them were dead, piled up in the leeside barracks like logs of wood. Someone had done for them awful quick. A lot of puncture wounds, a lot of slit throats. Bloody streaks where they'd been dragged in there, but no footprints of those who'd done the dragging. As soon as I found the bodies, I ran back to where I'd left Cassandra. She was still there, sitting on the ground next to the unconscious Owen.

"I wasn't sure if you were coming back, or if I was supposed to come find you."

"And what were you going to do if he woke up?" I asked. She shrugged. "Well, better that I came back."

"You find your Culties?"

"Nah. Not all of them at least." The Elders weren't there. Simeon was in a hospital somewhere, accused of apostasy. Maybe Isabel and Tomas had been taken too. All those folks in the barracks, they had been initiates, servants, couriers. Chefs. Just folks. Dead folks, now. "We'd best be going."

"There some secret passage out of here?" Cassandra asked, struggling to keep up. I adjusted my stride.

"I haven't thought that far ahead yet. There's other stuff we need."

"We have food, we have weapons. We have the whole city of Ash on our tails. What else do we need?"

"You'll see. Gods-blessed thing it is. Damned, too. Oh, you'll see."

We hurried past the final resting place of most of my compatriots. Cassandra noticed the smears on the ground and gave me a look but didn't say anything. I just kept going on ahead. There were signs of struggle in a couple places. Small fights, quickly over. Blood on the tiles. I cursed myself for having taken Cassandra directly to the mess without checking out the rest of the monastery. All those dead, and no one to stand watch over their bodies in the Rest. No one to say the final rites, to invoke them to their graves. No one.

This would all have been alarming in less radical circumstances. I could hear the voices of Owen's companions below. Kicking in doors, securing rooms. Looking for me. Looking for us. I chanced a glance out one of the converted gun turrets. Sirens all around, the streets packed with whiteshirts. The military contingent hung back. Lot of people. Then again, how many people do you bring to arrest the Cult of the Warrior? Why not double that number, just to be safe?

Cassandra was starting to lag. She made a terrible mule. Two-thirds of the way to our destination, in twice the time it should have taken, and I had had enough. I grabbed the pack of food and cut it off her back, then tossed it down the hallway.

"But—"

"We'll find food. We'll be fine. Come on."

"I was going to suggest you carry it," she said.

"Right, great idea. Maybe next time we're on the run."

We made the rest of the trip quick enough. I chanced a look into my room on the way by. The Paladins' quarters were technically two floors below, but they had been empty since I was a teenager. I moved up here to be closer to the Elders and their attendants, but still far enough away for it to be quiet.

My room had been ransacked. Nothing for me there, anyway. We went on. The Elders' rooms were in especial disrepair. No sign of Isabel or Tomas, but no blood, either. Any fight they had gotten into would have involved plenty of blood. Then again, I didn't see them as the type to run away. These were strange circumstances.

"You're spooking me," Cassandra said as I tiptoed around Isabel's room. "Are we looking for something? Someone?"

"Nope. Looks like all the Morganites who're still alive have made good their escape."

"All but us," she said, nervously.

"All but me." I clapped her shoulder on the way out. "Let's not pretend you're warrior material."

I left the living quarters behind and made the final ascent to the ballroom without looking back. Cassandra kept up, but it was straining her. I wanted her a little wiped out for the bit that was to come. Wasn't sure how she was going to react when I showed her the artifact. If she really was some kind of Amonite spy, sent to gain my trust and then steal the machine, I'd rather find that out while she was good and tired.

We paused long enough on the landing to secure the grand entrance doors. The entryway was concealed from the main ballroom by a length of curtain. I looked Cassandra over.

"Doing alright?" I asked.

"Well enough."

"Okay. Just follow close."

I drew my sword and swept the curtain aside. I wish I'd done it sooner. I wish I had been alone.

Barnabas lay there, at the edge of the compass rose. Crushed. The wide, delicate window was shattered, and glass surrounded him like sharp confetti. I stumbled to a halt, the sword sliding loosely to the ground. Without thinking, I was by his side, kneeling, the shards cutting my knees and palms. I turned him on his back, but there was no point. He wasn't breathing, wasn't even bleeding anymore. He just lay there in a pool of stiff blood, his eyes pale and open, his hands clenched into dead man's fists. He had been beaten, while he was still alive. His face showed it. Angry bands around his wrists showed where he had been bound. His gums were bloody from a gag, and he smelled of offal and piss and long confinement. They had beaten him, an old man. They had beaten him, and they had killed him, and they had brought him here.

I closed his eyes, then went back and got my sword. Cassandra was standing by the entrance, her hands to her face. The bitch was crying. For all that it was her godsdamn fault that they had taken him, and she was crying. I knelt by the body of my friend, my only true father, and intoned the words of the Watchman's Dirge. Or tried to, but I was crying.

"We don't have time for this," Cassandra whispered.

"Shut up. I have to get the words right. I have to stand the watch I promised."

"We don't have time. You can pay your respects later, but we need to get—"

"I said shut up! I swore to him." I stood, pointing at the stiff old man at my feet. "I swore to the Fratriarch. There's no one else to stand his watch, and I'll be dead and damned if I'm going to let him just rot here. I don't care what they do. I don't care if they arrest me, or shoot me where I stand. I'm going to stand the watch I swore."

She stood there looking at me for a minute. I turned back to Barnabas and knelt, my forehead on the cool hilt of my sword. The words were hard to get right in my head, like everything was pouring out of my skull and all I could do was grab pieces of it. The Dirge went something like . . . like *A thousand walls, and I march my beat. A thousand walls to stand. A thousand nights to chill my soul, a thousand dawns to hope. A thousand—*

"And then what?"

I sighed against my sword, leaning against the steel. The words were slipping out of my head. *A thousand dawns, ten thousand more, and a spear for every star.*

"What will you do then? You'll stand this watch, fine. You'll bury the old man. And then what?"

"It won't matter. I'll be dead, like the others. It'll be over."

"It won't. Not for us, not for the people of Ash. Something's happening, Eva. Something's rising up. You think the House of Morgan is being knocked down because it's weak? Or because it's the only strong thing left?"

"The hell do you know?" I looked at her over my shoulder. She had the shotgun in her hands, squeezing it until her knuckles were white. "What the hell do you know?"

"I know that this was a good man. That he saved me, and he's probably saved you a couple times, and Brothers know who else. And they killed him."

I stared down at the Fratriarch. He looked better with his eyes closed. I could imagine the bruises were just from some brawl he'd gotten into, like when I was younger and he'd take me to the beater bars. To see the heart of the fight, he said. To see the ugly, violent, desperate, raw center of combat. Without the banners, the armor, the horsemen. Without the reason. Just the fight. And he always came away from those things laughing and bloody.

I pulled his arms across his body, pushed his fists into his sleeves. Arranged the body as it should be arranged. Then I stood up.

"A thousand spears against the sky, Brother," I said, and took out the pendant that he'd given Cassandra, and she had given me. I tossed it onto his chest. "You leave some for me, eh. I'll be there in a bit."

I turned to the compass rose. Bad luck that they'd brought the body here. Drama, I suppose. And with my mind in its present state, there was no way I was going to remember the little dance Tomas had done, even if I'd been trained to the invokation. But Morgan always finds a way.

Stacking invokations of strength, flaring them hard until a wave of energy burned out of me, layers of noetic power shimmering at my every edge, I raised my sword on high, the blade pure white with the mystery and majesty of dead Morgan. I brought it down on the center of the compass rose.

The building shattered.

The delicate pieces of the secret compartment burst open. The floor lurched beneath me, and I stumbled back. The artifact rose from the floor, too quickly, and tumbled across the ballroom like a jack. It came to rest under the glittering night sky, beneath the ruined window. I went to it.

"What is that?" Cassandra asked, creeping up behind me.

"A lot of dead people, and the end of my Cult," I answered. "Other than that, I have no damn idea."

She ran her hands over it, her fingers pausing gingerly on the Amonite runes.

"You know what it is," I said.

"An archive." Her voice was quiet. She looked up at me, briefly, then back to the artifact. "Like a library. A whole library, in this one space."

"No wonder it's so damn heavy." She started to put her hands under it, as if to carry it off. "Seriously, it's a *lot* heavy. You should—"

Cassandra turned some knob and a ring of runed light began to orbit the device. She lifted it carefully off the floor with one hand. It hovered, about two feet off the ground, level with the girl's kneeling head.

"Oh. Well, not so heavy."

"That's enough," a voice said from the shadows. I spun my sword into a guard and gathered up what little remained of the invocations of strength. A man stepped onto the dance floor. A thin man, a delicate man. A sharp man. Betrayer.

"We probably could have done that, if we'd known it was so simple. Barnabas led us to believe that there was a bit of magic to the opening of the secret space. I suppose that sort of brutality passes for mysticism around here. Nathaniel said I should wait and see what you would do. I have seen."

He wore white, trimmed with pewter, and his face was hidden behind an articulated mask of iron. Chain belts crossed his chest, an iron ring at the center protecting the icon of the Betrayer. He moved like a dancer. Displaying empty hands, he twirled his fingers with a flourish and produced daggers. Damn show-off.

I raised my guard, invoked the Wall of Orgentha, and apologized to Barnabas for being the last, and for giving him such a crappy watch. It was all I could do.

"Cass, run!" I yelled. I took a step forward, sword over my head, and then . . . then I was flying backward, out the window, into the night. The girl's hand was on my shoulder, and all I could see was the rapidly diminishing window of the ballroom, and the Betrayer, and Barnabas's tiny, dead body on the floor.

We landed in the framework of an iron water tower about two blocks from the Strength. Even now there were sirens stretching up into the sky from the street below. We'd been seen. Not sure how you'd miss us, honestly.

"That thing can fly?" I asked, when I'd reoriented to my surroundings. The flight had been a strangely weightless affair, and it was odd to be back in gravity's fist. Cassandra was bent over the archive, slapping controls and muttering invocations.

"Nope. Not really. That was an egregious misuse of the technology." She smiled and looked up at me, like a kid in a candy shop. "And now I've broken it all to hell. But it was fun, yeah?"

"You shouldn't have done that. I could have taken that son of a bitch."

"Your Fratriarch couldn't take that son of a bitch. He's the same creep who jumped us outside the mono car. And I know you're all ready to die in the glory of battle, but I think you're going to be more use alive. Yeah. I sure broke something, didn't I?" She sat back on her heels and stared mournfully at the device.

"I thought you said it was some kind of library? Why make a library that can fly?"

"Not the point. The empulsor . . . the flying bit . . . that was just meant to make it easy to carry from place to place. Just meant to offset the weight. All I did was break off the dial and point it at the sky."

"So now it's going to be heavy again?" I looked down at the swarms of whiteshirts below us. A flight of valkyn was powering up at the foot of the Strength. I didn't want to fight the mundane army. None of this was their fault. "Because we need to get a move on."

"I can squeeze some lift out of it. Just . . ." She loosened two straps from the artifact's side, spun some kind of dial at the base, then humped the whole thing onto her back. Looked all the world like a firefighter's breathing rig. "Oof," she said, and settled under the weight of it. Looked tricky.

"I can carry that, if you want."

"Nope, I got it."

I chuckled. "Ruck full of food and you can't manage. World's heaviest book and all of a sudden you're the damned strong man."

"Priorities, dear. Shouldn't we be going?"

And so we should. The crowd below had seen our flight but not our landing. Spotlights were washing across the nearby buildings. The valkyn were taking a slow orbit around the Strength, their feet dangling in the wash of their burners, wicked guns slung low from their shoulders.

We took a service walkway from the tower to a grubby-looking building that turned out to be a vertical farm. The glass windows were smeared with pollen, and the air buzzed with flies. Past rows of crummy stalks and into the central service core, and we never saw a soul. The main entrance to this place was below the streets, in the moldy, half-flooded worker tunnels that riddled the city. Bad lighting, bad mold . . . it was an unpleasant place.

I had to believe that Betrayer would be following us, but I had no idea as to their methods. I saw no value in hiding our tracks, not until we were good and safe from the mundanes. I was sorry to have missed a chance to fight Barnabas's murderer in open battle, but there was nothing for it now. The next time he would come in shadows. I'd be lucky to see the blade before it struck.

Which made the worker tunnels a less than ideal place to hide. Plenty of shadows for him to step out of. Plenty of dark tunnels to hide the bodies, and practically no witnesses. We had to get out of them, but the surface world wasn't too friendly to us either just then. We traveled about five blocks at a quick jog, the cobble road and ceiling of pipes slanting slightly down the whole time. The puddles became ponds, and soon we were walking on catwalks over the exposed waterways. The water below us was the lake, the same lake an army of coldmen had crawled out of earlier today. Or yesterday. I wasn't sure of the time anymore.

We stopped for a break and the girl collapsed against the railings, exhausted. I gave her my water bottle and spent a minute invoking rites of movement and fatigue. She looked better when I was done, but she still looked like hell.

"You have a plan, right?" she asked. "This is the sort of thing Morganites plan for."

"The collapse and betrayal of our Cult by those closest to us? Yeah, you'd think that'd be something we'd have a whole book of plans for." I sat down next to her and dangled my legs over the catwalk. The water below was smooth, and a babbling of currents echoed against the steel all around. It could have been peaceful, in a subterranean, buried alive sort of way. "Sadly, I left that particular book at the monastery. Also, I'm not much of a reader."

"So, no plan?"

"I was thinking of running for a long time. Killing anything that chases us. That's the core of it."

"Better than your previous tack of getting yourself killed and leaving the escaped Amonite slave behind to do your fighting for you," she said.

"Speaking of slave." I stood and bent her head forward. She still had the collar on, as well as the manacles. "Can't you just unmake these things? They make it kind of hard to hide who you are."

"One thing we can't unmake: the chains that bind us or our allies. It's part of the binding of Amon."

The collar was pinned shut. I brushed her thick hair away from the linchpin. It would be tricky to get a tool onto that joint without risking the girl's neck. I started looking around for something to do the deed.

"So how'd you get free of the chains you had when we took you from the Library? Those soul-things."

"Barnabas took them away. It was like an invokation, or something. He cut them with his knife, before we tried to break out of the car." She rubbed her nose and sighed. "Said I should have a chance to get away, even if he didn't."

"Sounds like the old man. But I'm not aware of any chain-cutting invokation. Then again, he was the Fratriarch." Was. I grimaced and kept looking for something to get the girl free.

"Not like he invoked or anything," she said. "Just laid his blade across the metal, and it parted like paper."

"Must have been a special knife. Then again . . ." I drew my two-hander and held it carefully in both fists. "Maybe you should hold really still."

I balanced the blade over the collar, calming my breathing. I wondered if I should invoke strength, but that didn't seem appropriate. Best to just take a light whack and see how it went. I lined up the blow, touched the blade lightly against the collar to set my aim, and . . . the iron parted like warm cheese. As I raised the sword, the collar fell open and clattered to the floor.

"Great," she said. "Now the wrists?"

"That's some bad metal," I said. "Cut way too easy."

Grabbing the manacles, I pulled and pushed and tested the strength of the rings. The girl didn't like the way the iron bit into her skin, but she kept quiet. The metal was good. And yet it split just as easily as the collar had.

"I will be damned."

She stood up and kicked the collar and cuffs into the water. They disappeared with a splash that was quickly swallowed by the current. I kept staring down at where they'd sunk until Cassandra had shouldered the archive and was tapping me on the shoulder.

"That plan of yours, about running? We should get on with that."

"Yeah," I said. "And while we're running, we can come up with a better plan."

"I'm just kidding," she said, smiling. "I've already got a better plan. But the first step is still running. After that, I want to find a place to hole up and give this archive some attention. Something about this thing has gotten a lot of people killed."

"Great. Glad not to be the only one coming up with ideas."

"Yeah. We're all pretty glad about that."

The instinct, when you are hunted, is to go to ground in familiar places. You know the land, you know the ins and outs of its paths. It's comfortable, and you need that when you're being hunted. You need the reassurance of the known.

The thing to do, then, is to go somewhere you don't know and are yourself unknown. It's unexpected, and going where you are not expected to go will offset your unfamiliarity with the terrain and its inhabitants. This was difficult, because Ash was my city, the only city I had ever truly known. There weren't a lot of places that I didn't know, where the last Paladin of Morgan wouldn't be known for what she was. The best path would have been to leave the city completely, but I couldn't bring myself to do that. Whoever had killed my Fratriarch and defiled my Cult, they were in the city. Whatever mystery would be uncovered with the Amonite archive, it was in the city. The collar countries around the lake could offer protection and anonymity. They could not bring me closer to vengeance, and I counted that higher than my safety, or the safety of the girl.

It shocked me a little to think that I counted Cassandra's safety for anything at all. Some part of me still distrusted her, as I distrust all scions of Amon the Betrayer. It was clear, though, that she served Amon in his aspect as the Scholar and had chosen a life of great difficulty to uplift this positive aspect of that fallen Cult. I had to respect that, albeit grudgingly.

Something more. I felt that she was my only link to Barnabas's last moments on earth. She had been with him, when I should have been. He had died to save her, holding off the Betrayer as she ran. That was the choice he had made, for whatever reason. I felt I could not dishonor that choice. That it was my duty, now, to carry on that choice.

So we sought some safety, but not so much that we could not strike when the enemy presented itself. We could have gone to the waterways, to the sketchily mapped and partially drowned corridors of the undercity, and there found peace. But I could not get my mind away from the coldmen and their aquatic assault on the Chanter's Isle. I wanted to be as far away from that threat as possible.

There are many high places in the city of Ash. Once, the ancient towers of the Spear of the Brothers and the Strength of Morgan were the greatest heights in Ash. No more. The inhabitants of the Library Desolate had advanced in their knowledge of architecture, and so now towers of glass and steel and light clawed their way to heaven. And not all of the space in these towers was occupied. There were service corridors, the empty floors abandoned to the strange disturbance of the impellors, iron-framed towers that supported airship docks, and communications towers that spoke in invisible voices to the rig that Owen wore when he needed to talk to headquarters. So many empty spaces, with so few people.

We took residence in an airship dock. It was a steel-frame tower, sheathed in metal cladding for a facade, perched on top of a middling height building on the edge of the outer horn of the city. An older building, but it afforded a grand view of the lake and the surrounding collar mountains. The dock wasn't built for people, but people had used it. There was a haphazardly constructed platform of wooden planks, allowing enough space for a half-dozen people to sleep, as long as they were friendly. Whoever had built the platform was long gone. It served the purpose we required: a place to sleep, to hide, to think about next moves. The constant docking and undocking of airships shook the tower, but no one came up to disturb us. It was ideal.

The girl spent most of the first night huddled over her archive, the pale green light of its runes bathing her face. I slept with my back to her, my hand over my sword. It was cold this high up, even though the facade kept most of the wind away. I was restless, kept getting up to peer between the slats of the wall. The airship traffic was constant, their cylinders glowing a warm orange from the burners as they eased into the dock. Behind them, the sky was crystal black and clear, the moon like a chip of ivory. It would be peaceful, in other circumstances.

"Where do you think they are?" Cassandra asked without looking up from the machine. "Your brothers of Morgan?"

"Dead, mostly," I said. I hadn't told her about the rooms of bodies I had found. Didn't need to tell her. It was written on my face, I knew, and in the set of my shoulders. "Some may have made it out. Some of the Elders."

"So there's hope. Your Cult will continue."

"It's been dying for a long time. It will keep on dying, regardless of what we do."

"Yeah, you Morganites have it real tough." She rubbed her eyes and cycled down the archive. It settled into itself, the runes flickering as they died. "Must be unbearable."

I looked back at her, then leaned against an iron spar and crossed my arms.

"There aren't many of us to bear it, that's for sure. And in case you haven't noticed, someone's trying to kill us off."

"And those who remain are free to defend themselves, or to run away." She busied herself with putting the archive to bed, closing valves and tightening dials. "You may be dying off, but it's not for lack of the opportunity to defend yourselves."

"You're talking about Amon. About the Library Desolate. Listen, you're the one who chose to enter the service of a fallen god. Not me."

"It's time you started thinking of Amon as something other than the Betrayer." She finished with the archive and stood to face me. "And his servants as something other than murderers. Our gods were brothers before they were enemies. Something led them to that path, and maybe something else can lead them back."

"One of them just killed my Fratriarch! Simeon is in the hospital with Betrayer steel in his guts. Elias and . . . hell, and Tomas and Isabel, for all I know. There are rooms full of my dead brothers back in the Strength, all of them dead at Betrayer hands. And you're talking about forgiveness?"

She watched me for a time, her eyes dark pools under her hood. Finally, she shrugged and went to the other side of the platform to lie down.

"It is an Amonite who will save you, Eva. And the knowledge of Amon that will get us out of this. Whatever we are, those of us who have chosen the life of the Library Desolate, we are not murderers. We are not the scions of the Betrayer."

With the light of the archive gone, the platform was very dark. I stared at the lump of her body, curled up at the edge of the platform. The wind and the passing of airships filled my ears, and in time I lay down and slept. My dreams were full of people I knew, people I had loved, and all of them were dead.

CHAPTER THIRTEEN

I was bored. Bored, bored, cooped up on a tiny platform in a tiny tower, listening to the wind and the airships and the girl and her archive, bored. When I woke up she was already at the feet of that machine, turning dials and muttering to herself, the crumbled remains of some of the flatbread I had stolen from a vendor cart scattered about her. All morning it had been like this. Dial, mutter, invoke, mutter, dial. I was going nuts.

"So how do you know how to work that thing?" I asked while cleaning my revolver. Again. This was the eighth time, I think. Cleanest gun in all of Ash, and no one to shoot.

"It's my nature," she said.

Silence. Mutter. Dial.

"Learned anything?"

She didn't answer for a long time. When she did, it was like she was answering a different question.

"He wasn't asking the questions I would think of." She pushed back from the archive and pulled a tangle of hair out of her face. "I suppose that's what made him the Scholar."

"This is the great secret that's gotten most of my Cult killed? That Amon asked strange questions?"

She smiled and shook her head. "I suppose that's the heart of it. But I'm not sure what this has to do with . . . anything else. You asked how I know how to operate the archive. Experience. We have one of these in the Library. Much larger, in fact. Our keepers tell us that it's the sum of Amon's knowledge, minus the profane knowledge that led to the Betrayal."

"Is that what this is?" I asked, rising to my feet. "The profanity?"

"I hope not. It would be the dullest blasphemy ever. Besides, everyone thinks Alexander keeps that close. If you show especial talent with the archive, with sorting it and plumbing its knowledge, the whiteshirts disappear you."

"Doesn't sound like it would pay to be good at that," I said.

"Who knows? We think they get taken off to a secret archive, hidden away. Something Alexander culled from the main body and kept for himself. Secret knowledge does have a certain appeal, doesn't it?"

"So this archive here, it's part of that secret knowledge?"

She shrugged. "I don't know all of the main archive, obviously. This doesn't seem like something you'd want to keep hidden." She turned the archive toward me, revealing a screen of garbled runes, flooding past like a waterfall. Images popped up, but they made no sense to me. "It's his research on the impellors. It looks like they're an offshoot of some kind of Feyr creation. When Amon wrote this, he was just beginning to apply the principle to the monotrains. Really, it's kind of dull, in a fascinatingly detailed sort of way. But I can't imagine there's anything here to justify . . . you know."

I paced around the archive, making one circuit before I stopped and sighed.

"And that's it? That's all that's in there?"

"Oh, gods no. I mean, it all seems to be related to this, but I've only just figured out the subject line. There are noetic pounds of knowledge in here—research, tangential investigations, technical drawings. It's a very thorough history of the process. And it's fascinating to see his mind at work. How he made the leap from the Feyr device to the monotrains."

"The Feyr didn't use them for transport?" I asked.

She shook her head, then leaned in to the machine and flittered through the text. "Near as I can tell, they just shot them up in the air. No idea why."

"Hm. Well, how much longer do you think—"

"I have no idea, woman. Knowledge is not something you can measure in time. It does not drip into our heads at a set rate. It comes suddenly, or not at all."

I sighed and started taking off my armor. She squinted at me in puzzlement.

"That won't make learning any faster."

"I'm going out. I can't sit here while your knowledge doesn't come. And I can't wander around in the armor of a Morganite." With my armor off, I unclasped the dozen icons and emblems that marked me as a Paladin. Even my holster and the articulated sheath went away. My padded coat and linen pants were plain enough. I shuddered at the thought of being separated from my oath-bound blade, but I just couldn't risk carrying it. I tucked a knife into my boot, and the bully into my waistband. "So I'm going out, like this, before I go nuts."

"Do you think that's wise?"

"You're the Scholar. I'll leave wise to you."

She didn't say anything else, and I climbed down the tower and through a garbage chute before making my way to the street. By the time I was there I smelled like cabbage and looked like a bum. Nothing like a Paladin of Morgan.

I bought a half-cape that buttoned down the front. It had a hood that hid my face without looking too much like I was trying to hide my face. And it let me keep a hand on my revolver without drawing attention. I had left the tower with no plan in mind, but as soon as I was on the street my boots turned toward the inner horn, and home. Toward the Strength.

It amazed me how life kept going in the wake of my apocalypse. Vendors were selling food, pedigears cluttered the roads, civilians went to jobs and came home. The streets were alive. Just like any other day. I felt as if a barrier had come down between me and the city of Ash. They had their lives and their futures and their plans. And I was just this hunted creature, alive only to run. I didn't like that. It didn't feel natural.

Of course, there were signs of change in the life of the city. There were more guards, especially anywhere there was open water. The canals looked like they'd been closed down. Patrol boats drifted lazily off the coast, and this was a city of many coasts. There were even valkyn in the air. There couldn't be more than, what, fifty of those beasts all told? It seemed crazy to have them on patrol. Then again, the city had been attacked. We had been attacked.

I approached the Strength from on high. There were elevated walkways that brushed up against the monastery's round plaza, public routes that were usually crowded with tourists from the collar countries. Today they were more crowded than usual. Almost impassable. I climbed higher, thinking the extra stairs might thin out the crowds, but no luck. Even on the top tier it was shoulder to chest. I kept my arms under my cloak, crossed over the cold weight of the bully. Wouldn't be good to have someone brush up against that.

It was a cloudy day, last night's clear skies betrayed by a low mass of pewter thunderheads that rumbled at the tips of the city's towers. My raised hood brought no comment as the first heavy drops of rain spattered down on the crowd. Even in the growing torrent, the crowds didn't thin. I worked my way forward slowly, listening to the gossip.

And of course, they were talking about me. I had gained quite a reputation. By my hand, the Chanter's Isle had split, and at my command the dead had flooded the hidden heart of that strange sect of the Alexian Cult. It was whispered that I was apostate, that I (along with my Elders of Morgan) had declared for Amon the Betrayer, and was leading a secret war against the godking.

None of it made sense. The whiteshirts had been helping us search for the Fratriarch, had lent us an Amonite, had guarded us against the attacks of the Betrayer and stormed out only at our command. We stood together against the Rethari. Why would we betray them? Why would they abandon us?

When finally I reached sight of the Strength, I was horrified. They had great spotlights thrown up against its side, and armed barricades all around the plaza. Smoke stained the windows and doors, and all the glass was broken. The front door hung intact but open.

"What in hell happened?" I whispered. But of course, in a crowd a whisper is a conversation. The man in front of me turned and answered.

"They had to break on in, did the Alexians. Thank the Brother they did, too. That whole Cult had gone bad in the soul. After the Chanters' bloody sacrifice, trying to hold one of them at bay, Alexander sent his boys up. Tried to talk, but those damned sons of Morgan suckered 'em in and killed a whole platoon. Whiteshirts had to go in in force. Burn the whole place out." He nodded to the wagons that were lining the promenade. "Still counting the bodies, they are."

I felt sick in my stomach. I looked at the stacks of blackened bundles, bleeding ash in the rain. My brothers of Morgan, my sisters of the Warrior. Murdered, and now burned and accused of murder. Of rebellion. Apostate.

A tinny voice echoed over the crowd, and I squinted in the direction of the main door. The voice was coming from a loudspeaker, erected on a stage. There were three platforms above it, hastily erected against the side of the Strength, and three spotlights on them. At first I had taken them for siege engines, but now I saw they were nothing but stationary wooden platforms. On the stage, a man was reading a list of accusations in a very proper, very precise voice. A familiar voice, distorted by the loudspeaker. I focused on him, and saw. And understood. Nathaniel, the man from the abandoned shrine of Alexander, the man Simeon had met with, the Betrayer. Hidden in the arms of Alexander. He was speaking accusations against the Cult of Morgan, gesturing widely up at the platforms above.

And on each platform, an Elder. And on each Elder, a sentence of death.

They stood chained, arms spread, their robes torn and heads shorn, blood on their faces and chests. A metal plaque had been struck with the ancient symbols of apostasy, the sigil of the godking as a blessing and a condemnation. Each of them stared down at the crowds in slack disbelief. Simeon. Isabel. Tomas.

"They're going to kill them," I said.

"Oh, they'll try them first. Then they'll kill them."

I fell back into the crowd, shoving people out of my way as I ran. I had the bully in my hand, and damn it to hell if anyone tried to stop me.

"We're out of time," I said as I rushed onto the hidden platform. "I need answers now."

The girl was facing away from me, her hands loose in her lap, her eyes closed. The screen reflected her face in pale green brilliance. She didn't move when I entered, didn't show any sign of caring when I strode over and shook her shoulder.

When she woke up, it was as if I hadn't been gone at all. Like a machine turning back on.

"You're back?" she asked.

"What the hell was that? I thought you were dead!"

"Yeah, pretty much. The forms of these machines can be tricky. Easy to get lost inside." She stood up and stretched, then noticed the look on my face and the revolver in my hand. "What's wrong? What's happened?"

"They've burned the Strength and declared the Cult apostate."

"We knew that—"

"They have the Elders. They're going to kill them. They say we, that I . . . that we're trying to overthrow the godking."

"Again, that's nothing new. We—"

I grabbed her by the collar and pulled her toward me. "Listen. To. Me. The man who tried to kill Simeon, the damned Betrayer—he's there. He's in charge of the operation. Right now he's reading the accusations against the Elders. He means to kill them."

She held my gaze with hers, trying to burrow into my head with her stare.

"That sounded an awful lot like an accusation."

"The Betrayer has infiltrated Alexander. He knew. He's the one who knew that the Fratriarch was at the Library Desolate. That I was his only guard. Where he was going. He stood guard while Elias was killed. Had Owen follow me around, keeping tabs on the Paladin. Gods know what else he learned, what Simeon or Tomas was telling the Alexians behind our backs. And now he has us falsely accused and on the run. And the people believe him! They're anxious for the trial, anxious to see the Cult of Morgan put down. They believe him!"

She peeled my hand off her cloak, one finger at a time, then pushed the bully away from her belly.

"Are you ready to trust an Amonite now?"

"I'm not ready to trust anyone, anywhere. Tell me what you've found, or get out."

She sighed and sat down by her damned machine. "Where did this thing come from?" she asked.

"We don't know. Just appeared in the Strength one day."

"That's what your Elders told you, at least. Fair enough. And you don't know who sent it to you?"

"I said as much."

She nodded. "Someone is trying to send you a message. A warning, really. They could have been more direct about it, but I don't think you would have trusted them if they had been."

"Who? And what message?"

"I don't know who. And I'm not sure of the message."

I spat. "You're being a hell of a lot of help here. Do you have anything that will help me prove the Elders are innocent? Anything that will save their lives?"

She turned and powered down the archive, then folded her arms and leaned back against the machine.

"It's a matter of belief, Eva. You're being led on a path, by some hidden agency. I don't know if they're the ones killing your friends, or if someone is doing that to drive you away. I don't know why I was the one chosen to interpret this device, why Barnabas gave his life to protect me. I think he knew what the device meant, but couldn't decipher it. Couldn't bear the message."

"Yeah, I'm going to barrel out of here and start shooting whiteshirts if you don't hurry the hell up."

She smiled and nodded. "Okay, okay. Let me explain, and then you can decide who needs shooting. I get the feeling it's going to be more people than even you're comfortable with."

"You'd be surprised."

She stood and fished out the cylinder of cigarettes. I hadn't seen her smoke since we'd left the Strength. When she was lit, she paced in a slow arc across the platform, trailing a blue haze.

"Amon discovered the Feyr device that we think of as the impellor, in the days after this city had been taken from the Feyr. Like I said, it appeared that the Feyr were just shooting them up into the sky. No real apparent purpose. Most of the devices were destroyed, or had shot down into the lake when their towers collapsed in the fighting. Amon retrieved what he could, and began to study them." She paused and toked a couple times, her hands shaking with the nicotine rush. "What do you know about godhood?"

"That there were three gods, and that we're down to one."

"And before us, before the Brothers Immortal rose up from their humble childhoods and led the tribes of man against the Feyr—who was god then?"

"There was no god. Just stories of gods, from ancient days."

"Yes and no. The ancient gods were from the race of the Titans. In their time, the Titans were just people, and a few among them ascended to godhood. Just like the Brothers, in their own way. They had more than three gods, so many in fact that most people don't realize there were regular Titans as well. Only the names of the gods come to us through history, and the mythologies of the Feyr."

"How do you know all this?" I asked.

"The archives of Amon. He studied such things. Especially in the early days of the Brothers, when they were just . . . becoming. He wanted to understand what was happening to them, in a very rational sense. And, of course, it wasn't a very rational thing. But he tried."

"Okay. So, many Titan gods, and then no gods, and then the Brothers. What's your point?"

"I didn't say no gods. The Feyr rose up against the Titans and over-threw them. Right here, in fact, in the city of Ash. They burned the city, and then they drowned the city. And in time, they tried to atone for that. I don't think they ever stopped trying to atone for it, actually. One of the reasons they fell to us so easily."

"Easily? Hundreds of thousands died in those wars."

"Yes. But how many would you expect to die in a battle with the gods?"

"Gods? They weren't gods, they were just . . . just the Feyr. Just funny little people."

She leaned against a steel spar and peered out between the slats of the cladding. The rain had passed, at least here, and the sun shone on her face, and on the aura of smoke that hung around her.

"They were more than that, I think. It's not clearly defined, but godhood seems to be . . . some kind of power. Power in the air, in the earth, in us. The Brothers assumed godhood by their actions, and by their actions we honor them. The Titans were the same way, raising gods from among their own, elevating them to godhood by their actions and their deeds. The Feyr did not take that route. They had no individual gods. They were a race of little gods."

"What?"

She shook her head and grimaced. "It's hard to explain. Godhood is a power that settles in people. It builds up in great people, making it easier for them to build up even more power. Someone becomes famous, and the power of god gathers in them, and then they are able to do more marvelous things, becoming more legendary, gathering more power. It's a cycle. But like any power, there are limits. There are capacities that can be exceeded."

"You make this all sound very rational. Are these Amon's theories?"

"No. These are the things he learned from the Feyr. While studying the impellors." She moved away from the sun and stubbed out her cigarette. "If you take a battery and keep charging it, it holds more and more power until it can't hold any more. And then what? Either you discharge some of that power or it explodes. The Titans had many gods, so they were able to hold the power for a long time. Their divinity was distributed across many people. Maybe it wasn't enough. Maybe they were losing control of it, and that's why the Feyr rebelled against them. Either way, when the Feyr assumed the mantle of godhood, they realized you couldn't just hold it in a couple people. You had to spread it out. And they figured, hey, why not spread it out across all of us?"

"They didn't seem like gods. Hell, they're still alive, still have some power."

"Very little, because they were only very little gods. But they were able to hold that power for a very long time, and gather a great deal of it."

I crossed my arms, my pistol forgotten, and sat down.

"So what happened when we threw them down, and the mantle of godhood came to us?"

"We had our three Brothers Immortal, and that's all."

"And now we're down to one?"

"Yeah. The math is terrible."

We were quiet for a while, listening to the airships and the wind. Finally, I stood and stared down at the archive.

"Something I don't understand. What the hell does this have to do with the impellors? And why does it mean people want to kill my Cult?"

"The Feyr used the impellors as a kind of pressure valve. They invented them late in their empire, when their numbers were dwindling and the accumulated power was overwhelming them." She lit another cigarette and blew a long, deep breath out into the room. "They were venting god."

"Do the impellors still do that?"

"Who knows? And as for why anyone would want to kill your Cult over this? Well, here we have proof that Amon knew about how godhood worked, and that you had to have multiple gods to keep it from destroying those who held that power."

"So?"

"So," she whispered, then turned and looked me in the eyes, "why would he want to kill his brother Morgan, if the idea was to have more gods, not fewer?"

I sat up and stared in confusion. My mind was unhinging at the implication.

"You're saying Amon didn't kill Morgan. That he wasn't the Betrayer."

"I am. Leaving only—"

"Alexander," I breathed, trembling. "Godking of Ash."

The throne of the godking sits in the Spear of the Brothers, the white tower in the old district of Ash. I was taken there for my acceptance into the rank of Paladin. At that time Matthew was still with us, before he led his fated crusade against the Rethari in distant Herion. Four of us went to the throne: Matthew, me, Barnabas, and an Initiate of the Bullet named Emily, who also went with Matthew on his little crusade.

The Spear sits in the oldest part of Ash, the quarters along the edge of the city-island where the forces of the Brothers Immortal first made landfall. There had been much bloodshed cracking the defenses of the collar countries, and the landing had been murderous. Amon, sickened by the loss of life, drove his spear into the ground and declared his part in the conflict over, swearing never again to take up arms. Morgan and Alexander took the rest of the city, and Amon came after, to sweep through the ruins and collect artifacts. When the harsh street fighting was over and the peace was signed, Amon came back to his driven spear and built a temple. That temple became a tower, and that tower became the seat of power for the three brothers. Later their Cults split, but the Betrayal left only Alexander. He settled into the tower, even reclaiming the spear Amon had abandoned and putting it on display.

I remember looking up at that spear as we entered the building. It hung in the grand foyer, suspended by wire in midair. The tip was polished iron, intricately barbed, with two flanged wings at the base of the head. The shaft was black wood, runed with the symbols of the secret language of the Scholar. The base of the shaft was capped with dull iron, and still bore the dents of a thousand counterstrikes and crushed helms.

"Why do we hold this thing up?" I asked my brother Matthew as I stood beneath it. "It is the weapon of the Betrayer, is it not?"

"There are stages to our lives, even for the Brothers," he answered. At the time I thought of him as an old man, but I realize now he couldn't have been much through his thirties. He laid his hand on my shoulder. "The Spear of Amon symbolizes his renunciation of the battle, of violence, and his commitment to knowledge. It is the holiest symbol of the Cult of the Scholar. That moment in our lives when we put struggles behind us, and commit to something pure."

"Like the broken plow, for Morgan."

"Yes. Morgan left behind his fields and his wealth, and warred against the Feyr in their madness. There was once a sect of our faith that worshipped Morgan the Farmer, did you know?"

"What became of them?"

"What becomes of all of us," Barnabas answered. "They passed on. Come, the godking awaits."

We walked ceremoniously up the wide, curving stairs of the foyer and past a line of stiff guards in shiny plate, and tabards of white and gold. Up to the terrace of the throne. It was not a large building, at least not this part of it. We waited patiently on the reception terrace while voices rumbled from beyond the curtain. When an attendant came out, we bowed once and then were led inside.

The ceremony was simple. Matthew carried my blade, Emily my revolver. The ceremonial garb of the Paladin was symbolized by a cloak, draped over the Fratriarch's arm. I walked barefoot, in simple linen. The marble floor was cold, and the room smelled like old books and too much incense.

Alexander awaited. He sat on the throne of the Brothers quite casually. Depictions of the Brothers always show them as larger than life, giants among men, their shoulders broad and their faces divine. But he was just a man. An ancient man, and a man of great thought and certitude, and a man who had seen a hundred thousand dawns and raised his sword to a million foes, certainly. But still, just a man.

Alexander's hair was dark, and his brows and lips were heavy. He looked at me with simple brown eyes, but there was a depth to his gaze that weighed on me. We lined up in front of the throne and knelt. When I looked up he was leaning forward slightly, like a bored man who has seen something unique. He raised a cupped hand, and we stood.

"You have brought my fallen brother's latest scion?" he asked.

"We have, Lord." Barnabas put a hand on my shoulder and indicated I should step forward. I did. "Eva, daughter of Forge, Initiate of the Blade. We have examined her, and recommend her for acceptance into the role of Paladin."

"Initiate of the Blade." He stood from his throne. No taller than any other man. No taller than me. But his voice was soft, and carried generations within it. "An unusual choice. A brave choice. It was always my brother's choice, as well."

"You honor me, Lord," I said.

He walked around the four of us, pausing to examine the vestments draped across Barnabas's arm. When he came to the sword, balanced across Matthew's palms, he lifted it and looked down its length before handing it back to Matthew.

"The Grimwield is a hell of a blade, Eva Forge. Even this figment of its dream will serve you well in battle. Have you seen my brother's true blade?"

"Yes, my Lord. I stood my night beside it, meditating on the acts of god Morgan."

"Of course. It is good that you follow the old ways." He returned to the throne, and an aura of fatigue seemed to settle about the room. "More should follow that path. Enrobe her, that she might stand before me."

I knelt, and Barnabas draped the cloak across my shoulders. I turned to Emily, and she presented me with the revolver and belt of bullets, laying them over my arm. Matthew stepped in front of me and presented the hilt of my blade. There were no words to the ceremony, as Morgan took the blade without grand speeches or stirring exultations. He led with actions, and with steel.

Sword in hand, robed and armed, I walked humbly to the feet of Alexander.

"I have never liked war, Eva Forge. That was my brother's calling, and his burden. When he fell, I took the mantle of his vengeance and carried it out. Since then I have offered the final blessing to his initiates in his stead. And so now I offer it to you. Will you serve the Fraterdom, in all your days, against all its enemies?"

"I will."

"Will you carry the sword and the bullet in true faith, protecting the weak, defeating the strong, opposing those who oppose you, standing with those who stand beside you?"

"So have I sworn."

"In faith Morgan raised you, and in faith he has clothed you. Find comfort in the actions of his life, in the deeds of his greatness. Find strength in his memory, and courage in his courage. Remember always his death, and his life."

"His life," my three brothers whispered behind me.

"In all things, honor him. Morgan, god of war and of the hunt, Brother of my Brother, Betrayed by the Betrayer. Stay true to him and he will guide you. Depart him, and he will depart you. Fight for him, and he will fight with you."

"Forever," we said in unison.

"Forever," Alexander answered. He touched his finger to my forehead, and then my sword, and finally my bullistic. He settled into his throne, and the energy went out of him. We left the room quietly, while he stared out the window at the lake. Just as we reached the door, he raised his head and called to me. The others were already in the hall.

"Eva," he said, though so quietly I could barely hear his voice. "Your sword may be Morgan's last. May your blade bear much fruit."

"I . . . yes, Lord," I answered, and then left. The others gave me curious eyes, but I shrugged.

"He seemed tired," I said.

"Alexander gets like that sometimes," Barnabas said. "Especially when discussing the Betrayal. It saddens him."

"I imagine it saddens Morgan, too," I answered. Matthew grinned, but the others didn't like it so much. We were quiet until we got outside the Spear. I pulled on the boots I had left with the attendant, then wrapped the ceremonial robe more tightly around me.

I told the others what Alexander had said, about my blade possibly being Morgan's last. At the time they chuckled nervously and changed the subject. Later, I thought he was speaking to the general dwindling of the Cult, and the lack of new recruits. He was right in that. No more initiates passed the Rites of the Blade, and very few even entered the path of initiate.

And now there were no more initiates, and no more Cult, but only my blade. The last of Morgan.

CHAPTER FOURTEEN

*J*sat cross-legged on the floor, the blade across my knees, sharp-stone in hand. The stone rasped as I drew it against the edge. It was a drone that was familiar to my ears, like a prayer for calm. The girl was still staring at me. Waiting for me to do something.

"You were in a hurry a minute ago," she said, after several long minutes filled only by the stone's song.

"Things change," I said.

"Just in the short time I've known you, you've always been the sort to act. Rather than sit."

"I am. But now I must also be Barnabas, and Tomas, and Isabel." I turned the sword over and started on the other side. "I am the Council of Elders, and the legion of Paladins, and the armies of the initiates. I have to be the whole Cult, Cass. The luxury of being only the Paladin is ending."

"And this is what the Council of Elders would do? Sharpen their blades and think things through?"

"In a way. They sit and they think and they ask questions. Like this: Where did the archive come from?"

Cassandra stood up, paced the room, peered out the slatting, and then sat down again. "I don't know. I don't know why it matters, either."

"Matters? It's probably the most important thing right now. It came to us at this time, in this way. You said yourself it was a message. But a message from whom?" I stopped my sharpening and put away the stone. "Better yet, why now?"

"Maybe this was only recently found. Maybe whoever found it didn't trust the Alexians to convict their own god—"

"A reasonable mistrust," I said.

"—and didn't think anyone would believe the Amonites. So they gave it to Morgan."

"No one would believe the Amonites. And yet here we are. You, an Amonite, asking me to believe what you've read on the archive." I got out a rag to polish the sword. "And what you've read is that your god is innocent, and the only god we have left is the true murderer."

"I swear, Eva, that's what it says."

"Perhaps. And if it does? What are we to do? Proclaim Alexander as the Betrayer, and lead a popular revolt among . . ." I waved my hand dismissively. "Among the civilians? Lead an army of trash pickers and fishermen against the Fraternal Army?"

"We would join you! Free the Librarians Desolate and we would provide you with—"

"Stop. No one will believe the scions of Amon. Joining you to the cause would only invalidate it in the eyes of the people." I leaned back against the tower and closed my eyes, the rag and sword forgotten in my hands. "I haven't said I believe you, yet. The more I think about it, the less I believe. It's too perfect, and too easy to conceal. Some Amonite cult mocked up a pretty-looking machine and snuck it into the monastery. It didn't make any sense to us because it's just a pile of junk made to look nice, so we summon an Amonite. The Amonite 'deciphers' the archive to reveal that the Scholar has been innocent all along." I opened my eyes and clutched the rag. "How could you expect us to believe that?"

"How do you explain the murders, then? Someone wants to keep this hidden."

"Or is willing to kill to make the story look good," I answered.

"Gods, why are you so stubborn?" She stood up and threw her arms wide. "They've declared you apostate! For no reason! Alexander has burned your monastery and is going to kill your Elders! And you're debating over who the enemy actually is?"

"For two hundred years we have carried the banner of the Fraterdom. We have hunted the scions of Amon throughout the earth!" I stood as well, because I looked more impressive standing than this skinny, curly haired little girl, and I didn't want her to forget that. "Amon has been the Betrayer for all that time! Do you expect us just to abandon that crusade, to make amends and turn against Alexander? On your word, you, an Amonite?"

We stood trembling at each other, fists balled, jaws set. I at least had my arm thrown over a mighty big sword. She didn't back down. She wouldn't back down.

"Really, I don't care if you take my word. But it's true. I don't know what has to happen for you to believe that, but it's true."

"The timing is crummy," I said, after a space of many breaths. "The Rethari are marching. They could have spies in the city. They could be spawning those . . . monsters, agitating the Betrayer Cults. They could have fed the archive to us, and fed false information to Alexander, implicating us in the attacks. The Alexians could be acting in true faith. The Rethari could be setting us against each other in the hope of finally throwing us down and raising up their own gods."

"You have a lot of theories," she said. "But I'm not hearing a lot of answers, and fewer plans."

I sighed and nodded. "Yeah. It's easy to ask questions." I sheathed the blade and buckled on my holster. "I need to know more, though. I need to know that this is true, before I act."

"Who else can you ask? The Alexians? They're not just going to say, 'Oh, yeah, right. We're the ones who killed Morgan. Sorry about that,' and go away."

"No, they're not. And if it's true, I'm willing to bet most of them don't know, anyway. No, I need to find a different source. Someone I can trust."

"Who?"

I looked around the little platform, at the wreckage of our short stay. This might be a holy place, someday. The last temple of Morgan.

"The Feyr. Amon's research led to them, didn't it? Maybe they still have the same answers to his questions."

"There aren't many Feyr still around."

"Nope. But I know where to find them." I motioned to the archive, and her shotgun. "Get that stuff together. We're going, and we're not coming back."

The echoing hum started up in my bones as we got closer, the period of the impellor's vibration getting shorter with each step. By the time Cassandra and I were standing outside of the tall, black tower, every second breath was washed in the invisible song of the impellor.

There was a time when these had been the tallest buildings in Ash, save the Spear and the Strength. Mostly for the comfort of the inhabitants, though even here at ground level the wave of the strange device inside was . . . distracting. Up at the same elevation as the monotrain, you couldn't stand this close to the impellor, not without jellying your meat. All across the city, any building this high had a couple empty floors, abandoned to the periodic thrum.

Cassandra hid in an alleyway near the tower. I had told her where we were going. There would be a signal for her to come inside. I was still wearing my new half-cloak, and the sword was bundled into a reed mat strapped across my back. Not the best disguise, but the best we could manage. No one had called the whiteshirts on us. Yet. Once Cassandra was good and hidden away, I braced myself and went inside.

The tower was really just a shell, stitched inside with catwalks that gave access to the central spinning core. Black-clad Amonites crawled all over the inside of the tower, checking fittings and monitoring the impellor's activity. They wore some kind of hard suit, with masks and goggles over their faces. The sheath twitched beneath the reeds on my back as a wave of adrenaline spun through my fingers. Up there, in their goggles and masks, they looked so much like the coldmen. Similar technology, maybe? I swore, every clue I got gave me more people to mistrust. My instincts yelled for guilt on the heads of the scions of Amon. Everything else pointed to Alexander. I didn't like it.

The impellor itself was . . . alien. The shaft was a blizzard of movement, like a tornado of twisting metal pistons and smooth, swooping cogs that meshed and danced at odd angles and impossible speeds. The structure rose to the top of the tower, spinning in a near silence that was actually a roar of movement just below the range of my ears. My skull ached to hear it, but could not. At the top of the column was a giant cylinder, like the head of a war hammer. It turned more slowly than the column, though it seemed dependant on its action. Each face of the hammer was made up of dozens of open drums, their skin glowing an arcane blue, each drum fed by a dozen conduits that coiled and were themselves fed by larger tubes that burrowed down into the column. The whole thing looked like something that had dropped out of the sky, to be worshipped.

I wondered how Amon had built such a crooked thing, based on that smooth, clean Feyr artifact that we had fished out of the cistern. Not a logical jump. Then again, for all that Amon was the Scholar, the Feyr were something more. Something different. I shrugged, then went to find someone in charge.

Wasn't even a Healer. Just a guy in city blues, peering at gauges and checklists through a pair of uneven wire spectacles. His hair was rusty gray, sticking out all around and bald on top, his naked scalp spotted with moles. I had to tug on his shoulder to get his attention. There wasn't much about me to keep his eyes, so I showed him the gun under my cloak. He took in the whole package, the hidden sword, the revolver, the poorly covered uniform, then nodded once.

"Yeah?" he asked.

"There are some people here I'd like to talk to."

"Those people are probably busy."

"I'm sure they are," I said. "But I'm sure they could be spared."

"What's it about?"

"Kidnapping. Murder, maybe." I picked up one of his checklists, flipped through a couple pages, then put it down somewhere else. He didn't like that. "Maybe a grand conspiracy to topple the Cult of Morgan."

"You're the Paladin," he said finally, after a long pause. "The heretic."

"That's what they're saying. Does that matter to you?" I asked, flashing the bully again. "Or this?"

"Neither, really. Were you hoping to threaten your way through this conversation?"

"Does it matter to you that someone has killed all my friends, burned the house of my god, and now falsely accuses my Cult of siding with the Betrayer?" I took the revolver out and placed the barrel squarely on the table, like I was pointing something out in his ledger. "Does it matter that I'll kill anyone who gets in the way of me hunting those people down, no matter who they are, or on what throne they sit?"

"Yeah?"

"Yeah."

He looked up at the catwalks, like he was doing a mental count of his crew.

"It wasn't any of my people," he said. "Whatever you're talking about, it wasn't these guys. I know where they go, where they sleep, what they eat. Who they love. It wasn't any of them."

"And if any of them *are* involved, I guess that makes you complicit?"

He snorted. "You're trying to threaten me. That's cute, little girl warrior comes in here to threaten me." He plucked the glasses off his face and tossed them on the table. "I'm not going to scare. You pull my people off that machine, you maybe put the Harking line out of commission. How you like that?"

I scraped the revolver along the edge of the table and passed it across my body. One long arm stroke and I backhanded him with the heavy tip of the weapon, the reinforced barrel taking him along the jaw. He spun away, drooling teeth.

"Took you long enough to lose those godsdamn glasses." I holstered the bully, shattered the mat of reeds, and drew the blade. I put the tip on the floor and leaned against the crossbar. The blade slid into the hard stone of the floor like a hot knife into ice. "Now, I'd like to talk to some of your crew."

He stood slowly, anger boiling off him in sheets. His voice was a barely controlled cauldron.

"I said, it wasn't any of my damned people."

"It's not your damned people I want to talk to. It's your damned Feyr."

He looked at me with steadying calm, wiped the blood off his chin, and laughed.

"Not my call to make. Those buggers come when they want, go when they want. And if they do a godsdamn thing while they're here, that's their business. No. They want to talk to you, they'll talk to you. Not my problem."

"How do I—"

He dropped like a cut puppet. I leaned away, surprised, then heard other things: tools falling, glass breaking. Above, an Amonite slid heavily against a railing, then spun over and fell against a lower platform like a bag of flour. No one to catch him, because all of his mates were out, too. I left the sword where it was, swaying slightly in the floor, and drew my bully.

The Feyr was standing behind me and slightly higher, up on a piston array. He was wearing a robe, white cloth wrapped tight around his tiny form. He had a hand raised in benediction, looking all around the tower with his wide, black eyes. He noticed me and nodded.

"We thought you should know," he said. His voice was tiny, small as his delicate, pinched face. His palm came around and I twisted, drawing a bead on his little chest. He shook his head and I faltered, though if that was something he was doing to me or just my own unwillingness to put lead into a child-sized target . . . who knows? Point is, I didn't shoot and he put his hand down.

"Know what?" I asked.

He didn't answer immediately, didn't even seem to be paying attention to me any longer. He looked around the room at all the fallen people, their eyes open, breathing steadily. Even the broken ones seemed comfortable, regardless of which direction their legs were facing. For the longest time he meditated on the silence, his eyes turned up toward the top of the impellor, breath shallow. He looked back at me.

"You wished to talk to us?"

"Yeah, about—"

"Then we shall talk. Your friend. You should give her the signal, now," he said, then turned and walked away, disappearing behind the array. I ran to the door and opened it, almost banging into Cassandra.

"Couldn't wait?" I asked.

"I heard something. Noises."

"Yeah. Just don't look around." The street was empty. Dusk was falling. "It's kinda weird."

We went around the thudding cylinders and caught sight of the Feyr ducking into a maintenance shaft. I snatched up my sword and fed it into the sheath's grasping mitts, then followed. Cassandra didn't say anything, though her eyes must have seen a lot of blood and a lot of sleeping bodies.

The corridor wasn't meant for big people. It made me wonder as to its origin. Amon, for all that he was a murderer and a mad assassin (and I corrected myself even as I thought it, but the thought came naturally), probably wouldn't have designed his engines to depend on child-labor parties. And he certainly didn't design anything for the Feyr. No one did.

I went to the impellor because I knew they would be there. Something about the energies that washed out of those machines attracted the little creeps. I had the beginnings of an idea why that was, now that I knew something of Amon's research into the impellors. If the stuff Cassandra was reading from the archive was true, of course. Whole little creepy Feyr villages gathered ramshackle beneath each of those towers, filling in whatever space they could find with clapboard buildings and driftwood catwalks. They even built little rafts to anchor around the water-bound impellor towers between the horns. The crews tolerated them because sometimes they were helpful, calling the Amonites' attention to things that were on the verge of breaking, or clearing out in advance of some disaster. Like little canaries. Some people thought they could see the future. I preferred to believe that they were simply very aware of their surroundings.

"What did you do back there?" I asked. It was hard to talk, bent over and squatting along with my knees in my face. I could crawl, but that was a bad position to try to react from. Not that this was much better.

"I made it night. For them, of course."

"Then why didn't they wake up, the ones who fell?"

He shrugged. "Night is when you sleep. When you wake, it is morning."

"Huh."

He stopped and looked back at me. "You would like a demonstration?"

"No, no. Just curious."

"It is good to be curious," he agreed, then continued on his way.

The path opened up, and I was in the expected hovel-town of the Feyr. This space must once have been a cistern, or some other storage facility. Muck lines on the wall of the wide, round chamber showed that varying levels of some liquid had spent time here. It smelled, mostly of burning timber and cooked food. The tiny houses were elevated on stilts, with porches that joined towers of buildings like wide catwalks. The stilts were water-stained and black. Maybe the place still flooded occasionally. It wasn't a big place, maybe a dozen small homes for small people. The largest building, at the center, did not share a porch with anyone else. We headed for that building.

All around, the Feyr watched us. Cassandra had the archive in her arms, hugging it like a child as she rushed forward. The little people were silent, and simply dressed. Their hair looked like the swept-back roots of an overturned tree, thick ropes branching out from their scalps, the same shade of brown or black or chalk white as their hard, knobby skin. Their eyes were large and black, without pupils or irises, deep and watery like those of a shark. The rest of their faces were pinched and tiny, mere sketches of a nose and mouth filled with tiny, sharp teeth. They had three thick fingers, each opposed to the other two, and their nails were hard and sharp. They looked like something grown in the dirt, yanked out by their feet and still caked in the mud of their birth.

My guide took me to the building in the middle. It was wide and flat, almost entirely porch, open to the rest of the room. Up the stairs, and the guy in charge was waiting for us in a tall chair. More of a cushioned platform than anything else. He looked distracted.

His skin was as brown as a chestnut, and just as shiny. He sat with his hands in his lap, and his eyes on his hands, unmoving. My guide bowed out, leaving us alone with the creepy guy. Elemental, I think they called him, the guy in charge. Strange name for a boss. I waited for a while, then grew impatient.

"I've got some questions for you."

"You do," he said, without looking up from his hands. "Old questions."

"Pardon me?"

He raised his head, tired, blinking those deep, dark eyes like a man just waking up. He looked from me to Cassandra, and then to the archive.

"Old questions," he said again. "We wondered when one of you would come to us again, to ask these questions."

"How do you even know what we're going to ask?" Cassandra said.

"When there is a flood, you do not ask about planting crops. When there is a fire, you do not ask about building boats." He folded his fingers together and clenched them in front of him. "Unless your boat is on fire, I suppose. And then you would have to ask very quickly."

"Amon must have been a very patient man," I said, "to learn anything from you."

"He was. Though it was not me, but my father."

"Making you how many hundred years old?" Cassandra asked. Which wasn't what we were supposed to be asking about, but I suppose the Scholar is the curious type. I was getting impatient.

"We do not think in such paths." The Elemental raised his hands to the dirty ceiling and nodded. "The days and years are like—"

"Like water drops, right? Or snowflakes? And we are the blizzard. Look," I leaned down to the tiny man, "we've got some people who might be dying right now, and they do think in such paths, so maybe we could skip the poetry lesson."

The Elemental looked at me, his hands still raised to the ceiling, his face placid.

"A child of Morgan, then?"

"Brilliant. And since you already know our question, why don't you go ahead and give us our answer, so we can get out of this sewer before it floods again?"

One of the Feyr, on a different platform, stepped forward.

"Flooding occurs on the third Friday of every alternating month, at a volume of—"

"Shut up!" I yelled across the porch to him. He did, and stepped back. Cassandra was taking notes.

"The question that you are asking, just so we are clear, it involves the cycle?"

"The cycle of . . ." I glanced back at Cassandra, who was rubbernecking the whole Feyr populace. "Of what now?"

"The Titans burned their candle slowly, and lived long. We burned ours even more slowly, so slowly that there was hardly a flame to be seen." The Elemental gestured nebulously, addressing us. "You burn quickly. Like a flare."

"Like a fuse," I corrected. "This is the cycle of godhood, then?"

"Yes. We can feel it in the air. The gods are changing, and you are changing with them. The days of mankind on the throne of god are limited."

"And after us, who?" Cassandra looked up from her notebook. "You?"

"We have had our time, and will have it again. But I think it will not fall to us."

"Then the Rethari? Or some other race that we've never met, across some other ocean?"

"A wise thought. Other oceans." The Elemental folded his hands beneath his chin and stared thoughtfully at the ground. "A good thought. But the power that will be released with your fall, I think it will go to the people of the scale. As you say."

"Alexander should hear this," I said. "I'm sure he'd be pleased."

"We have spoken. Not recently, but the nature of the formula is familiar to him."

"He knows this stuff?" I asked. "Knows that fewer gods means a quicker descent? That doesn't seem to make him likely to betray his brother either, does it?"

"Our conversation was after the death of your god. And only shortly after the death of yours," he answered, nodding to Cassandra. "He felt the change in power. It pleased him."

"Pleased him?"

"Before there was one fountain, and three vessels. After, one fountain, one vessel."

"More power for the godking," I said. "There's your motivation."

"You are implying that Alexander killed Morgan, and framed Amon." The Elemental shook his head. "We do not know that. To be clear, we stay out of the affairs of brief men."

"But it makes sense, doesn't it?" Cassandra asked, desperation in her voice. "Amon spoke with your kind, learned the truth of the cycle of gods. Why would he kill his brother, knowing that it would doom the Fraterdom?"

"Why does Alexander not raise up more gods? Why does he keep what knowledge he has secret?" The Elemental spread his hands wide. "Men do irrational things. Especially the Brothers."

"So it could have been Amon," I said, weighing the thought. "All along, Alexander could have told the truth of that. The rest he's hidden just to accumulate power."

"I will not lead you to answers like this. The ways of men are their own." He shook his head sadly. "I do not understand them."

"This has been a tremendous help," I said, rubbing my face. "You've revealed to us, through a series of overly complicated proclamations, that Morgan could have been killed by Alexander, or he could have been killed by Amon." I sat down and folded my hands over my knee. "And either way, it doesn't really matter because the cycle of the gods is rolling over, and we're all going to end up servants of the Rethari. Any idea how long until that happens?"

"We don't know how it hasn't happened yet. It should have been years, the way Alexander is burning. Like a fuse, as you say." He grinned and sat back. "Like a fuse. I like that. I will remember it, for the next time one of your kind comes to ask us these questions."

"So it should have happened already. And you have no idea why it hasn't?"

He shook his head. "Something is holding the water back. That was the point of Alexander's questions, when last he came to speak to us."

"The hidden archive," Cassandra said. "The full knowledge of Amon. He must be handpicking the best for the Library Desolate and putting them to work on Amon's research into the cycle."

"Which means he might have solved it," I said. "He might have figured a way to keep the cycle from turning."

Again, the Elemental shook his head. "The cycle will turn. The sky will turn. The waters will rise and the dam will burst, and everything will be washed clean. Our whole race could not hold the power. Madness and the Ruin were the cost of that. Who knows what's happening in Alexander's strange little head?"

"What did you say about ruin? The ruin of what?" I asked.

"Of nothing. Of everything. You know our sins, child of Morgan. The blackness that we created, the destruction that we wrought. It gave birth to a form, a form that lives in this lake."

"What now?" Cassandra asked. "Some kind of monster?"

"Some kind of darkness," the Elemental answered. "We built our temples to try to purge it. It absorbed all our pain, all our vile terror, and fed it back to us. More with each sin, always more."

"Is it still here?" she asked.

"It must be. We did not purge it, but it no longer speaks to us. Your Alexander knows of it. We always thought . . ." He paused, as if weighing us. "We always thought it was the burden of that sin that kept us from ascending completely. We may have been wrong. Alexander seemed to think it could . . . sponge up divinity. Swallow the light of the holy."

"And hold it," Cassandra said. "Like a battery."

"But what about—" I started.

The Elemental raised a hand. "I'm sorry, but there is nothing more I can tell you, because there is nothing more I can know." He stood and ritually brushed off the knees of his robe. "I wish you well, scions of Morgan and Amon. It is quite a task you face."

"Wait! You didn't actually answer any real questions!"

"You did not ask any real questions. I can hardly be blamed for that."

He turned and stepped off the edge of the porch, to disappear among the mass of Feyr that surrounded us. They began milling about, until we lost sight of the Elemental.

"That's great," Cassandra said. "You think we could come back later?"

"Maybe we can make an appointment," I answered. We went back the way we came, past the wooden houses. The place looked abandoned now. "I get the feeling that he doesn't talk to a lot of people, though."

"Other than the gods, that is. And neither of us is Alexander."

"No," I said. "We certainly aren't. Nor Amon, nor Morgan. And we don't know what Alexander knows, or what he's doing to maintain the cycle. If he's using that damned Ruin." I looked up at the brick-lined ceiling and grimaced. "Not yet, anyway."

CHAPTER FIFTEEN

The old part of Ash is nice, especially in the early fall. The worst of summer is past, the worst of winter far away. The air is clean, probably the only clean breath you'll get in the whole city. Distant winds come down from the Crow's Teeth Mountains, wash across the vast plains of the collar, and break over the lake, right into the Brothers' Spear. That air carries the smell of the harvest and the cold promise of snow.

There are a lot of old buildings on the lakeshore, stones that were raised under Amon's watchful eye. Picturesque arches cross canals that once fed the mercantile heart of the Fraterdom, but now serve nothing more than pleasure rafts and private boats. This district has been spared the modern touch. No monotrains, no glass towers, no waterway access to speak of. Just glorious old architecture and cobblestone streets, and the kind of boutiques that sell things no one really needs.

Which is why I hadn't been back since my acceptance into the Paladin. Passing through doesn't count, and the bit of sneaking I did on the edges of this district, following Simeon to his unfortunate meeting with Elector Nathaniel, doesn't either. No, for all my dedication to the old ways of my Cult, I had left this district to other pedestrians.

"The parade," I said, much to the surprise of my companion. "I suppose the parade comes through here. I'm usually too tired at that point from walking in formation to really notice."

"Notice what?" she asked.

"Oh. The buildings. The shops. It's really a nice area."

Cassandra looked around at the picture windows and colored awnings. I couldn't help but note how different this was from the Library Desolate. I wondered how long she had been in there, anyway. I asked.

"Five years, more or less. I've been visiting since I was a kid." I snorted at that. *Still a kid, kid.* "My parents didn't like it, but they supported my decision to dedicate."

"They still alive?"

"I don't know. I guess." She folded her arms into her sleeves and squinted out over the water. "I guess when I say 'support,' I mean they didn't physically stop me."

"Mm. Well. You ever been to this part of town before?"

"No. No reason."

"Yeah."

We had walked most of the way here, which in itself was unusual. Lots of pedigears here, rumbling down the street. Even at this hour. Easy enough to pass unseen, though. That lack of the modern touch also meant the street lighting was archaic. We were standing in an alleyway, not two blocks from the Spear of the Brothers. I could see the underlights splashing off the white stone and bathing the surrounding buildings in its pale reflection. We were in the worst part of the nice part of town, the sort of dark alleys that elected officials skulked down to find mistresses and vices and the like. Not a lot of that business going on tonight, though. The city was in upheaval. Even the vice making was in chaos.

"Let's assume that you know where the archive is," Cassandra said. "How do you propose we get in there?"

"That's assuming a lot. Specifically, it assumes something that's untrue." I leaned against the wall and sighed. "The good thing is that we don't have to worry about sneaking in. Not until we know where we're sneaking to, I suppose."

"I suppose," Cassandra echoed.

We had decided that we didn't know enough. That should have been obvious, but it took us a while to accept it. Cassandra thought the evidence from our little archive was more than enough to exonerate Amon and nail Alexander to a wall. Any wall. The girl wasn't picky. I wasn't ready to give up on Amon as the Betrayer, at least not on the scant findings we had in hand. I think I was just putting it off, really. Even if we had absolute proof that Alexander killed Morgan, what good would it do? Who would believe an escaped Amonite and the last of the Paladins of Morgan?

It didn't matter. We had to know. So we decided to seek out the theoretical hidden archive. If Alexander was keeping a body of knowledge to himself, grooming his own personal cadre of Amonites to care for it, and using that knowledge to prevent this "turning of the sky" that the Feyr Elemental had talked about . . . well, I wanted to know about it. If we found out some other truth about Morgan's death, that was fine. We would deal with that on discovery.

Thing was, this other archive was just a story. We didn't know it really existed. We certainly didn't know where it was. Just made sense to start at the Spear, close to the godking's throne.

I was done with waiting. The Spear was a simple building, surrounded by other administrative chambers that served as the seat of government in Ash. We would start in one of those other buildings and work our way to the center, or down, or whatever path felt right. I trusted the Hunter.

One thing bugged me most. Infiltration, spying, sneaking in . . . this was Betrayer work. And Cassandra was better at it than I was comfortable with. She had gotten us uniforms, even disguised the archive as some kind of street-sweeping gear. My sword and holster were hidden in an enormously complicated staff of office that I almost had to drag along. Administrators liked their relics of office, even if they held no noetic power. Mine at least had a revolver and a sword stuffed inside. The articulated sheath stayed on my back, retracted under the robes of state Cassandra had produced. She had gone out without me and returned with her gifts.

"These are good," I said when she handed them to me. "You practice this stuff?"

"Just a matter of hijacking an automated loom, tuning it up a bit. The owner will actually thank me, when he figures it out."

"You didn't steal anything, did you?"

"You're kidding, right? We're talking about breaking into the holiest house in the city, which will undoubtedly involve armed opposition, and you're worried about me stealing things?"

I shrugged. "I've got plenty of blood on my hands, but none of it was innocent."

"I seriously doubt that. But whatever you believe." She flipped a hand dismissively. "Just put on the robe."

I did, and so when we shushed our way across the last road and into the light of the Spear, we didn't look completely out of place.

The administration buildings were dull gray boxes against the Spear's white brilliance. Probably a psychological thing. Even though it was night, there were plenty of lights on in the various windows that looked down on the plaza. We moved purposefully, straight to the nearest door. No guards that I could see, so I put my hand on the knob and pulled.

Locked. I rattled the door and peered inside. Empty hallway. Cassandra was humming nervously behind me.

"I'm going to have to break it down," I said.

"You are not. We're administrators of the throne of god. We don't break down doors. We have keys, and permission to be wherever we are." She pushed me away from the door and knelt in front of the lock. "You break this door down and someone sees it, that's our cover blown. I'll pick it."

"You have a tool for that?"

"I can make one. Just give me a—People coming."

She was right. I could hear voices from around the corner of the building, approaching fast. There was a vehicle too. Moving slowly for a vehicle, but faster than was convenient.

"Open it now," I hissed.

"Can't." She stood. "Not enough time. Look natural."

"Not bloody likely." I turned away from the voices and hurried along the side of the building, toward the far corner. Cassandra was quick behind me. It was too much distance, and too little time.

The party that came around the corner got quiet when they saw us. I dared a glance back and saw an open-bed carriage, big knobbly wheels, with something huge on the bed. It was covered by a tarp and tied down with heavy rope. The carriage strained under its weight. Around it walked a circle of officials, carrying the familiar staffs and wearing half-masks over their faces. I turned around.

"Chanters," I said, and quickened my pace. They hailed us. Not much to do now. Run, or fight, or turn and be civil. Never my strength.

"Sire and lady!" the lead Chanter called, then stopped when I turned. "Ladies of the Throne! Can you give us a hand, perhaps?"

"What business have you at the Spear?" Cassandra called back. By the time they answered, they were upon us. The carriage smelled like bilge water.

"God's business, of course." The lead Chanter was a big man, heavy in the jowl and sweating profusely under his mask. He jerked it off, wiped his mouth, then returned the binding to his mouth. "We're delivering something, for his honor's collection."

"Alexander?" I asked. *Of course Alexander*, I thought to myself. *Don't be an idiot.* They were thinking the same, judging by the way they looked at me. "His collection. Of course."

"Yes. We were to meet an official, but he wasn't at the door as declared. So we thought we'd bring . . . this." He turned nervously to the carriage, then winced and turned back to us. "We thought we'd bring it around to the front. Perhaps you can lead us inside?"

"Are you late, or are you early?" A voice called from the corner, back where the carriage had come from. "Or do you simply not know when to stay put and follow orders?"

We all looked back. A man in a long gray robe was coming around the corner. He wore no sign of office and carried no elaborate staff. His clothes were plain, but his form was full of authority. The Chanters turned gratefully to him. Cassandra and I shrank behind the carriage.

"Someone told you to haul this abomination around front, did they?"

"No, your . . . sir. No. But we thought it would be best to get it inside."

"Yes, yes. You were wrong. Admirable thought, but utterly wrong. Come on, turn it around. Don't just stand there."

With a great deal of noise and drama, the Chanters got their automated carriage turned around and rumbling back toward the corner. We tagged along. The gray man noticed us and scowled.

"You brought your own administrators? They won't be necessary."

"Sorry, lord. They asked us the best way in, and we were about to direct them back to you. Your arrival was fortuitous," Cassandra purred. Again, too good for my comfort.

"Hm. Well, it's best you come along. Don't lag. No telling which Betrayers' eyes are watching, on a night like this."

Together we all made our way around the corner. When the man's attention was diverted, Cassandra tugged at my robe and leaned in.

"His wrists," she whispered. I turned and looked. Bracelets, one on each wrist, and matching rings. He even had a tight collar around his throat, made of thin chain. Very odd. Cassandra tugged at my elbow again. She had something in her hand. The light was bad so I leaned in to get a look.

It was her soul-chain, from her time in the Library Desolate. One of the links was snipped in half, the cut so clean it appeared to have been forged that way. I looked back at the man in gray.

Amonite.

"The Special Collections Agency is around the corner," the gray Amonite was saying. "Here." He led us to a nondescript loading door in a nondescript wall. It took some time for the door to open, time we spent listening to the lift chains rattle, loud in the silence of the street. The Chanters looked around nervously. Once the door was open they hurried inside as fast as the automated carriage would chug. The door closed behind us.

We were in a plain brick room, the walls and floor painted white. Another gray man stood just inside the door, his hands still on the mechanism that opened the door. The Chanters looked much more comfortable now that they were out of the open air. I was getting nervous. Cassandra felt it, and so did the neutered sheath on my back. Sheath without a sword can't do much but twitch.

"My dear brothers and sisters of the Song. I want to thank you for performing this duty for our lord Alexander." The Amonite put a hand on the tarp and smiled thinly. "Your god is pleased with you."

"We were lucky to save it from the drowning, your sir," the fat one said. "It seemed those bloody dead were coming right for it."

"And through your great works, we were able to prevent that most unfortunate event. We would hate for all the Chanters' work to have been lost in that tragedy."

"Aye. Many hours have gone into this. Though I was surprised his godship put an interest in this, rather than, say, the Song itself."

The Amonite shrugged. "Alexander will always have the Song in his heart. And you?" he asked, turning to us. "What was your part in this retrieval?"

"As we said, my lord," Cassandra answered. "Happenstance. We were leading them inside."

"Ah, well. Unfortunate."

The Amonite before us drew first. My guess was the guy by the door was already aiming, because three of the Chanters fell before this guy got iron clear of leather. Good shooting, for a Scholar. And they were putting the Chanters down, because they were the obvious threats. Couple pencil pushers weren't any kind of dangerous.

Cassandra unmade the weapon behind as the fourth bullet went into the chest of one of the Chanters. I heard the jigsaw tumble of metal parts, familiar from my previous fight with her. The guy in front of us had loosed one shot, killing the fat man. That guy had gotten off a couple notes, his mask rattling open, his chin wobbling as he incanted pure notes of destruction. Just enough to singe the air and leave us all feeling a little like we had met the sun. Not enough to kill.

I fractured my staff of office, the quick-fall shaft and flanges butterflying apart to present the blade and the bully. I took the sword and invoked hard, splintering the air with light as I vaulted across the room and opened the lead gray from teeth to ribs. He stumbled back, grinning at me from two sides of a bloody gash, his revolver snapping shots into the brick at my feet. Two quick revolutions and he stopped shooting. Clean.

Turning, I saw the other guy in a stance of meditation. He and Cassandra were in a battle of noetic will. Waves of force lashed between them, making and unmaking the bricks, the walls, the very stuff of the air and earth and time. The cadence of their voices was a wall of tectonic force. They seemed to be channeling the purest of power, forming energy out of nothing, and nothingness out of the bare rock. Both stood in perfect meditation, an invisible wind animating their robes and hair, the barest of auras pulsing from their closed eyes.

I wheeled my blade to the ground and snatched the bully out of the staff where it had come to rest when I dropped it, propped against the carriage. I walked around the circumference of their little disturbance, my feet buckling on the shifting plane of brick. When I was as close as I dared get, I put the barrel in line with the Amonite's head and pulled the trigger.

The bullet punched through the shimmering waves of their fight, slowing like a stone in water. As it slowed it peeled like an onion, the layers of lead spiraling outward until there was nothing left but a cloud of potential violence. Even that disappeared.

"Godsdamn Scholars," I spat, then emptied the cylinder.

Each shot followed the first, corkscrewing out of existence, each cloud wafting closer to the bastard. Waves of shock traveled out from their flight, cones of force that disturbed the balance of Cassandra's battle. Five bullets, five arcs of energy washing over each other, building and disturbing the patterns of energy that had accumulated between the two Scholars. An ever growing wave of shattered lead flowered out into the room.

The last bullet struck him. Just a glancing blow, and only the barest core of lead left from the aura of Unmaking. It was enough. He flinched as blood touched his cheek. Cassandra moved against him, viciously, with enlightened power.

The bricks of the floor roared up, stacking into a tower, the hollow core of which enveloped the man. He stumbled back, slapping his hands against the jigsaw horror that was swallowing him. There was no room for retreat. She built a tower around him. When she closed the cylinder, the shuffling whirlwind of bricks slid into place, clenching into the center, leaving no room for the man. One scream, and he was gone.

Cassandra collapsed to the floor. Her whole body was shaking, and a thin trail of blood leaked from her mouth. I put a hand on her shoulder.

"You alright?"

"I hope there aren't too many more like him. I hope he was their best."

"The doorman?" I stood up and started thumbing bullets into the bully's cylinder. "Probably not."

The Chanters were all dead. I'll say it again: good shooting, especially for a Scholar. These boys were a different breed from the Librarians Desolate, that was for sure. I lined the bodies up and did some violence to the door.

"What if we have to go out that way?"

"It's a door," I said. "I can open it."

We gathered up our stuff, the archive, and Cassandra's shotgun. I threw the disguises under the carriage, along with the remains of my false staff. If this was going to be a killing job, I'd rather do it in the full glory of Morgan. Before we left, we stood by the carriage and pulled down the tarp.

No idea what it was. Beautiful, for one. Complicated. Smooth and black and cut from some kind of wood. Like of which I'd never seen.

"They were building something," Cassandra said, quietly. "Something big."

"Something about this size, I would say." I put my hand against it. It pulsed in familiar time. Couldn't put my finger on it. "You're the Scholar. What is it?"

She circled it slowly, running gentle hands over its surfaces. First time the pulse vibrated through it, she snapped her hand back, startled.

"Is it breathing?" she asked.

"It's wood. Maybe it's some kind of instrument."

She shook her head. "Brothers know."

"I suspect one of them does," I said. "And let's be honest, we don't really have time to figure it out."

"Yeah," Cassandra said, then placed both palms against it, closed her eyes, and breathed in very deeply. Twice. When she opened her eyes, they were watering. "Yeah, okay. Let's go."

There was one big door that led to an elevator. The gears were running. Someone was coming up, so we went back to the room and took a different door. This led to a stairwell. Everything went down, it seemed. We followed the obvious path, trying to be quiet as we went. The stairs had a lot of horizontal sections, long hallways that moved us closer to the Spear before we descended again. We were probably underneath that old stone tower when we started coming across other doors to other floors. They were all locked. I could have gotten through them, but none of them seemed terribly compelling to me. By now the bodies would have been found. I didn't hear any alarms, but I had to assume that there was a search on. I was starting to taste something in my bones, too. Deeper we got, deeper it went.

"You've got that?" Cassandra asked me. "That feeling?"

"Got it," I said. It was like the impellors, but all the time. Made it hard to concentrate. "That can't be your hidden archive."

"Why else would there be Amonites here? Those two were his private stock, Eva. He's got his own little team of Scholars working on something."

"Yeah. Maybe. Or maybe he just uses them as guards."

"We make terrible guards."

"Those two did okay."

"Yeah, well . . ." she began, but I held up my hand. Voices.

One of the doors near us began to open, multiple locks being thrown and unlatched as we stared at it in terror. I cast about for an open door or hidden nook. We had just come around a corner, but after that the hallway was long and uninterrupted until the stairs. The direction we had been going was also a long hallway, pocked with doors. None of them looked unlocked. I grabbed the girl and ran. Best we could do was scoot around the corner and hope they were going the other way.

". . . the damned Chanters, if you ask me. Finley said they had been butchered."

"I thought we had a pretty good team in there," the second voice answered. They were getting closer. I pushed Cassandra farther back from the corner and whispered a quick invokation of speed.

"Yeah, we did. Not good enough, though. Someone must have tipped them off."

"We should have moved a dampener up there. I said we should have."

"Hindsight, Mal. Always with the hindsight."

They were right by the corner. I could hear their feet, their robes. The jingling of keys. They were opening the last door we had passed. I relaxed, just a fraction.

"I'm just saying that there'd be fewer dead now, and we wouldn't have to be doing this." The second voice was older. Cranky. "This is going to throw off the rotation. And for all we know, the Chanters fought just enough for one of them to escape and run for it."

"We have to assume more than that. This is a delicate time."

The final bolt was thrown and the door opened. There was a lot of open space in the new room, judging by the echoes. How much space could there be, this far under the street? We must be under the water by now, surely? The two voices paused in the open door.

"Our lot is not the one I would have chosen. That any of us would have chosen. But we are here, and we must play our part. It is all we can do for the Scholar."

"His name be praised," his companion intoned, like a prayer. "His body held tight."

The two men sighed, then moved inside the larger room. As the door swung shut I heard one more snippet.

"When we are done with the preparations, we can return to the archive and lock it down. The toll won't last forever."

"It will set us back weeks."

"Perhaps. But we'll still be alive."

And the door shut. I looked at Cassandra, but she was already past me and around the corner. I followed. She went straight to the door the men had come out of, and had her palm against it, her eyes closed.

"We can't wait around, Cass," I whispered. "They'll be coming back."

"Yes," she answered, and opened her eyes. "Coming back to the archive."

My eyes widened, and I turned to the door. The archive. I changed stance and began to invoke the Rite of the Sundering, as quietly as I could. Cassandra gave me a little slap and shushed me.

"We'll need to close the door again, Paladin." She produced a complicated tool, knelt by the door, and put her forehead against the metal. "This may take some time."

"It's in short supply, I think. They know someone is in the building."

"It will take more time if you keep talking."

I grimaced, but backed off. This was much too long of a hallway for me to be comfortable. Any of these doors could open with little or no warning. And if they had found the massacre upstairs, it wasn't like we'd be able to talk our way past a patrol. Sword in sheath, bullistic in hand, I paced. That was as much peace as I could give the girl.

Her whole body hummed with attention. She had the tool flat up against the lock. There were sounds coming out of her, out of the door, out of the tool. Like stones grinding. That had to be drawing someone's notice, didn't it? This was taking forever. A thousand forevers. I kept my eyes on all the doors, on the passageway, especially on the door that those two had gone through. Had they been Amonites? Alexians? They had referred to the Scholar, so probably some of Alexander's pets. They still wore the chains, I remembered. They couldn't be all that free.

The grinding sound stopped, and the door sighed open. Cassandra stood, smiling.

"Breaking things is not always the way," she said.

"Fine, fine," I said, hurrying her through the door. "Let's just get inside."

The door locked behind us. Inside was a square room with a low ceiling. The space was dominated by a brass dome that reached almost to the ceiling, and nearly to the walls. The only clear areas were at the corners, where the circumference of the dome did not reach. There were hooks all along the wall by the door, several of which were hung with some sort of suit. The dome looked pressurized, and in fact had several dogged portals leading into it at various heights, each one accessible by rungs soldered onto the dome. It was covered with Amonite runes, some painted on, some forged into the metal, or made of iron or copper or gold and bolted to the surface. I looked back at Cassandra.

She was standing in quiet awe, her eyes wide. She was whispering below her breath, and her free hand was making rites. The symbols of her faith.

"This is it?" I asked.

"Yes. The last archive of Amon the Scholar. It's . . . enormous."

"Well. We aren't taking this thing out of here, obviously. You wanna strap up and see what you can—"

"Can you give me one second of quiet, for Brothers' sake? Does Morgan have no holy place, no room of silence and meditation?" She turned to me, and I saw tears in her eyes. "Can we just be quiet for a minute?"

I gritted my teeth. "Battle, Cassandra—that is our holy place.

Everything else has been burned." I pulled one of the suits off the wall and tossed it to her. "And I've prayed enough today. I'd like to get out of here cleanly."

She looked unhappy, but she shucked off her robe and pulled on the suit over her skinny legs. I gave her what privacy I could. She was half into it when one of the pressurized doors unsealed with a gasp of frost, and an Amonite came out.

He was in a suit like the one Cassandra was pulling on. Without looking around, he hurried down the rungs and to the floor near us. He stopped long enough to release the mask and hood. His hair was white, but when he turned I could see that he was quite young. He didn't register who we were at first, instead rushing to one of the hooks that held a gray robe. He stopped, looked at me, at my revolver, at the blood still on my boots. Unphased, really. Then he looked at Cassandra, half naked, half suited, unchained and yet so clearly an Amonite. His eyes got wide. He jumped for a switch by the door, a panel that had a big red button on it. I got between him and it.

"Don't," I said. He stopped, his hand trembling as it reached for the button.

"They'll kill us all. If they find you here, they'll kill every one of us." He looked between us. "You don't know what you've done."

"And you have no idea what I've done. Or what I'm willing to do. Now get away from that switch."

"It doesn't matter," he said. "They'll kill us all." And he jumped for the console. I put two bullets in him, the report loud, the reverberations echoing around the dome. He fell, startled, and lay there with his mouth open.

"You didn't have to do that," Cassandra said as she rushed past me. She knelt at his side. "You didn't have to kill him."

"I think I did," I answered. She didn't look up. Blood was trickling out of the guy's mouth. He was trying to talk, but nothing was coming. He put a bloody hand on Cassandra's chest, right over her heart, smearing gore on her skin and undershirt. And then he died.

Cassandra nearly vibrated, she was so furious. She rolled him onto his back, cupped his hands over his eyes, and pushed his mouth closed. She was saying some kind of rite over him.

"We don't have time—" I said.

"We have more time than he does. Now shut up. This is not a place for blood."

"It's going to be, if you don't—"

"Shut. Up," she said, exasperation in her voice. "In Amon's name, be quiet."

I took a step back, but I was quiet. I remembered standing the watch over Elias. Who was I to deny her the comfort of ritual? She finished, stood, and buckled into the suit, all without looking at me, or the body of the Amonite.

"Watch the door," she said, and started up the ladder.

"He was going to sound the alarm."

"Watch the door."

She got up the dome and undogged the portal. White frost blossomed around her, turning the suit into a glittering sleeve. She disappeared inside, sealing the dome behind her.

I looked at the body, at the slowly growing pool of blood, at Cassandra's gory footsteps, and where she had knelt by the Amonite as he died. Then I turned, and watched the door.

CHAPTER SIXTEEN

The guy just lay there, dead. I usually didn't spend a lot of time with the people I killed. The advantage of a battlefield. You charge a position, sweep through, put down whatever resistance, and then redirect. Maybe get called back to reinforce the line, or forward to exploit a breakdown in the enemy. And then you move on. Plenty of time around dead bodies, of course. They were everywhere in the modern battlefield. But which ones did you kill? Which ones died at your brother's hand, or some other soldier's, or their own? Who could tell? Who could sort it out?

But this guy, I had killed him, and he wasn't going away. Cassandra's reaction had been wholly surprising to me. He had been about to call the heat down on us. Killing him was all I had. Maybe I could have subdued him, just knocked him out and tied him up, but it had been a split-second decision. This is how it had ended up.

I turned him over with the toe of my boot, so I didn't have to look at his gaping mouth and the weird way Cassandra had arranged his hands. That would probably upset her, too, but we can't all get what we want.

Look at me. What I want is my Cult back. Barnabas alive, the Strength intact, and a steady flow of initiates in the door. That was never going to happen. A long time, we'd been dying, little by little. Every potential initiate who passed us by to serve in the whiteshirt army was a little death. When the initiates stopped coming, it was only a matter of time before we stopped being. Just stopped. I didn't expect it to happen like this, of course. I didn't expect the Betrayer to come back, to start killing us off. But you can't turn back time. There wasn't going to be a Cult of Morgan, once this was through.

Scratch that. I didn't want the Cult back. It was dead, and had been dying for a long time. I didn't want to drag it out. What I wanted, what I really wanted, was revenge. I wanted the damn Betrayer dead, whoever he was. Alexander or Amon, it didn't matter to me. I wanted his towers thrown down. I wanted his Cult scattered, his scions persecuted and killed. I wanted to put my blade through the gut of that bastard Nathaniel. I wanted the Cult of the Betrayer to suffer what Morgan had suffered. Wiped clean from the earth. That would be enough for me.

And this guy. What did he want? Amon was dead. Even if the Scholar were cleared of the murder of his brother, people would never trust him. Never trust what they'd been taught for two hundred years to despise. And how would the Cult of Amon react, to learn that their god had been falsely accused? That they had lived in slavery or on the run for two hundred years to preserve a lie, all the while ruled over by the man who had put both of our gods to death. What measure of forgiveness would they be willing to pour out, and what measure of wrath?

I realized then the horror of what Cassandra and I were proposing. To expose the last god of man as a murderer. What would that do to the city, to the Fraterdom? If the cycle were about to turn, and Alexander was the only thing holding our divinity together, would it be worth our revenge to throw down the godking and open the door for the ascension of the Rethari? But what choice did we have? Bend the knee to a murderer, or lose our empire. These were the things we must face.

That's when the door opened. I was lost in staring at the dead guy and trying to juggle the gods of man, and didn't hear the bolts throw. When the door began to slide open, I only had time to step behind it. Good thing is, the Scholars were still talking, and that distracted them enough to get inside and close the door before they saw the body. Soon as the door was closed, I slid in front of it, right by their fancy panic button.

Two men, one old and stooped with age, the other young and thin. They wore gray robes, similar to the two we had killed upstairs. They wore their soul-chains openly, looped around their chest and neck, linked to their wrists and waist. A lot more chain than what the Librarians Desolate wore, I noted, though it seemed a much lighter weight. Almost delicate. Their heads were close together, and they were talking.

"The duration of the interruption doesn't matter," the old one was saying. "Any interruption is terrible. Alexander plays with these things like they're dice, but if we build up too much noet—"

"Yes, yes. Too much power, not enough conduit. I know, Malcolm, but—"

And that's when they saw the body. Malcolm just stood, staring at the twisted form, its back sticky with blood, the stink of meat and voided gut finally cutting through the antiseptic purity of the chamber. The other one, the young one whose name I had yet to hear, immediately turned for the button. Turned right into my bully, in his eye.

"What have you done?" he whispered. Malcolm turned and saw me. They both started backing up to the dome. "They'll kill us all."

"That's what he said. I'd like to hear a little more than that, if you don't mind."

"It's too late. You don't understand what you've done. As soon as the Holder learns that the archive has been found . . . he'll just kill us. He'll start over with a new batch from the Library."

"They can't afford that, Daniel," Malcolm muttered. "They can't get a new crew in here and hope to maintain the noet. The Ruin will break open, and then where will we be?"

"You're right, old man," Daniel said. "They'll just kill those of us responsible. Which is you, and me." He glanced at the body. "And Jeremiah, I suppose. But that won't really matter."

"You're assuming I'm not going to kill you first," I said. "Can we get back to paying attention to the girl with the bully?"

"You must be the Paladin," Daniel said. "Am I right? The last scion of Morgan?"

"I'm your girl," I answered.

"What happened to your Cult? Why did you turn against Alexander?"

"You're joking, right? We've been set up. The Betrayer has been hunting us down, disguised as one of the Healer's men. Guy named Nathaniel has a whole cadre of masked assassins skulking around. I think . . ." I went over in my mind what I thought, and found I didn't really know yet. "I think he's part of a sect of the Healer, which has been secretly worshipping the Betrayer all this time."

"Nathaniel Cascade? High Elector of the Cult of Alexander?" Malcolm's face wrinkled in a deep smile. "You're accusing him of worshipping the Betrayer. I assure you, my girl, that he is not of Amon."

"I didn't say that. But what makes you so sure?"

They both wrinkled their foreheads. I decided not to explain myself.

"Not of Amon. Well, no, he's obviously not. Nathaniel Cascade is the Chief Elector of this facility, Paladin. He's the Holder of our chains." Daniel raised his arms and displayed the links around his wrists. "When we say that they'll kill us all, we mean that *he* will kill us all."

"And smile through the whole butchery," Malcolm said.

"What is this place?" I asked.

"The hidden house of Alexander. He has gathered here all the stories of the forgotten gods, the mythos of the Feyr, even artifacts from the age of the Titans." Daniel raised his hands and presented his palms to me. "And the untold stories of the new gods, as well."

"What are you doing?" Malcolm asked. He had a bony hand around Daniel's elbow.

"New gods?" I asked.

"Yes. Do you think only the Brothers have ascended? That there is but one god by accident? Alexander has culled the harvest, my dear Paladin, and this is where he hides the chaff and stores the wheat."

"Stores the wheat," I said, mostly to myself, mostly to be heard. "Like that damned Feyr said. The Ruin could be used to swallow noetic divinity. Alexander must be doing that!"

"Has been doing it for two hundred years, little girl," the Amonite said.

"Why in hell did you tell her that?" Malcolm shrieked. "Do you want to implicate us in the murder of a thousand gods, boy? We'll be lucky if they only kill us, rather than—" He glanced back at me. "Rather than other things."

"You're saying that Alexander has been . . . has been hunting gods?"

"Young gods. New gods. Gods before they are truly divine. We can sense them with the Ruin, sense them as they draw power off. Only the ordained scions of the three Cults are allowed to survive, since their

216

development can be monitored and controlled." He turned to Malcolm and smiled. "It's okay, old man. I told her because he's already forgiven us. I told her because he already knows."

"What?" I barked.

"He monitors the chains," Daniel said, and raised his arms again. "Not always, and not all the time. But I sense his eyes upon me. His eyes upon you."

I skipped forward, drawing the sword as I moved and bringing it down in a long, sweeping arc. The blade parted Daniel's skull and exited at his hip. The boy slid apart. Malcolm was howling.

"You can't leave me to face him!" he yelled. "You can't give Daniel a quick peace and leave me to answer to that man!" He threw himself to his knees, his hands at my waist. "Please, for the love of mercy!"

"Mercy is in short supply," I said. I drove the sword down his chest and twisted. The blade became entangled in his chains, and when I twisted the links popped like glass. The whole length of it slithered to the floor. Malcolm fell back on his butt, his eyes wide with shock. He looked like he was having trouble breathing. I saw that where the metal had slid across his body as it came free, there were angry welts. I bent to him, and helped him to his feet.

"Last . . . push. He gave one last push, as the chain came loose." He held his hand to his chest and breathed in shuddering gasps. "How did you do that?"

"I'm not sure. The Fratriarch did it for Cassandra. I thought it was worth a try."

"You don't understand. Those links went into my soul. You severed them cleanly, like they were mere steel."

"Steel doesn't cut that easily, but yes. You are free."

He stood at my side, wavering on his feet. His hand was on my shoulder.

"Good to . . . good to breathe once more, my own breath. Even if it is at the end, even if we don't have much time. Even if he's already on his way here."

"You have to help me, then. There's little enough time without—"

The door began to unlatch. I threw myself against it. Whoever was on the other side began hammering at the metal.

"Help me, old man! Don't stand by and watch it end this way!"

"It's already ended, woman. You cannot stand against Nathaniel. I don't care what tricks they taught you in that monastery. Blades are blades. He will cut you down."

"It's no damn wonder they've been able to keep you people—" I grunted as a great deal of force was applied to the door. I staggered back, then threw myself against it again. Planting my sword, I invoked the Stones of Averon and set my shoulder against the steel. Malcolm was still watching me.

"No damn wonder they've been able to keep you on the leash for so long," I said through gritted teeth. "You give up before the fight is started."

"Not so," he said. "The fight has been over for a long time. Amon's Betrayal doomed us. We have been working to preserve the memory of the man, while shunning his darkness ever since. Any death is good for us."

"I would love to discuss theology, honest to Brothers I would." Another hammer into the door, another twisting of power against my shield. "But I think you're telling the wrong story."

"You would have us deny the Scholar, I know. The Cult of Morgan would like to line up all the scions of Amon and cut us down, but we are trying to make good on—"

"That's not what I meant." I nodded to the archive that Cassandra had dropped when she changed into the bodysuit. "That's an archive of Amon. Came into the hands of my Cult just—" I lost my breath and something nearly forced the door. "Just fucking look at it. Cassandra highlighted the important stuff."

He wrinkled his brow and, as if there weren't an army of men on the other side of the door trying to kill us both, knelt curiously by the archive and ran his hands over it.

"Fascinating. A lost archive. And how did you say you came across it?" I didn't answer, and he didn't seem to need me to. "It must have been from the final flight of Amon. When he was driven from the city, he took his closest followers and went north. Hid among the scattered tribes of the Rethari. The armies of the Fallen Brother had to fight their way through legions of those scaled bastards to get to him. Ah, but get to him they did. Much was lost, in those last days. Perhaps this was recovered there. But by whom, I wonder? One of your people?" he asked, and looked at me.

I was busy invoking mantles of strength and fortification, against the onslaught on the other side of that door. They had brought a lot of clever noetics to the fight, and I was having trouble holding out. I wished the guy would get to the reading, and stop blabbing on about the last days of Amon. Didn't have the breath to spare for the necessary obscenities, though. He seemed to get the idea.

"Oh, well. Perhaps those answers will come another day. Listen to me, prattling on about other days, when this is clearly our last. Ah. Some habits are hard to break." He spun up the archive and peered into the shifting icons of the screen. Even under duress as I was, I could tell that he was good with the machine, in a way that Cassandra couldn't approach. She had said that the ones picked for Alexander's special service were the best of the best. I believed it.

He took it all in quickly. The old man's face went slack as he absorbed the archive, wrinkles smoothing out, mouth hanging open. When it was done, he leaned back and looked up at the ceiling.

"The implications are . . . curious." He rubbed his face and stood, then began to pace around the bodies of his fallen comrades. Hardly aware of his surroundings, or the battle I was fighting at the door. "This must have been purged from the Library's records, and our access to the mind below is severely monitored. But the path taken does not match the knowledge."

"Uh-huh," I grunted.

"Why would he kill his brother, when he's just determined that the noet must be distributed? My gods, what does this mean for the Ruin? If we've been cutting off other conduits and simply venting the extra power, while keeping Alexander at the top of his game . . . What does this mean?"

"Uh-huh. Hm. Gah—" I was pushed away from the door, and had to draw my sword and fight back a brief tide of whiteshirts before I could get it closed again.

"I wonder if Alexander knew all this? I wonder if that's what led him to build this place? But he couldn't have, if he ordered Amon killed. It does reflect his understanding of noetic force, that there's only so much at a time and it can be distributed across many gods. That's the whole impetus behind the culling. But if Amon's observations are true—"

The door boomed open, throwing me across the room. I landed in a heap at the base of the dome. Malcolm watched me go, then looked curiously at the door. Realization dawned across his wrinkled old face.

"Ah. I see. Well, I suppose it was nice while it lasted."

"Quitter," I spat, and came swirling to my feet, blade already swinging through the stations of defense.

What came through the door was not what I expected. Not what I was prepared to face.

A group of coldmen, solid-looking guys with blades on their wrists, frost and fog wicking off their bodies as they walked in. And in their midst, standing taller than the rest, Barnabas Silent, Fratriarch of Morgan.

His skin was utterly pale against the harsh steel of his new garments. The injuries he had suffered while in captivity had faded away, though traces of the scars stood out in puckered white lines across his cheeks. He stood tall, as he always had. Pewter blue greaves and chest plate had been bolted on over his robe, and the lower half of his face was covered with a plate-mail bevor. His eyes were as clear as glass, and they leaked oily tears down his wrinkled face. In his hands he held a wicked hammer of blue steel, just as he had in his youth.

"Don't look at me like that, Eva. This is difficult enough," he said. His voice was a static-laced grating, only hinting at the gentle man who had raised me.

"What have they done, Barnabas?" I whispered.

"Killed me, Eva. Killed me and raised me and made me into something else."

"And have they sent you to do the same to me?"

He shook that great, heavy head of his and smiled.

"They sent me because there is no one else you would listen to. This has all been an awful mistake, Eva. They learned about the archive from their agents, but didn't know what it was. They kidnapped me because they suspected, because they were startled that the Fratriarch of Morgan would associate with an Amonite. It was a horrible, brutal thing to do, but it is done. What Alexander has done is unforgivable. What he has done to our Cult, to our god . . ." He placed the palm of his hand against his chest. "What he has done to us, Eva, can never be undone. And it can never be repaid. But this has to stop."

I put the point of my sword into the ground in front of me, like a statue at guard in the king's chamber.

"You have to be kidding me, Frat. Unforgivable? Does that even begin to cover two centuries of . . . of deception? I have no interest in that debt being repaid. You're right there. It can't be repaid, like some kind of bar tab." I drew the sword to my side, tip still on the ground, and leaned against the pommel with all my weight. "But what settlement I can make in Alexander's flesh, I'll take."

"Think about that. Think of the consequences to the Fraterdom, Eva. What will become of the tribes of man, if the last of their gods falls? And think about who would benefit from such chaos." He took a great step toward me. The air around me chilled, and my lungs ached with the sudden cold. "Morgan has been the tool of Alexander for too long. Do not submit yourself to a new master, just to spite your old."

"What are you talking about?" I asked.

"The Rethari," Malcolm answered. He was sitting on the archive as if it was a barrel, his hands folded neatly in his lap. "This archive must have come from them, yes? It was lost in their lands, and has not been seen since. The Cult of Morgan did not go looking for it, and yet here it is. Mysteriously."

"And who better to benefit from the turning of the divine cycle, Eva?" Barnabas said. "When mankind falls, it is the snakes that will feed on the body."

"You know about that?" I asked. "About the cycle?"

"I know now. Dying and living again have brought me a certain . . . clarity?" Another step closer. He whispered, "About you as well, girl. A great many strange things, about you."

"What?" I asked, backing up. The rest of them were looking at us strangely. They hadn't heard. Barnabas smiled and shook his head.

"They raised me to ask you to turn back. Yes, Alexander has sinned against us. In a moment of rage and weakness and jealousy, he struck down our god Morgan. Horrified, he tried to cover his action. Amon paid the price that Alexander could not stand. In the end, he has done everything he could since that time to atone for those twin evils. He has raised mankind up, and held the tribes together. He has arranged to keep the memory of his fallen brothers alive, through their scions. And he has kept the cycle from turning, for all these years. For that mercy, for that atonement, you must turn aside."

I sheathed my sword with a great deal more spinning and show than was necessary. I was furious. I needed both hands to express it.

"Mercy. Atonement. He murdered both of his brothers, one out of jealousy and one out of cowardice. His every action has been selfish, and his every purpose bereft of honor. You want me to stop, because if I don't that god may die? Honestly, Barnabas. How can we let a god like that live?"

"The Rethari will ascend, and the days of man—"

"Will be damned! And the Rethari should rise up! If this is the best we can do with that divinity, then let them have it for a while. Maybe we'll learn something of atonement, then." The rest of the room had pulled back. The crowd of whiteshirts at the door, the troupe of coldmen. Even Barnabas. Blasphemy felt good. It felt honest, for once. "You don't believe this, do you, Fratriarch? That we should honor the memory of Morgan by honoring his murderer? That the Betrayer should be protected because he's the only god we have left?"

"The alternative is unacceptable," he said, sadly.

"You speak as if there actually are alternatives. As if choosing between no god and that god were a choice."

"Eva, please." He raised his hammer between us, holding the shaft parallel to the ground, one wide hand under the steel head, the other grasping the base. "Please, no."

I stood straight as I could. There was a heaviness to the room, a cold void that was waiting to be filled with blood and fire. I drew my sword, and the rasp of it tore through me like a hook.

"Do what you must, Fratriarch. But I will not stand aside."

There was silence all around us. He bowed his head and touched a dead finger to his forehead. No one moved.

"I am not going to fight you, Eva Forge. The time for that is past. I think they hoped that I would, when they plucked me from the

grave. They did not believe you would be willing to strike me down."
He laid the head of his hammer on the floor with a mighty thud, and
crossed his hands on the base of the shaft. "They were wrong, on both
accounts. These others may try to oppose you, but I will not."

There was half a breath where the six coldmen exchanged querying
glances with their goggle eyes. They had not even raised their hands
before I struck. Best not give them the luxury of certainty. I invoked
as I moved, striking between words, rushing forward and falling back
with the rhythm of my invocation.

"The Fields of Erathis! The River that Roared and Bled! Having-
warry, Belhem, the Legions of Tin-Terra, the Legions of the Scale!" The
first coldman fell, even as my blade passed through him and the next one
was coming up. "Morgan stood there, he stood against them all. He
stood as the warrior." A spinning block, blade's edge against his knee,
blade's flat against his head, pommel to chest, upstroke and then down.
He fell. "The champion, the hero, the hunter. My blade is bound to
him!" And I realized I was just talking, but my blade traveled on. The
next two were circling me carefully, the final two rushing up to join the
circle. "I am bound to him! To the battle, to the grave, to the hunt! I
commit myself to blade and to soul, and never may the Warrior die!"

And something happened. I knew Morgan was dead, but his power
lived on. This was something I had never been taught in monastery,
never really thought about. Amon was dead, and yet his power was all
around us, in the machines that fed the city, in the Cants of Making
and Unmaking. Alexander lived, and his scions flourished. But
Morgan was dwindling. Because we had bound ourselves to the
memory of his days, and not the glory that had come after, to the battles that were fought in his name, with his power. To the heroes who
had followed in him. I had been serving a dead man, rather than the
living power that had sustained the Cult since his death. And yet I
could feel the power of Morgan welling up around me, though I was
speaking no invocation I had been taught.

"I bind myself to Barnabas," I howled, "hammers flashing, battle
raging. To Tomas, to Isabel." I racked my brains for the history of the
Cult, for the great Fratriarchs and Paladins who had come before me, and
after Morgan. "Clovis on the ramparts of Messit. Pure and High Yelden,

Paladin of the OverArch. Katherine, Kaitlyn. Sweet Anna, Bloody Jennifer. To the Paladins who held the walls of Dalling Gate for a hundred days, and the Paladins who marched against the Rethari, to bring the traitor Amon to justice. May they be forgiven. May we all be forgiven, and justified, and remembered forever. May the Warrior never die!"

And I struck, gods, I struck like lightning and fire and stone and blood. I struck with rage and purity, the light of three hundred years of divine service coursing through my skin and fire arcing from my blade, my face, from the strength of my arms. I blasted that room, those who stood against me, those who didn't get out of the way. That room saw the binding of this new god.

When I stopped, I was alone. The room was a ruin of broken bodies and fragments of arcane and noetic light, glimmering like snowflakes. Barnabas stood at the center of the room, hands still crossed on his hammer, head bowed, eyes closed. He was spattered with the black, cold blood of those monsters.

"What you have done, Eva, cannot be undone." He sighed deeply, hefted his hammer, and walked out of the room. As he went, he turned back to me, just once. "I hope you can carry this through. There is no other choice."

When he was gone I stood in the center of the room and gathered my wits. Energy was thrumming through my body and through my blade. There was a noise at the door, and I turned to it. A whiteshirt, peering into the room. I moved quickly to the corridor. There were a lot of them, and they had bullistics.

"What will you do, to stand against the Warrior?" I growled. Pulses of heaviness rolled off me, pushing against the walls and the floor, pushing against this cadre of gentleman soldiers.

The front row of Healers popped open their shotguns and let the shells clatter to the floor. Behind them, another whiteshirt emptied his clip, and then another. Soon the floor was rattling with unspent cartridges. When the last threat vanished—and I could feel that diminishment in them, could feel the empty weapons all around—when they were defanged, I nodded and stepped back into the room. Malcolm, who had retreated to the other side of the dome, came tottering back into sight. He was hugging the little archive against his chest.

"I'm not sure what to think of that, lady. I wish you hadn't killed my friends, but I don't think I'd have missed this for anything."

"I have freed you. I will free all of the Scholars. You may go."

"You'll probably want to rethink that. We've been under heel for two hundred years. That's an awful powerful grudge to bear." He scratched his brow and nodded. "And we aren't all pleasant old men. Hardly any of us are, actually."

"Be that as it may, I will see the wrong done to you righted. It is only just."

"Just isn't the best course, always. But I'm not going to stop you. Do you mind—"

He stopped and turned to the dome. One of the pressurized doors unsealed, and a cloud of fog vented into the room.

"There was someone in there? You sent some poor damn fool into the mind's archive? What the hell were you thinking!" He dropped the archive and ran to the bottom rung.

"She's an Amonite," I said. "She'll be fine."

"Oh no she won't. Hell, that'll just make it worse. Brothers damn hell, lady, do you just go around pushing all the buttons in a factory?"

The door finally creaked open. Cassandra stepped into view. My heart jumped. She was hurt. Something was wrong with her.

She stood just inside the door to the dome, wavering slightly. The pressure suit hung in tatters, her pale skin steaming in the air. The bloody handprint between her breasts pulsed through the remains of her clothing. She put a hand against the dome to steady herself and ripped the suit's mask from her head. Long black curls tumbled out and around her face. She was hunched over, like she was catching her breath. When she looked up, I could see that her eyes were nothing but ash.

"Cass!" I yelped, and jumped for the ladder. She collapsed forward, skinning her knee on the iron sill of the door before pinwheeling out into open air. I collided with her falling body, and we landed in a heap. I wrenched myself around and cradled her head, then laid her down. She looked up at me with empty eyes, tears that were nothing but soot smearing across her temples.

"Cassandra, what happened?"

"Amon," she whispered. "Amon lives."

CHAPTER SEVENTEEN

"The girl is mad," Malcolm snapped. He stood over the both of us, kneading his hands into his robe. "I don't care how talented an Amonite she was, looking into that archive without the proper training will have broken her."

"It's sure as hell done something to her," I said. I brushed a flake of ash from Cassandra's cheek. She didn't seem to be in any pain, but neither did she seem herself. I was starting to lean toward Malcolm's interpretation of her condition. She was sitting against the curve of the dome, her hands limp by her sides, looking around the room. Even though she didn't have any eyes.

"The archive is . . . How to explain it?" Malcolm sputtered. "That man who was just here, Barnabas. Who was he?"

I turned to the old guy. He did like the tangents. "Fratriarch of Morgan. He died at the hand of the Betrayer. I was supposed to be guarding him at the time."

"Then it wasn't him. Not really. The dead don't walk, or reason, or argue. But Alexander has a trick that lets him capture the essence of a man, and put it back in the body later on."

"The coldmen?"

"Oh, yes. What a name for it. The coldmen. That's exactly what they are. Anyway, to the point, the archive is like that. A bit of Amon's soul was saved. Bottled up, and kept in there. Just the thinking parts, mind you. Not the . . . Betraying things."

I sighed. "None of that matters, you realize. Alexander was really the Betrayer all along. What should we do with the girl?"

"Oh. Oh, I don't know. I'm not a Healer, am I?"

"The bottle doesn't hold the soul," Cassandra said. "And that soul hasn't been bottled, anyway."

"Elephants like penguins, but penguins aren't really elephants," Malcolm answered. "Gibberish."

"I can't imagine why you didn't go into the healing arts, sir. You have such a Healer's manner about you."

"Really? I never thought it would suit me, honestly."

The power of whatever I had invoked was long gone from my body. I was tired. Despite the surety of my words earlier, I really had no idea where I was going from here. Barnabas had been right, just as right as he had been dead. So what if Alexander killed his brothers two hundred years ago? From the looks of things, he was all that was holding the Fraterdom together. Even if I could challenge a god, killing him would get me nothing but an empire of ruin, followed shortly by an invasion from the Rethari. Which is probably what they were after. Probably why they gave us the archive in the first place.

On the other hand. He had killed Morgan, his brother. He had framed Amon, his blood. And he had used the Scholar's research to learn about the divine cycle, and to harness as much of the power as he could hold. He had tortured and oppressed the scions of Amon to perfect whatever process he was using to hold back the cycle. And now that the scions of Morgan had discovered the truth of it, he was hunting us and killing us. Had killed all of us, assuming the mock trials and authentic executions had taken place in the shadow of the Strength. Had killed all of us but one. And what was I supposed to do? Forgive that? Forget that?

So this is what I was left with. Bring down the Fraterdom, or let a murderer of gods off the hook. There was no winning. And when there is no win condition, all you can do is fight, as best you can, as long as you can. May the warrior never die.

Malcolm had his hands around Cassandra's wrists, and was peering at her face. "I think she'll live," he said. "Though her mind . . . Who knows?"

I looked at the girl's face, and wondered what she had done to deserve this. What any of us had done. That she would be so . . . maimed, just as Amon was being justified. Not that it would do the old, dead god much good. But it would have done her some good, I think. Something was boiling in my mind. I looked up at Malcolm.

"His name be praised," I said. "His body held tight."

Malcolm startled, but covered it quickly.

"I'm sorry, what?" he said.

"You said that. You or your friend. In the hallway, when you were going to the other room. We overheard you. It's how we knew where the archive was to be found." I stood up and crowded the old man's space. "What did you mean by that?"

"It's just . . . It's a ritual that we have. A blessing." He blinked rapidly and looked up at me. "May the warrior never die. That sort of thing."

"When I say that, I mean that we are all warriors, those of us in the line of Morgan. That he and I and every blade-wielding, bully-toting fool who has bled out on some gore-smeared battlefield far from home are of one blood. One spirit. That the warrior is all of us, and will always live. So." I poked him in the chest. "When you say that thing about Amon's body—what are you talking about?"

"Nothing, nothing. Forget you heard it."

"You have his body. Don't you? That bull about the archive being a bit of his mind, held in a bottle—"

"Bullshit," Cassandra sang, like a child.

"Bullshit," I repeated. "You have him in there, don't you? Amon, bloody Scholar of the Brothers Immortal, founder of the city of Ash. He really is alive, isn't he?" I stabbed my finger at the dome. "He's right in there!"

"Well," Malcolm said. "Not . . . right . . . in there."

This is the story of Amon's death. After the united forces of Morgan and Alexander punched through the Rethari homelands and dragged the Scholar back to Ash, there was a trial. A brief trial. When the sentence was read, Amon was bound in chain and placed in his famous boat. The boat was set on fire and then pushed out into the bay. The whole city gathered on the docks and watched the bastard burn, cheering as he screamed and cheering even louder when the boat failed and sank, and his screams were cut off by the black, cold water of the lake. Burned and drowned, and at the time we all felt that was too good for him, but it was the sentence Alexander, newly crowned god-king of all the Fraterdom, handed down.

This was before we knew he was innocent. This was before we knew that Alexander was our Betrayer, and all Amon had done was be a little too smart for his brother's comfort. Burned and drowned. But not, apparently, killed.

How do you kill a god? I had been giving this a lot of thought. Admittedly, I only started thinking about it when I learned that perhaps it was Alexander who had put a knife in Morgan's back. And my thoughts mostly involved ways in which I'd like to shoot him in the face. But these were unrealistic and, honestly, insufficient. Morgan had suffered grievous wounds in his life, wounds that would kill the strongest of mortal men. There was something special about the Betrayer's blade that killed the Warrior, probably something to do with the fact that it was held by someone he trusted so deeply, that the hand that pushed the knife into him was that of his brother.

I was no god's sister, and no scion of the Betrayer, either way. I had always assumed that, because Alexander bound the chains and kindled the fire, there was something special about it that could kill a god. But what if it had only been simple flame? Simple water? Surely these things wouldn't kill Amon. So what then? He sank to the bottom of the lake, undying? Eternal?

Apparently. Because, as I strapped on the suit that Malcolm handed me, a lot of what he was saying involved water.

"We don't know what's at the end of it. They monitor the chains, so we don't get near the pool. But the cable should lead the whole way. I've made the appropriate modifications, here," he said, tapping the new helmet, the tank that clipped on my belt, "that should let you make the descent. After that, I'm no help."

"How long have you known?" I asked.

"Since I came here. It's openly known, among the scions who are brought from the Library. It's why we work so hard to please

Alexander. To preserve the body. As long as we're useful to him, he keeps Amon alive."

"And when you're not?"

"Then? I would not want to be in the Library Desolate on that day. I would not want to be wearing the chains when Alexander drives in that knife."

"They'll be coming, soon," I said. We had secured the door, Malcolm applying various invokations to strengthen the steel and seal the portal. But it wouldn't last forever. "He'll discover that his gambit with Barnabas failed, and he'll send someone else."

"Don't worry. I'll keep the girl safe."

"I meant you, old man." I shrugged and fitted the helmet over my head. "The girl can keep herself."

"Of course," he said, patting my shoulder. "You meant me. Nevertheless, I assure you, the girl will be safe."

I looked across the room at her. Sitting against the wall, staring at her hands, and at the bloody print on her chest.

"Okay," I said. Then I unsealed one of the pressure doors, and went inside to the mind of Amon the Scholar.

Just about a foot below the lip of the door, there was a narrow walkway that went all around the inside of the dome. It was stone, and the first of many concentric steps that led down into a pool of water. The water came up to the third step, splashing lightly over it with each swell of the tide. The pool was cold and clear; I could see that the dome was in fact a sphere, and the steps went all the way to the bottom of it. A round opening at the bottom of the sphere, about five feet in diameter, led out into some darker space.

The archive itself sprouted like a flower from that opening. It was a series of thick cables, ranging in size from the width of a pencil to a couple that were as thick as my wrist. On the end of each cable was a cylinder of some translucent material, each sized according to the width of its cable. The cylinders glowed with an inner light, shimmering in the water like bottles of lightning, with the pulse turned way down. Most of the cylinders stayed below the surface, but those that had bobbed to the top shifted and hummed with a constant chiming sound.

"Leave it to the Scholars to make it all so damn complicated," I whispered to myself. I could see damp tracks where Cassandra had emerged from the water just a little while earlier. I put my hand beneath the surface and found it to be warm and . . . sticky. Not really water. Too thick. When I took my hand out it dried quickly, though where the water had splashed against the stone it remained. Water that wasn't really wet. Of course.

I sat by the edge of the pool and then slowly eased my way into it. The suit constricted as it came in contact with the water. The liquid. Whatever you want to call it. What had been comfortable a moment before was now too tight. Half in the water, warmth tingling along my bones and light flashing in my eyes, I pulled the helmet up and sealed it, then cut the bottle on and breathed in a healthy gasp of iron-laced air. *Do it quick*, Malcolm had said. *Do it quick, and don't look back.*

I plunged into the water and understood what he meant, right away. I also understood why Cassandra was out there, babbling to herself. And Amon wasn't even my god.

The water opened to me, opened fully to me, filled me with light and lightning and a glowing warmth unlike any I have ever known. Underwater, the chiming of the cylinders cascaded into more than sound, into pain and madness, and through it all there were voices, a single voice, a thousand times a single voice reciting prayers of madness and mathematics that slid over me without sinking in, drowned me without water, tore me without blood. I was no longer seeing a pool of water, a flower of light and sound, a dome in a building under the city of Ash. I was seeing formulas from the inside of numbers, knowledge from the inside of words. I was seeing the greatest mind our world had ever known, with an eternity of knowledge flowing out in a breath, half a breath, a never-ending sigh of . . .

What saved me was the mud between my own ears. I was an idiot. I mean that in the best possible way, the sort of idiot who can get by and take care of herself, but also the sort of idiot who looked at all this and could just let it slide over her without it sinking in. A duck in the water of genius, you could say. But I saw what had driven Cassandra a little insane. The initial blast had done a number on me, though. I was floating limp in the water, tangled in the cords of the mind, wasting the limited breath in my bottled lung.

I shrugged out of the coils of light and pushed to the bottom of the pool. The stalks of the cables thickened near the opening, and I dragged myself down by pulling on them. As I got close to the opening, the warm, clear water became mixed with patches of darker, colder stuff. Actual water, I thought. Lakewater.

The helmet had a tiny light. I turned it on, and could see that there was a disk, wider than the opening and about a foot below it, that held all of the bundles of cable together. I squeezed between the opening and the disk, and came out into the lake, at the bottom of the city.

I'd been underneath the city before, along the edges. Never this deep. The water here was impenetrably black, swallowing the beam from my lamp in a matter of feet. The underside of the city disappeared in blackness. I couldn't see any of the familiar blinking pathlight from the waterways, or swirling dock indicators or . . . anything. It was just watery night.

Examining the disk with my feeble light and my hands, I could see that it was shaped like a barrel, slightly bowed at the middle and warm to the touch. Metal, but old and pitted with corrosion. A single cable emerged from the bottom, heavy and thick. It descended into the depths of the lake.

Stay close to the cable, he said. It interacts with the suit, and keeps you from experiencing . . . something. Something to do with pressure and depth and blood. I hadn't understood most of that, but the illustration Malcolm had used when he could see that my eyes were glazing over was a tube of meat, filled with blood, and a hundred hammers hitting it from all directions at once. So I was going to stay close to the cable.

The water near the cable was warm and tingled across my skin, or at least it felt that way through the suit. When I put my hand on the cable the bones of my wrist hummed. Didn't like the feel of that, but I liked the idea of hammered meat even less, so I held on while I followed it down into the lake. Every once in a while one of my feet or the tips of my fingers would stray a little too far away from the cable as I swam, and an instant numbing coldness would fill them. That was all the instruction I needed, really. I was not a complete idiot.

It was a long, cold trip. The pressurized bag that held the sword and bully creaked on my back, the water tingled through my skin, the light disappeared, and my eyes swam as the cable and the darkness seemed to be the whole world. Down and down and down, lake without end.

And then there was light.

The structure looked like a madness of junk. It was nestled at the bottom of the lake, burrowed into the stony bed. It was ringed with light, coming from a circle of globes that whirled inside like starry tornadoes. Their glow leaked across the lake floor in murky blueness, picking out details of wrecked buildings and toppled pillars. These were the remains of the Titan city, drowned by the Feyr under this great depth of water.

And crouching at the base of the ruins, the cable's end. I descended toward it, the scale of the place slowly coming into perspective. Enormous. Larger than most of the towers of the city above, flat on its side, rippling with currents of light and shadow. The building shifted in the tricky light, pulsing like a drum soundly struck. I could feel the song of it in my mind, humming through the water. The closer I got, the bigger this place seemed, until I got so close that I could see that the building itself was quite small. Most of what I could see, what I had taken for structure, was just edifice. A web of beams and pillars and buttresses that arced and crossed through the water, supporting each other, building and descending without any central plan. The lights that pulsed through this open framework seemed to emanate from the stony arches themselves, without power or purpose. Beautiful, in the way that madness can be beautiful if seen from afar, like battle, or a storm cloud.

At the center of this openness was a single building. It looked like a pile of iron clamshells, carelessly shucked and stacked on top of each other. Long arcs of light lined the edges of the protruding shells, like rows of windows or the glittering bevel of a blade. When I got a certain distance from this structure, the cable branched and then branched again, a dozen times, each split diminishing the size of the cables until there was nothing but a thin vein-work of cables that led out into the stony arches around the building. Hoping that whatever magic kept me safe when I was close to the cable would transfer to this strange architecture, I let go and drifted toward that building of shells.

Luck held, and there was no more bruising coldness to greet me. I set foot on the sandy bottom of the lake. The grit was shallow, just covering a floor of sharp angles. Uncomfortable to walk on, but great traction. I felt light as air. Too light, in fact. I looked down at the iron lung, but the dials made no sense to me. I was getting featherheaded. That was indication enough for me. I rushed to the central building, kicking up in great long strides that bounced me across the lakebed.

Even dwarfed as it was by the brooding archwork all around, the building was huge. Maybe as large as the Strength, maybe larger. There was no perspective here, and I was running out of air. The swirling globes of light, embedded in the ground, were scattered around the approach to the building. Some of those were as large as buildings, some as small as eyes, all of them peering up out of the sand like crabs scuttling up from the tide. I stopped to put my hand against one, and felt the warmth of it shoot up my arm like a knife. I shivered and drifted away, smiling happily in the light and the lightness of my body. My body. My body was going away.

I bit my tongue and rode the pain toward the shell building. I panicked as I approached. Such a large building, but not built for people. Certainly not for intruders. I was going to starve for air, battering myself against its pebbled sides. I reached a near lip of shell, the band of light nearly as tall as I was, translucent and yellow-white in the murky water. I reached out for it but my hands were turning numb. I watched my fist beat senselessly against the colored wall, scrambling at the lip of it, striking my fingers on the smooth, cold edge of the shell building. There were no doors. There was no entrance.

The building settled, and I felt movement around me. Suddenly I was . . . breathed in. Inhaled. Shooting up, pausing some distance away from the building, then the water swirled and I was going up again. I turned my head and one of the upper decks of the building rushed at me, a black void at its center, flexing as I slithered bonelessly toward it.

A smack of air pressure, the suit spasming against my ribs and legs, and then I was through and flopping up onto a beach of smooth pebbles. I lay there, still gasping for air, my lungs starving, and then I got a tingling hand up to my mask and threw the dogged seal away. A rush of air and I was alive. Alive, but trapped at the bottom of the lake without a breath of air to get me back.

I lay there for a while, breathing, aching as the blood surged back into my hands and feet, my lungs shredded with the effort of inhaling vacuum. I tossed the bottled lung away and listened to it clang loudly off stone. A big room. I forced myself to my knees for a look around.

It was a cancer of a cathedral, drowning at the bottom of the lake. Swirling constellations of naves led to fluted columns, supporting gothic arches that climbed out into midair, themselves supporting nothing. The whole space felt like the inside of a dead thing's shell, chambers whirling into smaller chambers, stairwells that started broad and narrowed into nothing, melting into the wall dozens of feet over the floor. Everything was smooth and dry. Organic.

I stripped off the pressure suit and refitted what remained of my holy vestments. Still on my knees, I rolled out the sealed weapon pack and settled the revolver and articulated sheath properly on my body. I fed the sword into the sheath, checked the load on my bully, then got to my feet and headed down into the convoluted center of the building.

This place wasn't built for traveling through. I felt like I was behind the stage at a carnival show, with half-built sets and stage tricks that stretched away into forever. Stairways ended abruptly. Doors opened into nothing, or wouldn't open at all. Arching paths led to other framework catwalks that led back to the start of the path. More than once I found myself jumping from one tilted floorscape to the next, leaping over chasms that yawned down for hundreds of feet, maybe more. Wicked gusts pulsed through the building, like the startled breathing of a dreaming child. The air smelled of dust, then of fire, then of mold. The air smelled of madness.

I rested on a terrace of pews. It amazed me, how much this place resembled the Grand Library, in the Scholar's prison up above. The same wild logic of architecture and landscape permeated everything, though here the logic slipped into dream as much as reality. And no books, I realized. There were no books here.

The farther I went, the narrower things became. Ceilings dropped claustrophobically low; walls pressed in. The stairways were mere wisps between rooms. The logic of the place was compressing into a single, disjointed note. I felt more and more like I was pressing on into a dollhouse, hunching down to pass through doors, stepping over walls that had never been closed. I was about to invoke Morgan's strength to clear a little space when I passed through the final door, and came to the heart of it all.

The central chamber was enormous and smooth. White walls raised up dozens of feet, a cylinder of arches, each arch leading off to tiny rooms like the one I had just left. It was as if the architecture of the building was an ever-expanding note, and this was the bell that had sounded it. I looked around once, then saw what was at the center of the room.

A boat, tucked into a bank of sand, wooden sides charred and bound with brass. The nose of the boat was down, as if it had plummeted to this spot and burrowed into the earth. Lying in the bottom of the boat, but nearly vertical due to its orientation, was a body, bound in chains.

Amon the Scholar. Still breathing, his lungs rasping like steel on sand. His skin was charred and black, great cracks in the flesh open and raw. Not a tall man, but a god. Water from the lake burbled from his mouth with every breath, slopping messily down onto his bound chest. The chains sang with power, hovering inches over his body and orbiting, seemingly diving into his body and his soul to twist out in a complex knot that strained my eyes. I looked away.

Nathaniel was there, leaning against one of the arches. He held a cigarette cupped in one hand, the iron mask of the Betrayer tucked under his arm like a football. Other than the mask, he was dressed as an Elector of Alexander. Playing his full hand. Hiding nothing.

"I thought he had convinced you," he said, quietly, his voice carrying through the bell-shaped room like an infection. "I thought Barnabas had turned you aside. Thought that you weren't going to come to me at all."

"You won't run from me this time, Betrayer," I said, though my voice shook.

"Oh." He smiled, then stubbed the cigarette out on the wall and dipped his head to place the mask on his face. When he looked up, it was with a gray visage, articulated into the shape of a face, cruel and sharp. "I wouldn't dream of it."

CHAPTER EIGHTEEN

I held my bullistic on him, trained at his heart. He smirked.

"Bullets, Eva Forge? Black powder? Is that how you wish to resolve this?"

"You dead. That's all I care about."

He nodded slowly, looking down at the floor. His hands were clasped behind him.

"I understand that. Expediency." His voice echoed off the high walls of the chamber. Behind me, Amon burbled on his eternal bed, iron creaking through his chest. "The Betrayer follows a similar path, Eva. One knife, rather than two, rather than a legion. One knife in the dark."

"Driven home by a coward," I spat.

"Well. Why fight when you cannot win? Why not fight the battle you are guaranteed to win? Efficiency of force." He was getting close enough to make me nervous. I poked the revolver at him. He smiled. "And still you haven't shot me."

"Whatever you want," I said, and sighted the shot.

"We dream Morgan's death every night, Eva. His last moments. The blood on our knife. The sirens in the camp as the body is found. I close my eyes at night and dream that glory." He stood straight-backed, halfway to the Scholar's coffin, arms still behind his back. Like a schoolteacher, standing in front of a gifted though stubborn student. "Is there anything about that you wanted to know?"

"Nope." And trigger. The thud of gunpowder roared through the chamber, flash and shock shuddering up my arm.

His swing was quick, quick as a bullet. Quicker. He swung his right arm up, holding something loose and silver. Sparks showered the white of his armor, but he kept smiling. I backed away as he slithered forward, cycling hammer and cylinder, taking even breaths, timing the shots to match the quiet of my body, putting round after round on target. And every shot, every booming report, met by that arcing silver that ended in sparks and his smile.

We stood, separated by ten feet, immobile. That dry clicking sound was the hammer landing on an empty chamber. He was in a relaxed stance, swinging his weapon casually across his chest in a figure eight. It looked like a chain, mirror bright and as long as my leg.

"Reload, if you like. I'm in no rush."

I stared at him in empty panic and fought my way through the nerves, through the antiseptic terror of his defense. I flicked my wrist and emptied the shells, clattering, to the floor. Calmly as I could, I pinched bullets out of my belt and seated them in the empty chambers. He watched me with idle amusement.

"If you prefer, we can start again. I can go back to my wall, there. Light a cigarette—"

"What happened to the darkness, Nathaniel? What happened to the expedient blade in the middle of the night?" I slapped the cylinder shut. "Why are you toying with me?"

He bowed ever so slightly. "A final kill, Eva. We have been counting the days, praying for the sheath to be dropped, the cloak pulled aside. There have been many deaths in these two hundred years. In the house of Morgan, in the temple of Amon. Even in the halls of Alexander. But it is drawing to an end. I am savoring the last bite of a marvelous feast."

"The halls of Alexander? You would kill your own?"

"They are not all our own. Very few are, in fact. We kill those who must be killed."

"And Morgan? Why must we all be killed?"

"You come here, and do not know the answer? No, I think you do. Come," he raised a hand. "The feast is getting cold. Let us dine."

I slapped the cylinder closed then holstered the revolver. I was never a lady of the bullet, anyway. Blade was my soul, and blade my heart. I raised my hands, and the sheath fed me my sword. Nathaniel laughed.

"Excellent! I would have it no other way." He stopped spinning his chain and held it limp in front of him. The links of the chain were sickle sharp and barbed, oddly formed to let the chain lay nearly flat when it was still. It swung slowly by his chest like a pendulum. With a quick hand he snapped it to one side. The chain stiffened, the links collapsed together, and suddenly he was holding a sword, full of barbs and gaps and links and sickle-shaped cruelty. Idly, he twirled it in his hand, and it droned as it cut the air.

"What amuses me is how little curiosity you show for your brothers of Morgan. Tomas? Isabel? You have yet to ask if they still live, or if I have named their judgment and declared their—"

I struck, without invocations or rage, without thought. I was mesmerized by the pattern of his blade, its path burned into my mind, its farthest orbit, weakest point, just as I stepped forward and put my blade neatly into his chin. Just nicked it, like an accident you might have while shaving.

He stumbled back, blood coursing down his throat and onto that gloriously bleached doublet. The mask went flying, to crack against Amon's charred boat. It ended up on the floor, spinning like a dropped plate. I barked out a laugh.

"Show your face, coward," I said, and swung in again.

He answered, his face angry, the blade swift as he countered my stroke, countered again, then riposte. I took the stroke on the wide, flat face of my sword and twisted the handle to throw off his weight. I lunged again. He back-stepped from the attack, and collected himself.

"Not talking so much now, eh?"

"Why do you attack without your invocations, Eva Forge?" he chided. "Has Morgan left you? Have you lost your faith in the old Warrior?"

"I don't need the rites to put down a dog. Even Alexander's dog."

He settled his face, assumed a stance of defense, and swung the chain-sword in a close dance. That drone hummed off the high ceiling and drowned out Amon's unnatural chorus.

"You seek to unsettle me. You think that because we fight in shadows, we do not know how to fight. You demand proof." He skittered forward in a series of quick half-steps, his balance always at center. "Proof you shall have."

Proof I had. I didn't think that, of course. I knew damn well they could fight. Elias had put up a fight. I had crossed blades with Nathaniel's boys over Simeon's body. He could fight. I just didn't want to waste my noetics this early on. Reserves for the long battle. If he was going to gloat, then I was willing to stretch it out.

I did just enough to keep him away, and he did just enough to keep me moving. We retreated across the chamber in a slow circle, blades dancing through sparks, the room quiet except for the metal strike and the drone of his blade, the scratch of grit under our feet as we moved. One circuit, and I had seen enough.

"Barnabas, never dead, son of hammers, son of light," I incanted, and the room began to hum with power. "Elias, green life and dark soil, warrior of wood and woad, blood feeding the life of us all. Isabel, ink-stained and careful shot." As I spoke the timber of our blades changed, the drone muting to be replaced by the high song of my sword. The sparks began to mix with a clinging fog that trailed my swings. The air cracked. My voice snapped like a flag in a hurricane. "Heridas, who stood at Chelsey Gate against the Paupers' Tyrant, dead for a day and still fighting. Bloody Jennifer, two swords against the night, never to see the dawn!"

The tide shifted, and we balanced against each other, blade for blade, stroke for stroke, countering each counter and stepping past each heart strike.

"What sort of invokation is that, Paladin? I know the names of your dead."

"The dead and the living," I spat. "Simeon, barrels hot, chamber dry, his eyes the eyes of heaven, his bully the hammer of gods. May the warrior never die!" And the chamber echoed with my voice, the warrior never die, never die . . . "Jeremiah Scourge, last of the living shield-brethren of dying Morgan, carrying the flashing steel into the Straits of Armice, unyielding as the Rethari swarmed. The massacre at Middling Hall, the charge of Maltis, the siege of Or'bahar. The hundred years of the warrior, and a hundred more, and a hundred more!" I bullied into him, blade swinging wildly, fire in my eyes and in my hands, wicking from my sword as I struck again and again. "A hundred years forever, and may the warrior never die!"

He was in earnest now, falling back, sweat and blood dripping down his face and neck. Reckless with his blade, he left openings that I widened, revealed weaknesses that I pursued. He fell back, and I advanced, the warrior in me rising like the sun.

"I bind myself to the legions of the blade, to my brothers of sword and sisters of bullet. To the thousand years of Morgan, those who fell in his service, and those who fell in his defense. I bind myself to the battle unending, the hunt eternal." I spat the words, my voice rising into a crescendo of mad fury. "To the living sons of the warrior, and to the dead." And with each oath I struck, sword hammering against his defenses in glory and light. "To the dead! To the dead of Morgan! The dead of Morgan! Morgan!"

I threw him back and blood spilled out from his chest. He gasped and brought his sword around to defend. I hammered it aside and drew blood again. He was on his knees in the presence of the warrior god. I howled and rushed in.

The blade came from nowhere. From the shadows. It took me in the back, sliding smoothly between doublet and ribs, hot metal straight through me, and when it left there was nothing to fill that void but cold. I stumbled. I fell.

Nathaniel dragged himself to his feet, supporting his weight on the sword of chain. His servant ghosted behind me, shaking blood from his weapon and muttering invokations. I was on one knee, trying to get my breath against the pressure of the blood that was filling my mouth.

"The dead of Morgan," he said, and spat. "Morgan, warrior of the field. Champion of the people. Damned butcher." He raised his sword. "Hail to Morgan, the Brother Betrayed. Long may he die."

I twisted and swung my sword behind me, rising on one foot, just enough strength to drive the sword into the other ghost's belly, punch it in deep. The air smelled like piss and blood. I drew the sword out and up, rasping the blade against his ribs before exiting the steaming corpse just below the throat. He gurgled, already dead, slumped to the side. My return strike blocked Nathaniel's startled swing, corrected, then two quick punches that put the sharp base of the blade into his thigh, then his belly. We fell apart, leaving a pool of spilled life between us.

"The dead of Morgan," I burbled. He stared at me, face pale as his cloak, lips quivering. I was on my knees, gasping, grating my teeth.

Nathaniel leapt to his feet, hand on his opened guts, and invoked something short and arcane. Two quick steps and he was in the air, off the wall and higher up, disappearing into one of the archways. He left his sword and mask behind.

I knelt before Amon, my life spilling out into my lap, the chamber filled with the sound of the Betrayer's footsteps as he ran away, down the hundred hallways that led out of this place. Echoes of his feet, and my failing heart.

You come here, and do not know the answer? No, I think you do. His words ran through my mind as I lay before the undying Scholar god. *I think you do.* I did. Barnabas cutting the chain, the ease with which Cassandra's shackles fell away at the touch of my blade. The chains on the shoulders of the Librarians Desolate, and the chains twisting through their god. Before me. I knew.

The power of the soul-bonds came from this body, these chains. No Amonite had been able to remove his own chains, not since the Healer had taken possession of the Library Desolate. There must have been a ritual, with Amon as the sacrifice, and the chains as the reward. As long as these chains held Amon, the noetic chains in the city above would hold his scions. That was how these sorts of invokations worked.

But for every ritual, there had to be a price. An out. Chains had to have a key. And what better key than the Cult who hated Amon most? Only a scion of Morgan can free a Scholar. Barnabas knew, as the Fratriarch. Knew that when he laid his knife against Cassandra's chains, they would melt away. And Alexander must know, because he was the one who bound the rite to begin with.

And when Alexander learned that some secret of the Betrayal, some clue as to the assassin's true name, had fallen into the hands of the Cult of Morgan? What panic that must have caused. What fear. What desperation. Desperation enough to kidnap his brother's Living Sword, torture him, murder him. And when he learned that the archive had escaped his grasp, in the hands of the last Paladin and her Scholar companion . . .

That was the joke of it. Our greatest enemy had been our only ally. Every little thing Alexander did to undercut the Cult of Morgan during these past centuries—the civilian army, the protection of the Amonites, the factories that churned out rifles and bombs and fighting machines that made our glorious charges, our swords and our martial skill . . . made those things we held most holy irrelevant on the battle-field. I had always mistrusted Alexander, because I felt he humored us, coddled us. In fact, he had smothered us, one strength at a time, one recruit at a time. Until the time came when there weren't enough of us to oppose him. And then he struck. Declared us apostate, whipped up the populace against us, took our Elders captive and put them on trial.

It didn't matter that I knew the truth of it. No one would believe me. No one would trust a scion of the Warrior again, especially not in opposition to Alexander. The godking.

I stood, my chest rearranging itself, the blood flowing fresh down my legs and arms. *Such a damn mess, Eva. You're just all screwed up. You can't go to the city now, and tell them all about the lies of Alexander and the true betrayal.* It was up to someone else, now. It would have to be the Amonites who told the truth.

All I could do was let them go.

I raised my sword and stepped to the coffin. No invocation, no glory of the fallen church of the Warrior. Nothing but a ritual being broken. I brought the blade down, and it struck deep into the helix of chains that twisted around the Scholar's charred body. Metal parted like silk, the pattern of its orbit disrupted. I looped several bands of it around my sword, drew tight the tension of bonds, and then pulled back. The full length of the blade rasped through the metal and then they let go of their ancient station, with a sigh, with a clatter. The chains fell to the floor.

I stumbled back, weakened by blood loss and off balance from the blade. What would Barnabas think of his student, barely able to hold her weapon over her head? As if I were a child. As if I were weak. I went to one knee, holding myself up with the sword, tip biting deep into the pebbled floor.

Amon opened his eyes and looked at me.

"I will need champions," he said. His voice sounded like tombs speaking.

"I am bound to Morgan," I answered feebly.

"Morgan is dead," he said, then stood. His skin creaked like unkempt leather. He stood before me in the mutilation of his nakedness, and held a hand out to me. "And I am not. Stand as my champion."

"I am bound." I looked up at him, faint in head, weak of heart. "But I will fight for you, in what time I have left."

"That is enough." He breathed in deeply, then opened his mouth and let out a long, even breath that smelled of spiced meat and hot stones. The pebbled floor around my knees flaked and then rose. The shards drove into my flesh, sealing the wounds and patching the damage, but at such a cost. I jumped to my feet, panting and mewling in pain. The sword spun from my hands. When the pain stopped I was filled with a heavy coldness that touched my bones and weighed me down. Again I fell to my knees, my hands, gasping for air.

"You have paid the price of Amon," he said. "If only in part. As for my champion, I will find another. Another . . ."

He was still for a moment, then cocked his head to the ceiling.

"Or another will find me. Yes." Arms out, palms up. "A Champion of Amon."

The room shivered, but that might have been all the new rock in my gut. I was having trouble focusing. He inhaled deeply several more times, his breath curling out in oily wisps. Eyes closed, and then he turned to me. "I thought you were her, but you are not. The girl who found me, who touched my mind. Her spirit is in turmoil, but I have made repairs. It is done. Stand, let us rise to settle our scores."

"You're damned crazy," I spat.

"I have been bound in a tomb of my own making, held in perpetual sacrifice to the glory of my murderer." He set his feet in the center of the chamber and raised his arms. "Perhaps madness is the price of that. Rise!"

I didn't get the chance. The air shimmered around him, and a pulse of energy washed out from his lungs and pushed through the building. Everything shifted, and a sky of dust shook loose from the walls to hang in the air. The world groaned at our waking. The room pitched, and then we tore free.

The whole building was rising, rising, ripped from the bottom of the lake and rising to the city above. I looked at Amon and saw perfect calm there, perfect calculation. Perfect rage.

What had I done?

It began as a tide. The dark waters that slapped against the docks on the inner shore of Ash swelled against the pylons. Fishermen and watch captains noted the difference, and peered out into the artificial bay. That swelling became a tumult, and then water was rushing over the side of the city in a white-capped rush. Boats that were near the shore beached against cobbled streets. The new tide cracked open the glass shells of the closest buildings, washing through them in a wave of shattered windows and furniture and screaming citizens. Sirens sounded all across the waterfront, a droning wail that mingled with terror and shock and breaking glass. Deep in the city the domestic canals rushed their banks. The current flashed against bridges and walkways in a furious white foam.

At the center of the bay, a dome of dark water was rising, the disturbance sloughing off new currents. In a fury of foam and displaced depths, something white and massive broke the surface and rose, rose, burst from the lake and then settled into it. It trailed tendrils like netting, like a great fish torn free from a fisher's snare. It was a complicated object, like a deck of shells that had been poorly shuffled.

As the fishermen and the watch captains and ordinary citizens of Ash stared, the huddled structure began to shift and blossom. The overlapping leaves slid together, water still cascading off their grooved surfaces, some of them diving back into the lake as they shifted aside, others bursting from the water in a rainbow-laced spray.

The new island opened at the top like a flower opening to the sun. It was full of light. The inner workings of the island splintered apart, tumbling into the water like a discarded carapace. From the distance of the city, it looked like whole buildings were being turned inside out and disgorged into the lake. Another wave rose up to crash against the city.

From the new opening rose a figure. Telescopes and gunsights snapped to him all along the shore. Black, mostly naked, only the barest armor covering him and that looked to be made of charred wood. On his back he wore a wide, flat disk that silhouetted his upper body. The disk was of beaten brass, slightly elongated, and had some sort of aura filtering along its edge, like a blade that had been heated in the forge, distorting the air.

He rose above the building, above the lake, above the heights of the city. Arms spread wide, legs extended like a swimmer, he rose and the city watched him. Afraid. Unsure. Even the sirens quieted as their attendants left their stations to watch the spectacle.

He held out a hand and the towers screamed. Glass vibrated and steel hummed throughout the city in a wave. It passed through people, through stone, through water and steel. Finally, it rested on the Spear of the Brothers, tightening until the whole structure sang like a tuning fork. Something shifted inside the shining white marble tower, then a small section of the white stone crumbled like snow. An object flew out of the tower and smashed into a nearby building, raking along the glass walls and furrowing a trail of shattered windows. The object flew straight and true, breaking anything that stood before it, cracking walls and bending pillars with its passage. With a hammer's blow it struck a tall glass building on the water's edge, cratering the facade, burrowing through floors and stairwells before erupting from the other side in a shower of glass and noise. It flew to the figure and snapped into his hand, glowing with the might of its passage.

He raised it over his head like a benediction. The Spear of Amon, in the hand of Amon. The Scholar had taken up his weapon. War was upon us.

I clambered from the water, gasping and tired. I rode some of the detritus out when the building opened up, was lucky enough to find something wooden, and the wave brought me home. Lucky enough for that.

I sat on the shoreline, trembling, eyes wide at the ravaged coast. Waterfalls coursed out of broken windows; the harbor was choked with shattered furniture and churning pedigears and bodies. Lots of bodies. The sirens started up again as Amon raised his spear and pointed it across the city. Far away I heard stone shattering, and a pillar of debris towered between the buildings. The Spear of the Brothers, my guess.

From the wreckage of his throne, Alexander ascended. He rose into the air, white as the full moon, halberd in hand, half-shield on his back. And now he wore the articulated mask of the Betrayer. Alexander the Healer, Alexander the Betrayer, Alexander the godking of Ash.

The city stopped, the sirens and the pedigears and the monotrain. The impellors slowed and then halted. The gods of man faced each other across the landscape of the city of Ash, and we all stopped.

"Godsdamn," I whispered, easing my blade from its waterproof bag. "Gods and Brothers be damned."

Above me, the sky began to turn.

CHAPTER NINETEEN

The war between the Brothers Immortal was a thing seen and yet unseen, felt and yet unfelt. They hung above the city like rogue stars, one charred, one shining, hovering in poses of martial meditation. Around them the sky boiled and churned. In the city it felt like bad weather in a clear sky. Like everything was wrong with the world.

Massive pressure systems lumbered through the streets, causing windows to creak and eardrums to pop. Just as suddenly the air would vacate this alley or that building. People stumbled into the open, gasping for breath, blood leaking from their ears. The sky turned dark one second, then flared into brilliant whiteness the next. The air groaned with the passing of unseen energies.

It was worse for me, for all the scions of our erstwhile gods. Nausea swept through me, crippling weakness, then frenetic energy bordering on the psychotic. I was dizzy, I was high, I was tired, and I was scared. I focused on the ground in front of me, on each faltering step, on the sword in my hands. Around me the city was a hash of gunshots and oily smoke and breaking glass. The world was going mad.

The maddest part was around the Library Desolate. These were people who had voluntarily submitted to imprisonment, in order to serve the god they loved. And now they were free, and their god wasn't dead after all. Only he was clearly mad, and that madness was rippling through the community like a virus. Meanwhile, the citizens of Ash, who had grown up being taught that Amon was the darkest villain mankind had ever spawned, were just coming to grips with seeing the Scholar rise from the lake like an eclipsed moon. That his rising had killed hundreds of people, ruined the shoreline, and was now the subject of an arcane war that, simply, none of us could understand wasn't helping the public mood. Crowds had gathered at the Library, to be met by the newly freed Amonites. A thin band of whiteshirts stood between them, not sure who they were supposed to be holding back. My approach disrupted things even more.

"Paladin! Paladin of Morgan! Save us!" some of them shouted, from all three groups. Save them from the madness of their god, or the crowd, or their duty? I wasn't sure. And I was in no position to do any of it, anyway.

Others among them remembered the lies of Nathaniel, of the trials that had just been conducted, the judgments that had been handed down. Some of these same citizens might have stood in the shadow of the Strength, cheering while it burned.

My mind was in turmoil. I pushed my way to the whiteshirts, the hands of the crowd on me equal parts acclamation and condemnation. It was a gauntlet. By the time I reached the Alexian lines, I was twitching with restrained violence. Someone had to take control.

"Your god has betrayed you," I said to the frightened line of soldiers. "Amon did not kill Morgan. It was Alexander."

Okay, that probably wasn't the best thing to say, given the situation. Probably not a situation on earth where that would have been the right thing to say. But I was never a leader of men. More like a leader of the charge, and that's what this was. A rush to enlightenment, storming the walls of an ancient betrayal.

"What the hell are you talking about?" one of them shouted. We were all shouting, just to be heard over the crowd. Crowd. Riot, more like.

"Look up, look at your god." I pointed at the distant figure of Alexander, hovering among novas of power. "Tell me what you see!"

They peered up, squinting at the light. Finally one of them raised a set of binoculars to his eyes.

"He's wearing a mask," the man reported. They looked back at me.

"The articulated mask of the Betrayer," I said. "The fight is too dire, his brother is returned. He has to play all his cards, bring all of his aspects into play."

"To hell with you, lady. I swore to Alexander on my name, and with Alexander I'll stay," one of them said.

I nodded. "Fairly said, but consider: I am the last of the scions of Morgan. What reason would I have to stand with my god's betrayer?"

"Your god is dead. What reason do you have to stand with him?"

"She's a lady of conviction, fellows," said another in the crowd, and I turned to him. Owen, face smeared with ash, a bandage across his forehead. "You broke my skull, Eva."

"The cost of trusting me," I said.

"Yeah. But that up there? That's not the god I swore my name to."

"Then help me stop him."

He laughed and shrugged. "Of course. What else would I do with my time? But what are we supposed to do here?"

I looked around at the seething mobs on both sides of us. Even among the whiteshirts there were those who would knife me before they would follow me. Best to just defuse and get out. I went to the nearest Amonite.

"Who leads you?" I asked.

"Amon, risen again, Scholar and Saint!" he shrieked. I took his collar in my fist and slapped him once.

"Among these people here, who leads you?"

The Scholar looked at me numbly, so I dropped him and went to the next.

"Who leads you?"

"That is my calling," said someone deep in the crowd. He fought his way forward. An old man, face lined with ash and tears of joy. He looked calm, though. Not at all mad. "What do you need, sister of our brother?"

"You're never going to get out this way. These people will kill you. Go back inside, and wait. Let the Alexians guard you."

"Did that work for you, Morganite?"

"Well—"

"Then do not ask the same of us. We have been falsely bound for too long. The Library is being gathered and removed."

"Agreed. But if you come out this way, there's just going to be a lot of burned books and dead Scholars." I strained my neck to see around the crowds, then looked back at the old man. "There has to be another way out. The lake?"

"The lake," he said, considering. Eventually he nodded. "I think something can be done with the lake."

"Great. Everyone inside."

And they went. Peacefully, quietly, calmly. The whiteshirts followed them in and sealed the door. I stayed outside. When I turned to go, Owen was waiting.

"I said, you broke my skull."

"I'm sorry. Honestly I am. But now isn't the time for this."

He sighed, tore the icon of Alexander from his breast, and tossed it to the ground. Then he unhitched his shotgun.

"What is now the time for?"

"Follow me," I said, then left. He followed.

We found our way back to the Spear of the Brothers. Its remnants, at least. Just as I had feared, the central tower had turned to chalky powder and collapsed. There were bodies. I found a door, then a stairwell, then more doors. I got out from under that sky of madness and felt a little better. Even Owen seemed to be relieved to be out of the gaze of his former god.

The architecture had been shuffled, levels misaligned, doors hanging open and corridors flooded. I didn't think I would find my way back to Cassandra. Turned out not to be half as difficult as I was expecting.

Some kind of feedback had found its way to the chamber with the pressurized dome, where I'd left Cassandra and that cranky old Amonite Malcolm. The dome itself was cracked like an egg, steaming with frost and an aura of flickering light. The rest of the floor was leveled. Cassandra and Malcolm stood by the ruin of the dome, looking up at it. Cassandra was . . . changed.

She turned to me when Owen and I slid down a bit of wrecked floor and into the chamber. She wore little armor: pauldrons and a half-breast, gauntlets, armor for her hips and pelvis. Boots. She wore nothing else. Her nakedness reminded me uncomfortably of Amon, hovering above the city. The armor was metal, but charred. And the bloody handprint on her chest leaked through the metal, for all the world looking like it had soaked through the armor from her skin. When she turned to me, I saw that she was blindfolded. Smears of ash showed on her cheeks.

"You . . ." I started.

"I have accepted what you turned away, Eva," she said. Her voice was unchanged, only sad. "I am the Champion of Amon."

I shuddered at the sound of her voice. Malcolm looked between us, then at Owen, then shrugged.

"What happened here?" Owen asked.

"Place blew up," Malcolm said. "She started babbling, then she stopped, then the place blew up. She shielded me. When the smoke cleared, she looked like that. So." He clapped his hands and turned to me. "What's happening outside?"

"It's complicated," I answered.

"I figured." He looked back at the dome, then fished something out of his robe and threw it to the ground. The remnants of his soul-chains. "Complicated is good, sometimes."

"In this case, complicated will end up destroying the city," I said. "Those two are going to keep at it until one of them is dead. And they're too evenly matched for it to be a clean fight. The city won't survive."

"None of us will, in the grand sense," Malcolm said quietly. "Alexander was barely holding on to the power. And that was with the people behind him. He's played his hand now, revealed himself as the Betrayer. Tell me." He turned to us. "Do you think the city will worship Alexander the Betrayer?"

"No more than they'll worship Amon the Mad," Owen snapped.

"Some of us will," Cassandra said.

I nodded. "There will be split loyalties. And neither will let the other live, either way." I walked up to Malcolm. "What's that thing called? The damned holy battery?"

"The Ruin," he said. "They're both tapping it now. Even if it only held the power Alexander has gathered in the last two hundred years, this battle could last for weeks."

"But you said it goes back farther than that. Back to when the Titans fell."

"Aye. Don't worry. The energies will drive them mad long before then."

"Or they'll kill each other," I said.

The building shook, chunks of ceiling and tile clattering down into the chamber.

Malcolm nodded. "That does seem the more likely conclusion."

"What if we destroyed it?" I asked.

He turned to me, a quizzical look in his eyes. "Destroy it? What good would that do?"

"Drain them of their power. At least the stored stuff. I don't know, maybe it would weaken them enough to put them on their heels."

"Or it could destroy the city. It's a boiler, Eva. You don't just punch a hole in it."

"There are pressure valves, though. The impellors. That's what Amon was getting at, when he was working with the Feyr." I made a connection in my head. "It's what the Chanters were looking at, too. They were working with the Feyr, building something. They must have been figuring something out about the Ruin, and Alexander didn't like it."

"That's why he sent his little dead army, to crack them open?" Owen asked. "And we've been worshipping this guy?"

"There are valves. But emptying the Ruin through them . . ." Malcolm shook his head. "I don't know what would happen."

"Will it be something better than the city getting destroyed by those two bastards, throwing the entire Fraterdom into chaos?"

He bent his head to one side and thought, steepling his fingers against his lips.

"I can't guarantee that it will be."

"Close enough for me," I said. "Show us where these valves for the Ruin are."

"Hold," Cassandra said. She was standing between us and what remained of the door. "I cannot assist you in this. You act against Amon."

"But I act in his interest," I said, turning straight to her and clasping my hands across my sword. "If Alexander doesn't kill him in this fight, he'll be so badly wounded that he won't be able to hold on to the power of the Ruin anyway. Better to let it out now than have it tear free later."

She stared at me, hands clenched into a fist between her breasts, legs set to receive a charge. No other movement.

"We don't have time for this, girl." I walked up to her. "Are you going to stop me from doing this?"

Several breaths. She shook her head.

"Then move or follow. We're going."

And we went. When the room was empty she touched a finger to the bloody handprint on her breast, then smeared it against her forehead. But she followed us.

What the Feyr had told me of the Ruin was minimal. An ancient place. An atrocity lodged in the soul of their people, and then passed on to us. That it could be used to prevent the cycle of gods was a by-product, and one that the Feyr had never tapped. Leave it to man. Leave it to Alexander.

It did explain why we built our city on a lake, though. The Ruin itself did not float, nor did it sink. It simply was where it was, and the city was built up around it. The Elemental of the Feyr had described it like a sore, burned into reality. It looked like a rock, though.

Malcolm led us through the wreckage of the Spear and out. The sky resembled a white-water rapids now, conflicting currents rushing together and churning in near invisible turmoil. Whatever madness drifted down into the city was turning Ash into wreckage as well. Buildings burned, sirens called, but no one was answering them.

"I would take the 'train," Malcolm said, "but I'm pretty sure they're not running on schedule today."

"Smartass," I answered. Turned to Owen. "That wagon of yours available?"

He shook his head. "Do you honestly think the communications rig is going to work in this mess? And if it did, do you think anyone would answer?"

"Mm. Well. I guess we're walking."

Not a long walk, but a difficult one. Streets were flooded or had fallen through, replaced with sudden lakes and rivers that coursed through the infrastructure. Usually stable boulevards tilted, and buildings creaked dangerously. Lots of glass, lots of debris. Lots of bodies, and most of them dead at the hands of other citizens.

What had I done? What cost was I asking the rest of the city to pay?

"You've done nothing that should not have been done," Cassandra answered, though I'd kept my mouth shut. She looked at me with those blindfolded eyes. "These things have unfolded in a way that could not be expected."

"Are you going to be creepy like that forever now? Because if you are, I'm not sure we can still be friends."

"Maybe after the apocalypse I'll feel a little more chipper," she answered.

"Thank gods," I said.

What should have been five minutes by foot took us half an hour, and we were all on edge by the time we got where we were going. I'm not sure I could have found the place without Malcolm. As it was we kept getting lost, doubling back, finding new roads that hadn't been ruined.

The building itself was uninteresting. Long and flat-sided, cut out of granite, no windows. A sign on the front declared it to be part of the power grid.

"That supposed to be funny?" I asked.

"We don't get a lot of opportunity for levity in the Library Desolate," he answered. "Is it funny?"

I didn't answer. We went inside, with the help of Malcolm's passkey and a complete lack of guards.

"You'd think these guards would have stuck, at least," I said. "Alexander's true nature couldn't have been much of a surprise to them."

They had stuck, though, and died in their service. When we found them, they were stuffed into a closet. Dead, not hiding. Butchered. I immediately thought of the groups of coldmen Owen and I had found around the city. Similar slash wounds, similar savagery. We exchanged a look.

The foyer of the building led to a freight elevator. No stairs. We all got in, locked up, and began the descent. Quiet ride down, but when the doors opened we were all a little open-jawed.

The Ruin of Ash was a wide, flat stone, big as a hockey field, glossy black and pitted. It looked a lot like the Feyr artifacts we had seen, only huge. It radiated energy, like a hot furnace about to blow. It was nestled into a bowl-shaped room. The room was lined with drumlike receivers, gathering and emitting some invisible force. Just standing in the doorway was like being deaf in the loudest room you've ever heard.

"This is it," I gasped. Malcolm nodded, but kept his head down. "What do we do?"

"Nothing," said a voice from the corner. The two men, their tattooed eyes, their bulky robes. They walked toward us like monks, hands clasped at their waists, sleeves hiding their fists.

"Who are you people?" I said as I led my little contingent out of the elevator. "I mean, I've appreciated your help, but what's your part in all this?"

"This is our point," he said, nodding to the Ruin behind him. "And we have appreciated your help as well, Eva Forge."

"What the hell is that supposed to mean?"

The nearer one shrugged and tore out of his robe. Not a man at all, and not wearing armor. He was armor. Bulky chest and backward-bending knees, arms like a giant's. And the tattoos around his eyes? Scales, just like the rest of him. His mouth yawned with teeth, and was as wide as both my hands together. He wore shielded gauntlets, bound to sharp punch daggers. He smiled at me with gods so many teeth.

Rethari.

"Dramatic, my brother," the other one said, calmly drawing back his robe and then rolling up his sleeves to reveal similar weapons. "Can't we keep our dignity?"

"You sent the artifact, didn't you? To get us here, to this point? To reveal the betrayal of Alexander and drive us to war against ourselves?"

"Not at all. We had no idea Amon still lived. That was just icing. All we wanted to do was drive the scions of Morgan away from the godking. This . . ." He raised his hands and nodded. "This is just serendipity."

"We're here to destroy that thing," I said. "And we're really not going to let you stand in our way."

"What luck. We're here to destroy it, too. Just . . ." And he cocked his head to the sky. "Not yet."

This gave me pause. I didn't like that our paths aligned. I looked to Malcolm, but he just shrugged. Cassandra stepped forward.

"You mean to free the power entombed in the Ruin, to force the turning of the cycle and ascend your gods. I will stop you," she said.

"Stop us from doing what, little girl? You want to destroy the Ruin? Fine." The one still wearing a robe held out his hand. It contained a tiny wheel and chain. "Here is the plunger. We've already set the charges. We will give this to you. We'll even pull the trigger, so that you might escape and live."

"They won't blow it yet," Malcolm said. "Not until Alexander and Amon kill each other."

"Why?" I asked. "Why wait until then?"

"The power would release from the gods, but the cycle would not turn. Not immediately. Maybe a month, maybe a year, but it would stay in the mantle of mankind. New gods would arise."

"Not if you blow it up," Cassandra said. "That kind of release would overwhelm the city, no matter when you do it." She looked at me. "It might be enough to kill the Brothers, and leave the rest of us mad with divinity."

"Until the cycle turned," Malcolm said. "Which we would have no mind to prevent."

"So," the Rethari said, gripping the plunger. "We seem to be in something of a draw. If you'd all please step back . . ."

The ghost appeared from the direction of the Ruin, rushing up the bowl of the room without making a sound. He started as little more than a fog, quickly solidifying as he came. Feet away from the Rethari he struck. I heard the blade go into meat, once, twice, and then a tearing slash that buckled the giant creature's back. Those tattooed eyes bulged, and then he tumbled to the floor.

His companion howled and went to slash at the assassin. I drew iron and put him down before he could even take a step.

Nathaniel knelt behind the fallen Rethari, blood on his blade and mouth. He looked up at me, chest heaving, skin white, the wound I had given him still oozing into his shirt. Maybe not so much of a Healer, after all.

"I could not let that happen," he said. His voice was wet with blood. "Not to Alexander. All that I do, I do for him."

"I understand," I said. "Thank you."

"So. Redemption at last, Eva Forge?"

"Let's not be idiots, Nate."

I raised the bully and put lead in his eye. His skull pulped around the bullet's path, bright crimson on his white pauldrons. He tumbled back and was still. In the quiet that followed, I walked over to the Rethari detonation device and crushed it under my foot. When I turned around they were all staring at me.

"I'm not much of a forgiver," I said. "Now show me how to vent this place."

The sky was a nightmare of light and current and arcane shadow. The city of Ash was cast in stark and unnatural darkness. The surface of the lake rippled with the impact of unseen forces, like a giant rainstorm. A thunderhead of ash and fury was growing over the battlefield, and the two combatants faced one another in utter silence and calm.

With a roaring creak, the great circular tracks of the monotrains shuddered and strained into life. Behind their shrouding towers, the impellors sparked. Glowed with arcane power. Began to move. The trains inched forward on their tracks, slowly speeding up as the cycle of the impellors increased, each pass moving the trains forward a little quicker, each pass coming sooner and with more power. More strength. Strength unrestrained. Something was wrong.

Thankfully, no one was on any of the trains. A small grace, on a day of great tragedy, with more tragedy still to come. The trains turned and turned, howling around their tracks. The force of the impellors exceeded all that the tracks had been designed to withstand, and kept going. Sparks showered down from the iron wheels, the metal of track and train starting to glow as they continued to accelerate. All across the city people stopped their rioting and their persecution and turned to look at the howling iron horses. The smart ones ran.

When the tracks failed it was with a great sigh of straining metal and broken tolerances. In many places, freed Amonites ran to the failing system and tried to bolster them, but this was beyond their ken. Many died, only hours into the dawn of their newly liberated Cult.

Many ordinary citizens died as well, for standing too close to faltering tracks, or not realizing what was happening and trying to get close enough to see.

In most cases the trains just toppled from their tracks, skidding through towers and streets and across cobbled paths before burying themselves into a canal or building. Hot metal charred the ground as they rolled, flailing around like chain shot.

On the impellors roared, faster and faster, their power drums glowing to sun's brilliance as they spun. Their force peeled open the towers that hid them, shattering their skin like a struck bell. Feyr boiled up from their hidden places, screaming in mad ecstasy, clawing at their ears. The impellors roared, and soon the towers that had been built taller than the tracks were crumbling. Walls boomed, windows popped, the steel framework splintering like china. The city fell, tower by tower, block by block. Only the ancient buildings stood, those that had been built lower than the tracks. Even those structures sustained damage as the higher places collapsed on them in a cloud of glass and steel.

The impellors howled like sirens, like juggernauts, like the horns at the end of the world, calling damnation down from heaven. The horns sounded, and Ash fell into ruin.

Above us, the sky wrinkled and flexed. The two gods of man screamed along with the ruining of their Fraterdom, and when the last gasp had left them, the world was silent. They fell to earth like broken angels, to crater into the city. The storm broke, the sky cleared, and the world breathed anew.

CHAPTER TWENTY

The crater was twenty feet across, lip to smoldering lip. What had once been a smooth stone parkway was now fragmented like cracked pottery. The heat of Amon's entry had fused the stone as soon as it was shattered. He lay at the bottom, venting arcane steam from the fissures in his skin.

We pushed through the silent crowd that had gathered. Cassandra ran gracefully down the incline and knelt at the side of her god. I waited up top. The crowd began to mutter.

I heard a lot about Amon the Betrayer, about how he was dead and was back. To finish the job he had started, some said. Others, that he had allied with the scions of Morgan to put down the true godking. Others claimed he was someone else, some new god. Some devil, or a sign from the next ascendant race. Some knelt right there and swore allegiance to this unnamed deity. Some called for a lynching. Some stayed quiet, too scared or confused to do anything but stare.

When Cassandra looked up at me, the crowd stiffened. I hopped down and made my way to the girl.

"They'll kill him," she whispered.

"He might have killed himself," I answered, my eyes up on the crowd around us. "I think we're in a delicate place here, girl."

"He did what was natural. He did what you would have done, in his place."

"Aye. Doesn't make it right."

"Paladin," one man called down to us. His robe was singed, and there was a nasty scar along one eye. "Who is this new god, that we may name him?"

"Amon, Brother of Morgan and Alexander," I answered. "The Healer bound him. Morgan has released him."

"Why would you release the Betrayer?" he asked. Those who had knelt looked at me expectantly. I held a new religion in my hands. I wasn't sure what to do with it, whether to crush it or let it grow, set it free to find its own way. Nurture it. Cassandra tugged on my hand, pulling herself up. She was still so light. She faced the crowd with her blinded eyes and the dripping blood on her breast, the pale skin of her torso and the charred metal covering her shoulders.

"Amon was betrayed, as was Morgan. Alexander acted against them, to gain the throne," she said in a clear, loud voice. "Alexander is the Brother Betrayer."

"Well, I probably wouldn't have gone that far . . ." I hissed. The crowd was restless now. New gods were one thing. Casting down the old, established gods was something else. I took Cassandra by the arm and bent my head to hers. "Losing either of these gods is unacceptable, Cassandra. Divinity has been lost, and the cycle is turning. We can't put Alexander down without threatening the whole divinity of man."

"He murdered your god, Eva. He kept my cult as a pet and yours as a shield, until he burned the Strength and strung up your Elders. You would forget that?"

"No. But remember, your Cult has been tolerated for two hundred years because you served the god Amon was before the Betrayal. Now it is Alexander who is in need of that tolerance. Nothing's changed."

"How can you say that, woman?" she hissed. "Alexander must be punished for his crimes, his followers cast down and his temples leveled. Nothing short of justice must be seen. Nothing has changed? Everything has changed! Amon lives!"

I pushed her away, back to her prone god. "The only difference is that you are in the right, now, when before you thought you were in the wrong. Only you have changed."

"Eva—" she said, scowling. I held up a hand.

"Enough. See to your god. He won't be worth a miracle for a while. And when the power in him settles, I'm leaving it to you to see that he doesn't let his rage guide his terrible hand."

"You would dictate to your god?"

I climbed back out of the crater, then drew my sword and presented it to the girl and her god.

"I am Eva Forge, last Paladin of the dead god Morgan. Last scion of that god, his living blade and only initiate. I am the Cult of the Warrior, and I will hold you accountable. Amon is mad. Alexander is a murderer. Only the Warrior stands."

"The Warrior stands," several members of the crowd whispered back to me, and then more. The Warrior stands, rippling out into the mob, into the city, into the sky. I turned my back on them and headed toward the wreckage of the Spear of the Brothers.

I had another god to settle, and another score to count.

I could not walk alone. I hoped that the crowds would stay behind, but some followed, and more joined as I made the long walk across the city. He was easy enough to find. The sky was cut where he had fallen, a line of night in a bleached sky.

Halfway there, Malcolm appeared at my side. He was smirking. Looking back at the crowd that had gathered in my wake, he leaned to me and said, "Tell me something about your parents, Eva."

I gave him a look. Not a happy look. "What are you talking about, old man?"

"Your parents. Were they kind? Cruel? Did you run away from them, and swear to the Cult of Morgan to spite your mother? Or did they raise you holy and chaste, and cried tears of joy when their little girl chose the humblest of the Cults to call her own?"

I grit my jaw and marched on. "This isn't the time."

"It's not. It's a terrible time. But I have to know what I'm seeing, don't I?"

"I don't know what you're talking about."

"You don't," he said. He waved a hand behind us. "But they know. They can feel it."

I stopped walking, and the Amonite walked past me a couple steps before coming back. He was still smirking.

"Let's get something straight," I said. "I've got a hell of a lot on my mind. We have two gods, and they're both dangerous. My Cult is the last unspoiled Cult in the city of Ash, the last holy house in the divinity of man. And my god is dead. I don't have time for games, old man."

"No," he said, quietly. "You don't."

"I've already threatened one divine being today, Amonite. I'm on my way to maybe kill another, or maybe forgive him his life. I haven't decided. So do you have anything else you'd like to say, or can I be about the Warrior's business?"

"Of course." He bowed and held his hands out, palms to the sky. "Do what you must. Do what you were raised to do."

I grimaced at the formality of his pose, glared at the crowd behind me, then stomped off. The crowd followed, flowing around the old man like a river. When I turned the next corner I looked back. He was still there, unmoved.

Alexander had his own crowd. Mostly whiteshirts, from initiate Healers to patrolmen to Electors and ArchPaladins in full battle gear. A scarred valkyn lurked at the edge of the crowd, its glimmering eyes watching me, hissing steam from its neck. They were quiet as I approached. Past a certain point my followers held back. Some unconscious calculation of blast radius, I suspected.

I walked with intent, and without forgiveness. They parted silently to let me pass, closing up behind me, patrolmen and priests looking at me with eyes that ran from disbelief, to horror, to hate, to fear. Most of them looked lost, and furious at their loss. Near the inner edge of the crowd I passed Owen. He nodded to me, and I put a hand on his arm and squeezed. He looked shocked.

Near the center there was chanting. Arcs of light danced over the crowd. When I got there, I saw five High Healers standing around Alexander, hands joined, chanting the rites of fulfillment. I clambered down into the crater, so much like Amon's landing spot, and put my hand on the shoulder of the closest priest.

"What he has can't be cut away, Doc."

He stumbled in the invocation, and the arcs of light fell away. Murmurs rippled through the crowd, but the Healers split and faded back. Alexander was alive, awake, sitting up. When he saw me he winced and struggled to stand. The Betrayer's mask was nowhere to be seen.

"You would have a word with me, I suppose," he said. His voice was cracked and weak. I nodded. "Then have it. I have a city to rebuild."

"I want it from your mouth," I said, and shocked myself with the cold anger in my tone. "I want it in your words."

"Who are you, to demand—"

"Who are *we*, to demand. The city. The generations of Amonites who have suffered, the legions of Morgan you have thrown into battle. These, here, who have sworn words to your name, and knew not to whom they were swearing. Who are we? Your Brothers Immortal, Amon, Morgan. We demand it, Alexander." I raised my arms and turned to the silent crowd. I saw some who had followed me filtering in. "In your words. From your mouth."

He set his jaw and clenched his fists. Back stiff. Head high.

"I don't know what—"

Blade in hand without thought, metal against the softness of his neck, heavy against his blood. The skin parted and wet the steel.

"How many, just today? How many have died? I have emptied the Ruin with my own hand. You can feel it, feel the loss of power. The divinity has been spread, Alexander. There will be new gods. The sky will turn, and maybe it will fall to the Rethari, or maybe we will hold on. We can't lose a single divine body, not with things so delicate, but I swear to . . ." I stopped, trembling with sick rage. "I swear in my own name, if you breathe one more lie to me today, on this day, in this city you have ruined, among these bodies, I swear I will end you, Alexander. I will spill your holy godblood across these stones without a second thought."

Long breaths without movement, his eyes burning cold and bright. Eventually, he nodded.

"I, Alexander, Brother of Morgan and Amon, godking of all Ash, last of the Brothers Immortal . . . I killed my older brother, and cast the guilt on my younger. I am the Betrayer. But only for the good of—"

I pulled the sword away, slicing lightly through his flesh. Enough to sting. He gasped, then I wrapped my fist around the pommel and punched. Holy teeth and a divine nose crumpled.

"That's enough," I said as he fell to the cobbles. I flicked the blood from my sword, sheathed it, and turned to leave.

No one got in my way.

I gathered the bodies myself. Cut each one down, carried it, and laid it to rest in the charred ruins of the Chamber of the Fist. Tomas, Isabel, and Simeon. Stories were being told of the walking Barnabas, seen leaving the city shortly before the cataclysm of divinity. I swore to find him later, and offer him the quiet of the grave. The Strength was a ruin, but the stone still stood. The high halls were smoldering. It would be days before I could walk them, and gather the rest of my brothers. And then I would stand their watches, and lay them away in the Last Rest. Fire hadn't touched those cold stone walls under the monastery.

A crowd gathered around the plaza. None getting too close, but none going away, either. They watched me as I performed the duties that were my burden. When it was done, I sat in the nave and cleaned my revolver and my sword, clearing a space in the ash to lay out the rituals.

I went to the door and looked out at the sea of faces, burned robes, charred faces, and bewildered eyes. Behind them the city smoked in its ruin. The impellors were silent, burst in the might of their divine siren. I stood in the doorway of the Strength of Morgan, and they waited for me. They would continue to wait.

I turned away, closing the mighty doors of the Strength behind me. I had a church to clean, and then a city, and then a godhood. There was ash in our blood, ash deep in our flesh, a history of tragedy and betrayal that could not be denied, but that we could not discard. It was our history; they were our gods. A divinity of ashes and death, and we would have to burn them clean. The Warrior stands.

ABOUT THE AUTHOR

Tim Akers was born in rural North Carolina, the only son of a theologian. He moved to Chicago for college, where he lives with his wife and their German shepherd. He splits his time between databases and fountain pens. You can visit Tim's Web site at shadoth.blogspot.com.